GENA SHOWALTER

The Darkest TORMENT

HQN™

ISBN-13: 978-0-373-80373-6

The Darkest Torment

Recycling programs
for this product may
not exist in your area.

This edition published by arrangement with Harlequin Books S.A.

For questions and comments about the quality of this book,
please contact us at CustomerService@Harlequin.com.

® and TM are trademarks of Harlequin Enterprises Limited or its
corporate affiliates. Trademarks indicated with ® are registered in the
United States Patent and Trademark Office, the Canadian Intellectual
Property Office and in other countries.

www.HQNBooks.com

Printed in U.S.A.

CONTENTS

Dear Reader,

When I sat down to write the next Lords of the Underworld tale, I had some hard choices to make. Did I tell Cameo's story, the Lord readers most wanted, even though I hadn't set up the final threads for her plot? Did I tell William's story, a non-Lord but also a reader favorite, even though I hadn't set up his plotline at all? Or did I tell Baden's story, the character readers knew the least about? In the end, I had to go with the story I was most excited to tell, and the moment, the very second, Baden's dilemma and heroine came to me, I gasped. I shivered. I paced with anticipation, scenes already rolling through my head. Writing his book became a need, an undeniable passion, and it's my hope that that passion shines through every word. Because you get more than a story when you read *The Darkest Torment*. You get a little piece of my heart.

Love,

Gena Showalter

The Darkest
TORMENT

To Julie Kagawa. You are a treasure! Thank you for the phone call, conversation and dog training tips. (All mistakes are my own and purposely done to fit the confines of my story—that's my excuse and I'm sticking to it.)

To Beth Kendrick. Pecan pie rocks my world— and so do you! I would love to vacation in your brain!

To Kady Cross and Amy Lukavics. Amazing women, fabulous tour buddies and forever cherished friends. I am so blessed to have met you!

To Allison Carroll. Editor extraordinaire. You go above and beyond, and your input has been invaluable. Thank you!

To the beautiful, talented authors I'm privileged to call my friends (the ones above and the ones below) with hearts of gold:

Jill Monroe, Roxanne St. Claire, Kresley Cole, J. R. Ward, Karen Marie Moning, Nalini Singh, Jeaniene Frost, P.C. and Kristin Cast, Deidre Knight, Kelli Ireland, Kristen Painter and Lily Everett.

To Anne Victory and her Pippin!

And to my own Biscuit. You were a treasure, a gift from God, and I didn't deserve you. You loved me madly. I was your favorite person on earth. You're in heaven now, and when we're together again, I'm going to adore you for the rest of eternity!

"There's a time and place for killing.
Never and nowhere."
—Baden, the Gentleman of Mount Olympus,
pre-beheading

"There's a time and place for killing.
Always and anywhere."
—Baden, fearsome Lord of the Underworld,
post-resurrection

1

"Benefits to having me as your ally? You have me as your ally. Enough said."

—Hades, one of the nine kings of the underworld

Guilt could not change the past. Worry could not change the future. And yet, both followed Baden with relentless determination. One brandished a barbed whip, the other a serrated blade, and though he had no visible wounds, he bled buckets every—damned—day.

The constant stream of pain provoked the beast. Upon his return from the dead, the creature moved into his mind. His new companion was far worse than any demon. And he should know! The fiend resented the physical cage…was starved for prey.

Kill someone. Kill everyone!

It was the beast's war cry. A command Baden heard whenever someone approached him. Or looked at him. Or simply breathed. The urge to obey always followed…

I will not kill, he vowed. He was not the beast, but separate.

Easily said. Harder to enforce. He prowled from one corner of his bedroom to the other and yanked at the

collar of his shirt, ripping the soft cotton in an effort
to assuage the constant discomfort. His too-sensitive
skin needed continuous soothing. Another *perk* of returning from the dead.

The butterfly he'd tattooed on his chest hadn't helped
the pain, quickly becoming an itch he couldn't scratch.
But he couldn't regret getting the image. The jagged
wings and horned antennae resembled the mark of the
demon he'd carried *before* his death; now, the mark represented rebirth, a reminder that he lived once again.
That he had friends—brothers and a sister by circumstance who loved him. That he wasn't an outsider, even
if he felt like one.

He drained the beer he held and tossed the bottle
against the wall. The glass shattered. He was different
now, it was an undeniable truth, and he no longer fit
within the family dynamic. He blamed the guilt. Four
thousand years ago, he'd allowed the enemy to behead
him—suicide by proxy—leaving his friends to continue the war with the Hunters while mourning him.
Unconscionable!

But he also blamed the worry he'd been coddling like a
precious newborn. The beast hated everyone he adored—
the men and women Baden owed a blood debt—and it…
he…would stop at nothing to destroy them.

If ever that urge to lash out overshadowed Baden's
desire to right the wrongs he'd committed…

I will *right my wrongs.*

The dead can't collect their debts. Killlll.

No. No! He beat his fists into his temples, the metal
bands around his biceps pinching. He pulled at hanks
of his hair. Sweat rolled between the knotted muscles

in his back and chest, catching in the waist of his pants. He would rather die—again—than harm his friends.

Upon his resurrection, all twelve warriors had welcomed him with open arms. No, not twelve. Thirteen now. Galen, the keeper of Jealousy and False Hope—the one who'd orchestrated Baden's death—had moved in a few weeks before. Everyone believed the prick had changed his evil ways.

Please. Shit sprinkled with sugar was still shit.

Baden would love to hack Galen into tiny pieces. Five minutes and a blade, that was all he required. But his friends had issued a strict hacking moratorium.

Baden, no matter his own desires, would obey their rules. Not once had they ever castigated him for his terrible mistakes. Not once had they demanded answers. They'd given him food, weapons and a private room in their massive home. A fortress hidden in the mountains of Budapest.

A knock sounded at the door, earning a growl from the beast. *Enemy! Kill!*

Calm. Steady. An enemy wouldn't take the time to knock. "Go away." His broken voice made it sound like every word had swum upstream in a river of glass shards.

"Sorry, my man, but I'm here to stay." *Bang, bang, bang.* "Let me in."

Hello, William the Ever Randy. Youngest son of Hades obsessed with fine wine, finer women and the finest hair care. He was a savage, stubborn bastard, his best and worst trait the same: He had no concept of mercy.

The beast stopped snarling and started purring like a tamed house cat. A surprising reaction, but also…not.

Hades was the one who'd given Baden his new life. The king's family basically had a Get Out of Torture Free card now. Except the eldest son, Lucifer; his crimes were simply too great.

"Now isn't a good time," Baden said, fearing the beast would forget the card.

"Don't care. Open up."

He purposely inhaled deeply...exhaled sharply. As a spirit made tangible, he had no need to breathe, but the once-familiar action pandered to his calm.

"Come on," William said. "Where's the brave piece of shit who stole and opened Pandora's box? He's the one I'm here to see."

Brave? Sometimes. Piece of shit? Always. He and his friends ended up freeing the demons trapped inside the box. Zeus, king of the Greek gods, then punished them with a lifelong curse.

And so your body shall become the vessel of your own destruction.

Baden was possessed by Distrust.

Tainted and unworthy, the warriors were discharged from the royal army and booted to earth. As predicted, the demons soon *destroyed* them. Him most of all. More and more, his ability to trust eroded. He spent weeks... months plotting ways to murder those he should only succor.

One day, he reached the end of his tolerance. *Them or me* was the last thought to sweep through his mind as a human swung a sword at his head. He'd picked them— his family. But they hadn't emerged unscathed. Grief had haunted them. And so had Distrust!

The moment Baden's head fell from his body, the demon emerged, emancipated from his control. No longer was he able to check the worst of the fiend's impulses. Invisible chains then dragged his spirit into a prison realm created for anyone tainted by the box, his only link to the land of the living a wall of smoke that revealed real-time happenings.

He had a front row seat to his friends' spiral into a pit of agony and despair, unable to do anything but lament. The rest of his time was spent warring with Pandora, the realm's only other occupant—a woman who detested him with every fiber of her being.

Then, only a few months ago, Cronus and Rhea, the former king and queen of the Titans, appeared in the realm. They were Zeus's biggest rivals, and Baden's number-one targets. How many times had the pair hurt his friends?

He'd taken great pleasure in his escape with Pandora, leaving the other two behind.

Bang, bang, bang. "Yo! Baden! The wait is ridiculous. I'm pretty sure I'm going gray."

He jolted, pissed he'd gotten lost in his head.

"Fine. I guess we do this the hard way," William called. "In three seconds, I kick in your door."

Calm. No hacking. Baden yanked so hard the handle came off in his hand. Oops. "What do you want?"

Unlike the tornado he was, the black-haired, blue-eyed warrior leaned one shoulder against the frame, as gentle as a summer rain. He looked Baden up and down and grimaced. "Dressing for the job we want, not the job we have, I see."

Strong male. Too strong. Threat.

As feared, the Get Out of Torture Free card burned to ash. *No hacking!* But…punching wasn't hacking. It was pure bliss. Bone against bone. The intoxicating scent of blood would hit his senses, and the musical howl of someone else's agony would fill his ears.

He pressed his tongue to the roof of his mouth. *Who* am *I?*

"Go away," he repeated.

William scanned the room. "Drinking all by your lonesome? Tsk-tsk. Is your heart missing the demon?"

A few times, he'd thought he...*might.* The arrival of his new companion had set him straight.

Now Distrust had a new host. A woman. Her name was—his brow furrowed. He couldn't remember.

Whoever she was, she had supported Galen for centuries, helping him commit the most heinous of deeds. A few months ago, the foolish female had willingly accepted Distrust. In other words, she had willingly accepted unceasing paranoia. Who did that?

William sighed. "No need to respond. I can see the answer on your face. Don't you know looking back *pulls* you back? Fine, fine. I'll help you focus on the future. No need to beg." He drew back his fist—and punched Baden in the nose. "You're welcome."

He recoiled from the impact, his nose snapped out of place. Though Baden produced no blood, his body simply a husk for his spirit, the taste of old pennies coated his tongue. Delicious. Practically dessert.

The beast raged, hungry for more.

Glaring at William, he righted the cartilage in his nose.

"Oh, no. I've provoked you. Whatever shall I do?" A grinning William rolled up his shirtsleeves. "I know. How about I give you more."

Looking for a fight? He's found it.

The beast...*exploded.* Every muscle in Baden's body

pumped full of adrenaline while his bones filled with molten lava. Somehow, he doubled in size, the top of his head brushing the ceiling.

"I heard Distrust caused your hair to catch fire," William said. "Pity he's not here. Flames would make your coming defeat more interesting."

Defeat? I'll introduce him.

With a roar, Baden swung. Contact! Addictive… He swung again and again, his fist a jackhammer, brutal and unrelenting. William took the blows like a champ, miraculously remaining on his feet.

I like this man…kind of. Hurting him hurts me.

A glimmer of rational thought. Baden dropped his arm to his side and gripped his camo pants. "Sorry. I'm sorry," he rasped.

"Why?" William's teeth were smeared with crimson. "Did you soil your panties while you were giving me those love taps?"

Humor. He wasn't in the mood. "Walk away. Before you have to crawl."

Already the beast pawed at Baden's gray matter, ravenous for round two.

"Don't be silly." William waved his fingers. "Hit me again. Only this time, try to do some real damage."

The warrior didn't understand…*wouldn't* understand until too late. "Go! I'm losing control."

"Then we're making progress." William jabbed Baden's shoulder. "Hit me."

"Do you want to die?"

"Hit." *Jab.* "Me." *Jab.*

The beast snarled, and Baden…

Baden detonated like a bomb, whaling on William,

who made no effort to block or dodge the barrage of blows.

"Fight back!" Baden shouted.

"Since you suggested it…" William threw a punch of his own, a crack so powerful Baden reeled backward and slammed into the dresser.

Books and decorations the female residents had given him rattled before toppling to the floor. Everything made of glass shattered at his feet. William stalked forward and, without a pause in his step, bent down to swipe up one of the books. He struck, pummeling Baden's throat into his spine.

Pain. His body bowed as the warrior slammed the book into his side. Once. Twice. More pain. His kidney was puréed.

Opponent…even stronger than expected…cannot be allowed to live.

Before William could deliver another blow, Baden jerked up a knee. The book flew across the room. He punched William in the jaw. As the warrior stumbled, Baden picked up a shard of glass.

By the time he straightened, William had recovered. That fast. The warrior crushed a vase into the side of his head, new shards raining.

Different voices suddenly penetrated his awareness.

"Is that Baden? Duuude! That *can't* be Baden. He's three times his usual size!"

"He's going to make a retainer out of Willy's teeth!"

"I call dibs! On Baden, not the retainer. If my man ever kicks it, I get to hook up with Hulk-smash first!"

In the back of his mind, he knew his friends and their mates had heard the commotion and come running, intending to break up the fight. To help him. The beast didn't care.

Kill...kill them all...they're too strong, too much of a risk.

Evil like the beast had no friends, only enemies.

The group is dangerous to the rest of the world, but not to me. Never to me. These people would die for me.

Die...yes, they must die...

William kicked the door closed, blocking the others from Baden's view. "You focus on me, Red. Understood? I'm the biggest threat, so do us both a favor, take your arthritis medication and *hit me*."

Yes. Biggest threat. Hit. Rage gave him added strength as he unleashed a new stream of punches. William blocked the first few, but couldn't dodge the others. Baden failed to dodge his retaliation.

The brutal fight propelled them around the room, bouncing off walls and furniture as if they were animals in the wild, vying for position of King of the Jungle.

Pick up another piece of glass. Cut through the warrior's ribs.

Yes. The perfect finish. But as Baden swooped down, William flashed behind him—moving to a new location with only a thought—and punched him. He twisted as he stumbled, capturing the male's hand when he attempted to deliver another strike.

Baden purposely dropped, sinking to the floor, taking William with him. Midway down, he wound his legs around the bastard's neck, applying enough pressure to choke a rhino. The moment they crash-landed, Baden tossed William over his head.

Thud. His opponent smashed face-first into the pile

of glass shards. He grinned and drew himself up to straddle Willy's back.

Punch. Punch. William's skull cracked—and cracked Baden's knuckles. Before he could deliver his next blow, the low-down-dirty-sneak flashed again—but it was too late to halt his fist. Punch. A wood panel on the floor splintered. Pain vibrated up his arm and pooled in his shoulder.

William laughed with delight and, as if the sound opened a magical portal to calm, the beast quieted.

"There." Willy ruffled Baden's hair. "You feel better now." A kind statement rather than a smug question.

He performed a danger-check, just to be sure, and nodded. "I do." Even his throat had healed.

"Now we can have a conversation without you eyeing my trachea like it's a gummy worm."

"Conversation can wait." He stood, grimacing as he noted the condition of his room. Holes in the wall, broken glass on the floor, furniture overturned and missing pieces. "I've got some cleaning to do."

"You'd choose a broom over information?"

"Depends on the information being offered."

"If I said the serpentine wreaths and their side effects…?"

"I'd turn your pretty face to pulp." Baden loved the wreaths, but he also hated them. They were a gift from Hades, ancient and mystical, and they were responsible for his corporeal form.

Hades and Keeley—the mate of Baden's friend Torin—had come to him in what he'd thought was a dream. Through some kind of supernatural power, they'd removed the bands Lucifer, his jailer at the time, had forced on him and replaced them with bands that belonged to Hades.

As long as you wear my *wreaths,* Hades had said, *you will be seen...touched.*

The friendly gesture of an ally he supported in the war of the underworlds? He'd thought so in the beginning. Now he wondered... The trick of an underhanded foe?

Soon after Baden had donned the gift, William had looked at him with pity and said, "Have you seen *Pet Sematary*? Sometimes dead is better."

William wasn't wrong.

By that point, Baden had already begun to change. Not physically—maybe physically—but definitely mentally. Once even-tempered, he struggled for control, and he despised anyone who might be stronger than him. As proved. Memories plagued him, but they weren't his own. They couldn't be. He'd never been a child, had been created fully formed, an immortal soldier tasked with protecting Zeus, and yet he clearly remembered being around ten years old, running through an ambrosia field set aflame, thick smoke choking him.

A pack of hellhounds tracked him, *fed* on him and dragged him into a cold, dank dungeon, where he'd suffered, alone and starved, for centuries.

With the first memory, a horrifying truth had struck Baden. The wreaths weren't just an object, but a being. The beast. Not a demon, but worse. An immortal who'd once lived and now expected to *continue* living through Baden. A monster who always teetered on the brink of rage, violence and distrust.

The irony of the situation wasn't lost on Baden.

"Well." William pretended to be offended. "Try to do a man a favor."

Concentrate! "Yesterday you said you knew nothing about the wreaths."

A hike of his broad shoulders. "That was yesterday."

"And today you know...what, exactly?"

"Only everything."

He waited for the warrior to say more. "Do you require another beating? Tell me!"

"*Beating* is too strong a word for what transpired. I'd go with *massage*." William buffed his nails. "Just so you know, the wreaths' side effects are numerous and horrifying."

"I figured the horrifying part out on my own, thanks." Removing the wreaths wasn't an option. They were fused to him, and he would have to amputate his arms with a meat cleaver.

Before his death, his arms would have grown back. Now? He wasn't sure and wasn't willing to experiment. Well, not on himself. His hands were his first line of defense.

"Give me specifics," he demanded.

"For starters, if you want to keep your new temper tantrums at bay, you'll need sex and a lot of it."

The pronouncement was a joke. Had to be.

Baden arched a brow. "You offering, oh great and randy one?"

William snorted. "As if you could handle me."

To be honest, he couldn't handle *anyone*. When he wasn't fighting, he avoided any kind of contact, the sensitivity of his skin too great. Every brush of flesh against flesh was excruciating, like a dagger being raked across exposed nerve endings.

"You're going to leave Budapest today," William said. "You'll go…somewhere else. You'll collect a harem of immortal women, and you'll spend the next decade or two concerned only with pleasure."

Leave his friends? After they'd only just been reunited? No. He was here to help them, to guard their backs the way he'd longed to do for centuries. "I'm going to pass."

"And I'm going to insist. You can't beat the darkness."

"I *am* the darkness."

The warrior canted his head in agreement. "Here's the rub. Maddox and Ashlyn have children. Both Gideon and Kane have a pregnant wife. Not to mention the other females living in the house. And what about the traumatized Legion? The vulnerable Gillian?" His voice roughened with her name. "You go after any of the females the way you went after me, and your brothers-by-choice will gut you. No matter how much they love you. *I* will gut you."

"I would never—"

"Oh, princess. You so *would.*"

A new rage sparked. He slammed a fist through the wall and cursed, proving William right. The beast took advantage of him at every opportunity. "All right. I'll leave." The words pained him, but he even added, "Today."

"Your IQ just jacked to the next level." William beamed at him. "Any idea where you'll go?"

"No." He had very little experience with the modern world.

A sigh. "I'll probably regret this later," the warrior said, stroking two fingers over his jaw, "but what the hell. We only live twice, right?"

Baden waved a hand, a silent command to carry on.

"For the bargain price of a favor to be named later, I'll give you one of my homes and even set up a carnal buffet for you. And don't worry. By the time I'm done, even a man with your lack of game will be able to score a ten."

As the rapid beat of rock music blasted from surround-sound speakers, a pair of double Ds hit Baden in the face. He hissed in pain, not that—whatever her name—noticed as she gyrated on his lap.

She reached out to cup his nape, clearly intending to draw him closer.

Every man needs to motorboat at least once in his life, William had told her earlier. *Make sure Red gets his chance.*

Baden batted her hand away as gently as possible.

She grinned at him, though there wasn't a single hint of amusement in her eyes. "Performance anxiety, sugar? I know the perfect cure." She hopped off and spun, shoving her ass in his face.

"Twerking is the best, isn't it?" William said now.

Baden turned to glare at him. They were the only males in the room, and the prick was certainly living up to his original playboy reputation as he stuffed a hundred-dollar bill in the G-string of his own stripper. A blonde bumping and grinding on him with absolute abandon.

"Even though *you* should be paying *me*, I'm feeling generous." William gave her another hundred. "Don't think I failed to notice your orgasm. The first *or* the second."

She was too busy having a third to respond.

"This isn't helping me," Baden snapped.

William leaned forward to lick the blonde's collarbone. A practiced move he seemed to perform by rote. "Don't doubt my pimposity just yet. This is only the appetizer."

Pimposity?

"Listen to him." Miss Twerk faced Baden, brushing her fingertip along the curve of his jaw. "You're supposed to eat me up."

The pain! He endured it a few seconds more, but only to clasp her by the hips and set her away from him once and for all. "No touching. Ever."

His unintentionally harsh tone made her tremble.

"Go." Disgusted with himself as much as the circumstances, he motioned to the door. "Now."

As she raced from the room, he settled more comfortably on the couch and closed his eyes. He needed sex—supposedly—but he couldn't bring himself to have it. What kind of future awaited him? One dark rage constantly bleeding into another? Like before…

Another memory he'd never lived played through his mind.

He stood outside the dungeon he'd occupied for a torturous eternity, a sea of bodies and body parts all around him. Blood soaked his hands…hands tipped by sharp claws, bits of flesh and *other things*.

Footsteps thumped in a nearby hallway. A survivor? Not for long.

Grinning with anticipation, he climbed through the debris and—

The music cut off abruptly, drawing Baden back to the present. He opened his eyes in time to see the last stripper exit the room.

William tsk-tsked at him before flashing away…and

returning with two glasses and a bottle of ambrosia-laced whiskey.

Ambrosia, the drug of choice for immortals.

The warrior filled the cups to the brim. "Here. Lubricate your brain."

The sweet scent wafted to Baden, causing his stomach to churn. For a moment he was a child again, trapped in the burning field, running…running…his heart galloping like a horse at a race.

Not me. The beast.

Trembling, he drained the cup. A tide of warmth spread through him quickly, calming him despite the adverse association, grounding him deeper in the here and now.

"There. Isn't that better?" William reclined at his end of the white couch, the only piece of furniture in a room of white.

White walls, white floor tiles. White dais with a trio of mirrors in back. Baden's reflection—the only real source of color—glared at him in challenge. He'd become a soldier he no longer recognized, with shaggy red waves in desperate need of a trim. Dark eyes once filled with welcome only offered silent threats. A mouth that used to quirk up in amusement only ever curved down in anger. Laugh lines had been replaced by scowl lines.

No, not better. "I'm ready to leave."

"Too bad. I won't remember how to flash you somewhere else until you've gotten laid. And as soon as you appear less murdery, you will get laid. The girls will love you." William drained the contents of his glass in a single gulp. "Just do me a solid and inform your face this is supposed to be a *good time*."

"Skin-to-skin contact is painful."

The beast snarled at him for daring to voice such a damning vulnerability, even to one of Hades's children.

William frowned at him. "If you think the wreaths are responsible—"

"I don't."

"—think again. They're not. So grin and bear it or you won't live through your transition."

Transition? "Appearing less murdery, as you say, is the true challenge. I've forgotten how to smile."

"Are you *whining*?" William set his cup aside and traced a fingertip down his cheeks, mimicking tears. "Your new life sucks. So what? Do you think you're the only one with problems?"

"Certainly not." His friends were currently hunting for Pandora's box, determined to find it before some-one—anyone—else. It could kill them in an instant. Just boom…gone…dead, their demons removed. Normally a good thing. But evil so entrenched had to be cleansed first and replaced by its opposite. Like with Haidee, Hate for Love. Otherwise rot set in. Which was why the Lords were also hunting for the Morning Star—a supernatural being still trapped inside the box, capable of granting any wish. Capable of freeing the demons without killing the warriors.

Lucifer had mounted a search for the Morning Star, as well, though he had no plans to spare the Lords. He was at war with Hades and determined to win whatever the cost. He'd made no secret of his desire to eliminate his father's allies: William, Baden and all the oth-ers. And as the master of Harbingers—messengers of death—he might just be powerful enough to succeed.

"That's right," William said. "You're not. In fact,

my life makes yours look like a picnic hosted by naked forest nymphs."

"Now you're exaggerating."

"*Under*-exaggerating, perhaps. In a matter of days, Gillian will celebrate her eighteenth birthday."

"So?" Baden wanted the guy to say the words aloud—to admit to a vulnerability of his own. Tit for tat. "She'll be an adult. Old enough to handle you." He couldn't help but add, "Or any other man she wants."

"Me," William snapped. He'd never been able to mask the intensity of his emotions for the girl. "Old enough to handle *me*. Only me. But I can't have her."

When the guy said no more, Baden prodded him. "Because you're cursed?"

A pause. A stiff nod. "The woman who wins me will kill me."

Wins. As if *he* were the prize. *The same can't be said about me.* "Well, boohoo for you." Survival first, matters of the heart second—if at all. "You've been warned. You can be proactive."

What. The. Hell. Had he just suggested William kill sweet, innocent Gilly before she had the opportunity to kill him?

His hands fisted. He needed to put a tighter leash on the beast. So. He would pick a girl, have sex with as little bodily contact as possible, and maybe, for a little while, his head would clear. He would be able to think, to figure out a way to remove the wreaths, and the beast, keep all his body parts and remain tangible.

"Enough conversation." He forced the corners of his mouth to lift. "I'm less murdery. See?"

"Wow. Just when I think you can't look any worse,

you go and prove me wrong." Even still, William clapped his hands. "Ladies."

Hinges creaked as the door opened. A new crop of scantily-clad females sauntered into the room—a brunette, blonde, redhead and ebony-skinned beauty. Smiles abounded as they lined up across the dais.

The mirror suddenly made sense. Baden had a perfect view of the front *and* the trunk. His long-denied body stirred at last, even as a new heaping of self-disgust assailed him.

"Prostitutes." He should have known.

The blonde blew him a kiss.

"They prefer the term *freelance pleasure specialists*. They are immortal. A Phoenix, siren, nymph and pretty little kitty shifter, to be precise." William draped a muscled arm over the top of the couch. "Which one do you want to jones for your scones? Your wish is her command."

"I have no interest in feigned passion."

"Hate to break it to you, Red, but feigned passion is all you're going to get." The warrior offered him a sorry-not-sorry smile. "Right now, you have only two things in your favor. You're rich, thanks to investments Torin made over the centuries, and you're a dead ringer for Jamie Fraser."

"Who?"

"The male these females are going to pretend you are," William said. "Because you, my dear man, are lacking in charm and sophistication, which means your fat wallet and chiseled features are all you have to get you to the finish line."

"I'm not lacking in charm." Sometimes he was. Maybe. Probably always.

William ignored him. "Ladies, tell Baden how pretty his wallet and face are."

"*So* pretty."

"The prettiest I've ever seen."

"More beautiful than pretty."

"I'll ride your wallet *and* your face!"

Baden glared at William while stroking the hilt of the dagger hidden in a sheath at his waist.

William sighed. "If Jason Voorhees and Freddy Krueger spawned a love child, I'm certain that nightmare of a kid would look at me just—like—that."

More men he hadn't met. Which annoyed him greatly! He had no need for reminders that the world had ticked along just fine without him.

"My brilliant sense of humor is lost on you. Noted. Ladies," William said, reclaiming the bottle of whiskey, "tell Baden what carnal delights you're prepared to offer him."

One by one, they breathlessly described different scenarios. The shy virgin. The naughty librarian. The punishing dominant. The girlfriend experience.

When Baden had lived in Mount Olympus, he'd dated his fair share of women, but he'd never loved one. He'd wanted an equal, not a weakling merely using him for protection, placing his power before her sentiment. He was tempted to try out the girlfriend experience.

"Well?" William prompted.

"I will accept none of the scenarios offered." *Give me truth, or give me nothing.* He met each beauty's gaze. For the chance to tame the beast and return to his friends… "Who will bend over and simply take it?"

Perhaps he *was* lacking in charm.

William shook his head and muttered, "You should be embarrassed."

Meanwhile, two feminine hands shot into the air.

"Me! Pick me!" The brunette. The punishing dominant.

The blonde elbowed her in the stomach. "I'm the one you want." The naughty librarian.

"How are we friends?" William asked him.

"We aren't." Baden had twelve friends. Only twelve. The men and woman who'd suffered demon possession right alongside him. The warriors who'd bled with him and for him—the heroes he'd only disappointed since his return. They wanted him to be the man he used to be, not the bastard he'd become.

An-n-nd there was another log on the fire of his guilt.

"Tears. Sadness." William placed a hand on his chest, as if he'd been stabbed. "Now. Choose your girl. I'm going to do you a solid and take the other three."

"What type of immortal are you?" Baden asked the two contenders.

"Phoenix," the brunette said, her pride evident.

"Nymph," the blonde said, her voice smoky.

"You." He pointed to the blonde. "I choose you." Nymphs needed sex more than they needed oxygen. At least she'd get something other than cash for her trouble.

The brunette wilted with displeasure, surprising him.

"I'll make it up to you, petal," William told her with a wink. "With him, you'd have to work for every cent. With me, you can simply enjoy. I don't want to overhype my skill, but I invented the female orgasm."

Whatever. Baden stood and, without initiating contact, led the blonde to the exit. He opened the door and motioned her through. The faint scent of white oleander accompanied her. He followed her into a narrow hallway, maintaining a safe distance.

"Pick a room," she said with what might have been... anticipation? "Any room."

He selected the first one on the right, entering before her in case someone waited inside, intending to attack. No assailant jumped out, but he did find a camera hidden in a clock on the mantel above the hearth. William's doing? Why?

After disabling it, he conducted a more generalized search. The room had a king-size canopy bed with black silk sheets, a nightstand full of condoms and lubricants, and a recliner next to a bear-shifter rug.

The blonde traced a fingertip between her breasts. "What do you want me to do, gorgeous?"

The beast protested. Loudly. He didn't like her, and didn't want Baden distracted and vulnerable while in the presence of another—especially in an effort to quiet him.

Still Baden said, "Strip and bend over the edge of the bed, facedown."

"Ohhhh." She grinned. "Are you going to spank me for being naughty?"

The beast cursed him, then the girl. *You will leave. You will leave* now.

No threat. Just an order. Something about his tone...

A tone Baden had only ever heard from kings. *Who are you?*

With barely a pause, the beast replied, *I am Destruction.*

2

"Your hardest times often lead to your greatest moments. So get hard."

—William the Ever Randy

Baden reeled. The beast... Destruction...a demon.?

A king, he added.

The pride in the creature's voice was unmistakable. Nailed it. *A king of what?*

Right now? You. Leave the girl or kill her. Your choice.

There was one other option. Baden narrowed his focus on his chosen bedmate. "I won't be spanking you, only fucking you. Strip, and bend over the bed face-down," he repeated. "Please, and thank you."

Destruction hissed.

"For you, gorgeous, I'll do anything." She unhooked her bra and shimmied out of the matching underwear. Both garments floated to the floor. As she moved, the ring she wore glinted, the multicolored stone catching in the light.

Bang, bang, bang. The beast kicked Baden's chest

with so much force, the impact mimicked a heartbeat. *Can you not see the danger right in front of you?*

The girl had no concept of his inner turmoil and slowly pivoted, revealing her backside. She bent over the mattress, as requested, and spread her legs to present him with a view he'd missed all these centuries.

"Just so you know, I can take a lickin' and keep on tickin'." She looked over her shoulder, her smile returning. "Show me your worst."

She wouldn't survive his worst.

Destruction banged harder, hissed louder. *Kill her before she kills us.*

"No," he said through gritted teeth.

"No?" she asked, incredulous. She gave her ass a firm slap, leaving a red palm print. "You're going to walk away from *this*?"

Jaw clenched, he replied, "I will have you." *And I will* silence the beast.

Relief bathed her features as he moved behind her. As he fought the impulses of his companion, sweat poured from him. Soon his clothes were sticking to his too-sensitive skin.

Destruction grew even more frenzied. *She's the enemy. See! Know!*

All I see is a one-way ticket to paradise. It was time to nut up or shut up. No matter how agonizing. Risk... reward. Baden left his dampened shirt in place and merely unzipped his pants.

She continued to watch him over her shoulder, unabashed. "You really are beautiful, you know."

"Only on the outside."

"Even better."

He wished he had experience with modern women. Did they actually *like* assholes?

In four thousand years, the only other female he'd interacted with was Pandora, and she'd constantly tried to kill him. Now she was out in the wild, tangible because she, too, wore a pair of serpentine wreaths. She'd staked out the fortress and managed to sneak past security to ambush him. Twice! In both instances, they'd nearly killed each other.

Was she dealing with her own version of Destruction?

Fool! Already you're distracted. Without me you'll become a walking target.

Hell, no. A lie from a desperate creature. Baden withdrew a condom from his pocket, not trusting the ones in the drawer. As he ripped the foil packet with his teeth, a strange red glow bathed the room. He palmed a dagger, looking around, Destruction suddenly—strangely—calm.

The girl twisted to brace her weight on her elbows and face him fully. She gaped at him. "Your arms."

He glanced down and frowned. The wreaths were no longer black but crimson, and the brighter they glowed the more they singed his skin, little black rivers branching from underneath them, reminding him of the cracks in the foundation of his life—and his sanity.

What the hell was going on? He zipped up his pants, intending to find William.

His companion released a heavy sigh. "No wonder he wants you dead." With no other warning, she swung her fist at him.

Instincts honed on the bloodiest of battlefields spurred him into motion even before his mind processed what was happening. He caught her wrist before contact and twisted her arm behind her back, effectively pinning her down.

Now kill her, Destruction said. *Make her a cautionary tale for all who think to harm us.*

He would…not. "You said *he* wants me dead." The words were snarled. "Who is *he*?" William?

"Let me go!" She kicked at him to no avail. "It was nothing personal, okay? Not on my part. I only wanted the money." She beat her free hand into the mattress. "I should have stuck to the plan and waited until you were weak from orgasm."

He wrenched her arm higher, and she shrieked in misery. The ring caught his attention. The stone had been discarded, revealing the needle underneath. She'd intended to poison him?

Cautionary tale…

Enemies had to die. Always.

"William!" he bellowed, though he needn't have bothered.

The bedroom door burst open. William stomped inside, his narrowed gaze landing on the blonde. "Mistake, nymph. I would have been good to you." Blood drenched him. "Now you'll only experience my worst."

Tremors of fear rocked her.

"She said *he* wants me dead," Baden informed the warrior.

A muscle ticked below his eye. "He. Lucifer. And don't you dare refer to the male as my brother. I'll never claim him."

Baden should have guessed. Lucifer was power-hungry. Greedy. An unrepentant rapist. A killer of innocents. The father of lies. There was no line he wouldn't cross. No foul deed he wouldn't commit against men, women and even children.

William motioned to Baden's glowing bands with a tilt of his chin. "Prepare yourself. Soon you're going to face—"

Baden was yanked through an invisible black hole… only to crash-land on the other side. He oriented his mind as a massive ballroom came into view. Tendrils of smoke wafted from multiple bonfires, hazing the air as they curled toward a domed ceiling made entirely of flame. There were only two exits. The one in back, manned by giants, and the one in front, manned by even bigger giants.

A grandiose throne made from bronzed human skulls consumed the center of a long dais, and on that throne sat Hades himself. He was a large man, similar in size to Baden, with inky hair and eyes so black they had no beginning or end. He wore a pin-striped suit and Italian loafers, the elegance at odds with the stars tattooed on each of his knuckles.

Urbane and yet uncivilized, Hades spread his arms. "Welcome to my humble abode. Love it before you hate it."

Baden ignored the nonsensical greeting. He'd interacted with the king only once before, when the male gifted him with the wreaths and freed him from Lucifer's prison. "Why am I here?" The glow faded from the bands, the metal cooling, becoming dull and dark once again. Better question: "*How* am I here?"

Hades smiled slowly, smugly. "Thanks to the wreaths, I'm your master, and you are my slave. I called, you came."

Baden fought the urge to attack. "You lie." He was

slave to no one, not even the king. The beast, however…
might be. Realization stabbed him, and suddenly only
one question mattered. "Who is Destruction?"

The king was an expert strategist and donned a blank
mask. "Perhaps a man I cursed. Perhaps a being I created." His fingers formed a steeple in front of his mouth.
"The only thing you need to know? He will always
choose me over you."

The beast offered no response, a fact as annoying
as it was baffling.

"I will fight his compulsion to obey you," Baden
vowed.

Hades winced with something akin to pity. "When
I summon you again, you will come. When I give an
order, you will obey. Let's have a good old-fashioned
demonstration, shall we?" He lifted his chin, the picture of a male who'd never known uncertainty. "Kneel."

Baden's knees slammed into the floor with so much
force the entire room rattled. Though he struggled with
all his considerable might, he failed to rise.

Horror joined his rage. Bound to the will of another…

"As you can see, my will is your delight." Hades
waved a hand through the air. "You may stand."

His body unlocked, and he leaped to his feet, his
hand automatically resting on the hilt of a dagger. He'd
been tricked. And oh, the irony. The one time he should
have doubted, he'd trusted blindly.

Battling a redoubled rage, he gritted, "You can't give
orders if you're dead."

"An empty threat? I expected better from a fearsome
Lord of the Underworld. Excuse me, *former* Lord. But
all right. Do it. Try to kill me." Hades motioned him

forward. "I won't move. I won't even retaliate if you land a blow."

Without hesitation, he stalked toward the throne, a plan of attack already forming. The throat and heart were obvious targets, so he would go for the femoral artery. Massive blood loss would lead to weakness.

The moment he came within striking distance, he went low, the dagger at the ready.

Hades smiled with genuine amusement.

The rage redoubled, and Baden—

Froze, unable to move. A mere inch from contact.

Arching a brow, Hades said, "I'm waiting."

With a roar, Baden swung his other arm. It froze, as well.

The king smirked. "As you are clearly brain damaged, I'll help you compute what's happening. You are incapable of harming me. I could press myself into your weapon, but you would turn the blade on yourself before I started to bleed." He ran the tip of a finger along the edge of the blade in question. "The box bitch required a demonstration of that. Do you?"

Box bitch. The bastard had put Pandora through this same routine?

Protective instincts welled, appalling him. And yet, he thought he understood the source. Right now she was the only person in the world who understood his plight. Not only had they experienced the same horrors in the spirit realm—poisonous fogs, months without a single spark of light, plagued by a bone-deep thirst that could never be quenched—they were now experiencing these new horrors in the land of the living.

"Well?" Hades prompted.

Baden didn't need another demonstration. He needed a new plan. "Why are you doing this?"

"Because I can." Black eyes glittered like a night sky filled with dying stars. "Because I'll do *anything*, hurt *anyone*, to win the war against Lucifer."

A war Baden had supported for weeks. Of his own free will! There was no reason to force his hand. "Five minutes ago, I would have said the same."

"Five minutes from now, you'll say the same again." Hades reclined, stretching out his legs, and gesticulated with two fingers. "I've decided to delegate some of the more unsavory tasks on my to-do list. I'll hear your thanks now."

Unleashed from the freeze-frame, Baden stumbled backward. Comprehension delivered a punch as powerful as William's fists. He was to be an *errand* boy?

"To ensure your willing participation outside these walls, every successfully completed task will earn you a point," Hades continued. "Once the list is completed, the slave with the most points will be freed from the wreaths and allowed to live in the human realm."

New flickers of rage burned his chest. "And the loser?"

"What do you think? I have no use for incompetent weaklings. But by the end, you might actually welcome the blade, eh? That *is* your MO, is it not?"

Guilt...

"Don't bother going after Pandora in order to eliminate the competition," Hades added. "Kill her, and I will kill you."

He licked his lips with an aggressive swipe of his tongue. "I'm already a spirit. I can't be killed."

"Oh, dear boy, you most certainly *can* be killed.

Without your head and your arms, you will simply cease to exist."

At least there was a way out.

Hell, no. He would never purposely die. Not again. He would never hurt his friends in such a cowardly way.

"By enslaving me, you court the wrath of my family. An army you need if you have any hope of winning your war. You also court the wrath of William, your own son."

Hades rolled his eyes. "Nice try, but you know nothing about the bond between father and son. William will support me. William will *always* support me. As for the Lords, I doubt they'll ever back the monster who raped one of their own."

No, they wouldn't. Aeron, former keeper of Wrath, loved a demon-turned-human girl like a daughter. That girl, Legion…who called herself Honey…still suffered from the effects of Lucifer's abuse.

Lucifer deserved a stake through his black heart, not another realm to rule. Siding with him would never be an option.

Hades *was* the lesser of two evils.

Baden flicked his tongue over an incisor. He had to play this bastard's game—even though he suspected the outcome wouldn't be as straightforward as Hades claimed.

Buy time. Figure out a solution.

"What of your father-son bond with Lucifer?" Baden asked with a sneer. "I'm not exactly feeling your love for him."

"There is no bond. Not anymore. Now, that's enough chatter from you. I have two tasks for you. One will take time. The other will take balls. I hope you're wearing yours."

Bastard.

Hades clapped his hands and called, "Pippin."

An old man with a haggard face and humped back stepped out from behind the throne. He wore a long white robe and chiseled in a stone tablet. Never glancing up from his toils, he said, "Yes, sire."

"Tell Baden his first assignments."

"The coin and the siren."

Hades smiled with fondness. "You spare no detail, Pippin. A true master of description." When he held out his hand, the robed man placed a tiny piece of stone on his palm. "A male in New York has a coin that belongs to me. I want it back."

This was an *unsavory* task? "You want me to fetch a single coin?"

"Laugh now, if you like. You won't be laughing later." The stone caught fire and quickly burned to ash; Hades blew in Baden's direction. "You'll need time, as I said, and cunning."

He instinctively inhaled. A moment later, multiple images took center stage in his mind. A golden coin with Hades's face on one side and a blank canvas on the other. A luxurious country estate. A chapel. A schedule. A picture: a twenty-five-year-old male with the face of an angel framed by golden curls that resembled a halo.

Suddenly Baden knew a myriad of details he'd never been told. The male's name was Aleksander Ciernik, and he hailed from Slovakia, where his father built an empire selling heroin and women. Four years ago, Aleksander killed his father and took over the family business. His enemies tended to disappear without a trace. Not that anyone could concretely connect him to a crime.

"You now have the ability to flash to Aleksander," Hades said. "You can also flash to me and your home, wherever it happens to be. The ability will expand to include any new assignments you're given."

The ability to flash was something he'd always coveted. Today, his excitement was tempered with caution. "How did the human obtain your coin?"

"Does it matter? A task is a task."

True enough. "And my second assignment?"

Pippin placed a new stone in Hades's palm. More flames crackled…more ashes floated in Baden's direction. As he inhaled, a different image took shape in his mind. A beautiful woman with long strawberry-blond hair and big blue eyes. A siren.

Every siren could evoke certain emotions or reactions with her voice, but each familial line had a distinctive specialty. Her family excelled at creating calm during chaos.

The girl…she'd died centuries ago. Killed by—the details remained hidden. What Baden knew? She was now a spirit, though her lack of tangibility wouldn't be a problem for him. Despite the bands, he was still able to connect with other spirits.

"Bring me her tongue," Hades commanded.

As in, *cut out* her tongue? "Why?" The single word lashed from Baden.

"My sincerest apologies for giving you the impression I would assuage your curiosity. Go. Now."

Baden opened his mouth to protest only to find himself inside the fortress in Budapest, where his friends lived. He was in the entertainment room, to be exact, with Paris, the keeper of Promiscuity, and Sienna, the new keeper of Wrath. A Hallmark movie played in the background as the two reclined on the couch, eating popcorn and strategizing ways to sneak into the underworld without detection.

Amun, the keeper of Secrets, sat at a small round table, with his wife by his side. Haidee was petite, her shoulder-length blond hair streaked with pink. A silver stud pierced her brow, and the tank top she wore revealed an arm sleeved with names, faces and numbers. Clues she'd needed to remind herself of who she was every time she'd died and come back, her memories erased. She'd died *a lot*, the demon of Hate reanimating her every time but the last, allowing her to continue her mission: destroying her enemies. The last time, the incarnation of Love reanimated her.

Baden had once been enemy number one, which was why she'd helped kill him all those centuries ago.

The memory rose, one he'd actually lived, and he couldn't beat it back, as if—because he was both living and dead, body and spirit—he was trapped between present and past. He'd resided in ancient Greece with the other Lords. A distraught Haidee had come knocking on his door, claiming her husband had been injured and he required a doctor.

From the start, Baden had suspected her of malicious intent. But back then, he'd suspected *everyone* of malicious intent, and he'd been tired, so very tired, of the constant paranoia. He'd even begun to suspect his friends of wrongdoing, and the urge to hurt them, to kill them, had proven nearly irresistible on a daily basis. On several occasions, he'd stood at the foot of someone's bed, a blade clutched in his hand. One day, he would have snapped.

Moving to a new town would have done him no good. Distrust had been as hungry then as Destruction was now. Eventually, the demon would have driven him home. Loose ends could not be tolerated for long, the paranoia they caused too intense. Suicide by homicide had struck him as the only option.

Seeing Haidee now sliced him up inside. He'd hurt her years before she'd attacked him—had killed her actual husband in battle. She'd hurt him in turn. They were even. Now, they weren't the people they'd used to be. They'd started over with a clean slate. For the most part.

Destruction stopped playing dead and snarled at her, remembering her betrayal as if *he* had been the target. He craved revenge.

Not going to happen, Baden informed him.

Kane, the former keeper of Disaster, paced the length of a second table, while his wife Josephina, the queen of the Fae, studied an intricately detailed map. Long black hair tumbled over her delicate shoulders. Hair Kane stopped to smooth out of the way, revealing her pointed ears.

The warrior whispered something to her—something that made her chuckle—before kissing the scar on her cheek…the hollow of her neck. Her blue eyes warmed and sparkled.

"War is serious business." She ran her hands over her rounded belly, a loving caress for her unborn child. "Let's get serious."

Need to leave. Now. Baden wasn't stable. He

shouldn't be this close to the females, must less the *pregnant* one.

In unison, Paris, Amun and Kane noticed him. Each man jumped in front of his girl, acting as a shield while extending a bloodstained dagger in Baden's direction.

He thrilled at seeing them work together. After his death, the twelve warriors he'd only ever sought to protect had split in two groups of six, severely weakening their defensive line. *My fault.*

While the groups had mended their broken relationships centuries later, Baden had yet to mend his conscience.

Destruction kicked at his skull. *Kill!*

The moment Baden's identity clicked, the daggers were lowered and sheathed. Not that the beast was pacified.

"How'd your vacay with Willy go?" Paris winked. "As bad as the one I took with him?" The male was as tall as Baden, topping out at six-eight. He had multicolored hair, the strands ranging from the darkest black to the palest flax. His eyes were vibrant blue and, when not glaring at potential attackers, they almost always gleamed with welcome, inviting others to enjoy the party…in his pants.

Baden had always been the sympathetic one. Solid as a rock. There when you needed him. Sad? Call Baden. Upset? Show up at Baden's place. He would make everything better.

But not anymore.

"The vacation—" his excuse for leaving "—is over."

Amun nodded a greeting. The strong, silent one. He had dark skin, hair and eyes—guarded eyes—while the fun-loving Kane had happy hazels and, like Paris, multicolored hair, the shades tipping the darker side of the scale.

They were handsome men, created to be sexual lures as much as assassins.

"Don't *ever* sneak up on me like that, man." Kane wagged a finger at him. "You're likely to lose your apple bags. And when did you acquire the ability to flash?"

"Today. A...gift from Hades."

Amun stiffened, as if he could see into Baden's head. Hell, he probably could.

"Did the H-bomb do something to you?" Paris demanded. "Say the word and we'll take him out right along with his degenerate son."

"Speaking of Lucifer," Kane said, waving Baden over. "We're in the process of creating a step-by-step plan to ensure his downfall."

"Right now, we only have step one. Break into his dungeon to liberate Cronus and Rhea." Josephina rubbed her belly. "They know too much about you guys. Your weaknesses, your needs. We can lock them in *our* dungeon."

It was never a good idea to allow one of your enemies to be controlled by another of your enemies. But recently, Cronus, the former keeper of Greed, and Rhea, the former keeper of Strife, had been beheaded. The self-touted gods had been given a pair of serpentine wreaths, but theirs had come from Lucifer. Hades had not performed an exchange.

"Don't go after the Titans," Baden said. "Not yet. They're likely enslaved to Lucifer." The way he and Pandora were enslaved to Hades. They might have powers—and desires—the Lords knew nothing about.

"I don't see the problem." Sienna moved beside her

man. The slender woman had curly dark hair and a freckled face. The enormous black wings arching above her shoulders gave her a regal and slightly wicked quality. "An enslaved man is a weakened man. There's no better time to nab them."

No! Baden refused to believe her assertion. He was enslaved, but he wasn't weak. "Just…trust me on this. Lucifer might *want* you to rescue the pair. Let me do a little digging first." He knew the first place to use his shovel. Though Keeley was currently shacked up with Torin, the keeper of Disease, she'd once been engaged to Hades. "Where's the Red Queen?"

"With the artifacts," Haidee said. "Why do you—"

Baden strode into the hall before she could finish, and the beast roared with displeasure.

Never leave an enemy behind.

I didn't. I left friends.

He tuned out the shouts of denial, reaching the artifact room without incident.

Keeley was pacing. She stomped past the Paring Rod, the Cage of Compulsion, then turned and stomped past them again, twisting the Cloak of Invisibility between her fingers.

"I can't find dimOuniak, and if I can't find it, I can't find the Morning Star," she muttered. She was a beautiful woman who changed colors with the seasons. Summer had given her pink hair with streaks of green and eyes the color of an afternoon sky. "I have to find the box. I have to find the Morning Star. What am I missing? What am I doing wrong?"

Baden knew the danger of startling this woman who had powers beyond imagining, but cleared his throat anyway.

As she jolted, a lightning rod of pain sliced through him.

The beast kicked up another fuss, demanding Baden slay her.

He should thank her. She could have done far worse damage to him. This? This was nothing.

"Baden?" She blinked with confusion.

Forced inhale…forced exhale. "The wreaths have made me a slave to Hades."

"Uh, yeah." She flipped the long length of her hair over her shoulder, the action wholly feminine, hiding the otherworldly strength she somehow managed to contain inside such a fragile-looking frame. "You say that like it's a surprise."

She'd *known*? "It is. To me."

"If you didn't want to be Hades's yes boy, why did you accept his wreaths?" She anchored her hands on her hips. "You could have remained *Lucifer*'s yes boy."

When she'd appeared with Hades, she'd said, *This season's hottest accessory! You'll never regret the decision to wear them. You have my word.*

His jaw clenched so forcefully his teeth ached. He reminded her of her promise.

"I said that?" She shrugged. "Wow. You're gullible. But, uh, I'm *certain* I calculated the odds of something bad happening to you."

Oh, really. He crossed his arms over his chest. "I'd love to hear your math."

"Well, if you have two wreaths and one immortal, how many problems will he face? Gold. Obviously. Because the heart bleeds secrets and doggies have claws."

How did Torin remain sane when conversing with her? On top of being crazypants from centuries of captivity, she had a shit memory. She'd existed since the dawn of time and had often referred to her mind as a corkboard with too many pictures attached. Some things were hidden by others.

Focus on the task at hand. "Are Cronus and Rhea now controlled by Lucifer?"

"Oh, yes."

Finally. A coherent answer.

"But the blind cannot lead the blind."

An-n-nd back to square one. Lucifer, Cronus and Rhea were not blind. Baden switched routes. "Hades commanded me to fetch a coin."

"Well, don't look at me for a loan." She held her hands up, palms out, and backed away from him. "I might beat you with a pillowcase full of quarters, but I'll never share a penny."

"I'm not asking for money. I'm asking for information." He had to tap into the vast ocean of her knowledge. Somehow. "Think. Why would Hades want a specific coin?"

"Is he broke, too? Prick! If he steals the diamonds I stole, I'll remove his testicles. Again!"

Calm... "Listen carefully, Keeley. A human male has Hades's coin, and Hades wants this *most special* coin back. Does it have unusual powers?" Could Baden use it to his advantage?

She blew him a kiss. "I'm mighty and fearsome. Immortal royalty! I don't concern myself with mortal affairs."

Steady... "Forget the human." For now. "I'm supposed to remove the tongue of a siren. Why would Hades command me to do such a gruesome task?"

"Hello! Because two tongues are better than one."

Destruction shoved a roar out of Baden's mouth as a

memory rose… Keeley hovering in the air, her hair such a dark red the strands resembled rivers of blood. Others hovered in the air around her, their bodies taut, their limbs shaking…their lips parted in an endless scream.

One by one, the men and women burst apart, pieces of flesh and viscera raining down on him—on the beast. Blood splashed him, the only man left standing.

She smiled at him. "Better?"

"Much." He clapped, proud of her, but also leery. If her power increased any more, she would be able to defeat him.

All threats had to be eliminated.

Fingers snapped in front of Baden's face, and he blinked, returning to the present.

"Hey!" Summer Keeley looked him over. "You went zero dark thirty on me."

"I'm not sure you understand the term—never mind. I apologize." The beast had known and admired Keeley. Must have met her through Hades…must have been *friends* with Hades?

No better time to dispose of a future threat. Even if the threat is an ally.

Suddenly Baden's hands ached to wrap around her neck and squeeze.

Her spine will break as easily as a twig.

Horrified, he stepped out of reach. William had spoken true. One day, he would snap; he would be hated. The guilt he carried now would not compare to the guilt he carried then.

He had to leave the fortress, and this time, he had to stay gone. William's sex plan had merit but he now knew beyond a doubt it wasn't the answer. Because of his skin sensitivity, yes, but also because he couldn't trust anyone.

Again, the irony.

Lucifer would send another assassin. It was only a matter of time.

Destruction writhed with anticipation, practically foaming at the mouth to prove himself strong. *Attack me. See what happens.*

Let me guess. You'll kill. Broken record. The beast needed new material.

A sense of loss struck Baden. His friends wouldn't understand his continued absence. A second "vacation." They would worry, and they would wonder if *they'd* done something wrong.

Together we stand, or one by one we fall.

How many times had Maddox, the keeper of Violence, spoken those words since Baden's return? Countless.

This wasn't righting his wrongs, but it *was* putting the well-being of his loved ones first.

"Baden?"

He turned from Keeley and palmed the cell phone Torin had given him. Technology was a bitch he had yet to tame, but he gave group texting his best shot.

Meetinf in 5

He would explain his situation with Hades and, with the advice of the warriors who'd navigated this world far longer than him, plan his first move, gain his first point, and fight by fair means or foul to maintain the lead in his game with Pandora.

The sooner he won, the sooner he could say goodbye to Destruction and safely return to his family.

3

"All I want from a man is everything and nothing
at the same but different times, sometimes and
never but always."

—Keeleycael, the Red Queen

Katarina Joelle prayed for the end of the world as her
fiancé recited his wedding vows.

Aleksander Ciernik was a bad, bad man, and she
would rather eat rusty nails than pledge her life to his.
But he'd given her a choice: marry him or witness the
torture of her brother Dominik.

Earlier in the year, Dominik had signed up to work
for Alek of his own free will. So, after she'd laughed
in Alek's face and said, "Go ahead. Torture him," he'd
upped the ante. Marry him, or witness the torture of
her precious dogs.

Panchart! Bastard.

She'd stopped laughing and started calculating the
LGB. Likelihood of Getting Bitten.

To Alek, Katarina would only ever be a prized horse
to trot around his friends whenever the mood struck.

He would do nothing but make her miserable. But her dogs needed her. They had no one else.

The problem? If she saved the dogs today, Alek could hurt them tomorrow. Or any day after. He would continue threatening their welfare to control her.

But, if she saved them today, she would gain time. Time she could use to hide them. If ever she *found* them. Alek had hidden them.

His guards watched her every second of every day, but twice she'd managed to sneak out of her suite to search the estate. She'd been caught both times, no closer to success.

I'm going to get bitten one way or another, aren't I?

Throughout her childhood, she'd helped her father with the family business, training drug-detection and home-protection dogs. After high school graduation, she'd taken the reins of control. And despite the added weight of responsibility, she'd used her free time to rehabilitate the aggressive, abused fighters the rest of the world had deemed too dangerous.

Three of those victims—Faith, Hope and Love—had been so deformed most people hadn't had the cojones to look at them, much less to offer a forever home. So Katarina had adopted the trio as her personal pets, pouring her heart and soul into giving them the happily ever after they'd always deserved; they adored her for it.

Then Alek kidnapped them and held them for ransom. He'd also vowed to hunt down *every* dog she'd ever worked with—one bullet to the brain.

She loved her canines, remembered every name, every tragedy they'd suffered in their young lives, and every personality quirk. More than that? A trainer always protected her charges.

A lesson her father had taught her.

Mr. Baker—a sniveling coward on Alek's payroll who'd gotten ordained online—cleared his throat. "Your vows, Miss Joelle."

"Mrs. Ciernik," Alek snapped.

She smiled without humor. "Not yet." *Can I really do this?*

He scowled at her, and she rubbed her thumb over the words tattooed on her wrist. *Once upon a time…*

A tribute to her Slovakian mother, a woman who'd had the courage to marry an American dog trainer despite their different backgrounds and skin colors, even despite their language barrier. Edita Joelle had fancied fairy tales, and every night, after she'd read one to Katarina, she'd sighed dreamily.

Beauty can be found in ugliness. Never forget.

Katarina hadn't really liked the stories. A princess in distress rescued by a prince? No! Sometimes you needed to wait for a miracle, but sometimes you needed to *be* the miracle.

Right now, she could find no beauty in Alek. Could see no miracle in the works.

Did it really matter? She was the author of her own story—she decided the twists and turns—and often what seemed to be the end was actually a new beginning. Every new beginning had the potential to be *her* happily-ever-after.

No question, today marked the start of a new beginning. A new story. Perhaps, like the fairy tales of old, it would end in blood and death, but it *would* end.

I can endure anything *for a short time.*

Strong fingers curved around her jaw and lifted her

head. Her gaze locked on Alek, who looked at her with a shudder-inducing mix of lust and anger.

"Say your vows, *princezná*."

She despised the nickname. She wasn't pampered or helpless. She worked hard, and she worked often. Many of her patrons had called her a stay-at-home dog mom. A compliment. Mothers worked harder than anyone.

And I love my babies. Dogs were better company than most people, period. Better than Alek, definitely.

"You make me wait at your own peril," he said.

Quiet words, clear promise.

She wrenched free of his hold. He was a plague upon mankind, and she would never pretend otherwise. Especially when she should be wedding Peter, her childhood sweetheart.

Peter, who had always joked, always laughed.

Sorrow spurred her on. "With you, *everything* is at my peril."

This man had already ruined her. Dominik had spent her money on drugs, draining her accounts, before selling the kennel to Alek, who'd burned it down.

His eyelids narrowed to tiny slits. He might like the look of her, but he'd never appreciated her honesty.

Fun fact: provoking him had become her only source of joy.

"I'm not sure you understand the great honor I bestow upon you, Katarina. Other women would kill to be in your position."

Maybe. Probably. With his pale hair, dark eyes and chiseled features, he looked like an angel. But those other women failed to see the monster lurking within... until too late.

Katarina had seen it from the beginning, and her

lack of interest had challenged him. There was no other reason a five-foot-eleven man—who'd only ever dated short women in an effort to appear taller—would take a fancy to someone his same height.

Though she'd always been a jeans-and-tennis-shoes kind of girl, she had a feeling she would soon develop a love of stilettos.

"Honor?" she finally replied. His last three girlfriends had died in suspicious ways. Drowning, car wreck and drug overdose. "That's the word you think applies?"

"*Great* honor."

Alek liked to tell his business associates Katarina was his mail-order bride. And in a way, she was. A year ago, he'd wanted to buy home protection dogs from a fellow Slovak. He'd come across the *Pes Deň* website and discovered she was known for training the best of the best. Rather than filling out an application, as required, he'd flown out to meet her.

After only one conversation, she'd suspected he would abuse her animals. So she'd refused him.

Soon afterward, Peter died in a filthy alleyway, the victim of a seemingly random mugging.

And soon after *that*, her brother was invited to join Alek's import/export business—importing drugs and *prostitútky* to the States, exporting millions in cash to be hidden or laundered. Not surprisingly, Dominik quickly developed an addiction to Alek's heroin.

Just another way to manipulate me.

When Alek summoned her to his estate in New York—*Dominik owes me thousands. You will come and pay his debt*—she'd once again refused him. Later in the week, Midnight, a cherished mountain dog, was poi-

soned. She'd known Dominik—and thereby Alek—was
to blame. The once-abused canine wouldn't have taken
a treat from anyone else.

She'd quickly found homes for the other dogs. But
her fool of a brother had known the few people she
trusted, and had given Alek their locations in exchange
for a reduced debt. *Always one step ahead.*

"I'm here for one reason and one reason only," she
said, hating him, hating this, "and it has nothing to do
with honor."

Mr. Baker backed out of striking distance.

Alek grabbed her by the neck, squeezing hard
enough to restrict her airway. "Be very careful how
you proceed, *princezná*. This can be a good day for
you, or a very bad one."

"Your vows," Mr. Baker rushed out. "Say them."

Alek gave her one last squeeze before releasing her.

Breathing in…out…she skipped her wild gaze
around the chapel. Armed guards were posted throughout. The pews were filled with Alek's business associates, more armed guards and various other employees.
The men wore suits, and their dates were draped in formal gowns and expensive jewels.

If she refused, she would be killed—but only if she
were lucky. Most assuredly her babies would be killed.

To the back of the building, beautiful stained-glass
windows framed an intricately carved altar. Beside each
of those windows was a marble pillar veined with glit-
tering rose, and between those pillars hung a painting
of the tree of life. The frieze leading up to the domed
ceiling depicted angels at war with demons and complemented the swirling design of gold filigree on the
ivory floor tiles.

The room offered a fresh start, not damnation, and yet she felt damned to the depths of her soul.

Save the dogs. Save Dominik.

Scratch Dominik. Just the dogs. *Then escape.*

At last, she repeated the vows. Alek beamed with happiness. And why wouldn't he? She had, like so many others, allowed evil to win the battle.

But the war still rages...

"You may kiss your bride," Mr. Baker announced, his relief palpable.

Alek took her by the shoulders and yanked her against him. His lips pressed against hers, and his tongue forced its way past her teeth.

Her husband tasted like ashes.

There was no going back now.

How was she going to survive the wedding night?

As the crowd cheered, the sanctuary doors burst open, banging against the walls. An ominous *thud* heralded a quick silence. Alek stiffened and Katarina's heart skipped like a stone over water.

Three males stalked down the center aisle. They were tall and muscled and very clearly on a mission. Law enforcement? Here to arrest Alek? Oh, please, please, please!

The one on the left had black hair and blue eyes. He smiled at the men in the pews, daring them to make a move against him.

The one on the right had white hair and green eyes. He wore black leather gloves that somehow lent an edge of menace to a genuinely relaxed demeanor.

The man in the middle...he captured her attention and refused to let go. He was so beautiful; he put Alek to shame. Despite the specks of blood staining his

T-shirt—had he fought the guards outside?—he was an amalgamation of every fairy-tale prince ever written. The kind of man usually only seen in fantasies.

Her mother would have loved him.

He was the tallest of the three, with dark red waves that framed a fiercely masculine face. Every inch of him was defined by such incomparable strength, he could have been carved from stone.

Feminine awareness sparked—*this man is the incarnation of dark, dangerous desire, but I'm not afraid... I'm intrigued.*

A well-defined brow led to a straight nose and sharp cheekbones. His lips were lush and his softest feature. His square jaw, his harshest feature, was dusted with dark stubble.

But his eyes...oh, *tristo hrmenych*, his eyes. They were a combination of both, soft yet harsh and pure carnality. They were the color of a sunset, blazing with different shades of gold and copper.

He and his friends stopped just below the dais.

"Ladies and genitals." The black-haired soldier—agent?—spread his arms to encompass his audience. "You'll give us a moment of your time."

Alek puffed up with fury. "Who are you? Better yet, do you know who *I* am?"

The redhead took another step forward, his gaze doing a quick sweep of his surroundings. He even looked Katarina up and down, taking in the wedding gown Alek selected for her—a strapless monstrosity with a corset top and a wide, full skirt layered with satin roses. His mouth curved in distaste.

She raised her chin, even as her cheeks burned with embarrassment.

He focused on the glaring Alek. "You have a coin." His accent… Greek, perhaps? "Give it to me."

Alek laughed his patented you-only-have-minutes-to-live laugh. "I have many coins." Several of his guards unsheathed their guns, waiting for the signal to strike. "You'll have to be more specific."

"This one belongs to Hades. Pretending ignorance will do you no good."

Alek gave his most trusted enforcer, who now blocked the door at the back of the room, an almost imperceptible nod.

The signal.

The enforcer aimed. No. No! Katarina screamed out a warning. Which was unnecessary. The redhead was already mobilized, spinning and tossing a dagger. The tip sank into the enforcer's eye socket.

Blood spurted, a howl of pain echoing from the walls. The gun fell from his grip, useless, and he dropped to his knees.

Katarina's scream tapered into a whimper. The redhead had just…without any hesitation…so brutal…

The women in the pews jumped up and raced through the exit, their heels *click-clacking* against the floor tiles.

"My next victim will lose more than an eye," the redhead said with cool detachment.

The male with black hair and blue eyes grinned. "Baden, my man, if *I* were keeping score you'd get a ten-point bonus. *So* proud of you right now."

Baden. The redhead's name was Baden. The *killer's* name was Baden, and the black-haired man had just praised him for his violence.

Baden focused on her. "Test me. I dare you."

Anyone else would have cried and begged for mercy

when challenged by such a deadly force. For Katarina, tears were impossible.

She'd cried buckets in the months leading up to her mother's death, but not a single one after. She'd been too relieved. Her mother's misery had finally ended. But with the relief had come guilt. If Katarina hadn't been able to cry for the mother she'd revered, what right did she have to cry for anyone else?

Paling, trembling, Alek retreated—he never retreated!—stepping behind her and...using her as a shield?

In the first pew, her brother stood. He was six feet tall, though his emaciation made him a pin-drop in comparison to the newcomers. Did the *chruno* actually plan to fight trained killers?

Baden pivoted in his direction.

"No!" She scrambled from the dais to throw herself in front of Dominik. "My brother has nothing to do with this. You will not harm him." While her affection for her only living family member had withered, she remembered the boy he used to be. Kind, patient and protective. She had no desire to see him killed, would rather see him locked behind bars, forcibly removed from Alek's insidious influence and a ready supply of heroin.

Maybe, if Dominik got clean, they could try to be siblings again.

He pushed her behind him, astounding her. "Do not play the hero, *sestra*."

Baden lost interest in him. Radiating bloodcurdling malice, he closed in on Alek, the man so many feared. "This is your last chance. The coin."

Alek pursed his lips, an action she knew well. His

drug lord moxy—*I am master of all I survey*—had just switched back on. "The coin belongs to me. Tell Hades he can go to hell where he belongs."

The dark-haired man laughed. The white-haired man adjusted his gloves.

"Wrong answer. Perhaps you don't yet believe I'm willing to do anything to retrieve it." Baden grabbed Alek by the neck and lifted him off his feet, squeezing him with so much force his eyeballs bulged and his face reddened. "Does this convince you?"

The dogs! If he died… "Stop," she shouted. She tried to return to the dais, but Dominik snaked an arm around her waist to hold her in place. *"Prosím!"* Please.

Baden ignored her, telling Alek, "I'll leave with the coin…or I'll leave with something you value." He motioned to Alek's hand with a tilt of his chin, ensuring his meaning was clear. "You choose."

Alek sputtered, beating at his arm.

"Know this," the redhead added, unruffled. "I'll be back tomorrow, and the next day, and the next, until I have what I want, and I will *never* leave without a prize."

Who was this man? Who was Hades?

Alek grappled for the small gun hidden at his waist. Baden spun with him, using him as a buffer while firing the man's own weapon at the guards who'd taken aim.

New howls of pain erupted. Blood splattered, and bodies dropped. Katarina clutched her stomach to ward off waves of nausea.

Finished with the guards, Baden twisted Alek's wrist and broke the bones; the gun fell as her groom screamed. More and more men jumped up to help him, and more and more guns were aimed at the trio.

Even Dominik withdrew a gun from his ankle holster, though he didn't take aim. He hauled her through a side door, down a long corridor.

Boom! Boom! Boom! Multiple shots rang out behind her.

Had Alek been hit? She tried to fight her way free. "Let go!"

"Enough." Her brother was panting, already winded. "This is for your own good."

A gesture of kindness, even if it was executed the wrong way.

"I won't allow Alek's bride to suffer," he added, ruining everything. For him, everything always came back to Alek.

"I must stay with him," she said. "The dogs—"

"Forget the dogs."

"Never!"

The gunshots stopped. The pained grunts and groans quieted. The scent of gun smoke and corroded metal coated the air, following her.

Just before Dominik reached the doorway that led to the outside world, she stuck out her foot and tripped him. He maintained his grip on her, lugging her with him as he crashed. As he fought for breath, she was finally able to jerk free. He reached for her, but she kicked him in the stomach and stood.

Cursing, he hopped up. She leaped backward and—

Slammed into a brick wall. With a gasp, she whirled. Her gaze traveled up a man's legs…a torso ridged with muscle. There were thin rivers of black tattooed from the tips of his fingers to the edge of the black bands that circled his biceps. Three bullet holes marred his shoulder, but the wounds didn't appear to be bleeding.

Her eyes locked on cool copper irises. Baden.

He was hyperfocused, radiating challenge, determination and lethal intent…maybe even anticipation.

"Get out of the way, Katarina," Dominik commanded.

Baden reached around her to knock her brother's gun across the hall.

When confronted with an aggressive dog, stay calm. Avoid direct eye contact. Stand sideways and claim your space.

She peered beyond him while assuming the proper stance. Then, using her calmest tone, she said, "Your quarrel is not with us. We mean you no harm."

"Lately I need no reason to quarrel with anyone, *nevesta.*" *Bride* in Slovak. He spoke her native tongue? "But you…you give me reason. You worry for a piece of shit." His disgust had returned full force. "You *married* a piece of shit."

He thought the worst of her, had no concept of the truth. *Don't know him, don't like him. His opinion doesn't matter.* "Should you really cast stones? You have glitter smeared on your neck." Truth. "Courtesy of a stripper girlfriend?"

When he offered no reply, her spark of temper drained. She asked softly, "Is Alek still alive?"

"Are you worried for him, or the position of power you'll lose upon his death?"

Position of power? Please! "Is. He. Still. Alive?"

Baden inclined his head. "He even has all his body parts. For now."

Thank God! "Listen to me. I'll get your coin. Yes?"

"You won't do any such thing. And you won't hurt her," Dominik told Baden. "I won't let—"

Baden glared him into silence before returning his attention to her. "You know which coin I seek?"

"No, but you can describe it and I can search Alek's home." If Baden kept the guards at bay, she could finally hunt for her dogs without fear of getting caught. "Let's go there now."

"You've seen the trouble your husband is willing to endure to ensure the coin remains hidden." Dark red waves fell over his strong brow, swatches of pure silk. "It won't be in a drawer."

Probably not. "Perhaps it's inside a safe-deposit box. I can gather all his keys. If we leave now—"

Dominik squeezed her arm but didn't say another word.

"What do you think I did before coming to the chapel?" Baden asked.

He'd been to the house? "Did you see three pit bulls? One is brindle, one is gray, and—"

"There were no dogs of any breed," he interjected, his brow furrowed. "No cats, either."

Devastation mixed with anger, the deadly combination frothing inside her. *Where* had Alek hidden her pets?

The white-haired man sidled up to Baden and, after a slight hesitation, patted his shoulder. "We have a problem. William killed the last—" His green eyes landed on Dominik, and he nodded. "Never mind. You kept a messenger alive. We're good."

Bile nearly choked her. "Three of you managed to kill over fifty armed guards?"

The white-haired man regarded her, all *did the bride hit her head on the way out?* "Wasn't like it was a big deal. They were only human." He smiled and walked away.

Only human. She couldn't stop her gaze from seeking Baden's, despite her warning to the contrary. He still watched her with that air of challenge, and she gulped. "You don't consider yourself human? So what are you, the boogeyman?"

"Yes."

What!

He stepped aside and motioned toward the sanctuary, the muscles in his arm flexing. "You will return. Now."

Leave the crazy man? No need to tell her twice. She raced down the hall and burst through the doors. She would stand guard over Alek if necessary and—

She skidded to a halt. Blood covered the walls and pews and pooled on the floor. Bodies, body parts and other things she couldn't name were flung here, there and everywhere.

Alek was nailed to the podium, unconscious, his head slumped forward. The bile returned, and waves of nausea crashed through her once again; she closed the distance. Her hand trembled as she felt for a pulse...it was barely perceptible, but it was there.

"Happy now?" Baden came up behind her, his shadow completely engulfing her.

"No! You tortured—"

"Rapists and killers. Yes. They got what they deserved."

"What gives you the right to be judge, jury and executioner?" And...and...the amount of death...the level of destruction...the trial of the day... "I think I'm going to—"

Too late. She hunched over and retched.

Baden had dragged her brother alongside him, but

neither male did the gentlemanly thing and held her veil out of the danger zone.

She almost snorted as she straightened and wiped her mouth with the back of her hand. A brutal savage and a callous heroin addict hadn't come to her aid? What madness!

"Mater ti je kurva," Dominik snapped at Baden as he struggled for freedom. *Your mother is a whore.* "You will pay for the travesty done this day."

Unconcerned by the outburst, Baden looked Katarina over. A spark of *something* lit his eyes, making her shiver. With dread. Had to be dread. "Aleksander will be the one to pay, and in a most unexpected manner. I've decided to take—his bride."

4

"Only one thing should be infectious. Your smile."

—Torin, keeper of Disease

"You can't just...take me," the bride said, obviously alarmed.

What was her name?

"I can, and I will. Don't fight me." The blood in Baden's veins *sang*, Destruction purring in harmony. Tides of pleasure rolled through him. *Hate the beast, but love* this. Nothing in his life—this one or the one before—had ever compared. And all it had taken? The total annihilation of another man's army.

So sure the annihilation is the cause? What about the girl?

One look at her and he'd been overcome with the urge to rut, long and hard and often—and oddly enough, to protect.

It was insanity. She meant nothing to him.

William and Torin were busy searching the slain for the coin. Just in case. Baden watched them, and the bride watched Baden, the heat of her gaze scalding him.

She cursed at him. "You're smiling right now."

Was he?

"Violence *delights* you? That's sick. Sick!" She unleashed a stream of Slovakian profanity, calling him terrible names and accusing him of sleeping with everything from a rat to a goat. Her anger clearly freed her of all fear.

Destruction paid her no heed. She was puny, harmless.

She actually *amused* Baden. So much rage in such a tiny body.

If ever her passion was redirected...

He swallowed a rumble of need—to hurt, only to hurt, surely—no longer amused.

Her brother reached out to slap a hand over her mouth, but she batted him away and continued shouting, saving the male from a blade through the heart. Baden had claimed the girl as a war prize. For one night, she would belong to him. He would safeguard what was his.

"Do not touch her again," he said with undeniable hostility.

The color drained from the brother's cheeks.

The bride moved in front of Baden, demanding his attention. A clear attempt to shelter the male who should have done everything in his power to shelter *her*.

Her concern for the men in her life—the scum—irritated him. Delighting in violence was sick, she'd said, and yet she had bound herself to a human who'd left the bodies of both the guilty *and* the innocent in his wake.

"There's a better way," she announced. "Killing a defenseless man is unnecessary and cowardly."

"No man is defenseless. Not while he has his wits."

"If wits are a weapon, some men are better armed than others. Some, like yourself, are actually unarm—"

"Katarina," the brother snapped. "Enough."

Katarina. A delicate name for a delicate (looking) woman.

She pressed her lips into a thin line.

She was far, *faaar* from Baden's type. He preferred strong warrior-women. Someone able to back up her boasts with her body. Like Pandora. Once or twice he'd even considered pausing their war. In the end, the desire to defeat her had always proved stronger than the desire to pleasure her.

He studied Katarina more intently. Her dark brown hair was wound in an intricate knot at the crown of her head, not a single tendril free to frame her arresting face. Arresting, even despite its delicacy. Big gray-green eyes possessed a catlike slant, sensually complemented by thick, straight brows and a fan of black lashes. A light smattering of freckles dotted an elegant nose and blade-sharp cheekbones. Plump lips dared a man to taste...

Resist.

Her jaw was her boldest feature, the one he wanted to trace with his fingertips; it was almost triangular, coming to a blunt point at her chin.

Her skin was as smooth and flawless as a freshly polished onyx stone—except for her arms. Multiple scars stretched from the inside of her elbows all the way to her wrists, each in the shape of teeth. She'd been bitten. But by what?

On her right arm, she had a tattoo. *Once upon a time...*

It was the beginning of more than one fairy tale, and an interesting choice for a gold digger. And she *was* a gold digger. He could think of no other reason a woman with such an indomitable spirit would pledge to love, honor and obey a man like Aleksander.

"Please," she said, switching tactics. "Give me a chance to find your coin. Alek has other homes. He has businesses. As his wife, I'll have full access. I will gladly search them all."

"How quick you are to betray your new husband." It irritated him as much as her concern. "Though I doubt he wanted you for your loyalty."

Done with the conversation, Baden grabbed her by the waist and hung her upside down, tucking her against his side, effectively avoiding skin-to-skin contact.

She kicked and flailed to no avail. He was simply too strong and her dress was too big, creating the perfect cage.

The brother reached for her. A mistake. Baden kicked his feet out from under him, sending him crashing to his ass.

"Stay," he commanded. "Or end up like the others."

The brother stayed down but spit on Baden's boots. "You won't kill me. You need me to deliver a message for you."

"Do I? A note would work just as well."

Eyes the same gray-green as Katarina's blazed with fury. "Take the girl, and Alek will kill you."

Baden grinned—so did Destruction. "You can't kill someone who's already dead."

Confusion shadowed the male's features, followed quickly by fear as screams tapered to moans throughout the sanctuary. Did he finally grasp the full scope of Baden's ruthlessness?

"A note won't convey proper emotion," the boy said.

He disagreed but said, "When Aleksander wakes, tell

him I'll find him in the morning. Hiding from me will do no good. If he fails to give me the coin, I'll keep my promise and take something else he values. Something that will make him *bleed*."

As the bride continued to struggle, Baden strode down the center aisle. "Let's go," he called.

William and Torin finished their search and raced over to flank his sides. They were spattered with crimson, but unlike him, they were free of injury. Good, that was good. Seeing them hurt might have propelled him into an unstoppable rampage. Against them!

Destruction liked to kick a man while he was down. *Should have ditched the pair and come alone.*

When he'd told his friends about the life-and-death competition hosted by Hades, the entire group had insisted on accompanying him. Baden had protested. The warriors had families now. Wives and children, as William had reminded him. There was no reason to endanger any of them. And they had life-and-death things to do, like finding the box and the Morning Star before Lucifer. Even finding Pandora, who'd gone off the grid. What if she turned her rage to the Lords, now that she was forbidden from striking at Baden? Also, Sabin and Strider were exploring ways to free Baden from his bands, and therefore Hades's control, while allowing Baden to retain his tangibility.

In the end, the warriors had overruled him, drawing straws to decide who would have the honor of aiding him. The honor. As if he was a prize they adored rather than a piece of shit who'd abandoned them. His guilt sharpened and razed his chest. How was he ever going to right the wrongs of his past when he owed his friends more and more?

Cameo, the keeper of Misery, and Torin had won the draw. William, who'd returned from the sexual buffet slash murder-fest, had simply said, "Try to stop me. Dare you. Oh, and it goes without saying you'll owe me another favor."

They reached the chapel exit. Baden stepped over the first set of guards he'd felled then shouldered his way through the door, sunlight and warm air greeting him.

"Taking the human is kind of a creeper move. You know that, right?" Torin said.

His words rallied Katarina. She increased her struggles, saying, "I can't leave Alek. Please! Let me go."

Her fear thrilled Destruction. "Calm yourself, girl. I have no plans to hurt you."

"Plans can change, yes?"

Oh, yes. "The good news is, we'll be together for only one night." No matter how Aleksander felt about her—love or simple lust—he would move heaven and earth to get her back. Today his pride had been pricked. If he allowed another man to steal his woman, he would lose the respect of his men. Or what remained of his men. His authority would be challenged daily.

He would hand over the coin, and that would be that. Baden would be awarded his first point and take the lead in Hades's game.

Actually, Baden would be awarded his *second* point. Once he secured Katarina, he would be flashing to the siren. He would remove her tongue, as demanded.

A dagger pierced his conscience. One he couldn't remove. Aleksander was scum. The siren was not. How could he damage her?

Would her tongue grow back? She was immortal, but like Baden, she was a spirit.

How was he supposed to live with himself after committing such a foul deed?

Easy, Destruction said. *You live.*

When Katarina beat her fists into his side, Baden added, "Your actions will dictate mine."

"Panchart!"

The sidewalks were crowded, the streets jammed with cars. Baden's SUV was double-parked, Cameo waiting behind the wheel.

"Help me!" Katarina shouted, and he wasn't surprised. To her, there was no better opportunity to escape. "This is an abduction!"

No one paid her any heed, everyone too busy staring at their phones, pretending the rest of the world no longer existed.

"Give her to me," William said, making grabby hands. "I think I've proven I'm better with the opposite sex. And mission planning. And fighting. And basic hair care. Frizz isn't your friend, Baden."

Baden tightened his hold on the girl. "My prisoner. Mine."

"Wow. Selfish much?" William frowned at him. "And after everything I've done for you."

"You mean everything I'll have to pay you for doing?" The favors to be named later had seemed innocent enough at the time. Slay an enemy for him? Guard his back during battle? Sure. Now the possibilities were endless and the beast...wasn't pleased.

Kill him. A command, as always, though this one lacked any true heat because of William's connection to Hades.

Death isn't the answer to every situation.

William pouted. "You act as if payment makes my good deeds less altruistic."

"It does!" Baden noticed two stray dogs perched on the curb.

Destruction growled in warning, and the dogs growled right back, as if they heard the sound Baden never released. The two were big, both black and white with patches of missing fur. Mange?

Katarina went as still as a statue. Quietly, calmly, she said, "Don't you dare hurt those poor animals."

I will not be ordered, the beast snapped. *I will—*

Nothing. You will nothing. Baden stepped around the dogs. The pair watched him with intense fixation, ready to pounce, and yet they made no move to jump him.

"Have a heart and call a shelter," she said.

"Already messaged one." Torin shoved his phone in his pocket and moved in front of him to open the back passenger door.

Baden threw the girl inside the vehicle, followed her in and caught her by the waist as she lunged for the opposite door. A superfluous action. William entered, blocking her from the other side. Torin claimed the front seat.

"Testosterone sandwich." William pulled a moist towelette from a dispenser hanging on the back of the driver's seat and handed it to Baden. "You should clean the condiments off your side of the bun."

"Curak!" the bride sneered as Baden removed the blood from his face. The Slovak word for prick. "I've done nothing to you. Say yes to your heart and let me go."

Baden fought—yes. An actual grin. "You think I have a heart?"

Even Destruction snorted.

Adorable.

"A human hostage?" Cameo burned rubber, speeding away from the chapel. "Really, boys? Whose bright idea was that?"

Everyone cringed, lances of sadness accompanying Cameo's words. Baden, William and Torin were used to the sensation and rebounded quickly. Not the human. She paled and trembled, curling into herself.

"Only one of us stopped using our big-boy brain." Torin hiked his thumb in Baden's direction. "Our very own beastie boy."

"What just happened?" Katarina whispered. "I never cry, and yet suddenly I want to bawl."

Never? "Misery," he replied, and left it at that.

"But… I'm always miserable." Bitterness laced her tone. "You…this…this is nothing new."

What did she mean, *always miserable*? She'd just married her dream man, had she not?

Cameo took the next corner a little too swiftly, nearly tossing everyone out the window. "Almost there."

Again, the human curled into herself.

He snapped, "Not another word out of you, Cam."

"What's your name?" William asked the human, a clear tactic to distract her.

"Katarina Joelle," she said, tremors in her voice.

"Katarina Ciernik now," Baden corrected, unable to hide his disdain.

She bucked up, her temper once again pricked. "You're right. I am. And a bride's place is beside her husband."

"So eager to return to your doom?"

"As if staying with you is any better, *vyhon si*."

"Jerk-off? Words hurt, petal. Perhaps you need your mouth washed out with soap. Or the magic elixir. Lucky for you, I happen to have a little magic elixir right…" William unfastened his pants. "Here. A potion so strong it will take down Typhon."

Typhon, also known as the father of all monsters. Baden grabbed William's wrist to stop him from showing Katarina the source of the "elixir."

"So suspicious." The male tsk-tsked, and after shaking off Baden's hold, pulled a tiny glass vial from a hidden pocket sewn on the inside of his slacks.

You've got to be kidding me.

Katarina reared back. "*Nie. Nie* drugs. Please."

Finally, the proper human response from her. Baden stuffed the vial of "magic elixir" in his own pocket, casting her a *just in case* look. "No drugs. *If* you stay still and quiet."

Katarina took stock, calculating the LGB. By remaining still and quiet, as commanded, she would avoid sedation. Awake, she could listen to conversations, learn more about her captors, fight if necessary, and keep track of her surroundings to better her chances of escape.

Though she trembled, she did her best to settle comfortably against the seat. And, even more difficult, she kept her lips pressed together for the remainder of the drive.

Finally, the driver—a black-haired, silver-eyed beauty—parked at a busy curb. She turned to wink at Katarina. "You're in good hands. Promise."

The sadness! Katarina wanted to die. The sooner the better. All of her loved ones were dead. Midnight was dead, and not just because of the poison. Her brother hadn't administered a strong enough dose, had merely caused Midnight's organs to *begin* to shut down. Her precious dog had been in pain, so much pain, with no hope of recovery, the vet had told her. She'd had to put a dog in the prime of his life to sleep, holding on to his paw as he slipped away.

"What part of *not another word out of you* did you not understand, Cameo?" Baden asked. "The bride looks ready to scoop out her internal organs and set them ablaze."

He acted as if the woman's voice was the source of the problem. Which was impossible…yes?

Baden opened a door and wrapped an arm around Katarina's waist, his gaze locking with hers. "If you run, I'll catch you. If you scream, I'll make you wish you'd died inside the chapel."

She shuddered. If ever a man would do as promised—and enjoy it—it was this one.

"I won't run," she croaked. "Won't scream."

As he "helped" her from the car, a barbed lump grew in her throat. She studied her new surroundings, memorizing details for police. Myriad flower boxes bloomed with begonias and lined the road's median, separating the traffic running north and south. The design of buildings varied, everything from medieval Gothic to box-shaped chrome and glass.

She'd seen very little of Manhattan, having spent most of her time confined inside Alek's country estate, and had no idea where she was.

Baden ushered her toward the only brownstone with copper-framed windows. A doorman let them pass a set of large glass doors without impediment, saying, "Congratulations on your nuptials, sir."

Baden ignored him. Katarina silently begged for help.

When the man merely smiled blankly at her, her shoulders hunched with disappointment.

People sucked. Her dogs would have helped her without hesitation.

Summer warmth gave way to cool air-conditioning. Once again she searched her surroundings. The ornate interior boasted a colorful ceiling mural and four three-tiered chandeliers that dripped with thousands of crystal teardrops. To the left was a beautiful winding staircase, hand-carved cherubs perched along the railing. To the right, multiple sitting areas delimited a massive unlit hearth.

The people milling about the lobby stared with open curiosity at the leather-clad warrior and the gaudy bride, but only for a second, not wanting to appear rude.

Can't scream, can't scream, really can't scream.

"You can be reasonable," Baden said as the elevator doors closed, sealing them inside the small cart. Alone. "I'm impressed."

His condescension irked. Death would be a small price to pay for standing up to such a brute. "You can be an asshole. I'm *not* impressed."

"You have spirit." He used a key card and punched a button for the top floor. The key card must have programmed the elevator to continue ascending, despite anyone waiting for a ride on any of the other floors, because they never stopped to acquire new passengers. "Your problem is you can't back up your spirit with brute strength."

The comment only irked her further.

Be strong, Katarina. Her mother's final words echoed in her mind. *Without strength, we have nothing...we are nothing.*

I'm someone!

"I suggest you be careful when dealing with one such as me," Baden added. "I'm a monster."

"The boogeyman," she whispered. The only real emotion he'd displayed was delight, and all because men were in pieces around him. He was the kind of person who cheered and placed bets as dogs fought to the death.

Keep his mind on his goal. "What's so special about the coin you're looking for?"

"I don't know."

Her brow creased with confusion. Had she mistranslated his words? "You don't know?"

"No."

And yet, he'd killed dozens of people to obtain the thing. He even planned to dismember Alek. "Explain. Please."

Ding. He led her down a hall, past a door and into a spacious room with gleaming dark wood floors draped with Tibetan rugs. Every piece of furniture was antique, boasting a unique animal carving: a swan, an elephant, even a winged lion. The fabric bordering the large rounded windows matched the rugs, the sides pulled back to reveal elaborate stained glass.

"Sit." He gave her a gentle push, and yet she stumbled onto the couch, plopping onto the comfortable cushions. "Stay."

Two commands she'd often given her dogs. Her fists clenched around her gown's colossal skirt, wrinkling the material. *She* was the trainer, not the other way around.

When an aggressive canine was sent to her for tam-

ing, she would introduce herself slowly, often pretending she was alone as she puttered around in places
he could watch her without feeling as though she en-
croached on his space. What she didn't do was allow
him to scare her away. He would only lash out more
aggressively the next time she appeared.

Baden wasn't a dog, but he was certainly feral. The
same principle applied. So, she stood.

He said nothing as she increased the distance between
them. She pretended to scrutinize lamps, vases and the
portraits on the wall, each a different type of flower.

"You appear calm and at ease, and yet I can sense
your terror." He leaned against the edge of the desk and
crossed his arms over his chest.

Surviving a feral, rule one: *Never show fear.*

Basically, fake it till you make it.

Two: *Use a soft but assertive tone.* Anything else
could rouse hostility.

Three: *Remember you get what you reinforce, not
necessarily what you expect.*

In this case, she ignored number four: *Place the dog's
needs first.*

And skipped to number five: *Find out what will work
best with each individual dog.*

"How do you sense my terror?" she asked, her tone
soft but confident. "I have no tells."

His raspy chuckle held a note of self-deprecation.
"Trust me. You have tells. My more beastly qualities
enjoy them."

"Do your more beastly qualities think I should thank
you for kidnapping me?"

"Yes. I did you a favor, *nevesta.* Consider this a holiday from the terrible life awaiting you."

"You know nothing about my life. Or me!"

He scoffed, his disgust back in full force. "You are married to Aleksander Ciernik. I can guess."

Don't know this man, don't like him. His opinion doesn't matter. But…

What would he do if she told him about the dogs? Would he understand her plight? Help her? Or would he condemn her?

Will never tell him! He was a killer, as bad as Alek—maybe worse—and he might hunt down her babies just to spite her.

"Your greed will bring you nothing but pain," he said.

She blinked at him. "Greed?"

"You covet your husband's money and power."

Her fingers curled into her palms, her nails cutting. "What about his pretty face? And what of redeeming him? Could I not want to make an honest man of him?"

"A bad man is a bad man," he said, his tone flat.

"No hope for you, then, eh?"

Direct hit. He scowled at her.

Clearly, she'd stumbled onto dangerous territory. She backtracked, forcing a saucy grin. "Perhaps I spoke too hastily. Perhaps I just don't know you well enough. Yet." If she could get her hands on the vial in his pocket, she could drug *him.* She could escape, return to Alek, save her babies, and run…for the rest of her life.

Her grin slipped. "Why don't you order room service for us both, *pekný*?" Handsome. She winked at him. "I'm dying—hopefully not literally—to learn more about you."

Baden was no longer amused by the girl's outbursts. The angry ones…and the flirtatious ones. More and more, he disliked how she made him feel. She looked at him as if he was a disappointment—because he was. She considered him as bad as the human she'd married—with good reason.

By the time he finished with the siren, he would be far worse.

"I'm your captor," he told her, "not your provider." She was beautiful, somehow more beautiful by the minute, and she most assuredly had plans to charm him. How many men had she tricked over the years? How many had she bled dry before moving on to another one?

Power before sentiment.

"Do you plan to keep me weak with hunger?" She continued to meander around the room, the innate sway to her hips acting as a summoning finger. *Come here. Touch.* He found the strength to resist. Barely. "Fear I'll overpower you otherwise?"

"Hardly. I've never met a feebler female." How easy it would be to wrap his hands around the elegant column of her neck and end her.

Or better yet, he could chew her up and spit her out.

She whipped around to face him, anger crackling in her eyes. "I'm feeble because a he-man was able to cart me away from my wedding?"

"Yes. You are unable to protect yourself, or even to take care of yourself. You need others to do it for you."

Threatened by those with power, disdainful of those without it. Was there any type of person he liked?

Katarina looked as if he'd slapped her. Then she blinked away the wound and pouted at him. "Can *any* woman protect herself from you, *pekný*?" She picked up a vase, weighed it in her palm. Deciding if it would make a decent missile? "I bet you slay hearts…figuratively as well as literally. Oh, and let's not forget the panties you must melt."

Just. Like. That. He shot hard as stone.

William strode through the front door, spotted Baden's state, and rolled his eyes. He launched into a speech about necessary tweaks to security.

Focus. Engage. But Baden...couldn't. The bulk of his attention remained on Katarina. When she filched something from a side table, he stalked to her side and, ignoring the pain of skin-to-skin contact, pried open her fingers.

She gasped as he stepped back, taking...a pen with him. A simple ink pen?

"Fine," she said. "Keep it. I didn't want to write down the poem I'd composed about you, anyway."

A lie. She'd hoped to use the pen as a weapon. Silly woman. Did she not know her own limitations? She'd vomited at the sight of blood. She would never have the courage to attack him. "Tell me the poem." A command, not a request. "I'm brimming with anticipation."

She smiled sweetly at him, batting her lashes. "His beauty is terrible, just like his temper. I look at him and I can only whimper."

Funny. Baden leaned down, putting him nose-to-nose with her. "Do you like the beginning of *my* poem? I'm no better than a homicidal maniac right now. Mess with me, and you'll see how."

5

"If this situation sucked any harder, I'd have an orgasm."

—Paris, keeper of Promiscuity

Katarina remained docile as Baden ushered her down a long hallway. He probably viewed her passivity as another sign of weakness. Let him. His mistake, her gain. He would never expect her to act against him. Which she planned to do, in three…two…one…

She sagged into him, pretending to faint while reaching inside his pocket to filch the vial. Success!

She hid the drug within the folds of her gown as he snarled and hefted her into his arms. He carried her inside a spacious bedroom, the sleeves of his shirt lifting to reveal the metal bands fixed to his biceps. Bands warm to the touch. He tossed her unceremoniously onto the bed.

She maintained a smooth expression and lax body as she bounced.

"Behave, girl, and tomorrow morning you'll be returned to your husband in the same condition you left him." Footsteps pounded. The door snicked shut, sealing her inside. The lock engaged with an ominous *click*.

She waited one second...five...ten...before opening her eyes. Alone! Yes! She jumped up and rushed around the room, searching for a way out. Maybe Baden would take her to Alek tomorrow, maybe he wouldn't. Probably he wouldn't. She'd seen his face; she could identify him to authorities. Once he had the coin, he would be better off killing her.

The window had been sealed shut. The knob on the balcony doors had been removed and plastered over, preventing her from picking the lock. Fine. She switched gears, hunting for weapons. But all knickknacks had been removed. There were no paintings on the walls—nothing to smash over his fat head. In the bathroom, there were no brushes to use as shanks.

Either he'd expected to take a prisoner and prepared, or she wasn't the first person he'd abducted.

Think, think. She spun in a circle, eyeing every piece of furniture as if it was the answer to the question: *Will I live or die?* The dresser! Determined, she opened an empty drawer. A sense of triumph overtook her when she noticed the knobs were attached with nails.

The plan: *use those nails to gouge Baden's eyes and escape.*

Though she broke several of her own nails and ended up with multiple cuts on her fingers, she managed to unscrew two before the door lock clicked.

Her heart an unruly hammer against her ribs, she dove onto the bed, hiding her hands in the folds of the comforter.

Baden rolled in a cart of food. "Eat. You won't wither away on my watch." He threw a bundle of clothing at her feet. "Also, do us both a favor and change. I've never seen an uglier dress."

Then he hadn't rifled through the closet Alek had filled for her. "I'm curious. What poison did you use to flavor this food?"

He scowled at her, but took a bite of every dish before stalking to the exit.

"Don't you want to eat with me? We can—"

He shut the door and turned the lock.

Great! How was she supposed to drug him if he refused to spend time with her?

The answer ceased to matter as the scents of sugar, spice and everything nice wafted to her nose. *Can't... resist...* Her mouth watered and her stomach grumbled as she walked toward the cart. Since her arrival in New York...however long ago... Alek had basically starved her.

Have to maintain your girlish figure.

And, she was sure, the lack of nourishment had the added bonus of keeping her weak and befuddled.

Weak...

I've never met a feebler female.

Don't like him, his opinion doesn't matter.

As she lifted the lid from each dish, the scents intensified, and so did the grumbles in her stomach. She discovered creamy pasta with flakes of crabmeat, a bacon-wrapped filet with butter-drenched asparagus on the side, a strawberry-and-spinach salad, and a bowl of French onion soup. But her favorite? The pecan pie soaked in melting vanilla ice cream. Baden might be a bastard, but he was a bastard with excellent taste buds.

She inhaled the dessert first, shoveling in bite after bite. The pasta received the same treatment, and by the time she cleared the plate, she was moaning with discomfort, so full she might pop.

Battling a stomachache, she changed into the new clothes: a pair of shorts and a pink T-shirt that read "William Approved." Both were a little too snug, but she'd have an easier time moving in them.

She'd make him regret the gift.

She padded to the door. She could pick the lock as she'd done at Alek's home, but why? Baden would stop her. Maybe she could prevent him from getting in, at least for a little while, and figure out her next move without fear he'd harm her any second.

She struggled and strained to pull the dresser in front of the entrance, and finally succeeded. Not the best barricade, but adequate.

Her mind raced as she worked on liberating another nail. Considering Baden had accomplices, the more ammunition she acquired the better. But the stomachache only intensified, eventually welcoming bone-deep fatigue. Her adrenaline began to crash, her limbs growing heavier, until they weighed a thousand pounds each.

Don't fall asleep. Don't you dare fall asleep.

Sleep, even a light doze, would leave her vulnerable. The very reason she'd only catnapped since Alek entered her life.

Her best option for escape? The balcony. After stuffing the nails and the vial in her pocket, she dragged the comforter to the balcony doors. If she could get outside, she could flag help. She wrapped a pillow around her fist and punched, punched, punched. Finally a section of glass shattered. The tinkling sound was muffled, thanks to the comforter she'd draped, but it still made her cringe. She waited one minute, two, a seeming eternity, unable to breathe.

Baden never reentered the room. Was he even nearby? Or had he taken off, leaving her to rot?

She removed as much glass as possible and shimmied through the opening. Hot summer air had turned the entire area into an oven. She stood, expecting to see wrought iron, but the bright rays of sunshine highlighted six-foot-tall brick walls with ivy spilling over the sides. *Tristo hrmenych!* The balcony was completely surrounded by the brick, in fact. She could see no one, no other room and no other balcony.

She'd have to climb the wall to catch someone's attention. *Heart, don't fail me now.* She scaled up…up… using irregularities in the bricks as handholds and footrests. When finally she cleared the top, she straddled the ledge and held on for dear life.

Don't you dare look down.

She looked down, and oh, wow, her heart failed her, shuttering in her chest. She was a million flights up. Cars looked like ants and people mere specks. If she fell, she would become the definition of *splat*.

Sweat beading over her skin, she scanned the C-shaped building. Most of the window drapes were drawn. The few balconies within range were guarded only by wrought iron, not brick. A point in her favor. But no one stood—wait! A woman stepped onto the balcony to Katarina's right.

A striking twentysomething with shoulder-length black hair, the ends straight as a pin but uneven, as if she'd cut the strands with a kitchen knife—and no mirror. She had a strong, angular face and an equally strong body. The kind Baden preferred? Her black tank top put her toned biceps and the black bands wrapped around them on display. Bands just like Baden's. An American fashion statement?

Both of her arms were tattooed, but from this distance, Katarina couldn't catalog the designs.

A cigar rested between the woman's lips, black smoke curling around her. In one hand, she clutched a glass of amber liquid. In the other, she clutched a *bottle* of amber liquid.

"Madam!" Katarina whisper-yelled, waving her arms. "Madam!"

Eyes of indeterminate color focused on her.

"Potrebujem pomoc. Zavolajte políciu!" The words left in a rush. *Speak English! Right.* "My name is Katarina Joelle, and I need help. I'm being held prisoner by a man named Baden. He's a killer. Call the police—"

The woman stubbed out her cigar, turned around and entered her room, shutting the door behind her. Without ever speaking a word.

Katarina withered with disappointment. One of her dogs would have leaped across the building to reach her, but a fellow human being couldn't be bothered to reply?

Damn it, what was she going to do now?

The time had come to earn his first point.

Baden flashed to—

The spirit realm. A cottage by the sea, judging by the sound of lapping waves, the scent of salt in the cool evening breeze. The furnishings were sparse, offering only the bare necessities. A couch, a coffee table and a chair. There were no pictures or decorations. No personal items of any kind, the kind of things that made a house a home.

A sweet melody drifted from the back of the house. A woman was humming. More specifically, a siren was humming. The lush, magical quality of her voice swept over Baden and even…soothed Destruction?

A trick of the beast to lull him into a false sense of calm? Always a possibility. Or a wile of the siren?

Baden couldn't make himself care. He closed his eyes and enjoyed a rare and precious moment of peace.

Only when pots and pans clanged did he snap to attention. Anger burned through him, and Destruction growled. Not a trick, after all. The woman had managed to distract them both without trying. If she had the same power over Hades…

No wonder the male wanted her silenced.

Her, an innocent. Guilt razed Baden all over again.

Can't afford to lose the game. He still wasn't convinced Hades would keep his word and free the winner, but right now, he had no solution. He had to participate and buy time.

Determined, he stalked through the house. He stopped in the kitchen entrance, watching as the woman from his ash-vision dried and stored dishes. She moved slowly and always used both hands—one to hold the dish, the other to feel the cabinets as if…

She was *blind*?

He observed her for several more minutes, just to be sure, and decided, yes, she was blind. Twice, she'd turned in his direction but she'd never displayed a single hint of distress.

Horror joined his guilt. Hades expected him to mute a blind siren? No. Absolutely not. There were lines one simply didn't cross. Once you did, there was no going back. No being the man you used to be.

What if, when Baden returned without the girl's tongue, Hades sent Pandora to finish the job? Knowing her, she would act without question. She had centuries' worth of rage trapped inside her.

Damn it! There was no good option here.

The siren stiffened, quieted. Her ears twitched. "Who's there?"

Now or never. He flashed directly in front of her, wound his arm around her waist and, as she beat at his chest to no avail, flashed her to Hades.

"I will not hurt her," Baden announced, and the girl stilled. "You wanted her tongue. Now you have it—attached to her body. If you want to keep it, you will vow not to harm her."

The king sat upon the throne, the rest of the chamber empty. "You defy me right out of the gate. Shocking." Such a dry tone.

"If you wanted a devoted acolyte, you should have given the bands to someone else."

"What I wanted was a minion of darkness. What I got was a pussy! You need to get your shit together." Hades drummed his fingers impatiently. "I'll give you one more chance to man up. Let it be known henceforth. Hades, king of the underworld, shall grant his slave Baden one boon, good today only. You may use it any way you see fit. Freedom? A physical body?"

Baden blinked, and the siren vanished from his arms. Another blink, and she reappeared draped over Hades's lap. She trembled so violently she might have been having a seizure. Tears welled in her eyes and spilled down her cheeks, making him think about the tears Katarina *hadn't* shed. A pang in his chest.

Hades combed gentle fingers through the girl's hair, his gaze locked on Baden. "I *will* take her tongue. Unless you use your boon to stop me."

Rage—all his own. More guilt. Helplessness. Each bombarded him.

"Think carefully," Hades said. "You don't know the crimes this woman has committed against me."

What gives you the right to be judge, jury and executioner?

"Release her," he said through gritted teeth. "Vow never to harm her, and never to allow someone else to harm her."

Hades arched a brow. "This is your boon? You're sure?"

No. No!

He canted his head in agreement, earning a sigh from the king.

"I'll be damned," Hades said. "You're the first of my slaves to do so."

Others had worn the bands? What had happened to them?

A twinge of hope. With those few words, the king had revealed more than he'd probably wished. A fact Baden would use to his advantage. He would find the answers—and act.

Hades's days as his lord were numbered.

"I'm disappointed in you," Hades said. "One day you'll learn people are never what they seem. Isn't that right, siren?"

Her tears dried, and she laughed. "Wow. You really

are a pompous dick. Let me up. This position isn't exactly comfortable."

With a fond smile, Hades released her. She slugged him in the shoulder before she stood. Her eyes remained unfocused as she descended the dais steps, counting silently.

Realization hit. She was blind, but she was no innocent. She was wily as hell.

"What would you have done if I'd put a blade to her?" Baden demanded.

"*He* would have done nothing," she said, answering for the king. "*I* would have stopped you."

"She's one of my best fighters." How proud Hades sounded now.

People are never what they seem...

A trick. Only a trick.

"Await me in my chambers," Hades told her.

"Yeah, yeah. I know the drill."

Baden snarled at her when she passed him. She sensed his ire and flipped him off, unabashed, as she sailed through the door.

Were all the tasks Hades assigned him trivial? Or were they tests? What of Aleksander and the coin?

No, not a test. Baden had scented zero fear from the siren, but Aleksander had projected the emotion from the beginning.

Hades wanted him to do his bidding, never certain of the reason, never knowing what was real and what was fake. Perhaps so Baden would never scheme to keep something or someone for himself.

Well, Baden would treat every task with the utmost importance. He would watch and learn. He would find his moment...find a way to beat Pandora *and* Hades.

"You've made a grave error this day, *King*." He spat the title like the curse it was.

"Or have I learned more about you than you were able to learn about me?" Hades smiled at him. "Consider today's lessons freebies, Red. The next one will cost you dearly."

Katarina climbed the balcony wall throughout the night...the morning...cursing the height of the brick that blocked any type of view, hoping to catch the attention of someone else. All the while, she listened for Baden, thinking she'd jump down and dive on the bed when he busted through her blockade. And when he was within reach, she would finally put the nails to good use.

As she straddled the top of the balcony wall for what had to be the thousandth time, a hard hand wrapped her ankle and yanked. She tumbled into an equally hard chest. A hiss sounded—one she recognized—and strong arms caught her.

Baden was here!

He roared like a grizzly bear woken too early from hibernation as he set her away from him. His features tightened with...disgust?

Definitely disgust. It was his favorite reaction to her.

"Going somewhere, *nevesta*?"

Her blood flash-froze. *Keep it together.* "Just seeing the sights, *kretén*." Asshole.

"There's that naughty mouth again." Sunlight stroked him, unconcerned by the danger he presented. Or the darkness inside him.

Could she really blame the sun, though? Baden smelled edible. Like honey-and-cinnamon candles set ablaze in the heart of midnight. Delicious and seductive...wanton.

A killer shouldn't smell like that.

"Do you need the elixir?" he asked.

"Nie." Soon he would realize the vial was no longer in his possession.

Strike. Now!

In a lightning-fast motion, she grabbed a nail from her pocket and slammed the tip into his neck. Hissing again, he shoved her away from him. She stumbled backward and hit the balcony doors—the closed balcony doors. They sprang open on impact, and she toppled inside the room, skidding into the wall. Stars glittered in front of her eyes.

"Do not touch me," he barked. "Ever."

She was *that* repulsive to him?

When she caught her breath, she said in a dry tone, "But attempting to injure you is okay?"

He plucked the nail from his skin, not a drop of blood leaking from the wound. Was that a drop of...motor oil? "You tried to fight back the only way you could." He actually sounded impressed. Then he appeared irritated. "Don't try again."

Trembling with a mix of astonishment and fear, she lumbered to her feet. His gaze raked her scanty attire, and he lost his air of enmity. He suddenly appeared *appreciative.*

Had the heater just switched on? Because perspiration now sheened her skin. "Are you taking me to Alek?"

A blank mask quickly covered his features. "No."

"But why? It's a new day. He might have the coin ready for you." He wouldn't. He'd have an army ready instead. "Don't you want your treasure? You've worked so hard for it…"

Baden combed a hand through his hair, leaving the strands sticking out in spikes. Could he be *any* sexier?

Shame on her for noticing!

"I want it," he said, "but I don't want Hades to have it. So Aleksander can wait."

"Hades is—"

"Not a topic up for discussion."

She motored on, anyway. A distracted Baden was better than a roaring Baden. At first glance, he could pass for calm. Upon closer inspection, she realized his pupils were blown, his eyes wild. The muscles in his arms were clenched, the bands pressing deep into his biceps.

"You work for Hades but you don't actually like him? Why don't you present him with your resignation and—"

He crossed his arms over his chest. A warning?

"All right. You win," she said. "We'll talk about something else while we have a drink, yes?"

After a moment's hesitation, he motioned to the bedroom door. A door still blocked by the dresser.

She peered at him in question. "How did you get inside?" A secret passage?

Silent, he stalked past her and shoved the dresser out of the way with a single swipe of his arm. Such strength! Her heart pounded as she entered the hallway and followed the path he'd taken last night, snaking around a corner, stepping into the familiar sitting area.

She stopped at the wet bar, keeping her back to him as she poured two glasses of whiskey…and stealthily withdrew the vial; she emptied the contents into the bottle rather than a glass. There was a good chance

Baden would decline any drink she offered him, but an even better chance he would indulge on his own later.

As she drained the contents of one glass, she faced him and held out the second. He shook his head. With a shrug, she drained it, too. The alcohol burned going down but settled like melted honey in her stomach, soon warming her.

"Where are your friends?" she asked.

He glared at her as if debating whether to answer her or strangle her.

Maintaining a neutral expression, she looked him over. He wore yesterday's blood-splattered clothing. Had he slept in them or forced himself to stay awake, like her? Probably the latter. His features were so taut she wasn't sure he'd *ever* slept, the poor man.

Wait. Poor man? She had *sympathy* for him?

No, oh no. Unacceptable! But it made her wonder... what had shaped him into the cold, calculating monster he was?

Finally, he said, "The others are out buying essentials."

That sweet feeling of melted honey in her stomach? Gone in an instant. "Rope? Knives? Plastic tarp to protect the furniture from blood spray?"

"Monopoly. Candy Land. Jenga." He settled in the chair across from the couch, the floral fabric somehow showcasing his intense masculinity to perfection.

"Board games?" She chose to remain standing, the dominant position. "For children?"

"Apparently I'm boring. And immature. As soon as I returned from—" He white-knuckled the arms of the chair. "Anyway. The others left."

That grip of his...a sign his friends had hurt his feelings?

How sad.

No. It wasn't. It wasn't! A new plan formed. *Make nice with Baden while creating a one-way bond with him, ensuring he kept his word not to harm her, then escape, save her dogs, and run.*

Rule six of training canines: *keep interactions short and sweet.*

Seven: *always end on a positive note.*

"I'll get to know you," she said, feigning delight, "and I'll decide if you're boring or not."

"Your opinion of me hardly matters. We'll sit in silence."

Don't like him. "Poor dear. I'm a very excellent conversationalist, and you fear you'll struggle to keep up. I understand."

His lips pursed. "Did your *conversation* win Aleksander?"

"Please. I blinked, and he came running." Which was the truth. Unfortunately. "Don't you consider yourself stronger and smarter than Alek? Shouldn't you be able to resist my potent allure?"

He traced his tongue over his teeth and stood, the motion jerky. As he marched to the wet bar and poured himself a drink, he avoided her gaze.

Hope unfurled. Finally! Something was going her way.

"What do you want to know about me?" He returned to the chair, his glass half-full. "*Why* do you want to know?"

A sense of anticipation and triumph flared, one she tried her best to hide. "Why? I'm a curious creature. What? More than once you and your friends have mentioned the people around you are human, implying you yourselves are not. The white-haired man—"

"Torin."

"Torin even said you are something better. The boogeyman is not better."

He continued to hold the glass without drinking. *Don't stare. Shouldn't appear too eager.*

"I know you're not a *literal* monster," she said. Had she put a tad too much emphasis on the word?

"So you think we're...what?" he asked. "Delusional?"

No reason to lie. "Yes. But what do *you* think you are?"

"Immortal."

She barked out a laugh. "Like vampires? Were-wolves?" The current movie fad.

"If I were a bloodsucker, you would already be drained. If I were a wolf, you would be chained to my bed and used as a pack whore. A *kurva jebat'*, you'd call it."

There wasn't an ounce of amusement in his tone, and she sobered, realizing he truly believed what he was saying—believed creatures of the night existed.

"I'll tell no one," she said, raising her right hand. In fiction, otherworldly predators liked to keep their origins a secret, often killing the ones who discovered the truth. "You have my word."

"Tell whoever you'd like. You'll be labeled crazy. Insane." He shrugged and at long last drained the glass.

Relief bathed her, cool and sweet. She waited, watching him closely for any sign of sedation, but nothing changed.

Rule eight: *distract when necessary.* "Convince me. Tell me about your life."

"Again, why should I bother?"

"Because I'd really love to hear your story?"

"That's insufficient enticement."

"So...what do you want?"

His gaze heated. He inhaled sharply, as if he wasn't

pleased with the direction of his thoughts. Or maybe he was a little too pleased. His pants suddenly looked tighter.

The moisture in her mouth dried. She pressed her hands together, forming a steeple. "Just tell me. Pretty please. Please!"

The plea...actually softened his expression. "For centuries I lived in Mount Olympus, a guard to Zeus. I'm sure you've heard of him. Everyone has. My friends and I were vastly offended when he gave his greatest treasure, dimOuniak, to a female to guard. You know this treasure as Pandora's box. To punish Zeus, we stole it, opened it and unleashed the demons trapped inside it."

Wait, wait, wait. "Demons?"

A curt nod. "*He* decided to punish *us* and cursed us to host a demon inside our bodies. I was given Distrust, though I was liberated from him the day I was beheaded."

She snorted. "Beheaded? And yet, here you are, alive and well."

"Alive, yes. Well, no. No one, immortal or human, is merely a body. We have spirits and as you can see, my spirit is still very much intact."

"You're saying you're a ghost?"

"In a fashion." He set his empty glass on the side table, his arm disappointingly steady. "I spent the past four thousand years trapped inside a prison realm. Until a few weeks ago, when I was freed just like the demons in the box."

"Demons," she repeated hollowly. She accepted the supernatural and always had. The world, humans and animals were so amazingly intricate, so perfectly honed, and so clearly of intelligent design, she knew there was a God...and if there was a God, there were guardian angels.

Her guardian angel was on vacation. Obviously.

Also, she'd seen far too much evil *not* to believe there were demons ruled by a devil. But…but…

Baden wasn't an immortal. He couldn't be. Things like this didn't happen to people like her. Normal. Ordinary.

"Where's your laughter now, *nevesta*?"

Her eyes narrowed on him. He dared mock her? "Perhaps I'm too busy wondering if you're going to blame your crimes on the demon."

"No," he said, surprising her. "I'm no longer possessed. Not by a demon, anyway. I'm not sure what inhabits me now. A dark presence…a beast named Destruction. But I don't blame him for what was done at the chapel. I made my own choices. I pulled the trigger. I wielded the blade."

A beast? Destruction? "You hurt the men in the chapel so easily. I'm guessing violence isn't new to your wheelhouse, whether you are what you claim or not."

"No, it's not new to me. But sometimes it's a special treat."

Cold fingers of dread walked the length of her spine. "The more evil you do, the more evil you are," she said softly. For a moment, she closed her eyes and imagined she was safe in Peter's arms. A girl with a bright future. Happy. Hopeful. "What does your girlfriend…wife?… think of your proclivities?"

"I have no woman I call my own. There's no one strong enough to handle me."

Without strength, we have nothing. We are *nothing.*

"Strength is your only requirement in a mate?"

"Yes." He frowned. "No. I want no mate. I'm too dangerous."

He looked away from her, focusing beyond her. The color drained from his face, and flickers of red lit his eyes. No, no. His eyes were bloodshot, that was all. The horror of the situation—and his declarations—had affected her perception of him.

Sweat rolled from his brow as a tremor rocked him. Was he having a panic attack? Or was he fighting whatever he considered the beast?

She contemplated comforting him, but she knew better than to touch him.

"Sing," he croaked. "Sing now."

She wanted to snap at him for issuing such a harsh command, but she obeyed him instead. She'd often serenaded her dogs whenever they'd been frenzied. More often than not, they'd calmed. Within a few minutes, the red began to ebb from Baden's eyes. He released a heavy sigh, the color returning to his cheeks.

He rubbed his temple, as if to ward off an ache. Or a voice he couldn't silence.

Were the drugs finally kicking in? She licked her lips, suddenly nervous. If he suspected…

Keep him distracted.

"Well. It's my turn to share." Before he could order her to be quiet, she said, "I grew up with an American father. He was black. My mother was Slovak and as white as snow. Most people accepted our family, but there were some who didn't. I got in trouble on more than one occasion for fighting the *didn'ts*. Knock-down-drag-outs at school. Daddy used to say we can't fight fire with fire. We have to use water."

"I had…no mother." Baden blinked rapidly as his head lolled to the side. His eyes closed slowly, and stayed closed, his body slumping over the side of the couch.

What had he meant, he'd had no mother?

Did it matter? There was no better time to act. *Stay calm. Stay focused.* Katarina ran to the front door, searching for more weapons along the way. No knives, no guns. Nothing. Fine. She would go with what she had. Her hands shook as she flipped the lock. Hinges squeaked as the entrance swung open.

Ding. Elevator doors slid apart. Out strode the black-haired woman who'd smoked a cigar on her balcony. She had a big black bag slung over her shoulder—and headed straight for Katarina.

Humans weren't a waste of space, after all. She'd come to help.

"Thank you!" Katarina stopped in front of her. "We need to notify—"

"Where's Baden?" the woman asked, a raspy quality to her voice. Like Baden, she had a slight Greek accent.

The accent…the bands…

Unease overshadowed Katarina's sense of elation. "In there. Asleep. I drugged him."

The woman smiled with relish. "Well, well. Aren't you full of surprises?"

Katarina latched onto her wrist to pull her back to the elevators. "Come on. We must notify the authorities. They'll handle—"

"No. They won't. But *I* will." With that, the woman slammed her forehead into Katarina's.

She careened backward, pain and vertigo rushing her. Her last thought before darkness swallowed her whole: *Only I could escape a murderer and go from bad to worse.*

6

"Steal the box, they said. It'll be fun, they said."

—Baden, companion to Destruction

Baden fought through the oppressive taint of lethargy, Destruction roaring obscenities in the back of his mind. Katarina had drugged him, obviously, and escaped.

As weak as she was physically, she was strong mentally. She'd proved to be smart, resourceful and sneaky. He'd underestimated her. A mistake he wouldn't make again.

He almost…admired her right now. Almost.

Enemies must be dealt with swiftly and harshly.

Destruction wasn't so easily impressed.

Only a few minutes ago, the beast had raged inside Baden's head—the discussion about parents had made him think of his mother, Jezebel. A witch who'd ruled a section of the underworld before Hades. The bitch who'd sold Destruction to one of the (former) kings— the male who'd locked him in the dungeon all those centuries ago.

Remembering the calm the siren had caused with her voice, Baden had command Katarina sing to him. She wasn't a siren, or even part siren, and yet she'd caused a stronger reaction. The beast hadn't just calmed, he'd purred, utterly content.

She had power over him. Another reason she had to die.

Baden's ears twitched as the front door opened. Booted footsteps thumped against the floor. Too heavy to belong to Katarina.

A tension-laced pause ended with a soft chuckle he recognized. Pandora had found him.

She must have passed Katarina at the bank of elevators. Had she harmed the human to get to him?

Baden raged, and yet the beast quieted.

Pandora tsk-tsked. "Apparently females are your Kryptonite, my friend. This is the second time one has led to your murder."

Threat? Destruction asked. He wasn't sure?

Baden fought the lethargy with all his strength, his nerve endings beginning to tingle as they came back to life.

"Do you remember the feel of the blade slicing through your neck?" she asked, maintaining a conversational tone. "No worries if you don't. I'm about to remind you."

Something heavy whacked the coffee table. He managed to crack open his eyelids as a zipper opened.

Threat! Destruction snarled. *Must eliminate.*

"When I'm finished with you," Pandora said, digging inside an oversize duffel bag, "I'm going to kill your friends. And I'm going to make it hurt."

If she targeted Baden, not fine, but whatever. Just more of the same. But to turn her murderous intentions to his brothers and sister? Too far!

The beast snarled *louder.*

She continued blithely. "You and the others…you didn't just take the box from me, didn't just end my life. You ruined my only chance to—" She pressed her lips together, and her nostrils flared.

Her only chance to what? In all their years together, she'd never revealed the secrets of her past.

She slapped different metal parts together, creating a battery-powered chain saw. She smiled as she pushed a button, the motor revving and blades spinning.

She had come to *play.*

Rage consumed him; the rivers of black the wreaths had etched into his skin now chewed through his veins and burrowed deep into his bones, forcing them to expand. All the while, Destruction slammed against his chest—a chest that expanded, as well. Unnatural strength flooded him, dark and intoxicating, more than he'd ever experienced, as if the beast was taking over his body.

The beast *was* taking over his body.

Pandora looked him over and frowned. "How did you—never mind. I can guess. The wreaths have done weird things to me, too. But your reaction is too little too late, I'm afraid." She lifted the chain saw overhead. "This is goodbye, Baden. I'd say it's been nice knowing you, but I never lie."

He worked his jaw, finding his voice. "What of Hades's warning?"

"If killing you means dying myself, so be it." She stepped toward him, and he sprang into motion at last, kicking out his leg to knock her ankles together. She crashed to her ass, losing her breath; she managed to retain her hold on the chain saw, even as the blade cut through the wood floor, shavings flying in every direction.

He latched onto her foot and twisted, hard, breaking the bones in her ankle and hobbling her. At least for a moment.

She yelped, and then she swung the chain saw at him. Target: his neck. He ducked and, when the opportunity presented itself, booted the back of her hand, causing her grip on the weapon to finally loosen.

The chain saw dropped, the motor dying.

He stood while she crouched, her hair standing on end as if she'd just jammed her finger into a socket. Fangs extended past her bottom lip, little growls rising from her. The chompers were new; they were bigger than a vampire's but smaller than a bear shifter's. She had lines of black running from the bands, just like him, but hers were intermixed with the many butterflies tattooed on her forearms.

When Baden and the others were first possessed, a butterfly tattoo appeared on each of their bodies. Same basic shape, but in different locations and colors. Pandora's tattoos were self-inflicted, each representing one of the demons. Violence, Death, Pain, Doubt, Wrath, Lies, Secrets, Defeat, Promiscuity, Disaster, Disease, Jealousy, False Hope and Distrust. There had been other demons, but they were given to the immortals trapped in Tartarus. A prison for the worst of the worst criminals.

Pandora had no problem with those prisoners, only the people who'd stolen her box.

The butterflies were an obvious kill list.

She's a threat.

Yes. Oh, yes. "Where's the human girl?" he demanded.

"She's sleeping soundly at the elevators. Why? Were you hoping she'd come to your rescue?"

"You're the only one in danger today." Hades wouldn't punish him for defending himself. How could he? "You made a grave mistake, coming after me." The beast already envisioned how best to end her. Using the chain saw to hack off her limbs...then her head. "You should have focused your efforts on earning your first point."

"How adorable." She circled him, her chilling grin widening. "You don't know. I've *already* earned my first point."

His hands curled into fists as he turned with her. She was the head, and he was the tail? Unacceptable!

"Enjoy being in the lead while you can, *skýla*." Bitch. "It won't last long. You're weak." He pricked at her pride, determined to send her into a rage, to make her vulnerable. "You've always been weak. I remember how Haidee killed me, yes...but I also remember how easy it was to steal dimOuniak from you. I remember how Maddox swiped up a sword upon his possession and stabbed into your vulnerable belly six different times. You were utterly defenseless, unable to stop him. You couldn't even—"

Cursing him, she swung at his head. When he blocked her fist with the palm of his hand, she swung at him with her other arm, going for his throat. He leaned back, avoiding impact, while catching her other wrist. A single twist spun her around, allowing him to pin her arm behind her back.

"See? Weak," he whispered into her ear.

"Bastard!"

Destruction laughed as Baden wrapped an arm

around her neck to draw her against him, the pressure he applied enough to choke anyone else.

"Asshole," she managed to rasp.

A sharp pain exploded in his thigh before his entire leg went limp. He released her, stumbling back. The hilt of what had to be a poison-tipped dagger protruded just above his knee.

"I'm going to rip out your—"

A pained moan drifted from the hallway, snagging his attention, silencing him.

Katarina was waking.

"Dibs on the first kill," Torin said with relish. A gun cocked.

His friends had returned.

Pandora stiffened. Baden yanked out the dagger, and for the second time since his return from the dead, he bled. But just as before the blood was thick and black. He could only guess at the reason: the beast, who was more alive to him with every day that passed.

With Destruction shouting obscenities, Baden tossed the weapon. Pandora dodged left, but not swiftly enough. The blade grazed her shoulder. She sprinted toward the window, jumping…diving. Glass shattered, warm air blustering inside the living room.

He raced over, seeing she'd left smears of black behind. As she soared down, down, she used a retractable wire to slow her momentum. Swinging forward, she crashed through a window in the middle of the building.

He wanted to give chase, to attack, but the urge to safeguard Katarina—the key to *his* point—proved stronger.

William had her draped over his shoulder. "Where do you want her?"

Torin and Cameo flanked his sides, weapons drawn and at the ready. Baden wanted to make their lives easier, and yet he kept adding complications.

"The couch," he said. The scene of the crime.

"There's no one to kill?" Torin pouted. "I always miss the fun."

William tossed Katarina onto the couch cushions. When she finished bouncing, he noticed the large knot on her forehead. One *he'd* sported on several occasions. Pandora had head-butted her.

Scowling, he shoved William in the shoulder. "Be more careful with her. She could have a concussion."

"That's not exactly a me problem, now, is it?"

Cameo gave her semiautomatic a little toss, caught it by the barrel and pistol-whipped the shit out of William. As he cursed and rubbed the fresh wound, she said, "Consider it a you problem from now on. Any injury she sustains, I'll make sure you sustain as well."

Baden and Destruction shuddered in unison.

Note to self: *Earplugs are my best friend.* He had no idea how Cameo lived with her demon. Anytime she experienced a moment of happiness, the kind that would change her life for the better, the demon erased the memory, ensuring she remained forever surrounded by darkness.

Without light—hope—there was no desire to live. A fact he'd suffered firsthand.

"You're worse than my children," William muttered. "You know that, right, Cam?"

The male had four children. Three sons and a daughter. The daughter was murdered months ago, and the sons were now in the midst of a vicious war with her killer's family. A war the killer's family would not win. William had fathered the Horsemen of the Apocalypse.

Cameo—thankfully, blessedly—shrugged.

Torin holstered his gun and held up a shredded box. "Monopoly, anyone? Got the M&M's edition. The stray dogs outside the hotel used it as a chew toy, but I think I managed to salvage most of the pieces."

More stray dogs?

Katarina moaned before bolting upright. Panting, she gave the room a panicked scan. Her gaze met Baden's, and she scrambled to the edge of the couch, holding out her hand to ward him off, as if she expected him to attack.

"The woman," she said. Most of her hair had fallen from the topknot, long dark waves now framing her face. The sight of her in such disarray caused his gut to clench. So fragile—the weak died swiftly—but so damned beautiful.

Destruction snarled at her, but made no new demand to kill her.

"She is Pandora, the one I told you about," he said. "She's my enemy."

"*That's* who attacked you?" Torin laughed. "Wow. The chick has balls, that's for sure."

Baden frowned at him. "She plans to kill me, to take me out of the game, before coming after the rest of you."

William nodded, impressed. "That's not exactly a bad strategy."

"And," he added, wanting to punch something, "she's already earned a point."

"A point?" Katarina asked. "What game are you playing with her?"

With a scowl, he focused on her. Any other human

would have cowered. This one lifted her chin, a now familiar action, refusing to back down. Brave, but foolish. Merely another weakness.

"A dark and dangerous one. At the end, the one with the most points lives and the other dies. As you might, very soon. You drugged me," he snapped.

She flinched. "If you wanted a passive prisoner, you should have chosen someone else."

He'd thrown similar words at Hades.

I'm nothing like the king. I have limits.

Easier said…

"The human drugged you?" Torin barked out another laugh. "Dude. Are you embarrassed? Because I'm embarrassed for you."

"Like you have room to talk." William poked him in the shoulder. "Your girlfriend has spanked you on a number of occasions."

"Yeah, but I was a very naughty boy. I started worldwide plagues, and I needed to be taught a lesson."

"Plagues?" Katarina gasped out.

William winked at her. "Don't worry, petal. If he touches you skin-to-skin, you'll sicken…but you can cure yourself by sucking on his—"

Baden punched him in the mouth, shutting him up. "She's had enough of our world. And I have things to do." A sense of urgency overtook him. He was still without a point. "I'm taking her back to her groom. Give me your gloves," he said to Torin, already resenting the barriers that would prevent skin-to-skin contact with Katarina.

The few times they'd touched, the warmth of her flesh had tantalized him even as it had agonized him.

His friend understood his affliction better than most and pulled the leather from his arms without protest.

Baden claimed one then the other, encasing each of his arms before extending a hand to Katarina. "Come."

She stood eagerly, curling her fingers around his.

"So determined to return to hell." A dark tide of... something rolled through him. Not jealousy. It wasn't!

She's a means to an end, nothing more.

"I have my reasons," she said quietly.

"Of course you do. Money, power and protection."

Baden yanked her against him, wrapping his arm around her waist. An unbreakable shackle. She gasped, and he wondered what she'd sound like when she surrendered to her man, incomparable pleasure consuming her.

Destruction prowled through his mind, more restless with every second that passed. She peered up at him through the thick shield of her lashes...and both he and the beast lost their concentration. The faint scent of vanilla wafted from her. Delicious. Edible.

Must taste her...

With so much evil in the world, beautiful things should be cherished.

"This is way past awkward, right?" William asked, ruining the sensuality of the moment.

"Definitely," Torin said as Katarina blushed.

Cameo did everyone a favor and merely shrugged.

Baden glared at the lot of them. "Patch the windows and doors and meet me at the fortress in Budapest. I'll return as soon as I can."

Torin got real serious real fast. "Going to visit Aleksander alone? I'm not sure that's wise, my man. He'll be armed, and he'll have more guards, guaranteed."

No human would ever be strong enough or fast enough to behead Baden and remove his arms. "I'll be fine."

William clasped his shoulder. "Your reasons for avoiding Budapest are still valid. Don't forget. And if you decide to move, stay away from Fox. Bad for your health and all that."

Why would he go around a fox?

He secured Katarina even more firmly against him, a pang in his chest, an ache in his groin. He ignored both. *Can't want her.* Won't *want her.* A seductress who used her man would ultimately betray him.

"Unless you're planning to carry me," she said, "you can let me go. I can walk."

"I won't be carrying you, and we won't be walking. And you aren't the one who gives orders. With us, I call the shots. For your safety, not my enjoyment."

"The excuse every bossy man uses, I'm sure." She flattened her palms on his chest and pushed...without results. Glowering, she snapped, "I don't understand how we can travel without movement."

"You don't need to understand. Close your eyes."

A single shake of her head. *"Nie."*

"I said—" Never mind. The stubborn female could deal with the consequences. Reyes and Gideon always vomited after being flashed. Paris passed out. "Keep your eyes open, then."

"Reverse psychology? Nice try," she muttered. "I'll never purposely make myself vulnerable."

And yet she'd done just that by wedding Aleksander. Maybe there was more to her—to her circumstances— than he'd realized, just as she'd claimed. Maybe not.

Not that it mattered. Soon she would be out of his life for good.

A fact that *pleased* him. Greatly.

He brought Aleksander to the forefront of his mind. One moment he stood in the penthouse with William, Torin and Cameo, the next he stood in some kind of an underground bunker richly furnished with plush rugs, a mahogany desk, a king-size bed and, off to the side, a private bathroom.

There was a large metal door next to the bed, but it was bolted from the inside.

Katarina gasped. "How...we just...we couldn't have...this isn't possible."

Aleksander sat at a desk, the lone occupant of the room, looking through a stack of photos. When he heard his wife's voice, he jumped to his feet, his chair skidding behind him. Paling, he swiped up a .44 and aimed at Baden.

"How did you get in here?" Aleksander demanded.

No concern for his wife's safety? Fool.

Baden released Katarina and stepped in front of her, blocking her from the line of fire. Destruction raged over the action, but directed the heat of the emotion at Aleksander.

Kill him. Kill him now.

Soon.

"Y-yes," Katarina stuttered. "How did we get here?"

Baden smiled at Aleksander but spoke to the girl. "I told you, *nevesta*. I'm immortal."

7

"Dude. You should *not* have put a ring on it."

—Bianka the Terrible, Harpy from Clan Skyhawk

Katarina's mind threatened to shut down. Too much to process! She couldn't have...how had...no, no, there were *zero* ways what she thought had happened could have actually happened. But truth was truth, and like any apex predator, it could defend itself. She'd traveled from one location to another in only a blink. Without taking a step. Without being carried. Without flying inside a plane or driving in a car. Just boom, the scenery had altered.

Baden had been honest about his origins, hadn't he? He really was immortal. And if he was immortal, he was also formerly demon-possessed—was now playing host to some kind of beast. A beast with an insatiable craving for violence.

Her hand fluttered over her throat. He said he worked for Hades...who was the ruler of the underworld, according to mythology.

Hello, vertigo. We meet again.

"The coin," Baden barked at Alek.

Alek gave a violent shake of his head, the barrel of his gun wavering. "I don't know where it is, someone must have stolen it."

"You lie. Unfortunately for you, I tolerate only one liar in my life." Baden pulled a dagger from the sheath in his belt. How many other weapons were hidden on his body? "And Gideon is way better at it than you."

"Go to hell." Alek squeezed the trigger. *Pop! Pop! Pop!*

As Baden jerked from impact, Katarina covered her mouth to silence a scream. Anyone else would have fallen, but he didn't flinch or even stumble.

What he did? Stalk across the room and turn the gun while it remained in Alek's grip. He pressed his finger over Alek's and forced her miserable excuse of a husband to shoot himself in the shoulder.

Alek—a mere human—toppled into his chair, blood spurting from his wound.

Men banged at the door, but it was locked and barred from the inside. No one could enter. No one could help him.

His own safety measures would aid his downfall.

"Last chance," Baden said, as calm as if they were discussing today's lunch menu.

Almost hysterically, she thought: *Death with a side of pain.*

"I can't give it to you." Alek panted for breath. "I just can't."

"You can. You choose not to, and you'll forever regret it." He dropped the gun on the desk and very slowly, very deliberately moved in front of Alek. He still held the dagger. "*I* am not a liar. I told you I'd take something else you value. Today, you lose a hand."

Alek tried to stand and run. Baden contained him easily and with a quick, downward swing, chopped through his wrist. Just—like—that. The hand plopped on the floor, and an agonized scream echoed from the walls.

Slak to trafil! Baden had done it. He'd really done it. The viciousness of the action…the sight of the blood… the stench it released into the air… Katarina clutched her stomach.

Baden wiped the dagger on Alek's cheeks, leaving smears of crimson behind. "Get me the coin or tomorrow I'll take a foot." He returned the weapon to his belt before closing in on Katarina.

She backed up. "What are you doing? You said we'd only spend one night together."

His gaze narrowed. "I hoped we'd part. I was wrong."

"I'm not going with you." She couldn't leave Alek a second time. He'd just lost a hand, he was in pain, and he would be enraged, violent; he would hurt her dogs just because.

"I insist."

"And I pass." She faked left and darted right, closing in on Alek. "Where are they?" Her voice cracked with desperation. In the back of her mind, she understood she'd just handed the immortal—and unstoppable— Baden information about her. Information he could use against her. But she was beyond caring. The need to save her animals far outweighed the need to protect herself. "Tell me!"

Alek gasped for breath he couldn't catch and clutched his spurting limb to his chest. Tears of pain streamed down his chalk-white cheeks. With his uninjured arm, he reached for...the gun? Did he fear her now? He should!

Merciless, she pushed the weapon, photos and computer to the floor. She leaped onto Alek's lap and cupped his cheeks, forcing his gaze to meet hers. "Tell me where they are, or I'll remove your other hand." She would do it, too. Without hesitation. She might hate herself, might retch before, during and afterward, but she would do *anything* for answers.

"Tell me!" she shouted, shaking him.

"Let him go," Baden commanded. He *always* commanded, but this time he wasn't getting his way.

"Tell me!"

"Dead. They're...dead," Alek said through chattering teeth, shock setting in. "Killed...last night."

No, no, no. No! She couldn't believe...*wouldn't* believe... "You wouldn't have acted so soon—"

"Was going to...use them to find you...but they attacked...had to...put down."

Her gaze homed in on the bite marks that littered his arms. Marks he'd been without yesterday. The dogs must have smelled her scent on his clothing—smelled her desperation—and acted out to protect her. To save her. And he'd killed them for it.

Rage bubbled over, spilling through her. She hammered her fists into his ugly, wretched, despised face. He was too weak to dodge her and couldn't shield himself from the blows, could only sit there and take what she dished out. His teeth scraped her knuckles, and his bones cracked hers, but she didn't care, couldn't stop, would never stop. Her babies...dead...gone forever.

Strong arms wrapped around her waist and wrenched

her from Alek. "Enough, Katarina. You've hurt yourself."

Baden's calm voice only made her more furious.

"Hate you!" she spat at Alek, then at Baden. He'd absconded with her. If he'd left her behind, if he'd allowed her to remain with her despicable husband, the dogs would still be alive. "Hate you so much!" Using her captor as a pulley, she kicked out her legs, nailing Alek in the face. "*Odjebat!* You are horrible men! Horrible! And yet you live and they...they..."

Baden carried her around the desk, out of striking distance.

"Let me go!" She fought him with all of her strength, scratching his arms, punching, kicking. "Don't you dare whisk me—"

The bunker vanished, a bedroom quickly taking shape around her.

She wrenched free and tried to orient herself. Little details hit her awareness. Masculine furnishings. A massive sleigh bed with a dark brown comforter. Aged stone walls, like those she'd seen when her family toured the abandoned castles in Romania and Budapest—when life was wondrous, happiness the norm. Wrought-iron sconces and a cracked marble fireplace boasting hand-carved roses.

Another prison? Well, this one was well earned. She hadn't protected her babies. When they'd needed her most, she'd failed them. They'd died in pain, alone and afraid, after she'd promised to always protect them.

Guilt and sorrow joined the rage, leaching what remained of her strength, and her knees crumpled. She would have crashed into the floor if Baden hadn't caught her and eased her down.

She kicked him. "*Panchart!* Don't you dare touch me." She'd tried to scream the words at him, but the lump in her throat caused her to whisper. "I hate you."

He straightened and held up his gloved hands in a sign of surrender. A lie! This male *never* surrendered.

"Hate you," she repeated. The toxic mix of emotions wrapped her in a cold embrace. She wanted to cry. She wanted to cry so badly. The dogs deserved her tears, but there was no telltale burn in her eyes.

Baden rubbed the spot just above his heart. "You lost loved ones?"

For the first time in their acquaintance, there was a note of gentleness in his voice. A note she resented. Where had this softer side been as she'd begged him to let her search Alek's homes?

"Katarina," he prompted, still gentle.

"My dogs, the most precious fur babies ever born, are dead. Gone." She didn't even have pictures of them. The fire had destroyed physical copies, and Alek and Dominik had crashed her website. "They were murdered. And you are the man who prevented me from saving them. Does that please you and your beast?"

"No. I'm sorry, Katarina." He crouched beside her and reached out, running a fingertip along the corner of her eye. Was he searching for a teardrop?

"Save your sorry and get out of my face, *kretén.*"

"Had I known—"

"Get out!"

He blanched, but stubborn bastard that he was, he remained in place.

The protective sheath around her heart suddenly cracked, all the rage, guilt and sorrow spewing out;

the emotions became a gale force she couldn't fight, *destroying* her.

She curled into a ball, shaking so forcefully her muscles soon gave out, her bones as limp as noodles. She hated anyone—especially this man—seeing her in such a helpless state, but she no longer cared to maintain a brave face.

"Katarina." He reached for her again. "I need to—"

She rolled away, done with him, done with the conversation—done with life.

Besieged by helplessness, Baden plowed a hand through his hair. Katarina loved her dogs the way he loved his friends. All-encompassing. Never-ending. Nothing held back. He had no doubts about that. Even without a flood of tears, so much sadness and misery radiated from her, she rivaled Cameo.

In an attempt to save her dogs, Katarina had sacrificed her happiness and her future. And, during Baden's short acquaintance with her, he'd repeatedly mocked her for it. He'd sneered at her and insulted her. His actions had even spurred Aleksander's, leading to the untimely deaths of the animals.

She hated Aleksander, and she hated Baden. She had every right.

She's just a means to an end. I don't need her admiration.

But there was an ache in his chest now. One he couldn't shake. He knew the horror of losing loved ones, of feeling as if you'd been dropped in the middle of an ocean during a turbulent storm, wave after wave crashing over you, rocks scraping you; again and again you swallowed too much water, but still you fought to breathe, to rise. The moment you breached the surface, hoping you were in the clear, you were swept under again.

How many centuries had passed before he'd stopped missing his friends? Trick question. He'd never stopped.

Far too vividly he remembered the centuries he'd been imprisoned, the rats his only friends. He'd adored those rats…had cried when he'd had to eat them to survive.

Survival before sentiment.

No, no. The rats…not Baden's memory but Destruction's.

With a grunt, Baden pulled at his hair. "You'll be safe here, Katarina. You have my word." He owed her, and he would pay his debt.

The beast began to utter a protest, only to quiet. The girl's misery touched a chord in them both.

Silence met his pronouncement, somehow worse than a torrent of curses.

He'd brought Katarina to the fortress in Budapest. The other women would care for her, hopefully soothing her as they'd so often tried to soothe him; the men would guard her from any and every danger while Baden saw to Aleksander's punishment. For killing the dogs, he would lose his eyes. To start.

Anticipation…

Suddenly the wreaths began to warm. Baden glanced down as a soft red glow pulsed from the metal.

Another summons from Hades.

Knowing what was coming, he raced to the door, shouting, "Maddox. Ashlyn. Anyone! Do not harm the—"

The fortress vanished, and the throne room materialized. Hades was nowhere to be seen. Nor was the siren. Instead, a black tornado swirled over the bottom step of the royal dais, a thousand screams assaulting Baden's ears.

The tornado slowed...stopped, the wealth of black shadows thinning. Hades appeared in the center, standing over what might have been a body, the flesh and muscle picked off, the bone pitted. A bloody heart rested in his hand. He'd ditched the suit and tie in favor of a black T-shirt and leather pants, chains wrapped around both of his wrists.

From business formal to punk rock. The man was a chameleon.

Destruction played the quiet game, just as before, irritating Baden. "What do you want?"

Hades smiled, and there was blood on his teeth. "We're just waiting on— Ah. There she is."

A movement at Baden's right. He twisted and came face-to-face with Pandora.

"You." She scowled at him, her hair standing on end, her fangs beginning to grow. Claws extended from the ends of her nails.

Baden's body expanded, preparing for battle.

"There will be no bloodshed in my throne room," Hades announced. "Well, no more. Not today."

His muscles locked onto his bones, preventing any kind of movement. The same freeze-frame clearly overtook Pandora, her expression strained as she fought the immobility.

Only when he made a conscious decision to stand down—*won't act, not here*—did he gain his freedom.

"Now, then." Hades stalked toward them. "You broke my only rule. You tried to kill my other slave."

"You never said *attempting* to kill Baden was a problem," Pandora replied. "Only that I'd be killed if I succeeded."

How did he know of Pandora's crime?

"Pippin." Hades clapped his hands.

The white-robed man appeared in a puff of dark smoke. Like before, he clutched a stone tablet.

"Yes, sire."

"What's my only rule?"

"That there are no rules, sire."

"And?" Hades prompted.

"And whatever else you decide, sire."

"That's right. Whatever else I decide." Hades spread his arms, the very picture of smug masculinity. "I've decided even an attempt to kill each other is a punishable offense. You won't be beheaded for it, even if you succeed, but you will be penalized—and wish I'd killed you instead."

Baden swallowed a curse. "If you're allowed to change your mind whenever you wish, how can we trust you'll keep your word and liberate the winner?"

"Do you have any other choice?" The king pinched off a piece of the still-beating organ and popped it into his mouth. He closed his eyes, as if savoring the taste. "Spy is so much better than chocolate."

Pandora flinched, and Baden frowned. Had *she* sent someone to spy on Hades?

"Send another one, Pandy girl, and you won't like what happens." Hades dropped what was left of the organ and wiped his hands together.

Well. That answered that.

"Now," the king said. "You're lucky I have a heart today." He kicked the one he'd dropped like it was a soccer ball. "I'm going to go easy on you. For attacking Baden, you are hereby stripped of your point." He glared at Pandora, daring her to respond. "And you." He focused on Baden, his anger seeming to double.

Baden waved his fingers, all *bring it*. He would not apologize for defending himself.

"You have yet to acquire my coin."

That was the male's beef? "This particular task requires time. Your words, not mine."

Hades winced on Baden's behalf. "Time, yes. Eternity, no. To speed things up, Pandora will aid you."

A roar rose from deep in his chest. *Calm. Steady.* With or without the game, Baden would be the one to find the coin and slay Aleksander. *My point. My right.*

"I'll ensure Pandora can flash to the male. In the meantime, I have a new task for you." Hades held out his palm and Pippin placed a piece of stone in the center.

The stone caught fire, turned to ash and when that ash drifted Baden's way, he inhaled it.

New images popped up in his mind. A bearded man with six fingers on each hand and six toes on each foot. He had multiple scars on his arms. Thin straight lines, as if sliced by a blade.

Baden's mind jumped the track to Katarina and *her* scars.

The pang returned to his chest. The pain she must have endured—

Stop. Concentrate!

New information continued to barrage him. The man was a sociopath, killing without concern for the age and gender of his victims. After every murder, he notched both of his arms as a memento.

Baden ran his tongue over his teeth. "What do you want me to do?"

"Bring me his head. Today."

In the past, Baden had only ever killed during battle. And he'd never enjoyed it. This time, he thought he might cheer alongside the beast.

What gives you the right to be judge, jury and executioner?

Katarina's words danced through his mind, and he frowned.

I have a mission to do, a point to earn. An evil act against an evil man.

Would Katarina understand? Would she castigate him for his actions?

Concentrate. Why did Hades want the head of a human?

The answer rose. The target played host to some sort of dark presence. Not a demon, not even a creature like Destruction. But something even worse. Something Lucifer hoped to obtain to use against Hades and give himself an edge in the war.

Baden would catch it and escort it to the underworld along with the head. Because, as much as he disliked Hades, he wouldn't allow evil to roam free on the earth. Not if he could stop it. He would also do anything, even remain a slave, to prevent Lucifer from ruling supreme over any more territory.

"Consider it done. A point earned." He pictured his target… flashed to a small log cabin. Despite the light cast by multiple kerosene lamps, doom-and-gloom tainted the air—or maybe the blame was the scent of rot.

Baden strode into the kitchen…found a dead body

strapped to a long wooden table, the chest cavity opened, and several organs removed.

His target perched at the end of the table, eating what looked to be a liver. Nice. He was talking to the corpse.

"—was nekkid as a jaybird. I almost spit my soda—" He noticed Baden and grabbed the rifle propped against his chair. "You stay right thar, now, you heer."

Baden flashed to his side, grabbed the gun and slammed the handle into his temple, then his yellowed teeth. *Jab, jab.* Impact sent him tumbling to the floor, but he wasn't out for the count. He crab-walked backward, blood trickling down his face, catching in his dirty beard.

"Don't be hurtin' me. Please." He tried to stealthily reach inside his boot, where a dagger hilt peeked out.

Thinks to stab me?

Baden flashed over and stomped on his hand, breaking the bones.

As a scream of agony cut through the air, Destruction laughed with delight—so did Baden. Then the man pissed himself, and one of the beast's memories knocked on the door of Baden's mind.

He fought to remain in the present...but he...he... the cabin was replaced by a cell. No longer a child but finally a man, he stalked to the first person he'd seen in centuries. The lord of the castle. The one who'd paid his mother a few measly coins for the privilege of "taming" him. The one who'd ordered his imprisonment when he'd resisted the taming.

The lord was draped in expensive velvets, with different medals pinned to his shoulders and chest. How many battles had he won? Countless. And yet, he urinated as the distance between them vanished, knew his time had come—

In the present, Baden's feet were knocked out from under him. He blinked and shook his head, breaking the tight grip of the past. His target stabbed him in the chest and raced toward the front door.

Baden grabbed his ankle, tripping him. His jaw shattered, blood and what remained of his teeth spewing over the wood panels.

Smiling, Baden removed the dagger and stood. The man stayed down.

What gives you the right to be judge, jury and executioner?

Act. Now, Destruction demanded.

Survival first, nothing else second.

"You showed no mercy to your victims. Now I show no mercy to you." Baden seized a fistful of the man's hair, lifted his head—*just do it!*—and sliced the dagger across his throat. Blood spurted from the wound, and down below, the male's bowels released.

Death was never pretty.

Baden hacked through the remaining tendon and bone, the head detaching. As he straightened, a dark mist rose from the body. The presence he'd seen in the ash-vision.

A set of neon red eyes found him, and crimson lips parted with a hiss. Baden reached out, expecting a fight. But the darkness lunged at him—and sank inside his arm. Before his eyes, one of the lines etched into his flesh thickened.

He ground his molars, a white-hot burn searing him. What. The. Hell?

He stomped through the kitchen, searching for a gar-

bage bag. He found a potato sack, stuffed the head inside and flashed to Hades's throne room.

Destruction went silent, as usual. Pandora was gone.
The king stood in a half circle with a group of warriors
Baden had never met. They were tatted up, pierced and
radiated the kind of acerbity he'd only ever encountered
from Hades and William.

They were young, looked to be Baden's age, a mere
four or five millennia.

A spark of memory—of recognition—courtesy of
Destruction. Most of the supernatural world believed
there were only three realms in hell. There were actually nine. The other realms had always preferred to remain hidden. No longer. They had taken sides in the
war.

These four men were kings of their own realms. The
tallest was known as the Iron Fist; he was the reason
the phrase existed. The others were equally notorious.
Merciless killers. Coveted by lovers. Powerful in the
most wicked of ways.

"—to win," Hades was saying, only to stiffen.

They *all* stiffened. In unison, they turned to face
Baden.

Don't want me here? Too bad. He tossed the sack at
Hades's feet. "I've earned my point."

Hades gazed at the bolder mark on Baden's arm,
satisfaction glinting in his eyes. "Yes, I can see that."

So. The king had known the presence would attach
itself to Baden, had even wanted it to happen. "What is
it, exactly?" More important, how did he get rid of it?

"That, dear boy, is my gift to you. A monster other
monsters fear. One the human you killed was unable

to control or use to his advantage. You, however, will not be so lacking. You're welcome."

"I want it." The Iron Fist stroked the handle of his sword. "Give it to me."

"You think to order *my* assassin?" Hades asked with quiet venom. "To take from him?"

The threat in his voice was unmistakable, and Baden blinked in amazement. Hades was *protective* of him, even though he himself had threatened Baden's life?

A development worth exploring.

"I order and take at will." The warrior kept his hand on the sword. "Have destroyed entire kingdoms for a single trinket I later deemed unworthy of my greatness."

"Which is why I like you," Hades replied. "Don't make me *dis*like you."

The other kings bristled. A fight brewed.

"If I'm no longer needed…" Baden had no desire to deal with Destruction, who would insist on participating in the battle between kings, if only to show himself strong. He longed to return to Katarina. They had unfinished business.

Hades smiled at him, colder than ice. "I will have another mission for you. Soon. Until then, stay alive."

8

"They called me a bitch. I called them an ambulance."

—Cameo, keeper of Misery

Katarina lay on the floor of the unfamiliar bedroom, strange men and women surrounding her, talking about her as if she wasn't there.

"Baden told us to protect...*her*?"

"Maybe he needed protection *from* her. Let's lock her in the dungeon."

"That's your answer to everything, Maddox."

"Because our enemies are wily."

"The girl's not a danger to anyone, least of all mad, bad Baden."

"Speaking of, where is he? Why'd he leave? And why'd he call for Ashlyn?"

"I can answer your last question right now. He called for me because of my ability. Which means I can answer the other questions as soon as you leave the room..."

"Not happening, sweetheart. This girl is an unknown and—"

"I know, I know. Unknowns are our foes. *Been there.*

But Baden *isn't* an unknown. You trust him. He would never bring a vicious woman into our home."

Katarina tuned out the woman's sweet voice, the man's reply, and the myriad of responses that followed. If the group decided to lock her in the dungeon…whatever. What did she care about another location change?

Grief enveloped her, choked her.

Someone picked her up and carried her to the bed. The covers were lightly tucked around her, and one of the women—a plump beauty with light brown hair and matching eyes—stayed when the others exited, sitting beside her and tracing soft fingertips over her brow.

"My name is Ashlyn. I'm not sure how much you know about the men who live here, but I'm married to one. I have a very special ability that allows me to hear every conversation that's taken place in a room as long as my husband isn't with me. As soon as he left us, I heard about your dogs. I'm so sorry for your loss, Katarina."

Shut up, she wanted to shout. Maybe the girl had a special ability, like Baden, or maybe there were bugs in the room, and she'd eavesdropped. Either way, the dogs weren't up for discussion.

"You're safe here. You have my word."

Katarina closed her eyes and drifted to sleep. Well, in and out of sleep, always fitful. She had no idea when Ashlyn took off. The other people visited throughout the day, checking on her, and someone even brought a tray of food. She had no desire to eat. The only thing she wanted to do was continue sleeping. And cry, the way she used to as a child. But as always, no tears were forthcoming, which meant she experienced no cathartic release.

Eventually the needs of her bladder plagued her. She rose to unsteady legs and shut herself in the spacious en suite. Mosaic tile decorated the floor, the pattern floral but dizzying. The walls were cream-colored stucco, the countertops gold-veined marble, and the shower encased by stone and glass. Behind two white columns was a sunken tub.

Overall, as luxurious as Alek's. She laughed without humor. Monsters and their money.

When she exited, Baden was seated at the edge of the bed. He'd recently showered, his damp hair darker than usual. He stood when he spotted her and held out his hand. "Come. I'll give you a tour of the fortress."

She ignored him, crawled under the covers and fell back to sleep.

The next time she awoke, she was alone. Alone with her thoughts. Alone with her misery…her memories.

Faith, Hope and Love adored her. When they were excited, they had hopped around her feet like bunnies. They had panted and smiled every time she'd walked through the door. She remembered playing fetch and going on walks, and she began to shake. She remembered slobbery kisses and cuddles on the couch, and she dry heaved.

She needed a distraction. Like, now.

She stood, her legs even shakier, and pulled on the first oversize sweatshirt she found in the closet. I Would Die For Lucien was scripted over the center. Using a string she cut from a bow with a blade—there were weapons stored in an unlocked trunk at the foot of the bed—she anchored her hair in a ponytail.

Why hadn't Baden hidden the trunk? Did he not fear her rage?

Whatever. She wandered through the massive home. No bedroom or sitting room was off-limits. There was an entertainment room fully stocked with all the latest technology. Antique furniture abounded. Portraits of muscled men wearing tiaras littered walls that were marred with cracks and fist-size holes.

At some point, she ran into Baden.

Keeping pace beside her, he said, "Aleksander is locked in the dungeon below. Pandora has done her best to steal him, but I've taken measures to stop her." Satisfaction dripped from his voice. "Would you like to torture him?"

Yes, oh, yes. Would she actually do it? No. "Torturing another living being is something you and Alek enjoy. I have no desire to become a reflection of the men I despise."

He flinched.

Different people stopped to speak with them and introductions were officially made, but she remained quiet, uncaring, and ultimately retreated to the solitude of the room.

Baden followed close at her heels. "Are you hungry? You need to eat. You're—"

She climbed in bed and burrowed under the covers.

Over the next few days—weeks?—she developed a routine. She slept and, whenever her shattered heart pained her too greatly, roamed the fortress like a ghost. The residents soon became used to her presence and, for the most part, ignored her as thoroughly as she ignored them. If they even noticed her at all.

Once, she encountered a beautiful blonde with the saddest eyes she'd ever seen. The girl was young, perhaps even younger than Katarina. Some people called her Legion. Others called her Honey. Whatever her name, she kept her head bowed and her voice low, as if she feared being heard.

Poor thing. Katarina lost track of her, though, when she ran into Baden, who was in the middle of a conversation with Torin.

"She's a liability," Torin said. "She trains dogs for a living. And you know what that means, right? She relies on the canines to see to her defense."

Baden rubbed the back of his neck.

She almost backtracked, determined to avoid him, but curiosity held her in place. How would he respond?

"The scars on her arms finally make sense. She's been bitten. Repeatedly." He paused for a moment, nodded. "If trouble comes, we'll protect her like we protect the children."

That galled. Not that she reprimanded him. His opinion mattered less now than it had the day they'd met.

"Trouble *is* coming," Torin said. "From the info I've been able to gather, Lucifer is doing his best to take out Hades's closest allies. So far, two realms in the underworld have been hit. It's only a matter of time before the bastard comes after us."

"Perhaps I'll send him a message," Keeley said as she strode into the room. "Mess with mine, lose yours."

Torin chuckled as he wrapped his arms around the pink-haired beauty. "That's my sweet girl."

"No," Baden said with a shake of his head. "No making out in front of the dead guy. I'm— Katarina? Do you need—"

She slipped away without a word.

A day—two? three?—later, she stumbled upon a conversation between a woman named Anya and the black-haired warrior named William.

"He shouldn't have come back," William said. "And he shouldn't be digging into the history of the bands. We have to stop him before he finds out…you know."

"Your secrets." Anya rolled her eyes. "Yeah, yeah. But it's not like he'll discover the truth. Hades ensured only lies are known about them, right?"

"A specialty of his. But you know as well as I that the truth is like the sun. It always finds a way to shine."

"So what? If you try to stop Baden from digging, you'll only pique his already piqued interest—and probably learn what it's like to be split in two. Just leave him alone and let him stay here, okay. He hasn't lost his temper more than twelve times."

"A miracle, yes, but he's only going to decline. Clearly he's not laying pipe. If you know what I mean. Not playing hide the sausage. Not giving his new roommate a ride on the carnal—"

"Yeah, yeah. We both wish his girl's favorite color of lipstick was penis," Anya said with a shrug. "But it's not, so we deal. The guys need him, and if they need him, he'll fight to hell and back to ensure he's here to help. You're a man-boy so you're as dumb as a box of rocks, which means you haven't noticed he regrets leaving in the first place. And now, with the war between your daddy and Lucifer racing to level two…"

William sighed. "After Lucy's defeat, I'm going to spank Hades for giving Baden those bands. Daddy Dearest should only be willing to die for *me*. I shouldn't have competition for his affections."

"Now you're talking nonsense. Hades cares for no one but himself. Not even you." Anya patted the top of his head. "You need rest. Why don't you lie down and watch a movie with the lights off. And your eyes closed. And the TV off."

Katarina padded off...and though she would never admit it, she searched for Baden this time. Where was he? What was he doing?

She had no luck finding him. In fact, he didn't reappear until bedtime, and he was splattered with blood. After he showered, he made a pallet on the floor. All without speaking a word.

The next day, she overheard a conversation between Maddox, the warrior possessed by Violence, and Sabin, the warrior possessed by Doubt.

"How many points has he earned?" Sabin asked.

"As of this morning, eight. But Pandora has nine. Damn it!" Maddox punched a wall, which explained the many holes Katarina had found. "Hades has turned the Gentleman of Mount Olympus into a guilt-ridden assassin."

"And that's not even the worst of it. Baden says many of his points mark the death of a human possessed by— he still doesn't know what. Hades called the creatures a gift. Monsters other monsters fear."

"I'll ask around. Maybe someone knows something."

"Good. Torin's been searching for immortals who might have worn serpentine wreaths before Baden, but so far he's had no luck."

Katarina walked away. As she turned the corner, she heard another warrior mutter, "Are you sure Katarina is legit?"

"I'm not." The reply came from Lucien, keeper of Death. "But Baden is sure. Says he'll kill anyone who harms her."

How...almost sweet.

That night, she noticed Baden moved his pallet closer to the bed, and she couldn't bring herself to protest. Because she didn't care what he did. She didn't!

The next day, she ended up in a room where the girl-friends, wives and consorts trained with swords, guns and crossbows.

"Well, Gillian's birthday party is officially canceled. She's supersick," Ashlyn said. "William's on a rampage, mumbling about his book and how this must be the curse in action, and how he has to do something."

Book? Curse?

"And that's the good news," Kaia the Wing Shredder announced. The beautiful redhead was a Harpy. A bloodthirsty race of thieves and pranksters. She appeared human, except for the tiny wings that fluttered between her shoulder blades. "I've spoken to Bianka. Lysander and Zacharel are looking for the box, too. How are we supposed to battle Sent Ones *and* the evil minions who don't exactly like our jam?"

Bianka... Kaia's twin, Katarina thought she remembered hearing. Lysander... Bianka's husband. Zacharel...she wasn't sure. Sent Ones...a term she couldn't identify.

"We have to intensify our search," Anya said. She was the goddess of Anarchy and, according to everyone in the fortress, an unholy terror. "Those goody-goodies might help our men, they might not. The problem is Lucifer. If he gets hold of the Morning Star..." She shuddered.

Morning Star. Another term Katarina couldn't identify.

"Actually, the problem is our men," Gwen interjected. She was Kaia's younger sister and often teased about being the "nice" one. "They worry about Baden. When he's here, they hover around him, as if they're afraid something bad will happen to him."

The girls brainstormed ways to fix the situation—until they noticed Katarina.

"You need to snap out of this funk, like, el pronto," Anya said. "You think you're the only one with crises? *Chica*, you should try living a few thousand years and see how many losses you suffer. You're being a baby and I'm sick of it. You're stealing my thunder!"

"I'm totally willing to gut the piece of scum who killed your dogs," Gwen said. "Blink twice if you want me to get started…waiting…waiting…fine. But the offer will forever stand."

"Listen. I've been meaning to talk to you but time got away from me." Danika was a petite blonde whose nickname confused Katarina. The All-seeing Eye. "I see into the future and what I've seen…well, if you don't step up, it's not pretty, Katarina. Please help him. Help us all."

What did Danika mean, she saw into the future? Was she psychic? Well. That explained the name, didn't it?

Katarina managed to escape the group without making any promises.

That night, Baden placed his pallet right next to the bed, so close she could touch him with her toes if she stretched out her leg. She still didn't care what he did… but for some strange reason, she took comfort from his nearness.

The next morning, she stumbled upon a make-out session between Danika and Reyes, the warrior possessed by Pain. Knives were involved, and it made Katarina gasp with horror. She raced away before the two realized they had an audience, trying to wipe the memory from her mind. But...

The two had looked so happy.

As the rest of the week ticked by, Katarina witnessed several other make-out sessions. One couple couldn't wait to get to their bedroom before ripping at each other's clothes. Another couple chased each other through the halls, laughing. Through it all, a startling fact became very clear. These people might be vicious and bloodthirsty, but they loved each other. Deeply. Madly. Their devotion was palpable.

And, in the quiet darkness of Baden's bedroom that night—with the redhead asleep on the other side of the mattress, the pallet forgotten—Katarina could no longer deny the truth: that devotion had lured her out of isolation. These people kept each other going. They had troubles, but they never gave up. Bearing witness to their bravery and determination to live life to the fullest had eased something inside her.

When morning sunlight streamed into the bedroom, she was once again alone. Thirsty for the first time in forever, she padded to the kitchen. As she poured herself a glass of orange juice, Baden crossed the threshold. He noticed her right away, as if his gaze was drawn to her, and closed in on her.

"I can't get you out of my mind, and it's twisting up my insides," he said, his voice a mix of anger and concern. "I'm worried about you. One minute I want to shake you, the next I want to...hold you."

He wants to hold me?

"Welcome to a non-relationship," Gideon said as he

entered the kitchen. The keeper of Lies. "Please tell me you drank all the—"

Baden pointed to the hall.

"*So* cool." The warrior with blue hair and multiple piercings backed out of view.

"You've disconnected from life," Baden continued. "I understand why, but now you need a reason to connect again."

She turned away from him. Even though he was right. She *had* disconnected, and this wasn't the first time.

After her mom died, she'd disconnected from the more rambunctious aspects of her personality. The girl who loved to laugh had soon become the somber girl who focused on her work with her father. Then she'd lost her father, then Peter—new reasons to throw herself into her work. Then she'd lost her work…her pets. Her only source of unconditional love.

Katarina slammed the juice on the counter. The glass shattered, liquid spilling everywhere. She rushed from the kitchen and into the safety of Baden's room, where she climbed into bed and buried herself under the covers.

A few seconds later, Baden stretched out beside her. Because he wanted to *hold* her?

He combed his fingers through her hair, making her gasp—tremble. Purposeful contact? "I know words can't make this better for you, nothing can, but I *am* sorry for your loss."

Guilt clogged her throat. Wasn't the blame partly hers? She could have told Baden the truth their first night together. Maybe he would have helped her rescue the dogs, maybe not, but she had denied him the chance, allowing fear to lead her.

"I know what you're doing," she croaked. *What was he doing?* "Stop."

He continued combing her hair. "I'm familiar with the pain of saying goodbye to someone you love. There were more of us created, you know. More immortal warriors meant to guard Zeus. Before the box, we lost eight brothers and six sisters during battle, and I still bear the scars." He expelled a forced breath. "After *I* died, my thoughts free of the demon for the first time in hundreds of years, I realized just how thoroughly I was separated from the ones who still lived. I hated every second."

What if he'd left her with Alek, as she'd asked? What then? Alek probably would have killed the dogs anyway, since he'd gotten what he'd wanted: control of her life.

Still, she rolled away from Baden to end the heart-wrenching conversation.

He wasn't deterred. "Want to hear something messed up? I warred with Pandora for four thousand years, and yet she's the reason I remained sane. I owe her, but I'll still do whatever proves necessary to beat her at our game. I have to. Victory might be my only way out of these bands." He laughed, the sound sharp with a bitter edge. "I've never had more reason to give up, but I've never wanted to live so much."

Her chest constricted. For her pain, yes, but also for his.

"Sharing is easier than I expected," he remarked.

Curiosity got the better of her. "You've never done it?"

"Why would I? I'm a warrior. Bearing burdens is my job. My privilege."

"I disagree. The more burdens you carry, the fewer battles you're able to fight. You're too bogged down."

He frowned at her.

"Why share with me?" To help her reconnect, as he'd said, but there had to be more to it than that. "You don't care about my opinion, remember?"

"I...care. I did you wrong, now I do you right."

What a sweet—and baffling—response from a man she shouldn't trust but couldn't bring herself to spurn.

He left her then. Rather than puttering around the fortress to calm the tempest in her head, she cleaned his room. And that night, as fatigue settled over her, she drifted off, enjoying her first peaceful rest since meeting Alek.

She woke when the bedroom door opened, hinges squeaking. A stoic Baden strode toward her, breakfast tray in hand.

"You will eat," he said, putting the food in front of her.

Hunger pangs failed to overshadow the sudden burn of anger. "You need to stop ordering me around."

"I've lived longer. I know what's best for you. Besides, you're fragile. You need my help."

Her anger only escalated. "I'm fragile... I'm weak. I admit it." *I'm nothing without my dogs.* "But *you* are a patronizing asshole."

"This, you've told me before."

"Well, it bore mentioning again."

A knock sounded, and relief glinted in his eyes. Hadn't liked the direction of the conversation? He moved to the door to speak to the intruder and Katarina sneaked an avocado slice.

When he returned to her side, he held a large black-and-white mutt. The dog had fleas and multiple scars, as if he'd once served as bait in a fighting ring.

She recognized him. One of the strays from outside the chapel.

"I know this boy can't replace the others," Baden said, "but he clearly needs an advocate. He showed up on our doorstep."

What! No. Absolutely not. She'd lost so much already; she couldn't bear to lose more. "Take him to the nearest shelter. They'll check for a microchip. If he doesn't have one, they'll put up posts to find his owners."

The wiggling dog growled at Baden, who shifted from one foot to the other, struggling to maintain his hold. The action only aggravated the dog further, and he snapped and snarled, baring the sharpest set of teeth she'd ever seen.

"Katarina—"

"No." *Too raw and ragged to offer any more help.*

With a sigh, Baden carried the dog away.

She set the tray on the floor, no longer hungry, and drew the covers over her head.

When he returned, Baden settled beside her and draped a glove-covered arm over her middle. Strangely enough, she fell into another peaceful rest—

Only to awake with a jolt as he muttered, "Kill. Kill!"

She stiffened. He wanted to kill her? She scrambled up. Lamplight trickled over him. His eyes were closed, his features pale and taut. He was sleep talking?

"Shhh. You don't need to kill anyone," she told him softly.

"Threats...too many threats." There was a husky quality to his voice, one she'd never heard before. "They can't be allowed to live."

"Who dares to threaten you?"

He answered as if he heard her, even understood her, despite his current state. "Everyone."

"Why?" She brushed her fingers over his furrowed brow, and he actually leaned into the caress. When she remembered the command he'd once bellowed at her— *Do not touch me. Ever*—she drew back.

He frowned and kicked at the covers. "I won't be imprisoned again. Never again."

How long had he been locked away?

This man had lived, in some capacity, for a very long time. Considering the violence of his world, he must have grappled with his fair share of ordeals. "Shhh," she repeated. "No one's going to imprison you. I'll keep you safe."

"Can only trust myself."

Because he'd responded well to her singing in the past, she hummed. Gradually, the tension drained from him. He relaxed against the pillows.

So beautiful, she thought. And like this he was almost...innocent. Like one of the abused dogs she'd rescued. Once forced to fight to survive, desperate for a safe home, hungry for affection...finally safe and able to hope for better.

In a fairy tale, he would be cast as the prince *and* the dragon. Right now, she would be cast as the princess, once again the damsel in distress. Well, things were about to change. Today they would switch roles. She would be the dragon prince, and he would be the princess. In the morning, she might even kiss him awake.

Kiss him? Whoa! Too far!

But his perfect lips snagged her attention, delicious warmth uncoiling in her belly.

Ignore it! Determined to use her energy to protect him—this man who'd fed her and comforted her—she remained awake the rest of the night, just in case. But no one attempted to sneak into the room; no one even knocked on the door.

When he sat up with a jolt, fully awake and aware, she yawned and muttered, "We're alone. Everything's okay."

"Of course it is." He climbed to his feet. "Why would you think otherwise?"

Was he kidding? "Because of what you said last night."

He went still, his back to her. "What did I say last night?"

He couldn't remember? "You said I'm the reason you breathe—or used to breathe—and you'd be lost without me."

The muscles between his shoulders knotted, pulling at the shirt he wore. "You're lying."

"No, I'm teasing. There's a difference."

"Teasing?" He spun. "You're healing."

She was, wasn't she? An-n-nd with the realization, grief and guilt enveloped her. But even still, the waves weren't as big and didn't quite tug her under the tide.

"You're going to shower," he said with a nod. "Today."

She sputtered. "I *would* have showered if you'd asked nicely. Now you can take your order and shove—"

He picked her up and carried her to the bathroom, his delectable scent tantalizing her, his protective arms keeping the worst of her emotions at bay.

"You can't manhandle me to get your way," she said on a sigh.

"I believe I just proved otherwise."

"You're strong, blah blah blah. Do you really think this will end well for you?"

"I'm willing to risk your ire." His amused smile galled her.

When the water heated and steamed, he placed her inside the shower stall. He even followed her in, clothing and all. And, oh! This had to be heaven.

Her mind betrayed her, failing to supply a reason to protest as he stripped her of everything but her bra and panties. Instead she entertained a crazy thought: *Let's see where this goes.*

He kept his own clothes in place and even wore the gloves. He sat down, taking her with him, and anchored her between his legs. She trembled with…anticipation?

"You have a rat's nest of tangles," he said. "We have two options. Shave your head or use the conditioner I stole from William, who will protest. With knives."

"Shave it." Hair was hair. It would grow back.

"Singular creature. Most women—and that includes William—would fight to the death to protect their locks."

"Would you?"

"No. I fight for enough already. Although I realize now I'll gladly fight for *your* locks." He slathered her hair with a sweet-smelling cream and, while it soaked into her scalp, soaped up the rest of her, avoiding her intimate areas. In fact, his touch remained impersonal.

And why would it be anything else? She was fragile, weak. The worst attributes ever, according to Baden. And her mother, who'd hoped to prepare her for the day the cancer would win.

He handed her a toothbrush and toothpaste, and she scrubbed her mouth clean.

He rinsed out the hair cream and finally shut off the water. He placed her on the toilet lid, dried her with a soft towel and gently untangled the locks of hair that had dared defy the deep conditioning treatment.

"Are you still unwilling to torture Aleksander?" he asked, his tone cautious.

"I'll *always* be unwilling." She chewed on her bottom lip. "Has he given you the coin?"

Anger colored his cheeks. "He resists me at every turn."

"I'm sorry." In the bright light, she noticed the cuts and bruises that littered his face. He'd recently been in a fight. Probably multiple fights. "Did he hurt you?"

"No. Of course not."

But others had.

Baden says many of his points mark the death of a human...

He'd had to fight to survive. "I'd like to doctor your injuries," she said.

He frowned at her. "I'm fine."

"But—"

"No. No touching," he reminded her.

Seriously? "We *just* took a shower together. Our bodies were pressed together."

"That was different."

"How?" she demanded.

He scrubbed a hand over his strained features.

"You're no longer my captive, Katarina. I'll take you anywhere you wish to go."

Subject changed. Fine. What else had changed? Her! She didn't want to leave him, her junkyard dog, even though she should return home and rebuild her kennel. And her bank account.

This man needed help. The game he played with Pandora was a tether. A chain. Through it, he suffered mental and physical abuse. His friends thought she could soothe him and she, well, she really wanted to prove them right. How foolish!

"No need to take me anywhere," she said. "I'm where I want to be."

"Why?" He was suspicious...hopeful?

"Why else? I like living on someone else's dime."

He stared at her, as if trying to see inside her head. "Very well." He nodded. "You may stay."

No protests about her gold-digger status? Bastard.

"Dress."

Another command. Would he ever just ask?

Maybe he needed a proper example. "Would you please turn around?"

He hesitated, his features tight, before doing as requested. She hopped up, removed her soaking wet undergarments and tugged on the T-shirt and shorts that were folded at the edge of the sink. Once again, the clothes he'd picked for her were meant for a much smaller person; the hem of the shirt ended well above her navel, and the shorts barely covered the curve of her ass.

"All done," she said.

As she strode past him, he sucked in a mouthful of air. "Your legs..."

She paused to look over each limb, but everything appeared normal. "What's wrong with them?"

"Absolutely nothing."

Was that...*reverence* in his tone? Did she want it to be?

Her insides heating, she toyed with a lock of hair. He strode to the closet and changed into dry clothing, unabashedly giving her a peek at his naked form, and oh, wow, he was a magnificent specimen. More muscled than she'd realized, a carnal buffet of strength and sinew.

"Your tattoo," she said, certain she was drooling. "The butterfly on your chest."

"Yes?"

"It's..." Delectable—edible. "Beautiful."

"We were marked with a butterfly when the demons first entered our bodies. I lost mine when I died and thought getting another would help me become the man I used to be."

How very sweet, and very sad. "Why would you want to become the man you used to be? From everything I've heard, he sucked ass."

He looked at her as if she were a strange creature. "The others loved him."

"But they sucked ass, too, yes? Not really a high recommendation for his character."

His lips twitched. "Perhaps I got the mark because I secretly wanted to be more like the honorable men my friends had become. To be bonded to them."

"Silly warrior. You didn't need a tattoo for that. You guys are bonded by your love for each other. But maybe the mark can have a new meaning now. You were Distrust, then you were dead, but you emerged from the abyss able to fly."

A strange and *wonderful* creature.

She preened. "Did you and Pandora hook up when you were trapped together? She's tough. Totally your type."

"Yes, she's very tough. But no, we didn't." He stepped toward her, his pupils expanding over his copper irises. His hands fisted…to control a need to reach for her? "You've proven to be even more fragile than I realized. You're also married."

The disgust had returned, and yet…no matter his feelings about fragility, no matter his prejudice about her sham of a marriage, he obviously found her attractive. As he studied her, the telltale signs of excitement only grew more pronounced.

The most feminine parts of her began to *throb*. "I'm married, yes, but not for long. This girl will be getting a speedy annulment."

Another step. "No need. I'll make you a widow."

How easily he spoke of murder. As easily as he committed it, she was sure.

And he was staring at her lips now, she realized. Wondering how they tasted?

She shivered with longing.

A harried knock stopped him while making her jolt guiltily. Would he have kissed her? Would she have let him?

"Baden?" Ashlyn called. "Is Katarina in there?"

He'd stiffened. "She is. Why?"

"Are you both dressed?" the woman asked.

"Yes," he grated, not sounding pleased by that fact.

She rushed inside the room, her hands wringing together. "Another stray dog showed up, and I'm begging you to take care of them both, Katarina."

No way, no how. She wasn't taking another animal under her wing. She absolutely one hundred percent was not falling in love and losing another piece of her heart. Why bother? Death was inevitable.

"Like I told you last time. Take him and his buddy to a local shelter."

"They bark at me every time I approach them. If I take them to a shelter, they'll be labeled aggressive and euthanized. And I can't ask anyone else to help. Everyone is too busy worrying about Gilly and planning William's murder." Ashlyn pressed her hands together, forming a steeple. "It has to be you."

She spoke of murder just as easily as Baden.

"I know Gilly is sick," Baden said with a frown, "but why turn on William?"

"He flashed her somewhere else. We don't know where. He's ignoring all calls and texts." Ashlyn looked to Katarina, beseeching with her gaze. "I've never had a pet, but I know suffering when I see it. Please."

"I…" *Can't say no, but must protect my heart.*

"Katarina," Baden prompted. "Help her."

That wasn't the first time he'd used her name, but it *was* the first time his tongue had caressed all four syllables and made her shiver.

"Another order," she told him with an arched brow.

"As I told you before, the strays won't replace the ones you lost, but the loss of one doesn't stop the need for another."

Wise words. And really, deep down—underneath her fear of loss—she *was* tempted to work with the dogs and offer all the love she'd once had to give. Love they clearly needed. Love they'd probably never received.

Likelihood of Getting Bitten? A solid one hundred percent. One of the dogs had already tried to bite a person, his instinct to attack first and trust later—if ever. He needed guidance as much as food. New surroundings, with new people and smells, could be frightening, and frightened dogs acted out. Not all humans reacted with understanding, patience or even compassion.

"Fine," she said on a sigh. "I'll do it."

Relief softened Baden's expression. "We'll have to muzzle—"

"No." She shook her head, adamant. "No muzzles unless absolutely necessary."

"Yes," he insisted. "There's no reason to risk a bite."

"I'll decide what I risk."

"That isn't how our relationship works," he reminded her, as if speaking to a child. "I'm the general, and you're the lowly soldier. I order, *you* comply."

"For my safety, blah, blah, blah. Well, this lowly soldier is doing things her way. You can deal."

"Thank you, thank you, a thousand times thank you!" A clapping Ashlyn jumped up and down. "The dogs are locked in one of the downstairs bedrooms. My children have named them Biscuit and Gravy."

Children…she'd heard about the twins in her many wanderings, but she'd never actually seen them. "How old are your kids?"

Ashlyn beamed with pride. "Urban and Ever are eight mon—years," she corrected as her happiness faded.

An odd reaction.

Whatever. Katarina had aided her dad as soon as she

could walk. "They're welcome to watch me work, but they have to do everything I say, when I say it."

"How kind of you. I'll let them know. Oh! And they've already been instructed *not* to hurt you, so you don't need to worry."

Eight-year-olds were a danger to her? Please.

Unless they were immortal?

Right. New world, new rules. She had to adjust.

She met Baden's probing stare. "Are you coming with us?"

"No." He rubbed the band hidden under his shirt-sleeve. "I have a job of my own to do."

What job? she almost asked. With him, it was probably best if she didn't know. "Be careful." The words slipped out, and though she wanted to take them back—*too concerned, almost clingy*—she didn't.

He blinked in surprise. "I will. You, too." A tension-laden pause stretched between them, and she couldn't quite pinpoint its source.

Perhaps he couldn't, either. He frowned and stalked from the room.

Ashlyn skipped over and linked their arms. "According to the other warriors, Baden used to be the nicest male on the planet, but death changed him. So have the wreaths he wears. He's harder, colder. But I know for a fact he'll never hurt you."

Her heart suddenly felt like the drum at a rock concert. "What makes me an exception?"

"Oh, honey. The way Baden just looked at you…well, I'm sure you'll learn the answer firsthand. And soon!"

9

"Looks like it's fuck-this-shit-up o'clock."
—Kaia the Wing Shredder, Harpy from Clan
Skyhawk

Gillian Bradshaw—Gilly to her friends, though she despised the nickname more and more, wanting to prove herself an adult rather than a child—tossed and turned atop a soft mattress as a terrible fever ravaged her from the inside out. So much of the past few days had become a blur, but she thought she remembered Keeley giving her something cool to drink.

Happy eighteenth birthday, little one. This is going to make all your dreams come true...dreams you don't even know you have. You're so welcome.

Then, as Gillian screamed in pain, Keeley had said, *I'm one hundred percent certain that I'm ninety-three percent certain that I gave you the correct dose. Hmmm. Your symptoms are...well, this doesn't bode well. Maybe we'll have to go with Plan B?*

Gillian also thought she remembered William gathering her close later that day and carrying her...somewhere else. He must have. None of her friends had visited her to command she get well soon.

Warriors. *Can't live with them, don't want to live without them.*

"There, there, poppet." William gently wiped her brow with a damp rag. "You'll heal. That's an order."

She opened boulder-heavy eyelids. He sat beside her, his image blurry, as if a gossamer mist surrounded him. Her mind supplied the details she needed: he was the most beautiful man ever born, with hair blacker than any night and eyes bluer than any ocean.

"What's wrong with me?" Her voice was weak and raspy, the words nearly impossible to understand.

Thankfully, he wasn't human, his hearing better than most. "Something supernatural. But I've got the best immortal doctors in the world running tests."

Yes. She remembered poking and prodding, William snapping, "Be gentler or lose your hand."

"I want to go home," she said. She wasn't just weak and pained; she was weirded out. Her every cell felt as if it had sprouted legs and now crawled through her veins. A familiar setting would help.

She didn't have the strength to get up and walk to the bathroom. She had to have help—William's help—or she had to use a bedpan.

A freaking bedpan. Oh, the humiliation!

She wanted the girls.

Cool fingers sifted through her hair. "Baden returned to the fortress, and his temper is…unstable. I know better than most what he's capable of doing. I experienced the same—" He quieted, then smiled a smile devoid of humor. "You're safer here. This realm is hidden. No one comes or goes without my knowledge. Sleep now, poppet."

No, no. Not ready to drift away just yet. She wanted more time with him before they were separated forever...

Panic. *Don't think about dying.* What if her thoughts opened the door to Death?

"You're not sleeping," William said.

Sweet William. From the first moment she'd met him, she'd been drawn to him in a way that both scared and excited her. He was just so wonderfully mesmerizing. And powerful. And wicked and smart and sexy and kind—to her. Always to her. His friends, too, but only sometimes.

His enemies, well, they died badly.

Men feared him, and women craved him like a drug. When he smiled, panties dropped. Or melted off. She wasn't sure which, only knew he worked the situation to his advantage. The guy slept around, though he never stuck around. Because he always came back to Gillian.

As much as she hated the thought of him getting naked with another woman, she never ever never *ever* wanted to have sex again. She despised everything about the act. The smells, the sounds, the sensations. The pain...the humiliation...the helplessness...

The thought of joining her body with another person's made her break out in hives, not shiver with desire.

"—friends are looking for you," an unfamiliar voice said, breaking into her awareness. It belonged to a male. Was deep and raspy, with the same cocky and perpetually amused timbre as William. "I think they want your head on a platter."

"Thanks to you, Baden brought trouble to Buda," William replied, utterly unconcerned by the threat. "Gillian needs peace and quiet right now."

"I told you not to befriend her. She's human."

"And I told you to go fuck yourself. More than once!"

"Is that any way to speak to your dear father?"

"Adopted father," William grumbled. "And I'm tempted to say worse. Let's take this conversation outside."

So. He was speaking with Hades, she realized, sweat beading on her brow. The bad boy of the underworld. And that was saying something!

William didn't know it, but Hades had appeared to her one night. He'd warned her: *Stay away from my son. You aren't the one for him. Don't make me prove it.*

He'd scared her, but she hadn't heeded him. William was too important to her.

"Not being blood related to me is an embarrassing secret you'd do well to hide," Hades remarked now.

Gillian cracked open her eyes...caught sight of two towering shadows on the balcony. *I have a balcony?* The sound of cascading waves caressed her ears, the scent of salt teasing her nose. An ocean!

"She's deathly ill. She's going to die if you fail to make her immortal," William snapped. "So, make her immortal."

"I have the power to change her, yes. But in her condition, she'll die before she's turned."

"Then you're useless to me. Leave."

"Tsk-tsk. So rude. You might want to be nice to me, my son. I'm the only thing standing between you and scores of angry husbands you've cuckolded over the centuries."

"As if a legion of them would be any match for me."

"True. I trained you well. But the girl...they'd hurt her without a qualm."

William unleashed a storm of curses. "Anyone touches her, and I'll spend the rest of eternity ensuring they and everyone they love suffer unending torments."

"Your dedication to her is baffling. She's so...ordinary."

Ordinary, huh? Well. She'd been called worse.

"Eyes on me," William barked.

"What's so special about her?" Hades asked.

Yes, Liam. What's so special about me? She'd always wondered.

"I'm not discussing her with you."

"I'm discussing her with you, then. You can't be with her. You can't be with anyone. You know as well as I that your happiness walks hand-in-hand with your doom."

Gillian had heard a little about William's doom. Aka, his curse. The woman he loved was destined to destroy him.

Did Gillian believe in curses? Yes and no. She'd lived with demon-possessed immortals forever it seemed. She'd seen things. Supernatural things. Wild things. Impossible things. But curses...good luck versus bad luck? No. Bad things happened because bad decisions were made. End of story.

If William expected the worst, he would only ever see the worst. He would act accordingly, and turn the supposed curse into a self-fulfilling prophecy.

Seek and you shall find.

"I'm searching for a way to break—" William began.

"You've been searching," Hades interjected. "For centuries."

"My book—"

"Is nonsense. A trick to make you hope for what can never be so that your demise will be that much sweeter. If the book could be decoded, it would have been decoded by now."

Another tense pause. Then William spat, "Did you come here to piss me off?"

"Pissing you off is a bonus. I came to warn you."

"Well, you've done both."

"No, son, I haven't." Hades's voice hardened. "The warning is this: if I think you're falling for the girl, I'll kill her myself."

"You'll *try*."

A rustle of clothing. The crash of toppling furniture. The pop of breaking bones. Grunts of pain and satisfaction. Panting. A whoosh as the shadows fell over the balcony railing—a *thud*.

Of course, she didn't have the strength to scream.

"Answer me this," Hades said, and she could hear him just as clearly, despite the greater distance between them. How was that possible? "Are you thinking about bonding with her?"

Her heart, the treacherous organ, dropped into her stomach.

"No," William replied after a centuries-long pause. "I will never bond with anyone. Especially a human."

Ouch. But really, his refusal mirrored her own. She would never bond with a man—would never marry. She was too screwed up.

As a little girl, she'd had a very good life...until her biological dad died in a motorcycle accident and her mom remarried a few short months later. Her stepdad had two teenage sons—and all three males had turned her life into a living nightmare.

Take off your clothes, Gilly. The boys need to learn how to touch a woman.

The terrible things they'd done to her...

Even now, years later, nausea struck whenever she

remembered. Those boys…they'd broken her, spirit, soul and body, and by the age of fifteen, she'd had only two options: kill herself and finally end her suffering, or run away. Though she'd leaned heavily toward option one, she'd still gone with option two, hoping, praying, her life could actually end on a high note.

After hitchhiking to LA, she'd gotten a job at a trashy diner. A few months later, Danika—who'd run from Reyes, whom she'd later married—had showed up. They'd bonded. And after Danika and Reyes worked out their problems, the pretty blonde invited Gillian to Budapest.

If she hadn't been dealing with a creepy super, spending every night watching her door with a baseball bat in hand, expecting the guy to sneak inside, she would have said no. All those muscled warriors… all that testosterone and evil…well, *scared crapless* didn't even scratch the surface of her reaction. But the guys had maintained their distance, giving her space and time to cope.

Except for William, who'd walked into the entertainment room one day, plopped beside her on the couch and said, "Tell me you're skilled with a game station. Anya sucks."

They'd played video games every day for months, and she'd felt like a kid for the first time since her father had died.

The side of the bed suddenly dipped, and her mind returned to the present. William sat beside her once again, and as a bit of the fog cleared from her vision, she got an up-close-and-personal view of his cut and bruised face.

"I told you to sleep," he said gently. He was always gentle with her.

She loved it, but she also kinda hated it. And she had no idea why!

She opened her mouth to respond—*When have I ever obeyed you?*—and noticed the dryness of her tongue. "Water. Please."

A strong hand slid under her head and lifted. A straw pressed against the center of her lips. She sucked, the cool liquid soothing her raw throat.

As William eased her onto the pillow, she asked, "Am I going to die?" She knew nothing about supernatural illnesses, but figured they were worse than natural ones.

"No!" he shouted. He breathed in, out. "No," he repeated softly. "I'll find a cure."

What if there isn't a cure?

Okay. Time for a distraction. "How did Hades adopt you?"

William smoothed the damp hair from her brow. "He says he found me. An infant left to die."

A twinge of sorrow. A boy rejected by his parents? Been there! Her mother hadn't believed her—hadn't wanted to believe her—when she told on her stepdad. Had picked the male over Gillian. "Found you where?"

"The underworld."

Even worse! "You have no idea who your real family is?"

"I have an idea, but I'm not interested in a reunion. I have you, and I have Anya and those fools she refuses to let me kill. That's enough."

He considers me family. Tears burned her eyes, and her chin trembled. "Why do you like me?" He hadn't answered Hades, but maybe he would answer her.

"Don't be silly, poppet. What's not to like about you?"

Where to start? She was scared of the dark, she was damaged mentally and she would never have any interest in sex.

Your tits are too small. You need a boob job.

I shouldn't have to lube you up to make you wet.

Nausea struck...

"You're immortal," she said. "You've had experiences I can't even fathom. You're worldly and sophisticated and I'm—"

"*You* are wonderful, and I don't want to hear another negative word come out of your mouth. Sleep. For real this time, or I'll punish you."

She snorted. As if he'd ever hurt her.

He ruffled her hair and stood. "There's a bell on the nightstand. If you need anything, anything at all, ring it. I'll be here in seconds."

Where was he going? What would he be doing?

She swallowed both questions. *Won't cling!*

Footsteps...the lights switched off, and she gasped with fear. The lights switched back on, and she sighed. Hinges squeaked as the door opened and closed.

Silence reigned. Ugh. She was alone with her thoughts. Which was never a good thing.

Drawing on every bit of strength she possessed, she rolled to her side. Dizziness swam laps in her head and oh, crap, when had the ceiling and floor traded places? She wanted to reach for the bell—William would make everything better—but moving again proved impossible. *Breathing* was barely possible. She had zero juice left in her system, her limbs suddenly a thousand pounds each.

The tears returned to her eyes and through the haze,

a pair of furry boots appeared. William had returned? In snow boots?

A soft sigh drifted to her ears as he crouched down. She frowned. He smelled different. He smelled like peat smoke and lavender, and it was nice, *very* nice, but still different. The heat he exuded was wonderful, but also wrong.

This wasn't William.

She tried to scream, but only managed to moan.

"There'll be none of that, now." The intruder had an Irish accent, his voice rough, and yet it held no note of viciousness. No note of any emotion, really. "I'm not here to hurt ye."

A lie to keep her calm?

Again she tried to scream. Again she failed.

Have to warn William. He would never allow a man in her bedroom. Not even a friend.

One of those jealous husbands Hades had mentioned?

Couldn't be. *No one comes or goes without my knowledge,* he'd said.

As the newcomer tucked the covers around her, her panic...ebbed? He gently wiped away her newest flood of tears and suddenly she had a clear—well, clearer— view of him. He was...what *was* he? He had the top half of a man and the bottom half of an animal. A goat, maybe? His legs were furred, a loincloth draped between them. He had hoofs.

"Eyes up here, lass."

Cheeks heating, she looked up—and gasped. He had the most mesmerizing face, a rival to William. He had dark skin and dark eyes, an aquiline nose and blade-thin lips. His hair was long and black with razors woven through the strands. And he had horns! Small and curved, but definitely there. They rose from the crown of his head. Wide shoulders led to strong arms and clawed hands.

Claws... Monster!

Can't be real, can't be real. A hallucination?

"I was told I could aid you," he said. "That we could aid each other. I wasn't told you belonged to William of the Dark, or that you were sick. And human." He sneered the last, as if there was something wrong with her race. "What are you doing with a male of his... reputation?"

"Wh-who are you?" she asked.

He frowned and reached for a lock of her hair. She cringed, and his frown deepened. Still, no emotion touched his eyes as he dropped his arm to his side.

"I'm Pukinn."

Puck-en. Never heard of him.

"You may call me Puck. I'm the keeper of Indifference."

So. He was one of the demon-possessed warriors, but not one of the ones she'd met. He hadn't stolen and opened Pandora's box. He'd... She racked her brain and dug up a vague memory about the leftover demons being given to the prisoners of Tartarus, a prison for immortals.

Her mind played a little word-association game: prison...criminal...dangerous...no moral compass— and the panic kicked into high gear.

The man sighed again, as if disappointed with her. "I'm not sure you can aid me, but I think I'll allow you to try. I'll return after you've gotten used to the idea." With that, he stalked to the balcony, climbed the rail and jumped.

Gillian sagged against the mattress, a fine sheen of sweat covering her skin. Gradually, though, her heart-beat slowed and the sweat cooled.

By the time William returned to check on her, she felt normal again. Well, as normal as could be, considering she was dying. He paused halfway to the bed, sniffed the air and frowned, then looked her over.

She opened her mouth to tell him all about her visitor, only to change her mind. The guy—Puck—hadn't hurt her and if she mentioned him, William would hunt him down. Maybe kill him. Definitely torture him. She'd heard stories about William's expert torture techniques and absolute love for the task.

Which made her comfortableness with him even stranger.

"You up for seeing another doctor, poppet?"

"My lord…sir," an unfamiliar voice said. Only then did Gilly notice a short, rounded man with scales instead of skin standing beside him. "I've spoken to my colleagues, and we agree. She has *morte ad vitam* and as you know, there's no cure."

"Remember. Come on! Remember." Cameo, keeper of Misery, pulled at her hair, banged her fists into her temples and when that failed, banged her forehead into the wall. No matter what she did, her mind remained a blank slate.

Frustration ate at what little control she had left. Ever since her possession, she'd experienced memory loss whenever she stumbled upon a road that would lead to her happiness. A few weeks ago, ancient artifacts had sucked her into a different realm. Apparently. She couldn't remember, which meant someone she'd met or something there had the power to change her life for the better.

The guys told her she'd mentioned a name upon her return home. Lazarus.

Lazarus, Lazarus, Lazarus.

Still no memory, only a vague craving for chocolate...

Were the two linked?

Of course, the answer eluded her.

With a screech, she picked up the biggest vase on her dresser and threw the stupid thing across her bedroom. Glass shattered, pieces tinkling to the floor. One taste of happiness she could stroke like a lover deep into the night, that's all she wanted. But noooo. It wasn't even possible in her imagination.

There had to be a way to remember Lazarus. Whoever he was. *Was* he the road to her happiness?

Her bedroom door burst open, the hinges shattering just as surely as the vase. Maddox stalked inside, a dagger palmed and at the ready. His violet gaze scanned every shadow in the room in a single second, and she knew he'd already cataloged every bit of damage.

"I'm fine," she said, and he cringed. Everyone always cringed.

Had Lazarus?

Don't think about him.

Rather than saying anything else, she shooed Maddox away with her hands.

He stood his ground. "You don't look like you're fine."

She arched a brow, giving him an *I'm Misery, asshole, what do you expect* look.

He shrugged, his shoulders brushing against the ends of his shaggy black hair. "So there's no one I need to kill for upsetting you?"

She shook her head.

"Very well." He backed out of the room, only to

pause to tap the shredded doorframe. "You should probably have someone fix this."

Little shit. Laughter bubbled up…and died a painful death in her throat.

Laughter wasn't allowed. If even a chuckle managed to escape, she would suffer.

Wow. What a life. And, even better, this was what she had to look forward to *forever*.

Long ago, she used to wonder why Baden allowed himself to be killed. And she'd always suspected he'd allowed it. He'd been too strong a fighter for anyone to get the drop on him. So, why? Even as miserable as she was, she'd never contemplated such a fate.

Until now.

Baden's female was so depressed she walked around the fortress like a phantom. And Cameo felt partly responsible, as if the taint of her demon had infected the girl. Had it? What about Gilly and William? Gilly was sick, and William was inconsolable. Her fault?

Probably.

The world would be better off without me.

Heart-heavy, she plopped onto the edge of the bed. She longed to sob, but crying would do her no good, would only feed the demon, making him stronger.

Finding the box would free her from the fiend at long last, and on the surface, appeared to be her best bet. But finding the box had never been more impossible, every edge they'd gained now dulled.

What could she do?

She had some thinking to do…some decisions to make about her future. What she knew? She couldn't go on this way.

10

"Only one of these sentences is true: I never chase, I replace. I will eat my words."

—Galen, keeper of Jealousy and False Hope

Baden—needed—sex.

He needed it hard, and he needed it fast. Most important, he needed it *now*. The fate of the fortress depended on it, as William had predicted. Destruction frothed inside his mind, banging on his skull.

Every minute—correction—every *second* in Katarina's presence had become a special kind of hell. Yesterday he'd showered with her, and though he'd been in agonizing pain he'd done his best to hide, every point of contact like dusting salt on an open wound, the pleasure of having her in his arms had almost proved greater.

Her nipples had tightened against his palms as he'd rubbed soap into her flesh, and he'd had to fight the urge to grind into her back. And afterward, when she'd walked across the bedroom, her mile-long legs on display, he'd wanted to pick her up and throw her on the bed, strip her naked and plunge deep, deep inside her.

His body had yet to calm.

His mind had even begun to rationalize. Katarina might not be his type, might be weak, but strength wasn't necessary in a temporary lover. So she belonged to someone else. So what? She belonged to Aleksander in name only. For now. Hardly a big deal. She could belong to Baden, too. For a little while.

But if he lost control of the beast and hurt her? Or worse?

He didn't want to hurt her. He actually *cared* about her well-being. When he'd shared bits and pieces of his life with her, attempting to draw her out of her depression, he'd created an unexpected connection to her. A bond he'd been unable to break. And he'd tried!

Destruction wanted her, too, which was part of the problem. The beast was now leery of her, unsure of what to make of her.

Baden stalked down the hallway, heading for Strider's bedroom. "Any sign of Pandora today?" he asked. He was alone, but Torin monitored the halls through a series of cameras and mics.

"Not yet," the warrior replied, his voice spilling from overhead speakers.

Though Pandora had flashed into the dungeon at least once a day in an attempt to snag Aleksander, she'd managed to avoid the trap Baden set.

No matter. She was impulsive and impatient, and soon, she would make a mistake.

She had to make a mistake.

Earlier in the week, when Baden refused to dismember a teenager, Hades gave the task to Pandora. She'd done it without hesitation, earning an extra point, putting her in the lead. Only later had Baden learned the teenager in question wasn't actually a teenager but an older witch cloaked by magic. A witch on Lucifer's pay-roll, who received a bonus for every human she lured to the dark side.

The king of Harbingers wasn't content with his im-mortal army. He planned to raise a human one, too.

Hades grew more agitated by the day. He'd even in-creased the number of assignments he doled out, pre-senting both Baden and Pandora with a list.

And Baden, well, he was beginning to *not* hate the male. There was a method to his madness, whether Baden understood right away or not.

He reached the keeper of Defeat's door and knocked hard enough to crack the wood.

Note to self: *Buy a new door.*

"Coming, coming." A patter of footsteps rang out and the door swung open, revealing Strider's mate, Kaia. She greeted him with a dagger in hand, her mass of red hair anchored in pigtails, her eyes bright with fury.

She's armed...a true threat. Kill her!

Baden did his best to ignore the beast, staring over Kaia's shoulder. He scanned the room, checking for hidden threats out of habit. Well. Her decorating style could probably be classified as *a hoarder died here.* "Did you reach your sister?"

For his next assignment, he was supposed to steal a pair of panties from Taliyah the Cold Hearted. Without touching or harming her. Taliyah was a Harpy, Kaia's older sister, and a snake-shifter hybrid. She was almost as bloodthirsty as Destruction.

Why Hades wanted him to do this, he couldn't yet fathom, but he was done questioning the man's orders.

"Yep. She'll meet you at Downfall in an hour."

"Thank you."

"Save your thanks and do me a favor." She gave the hilt of her dagger a kiss. "Next time you're with Hades, demand to know each of William's hideouts."

The urge to protect suddenly overwhelmed him. Protect William? Or Hades?

Both. Destruction snarled inside his head. *They are mine, and I will annihilate anyone who even* thinks *to harm them.*

That was far more than just a Get Out of Torture Free card. That was determination, caring and concern.

But the beast wasn't done. He fought Baden's domination—and he fought hard, finally managing to take over his body and mind.

His mouth watered. *Her blood, I'll taste it.* His hands itched. *Her bones, I'll break them.*

As a predator, Kaia sensed his intentions and reacted accordingly, crouching, readying for attack.

Rational thought intruded: *No, no. Not her.*

But Destruction had already pulled back his fist to strike. At the last second, Baden regained a semblance of control, raining the fury upon the wall with punches and kicks.

The beast roared as more and more of Baden's friends sprinted from their rooms, grabbing hold of him to try to stop him.

They dare try to restrain me?

Again, the beast was able to overtake him, flinging one warrior after another across the hall. The males crashed with so much force they left body-shaped cracks behind. Dust and bits of plaster thickened the air.

He laughed.

"How do we corral him?" someone shouted.

"Keeley." Torin's voice poured over the intercom. "You're needed in Strider's room. ASAP."

"No time. We need Katarina," a female called. "She calms him, I think."

A handful of warriors rushed him at once, tackling him to the floor, but again, flinging them away wasn't difficult. Power expanded his limbs, reinforced his bones. He was able to work his way to his feet.

I might fall, but I'll never stay down.

A grinning blond stepped into his path. The male named Strider. Killing him would be a pleasure.

Baden screamed at Destruction. *He's my friend. They all are!*

"Hey! Over here." One of the women said, "I'm going to rip you a new asshole—in your face."

Not my friends, Destruction told Baden as he grabbed the woman by the neck and lifted her off her feet. Anya. Destruction had made of point of learning the identities of the residents. *Know your enemy...*

"No!" Lucien shouted, tackling him from behind.

The goddess of Anarchy twined her legs around Destruction's neck and, as he stumbled, squeezed with surprising strength.

From the corner of his eye, he spotted Katarina and the one named Ashlyn rounding the far corner. Both females stopped to gape at him. He paused, he wasn't sure why, giving Baden the opportunity to regain a bit of control. Not enough to claim ownership of the body, but enough to slow him down as their wills clashed. He bellowed to the rafters.

"Run, Ash, and take the girl with you," Maddox demanded. "She's only making him worse."

Katarina...leave?

Baden and Destruction worked together to pull Anya off their shoulders and drop her. They sidestepped Lucien and stalked to the woman who'd haunted them. The woman who belonged to them. If only for a little while.

"Go!" multiple voices screamed at once. The warriors were giving chase, trying to beat him to the object of his fascination.

Ashlyn attempted to tug Katarina away, but Katarina shook off her hold and stepped *forward*. Toward him.

The moment she reached him, she framed his face with her delicate hands. He had to crouch to allow the action, which wasn't exactly a prime position to mount a proper defense—*but worth it*.

"What's wrong with you?" she asked.

He drew in a breath, his usually useless lungs suddenly infused by the sweetness of her scent…as if he were coming back to life. "They are threats."

"Wrong. There are no threats here."

"They are threats," he insisted.

She brushed her thumbs over the rise of his cheeks, gentle, so gentle, and yet still the action stung. But he didn't pull away. The air between them thickened and crackled with awareness. He liked it.

The others stopped their pursuit and maintained a proper distance, whispering with incredulity.

"Is this really happening or am I hallucinating?" someone asked.

"Does the human have a magic hoo-ha?"

"You have a job to do," Katarina reminded him, ignoring the others. "Why don't you go do it, and I'll take care of the threats here?"

He snorted. "You're not strong enough."

That earned a raised brow. "So you've told me."

"Dude. Isn't she married?" Kaia asked.

He snarled at the Harpy, though his gaze remained on Katarina. She'd lost weight and looked more fragile than ever, and yet her beauty took his breath away.

Breath he now needed to survive?

"Baden," she said.

"Destruction," he corrected.

"Since he's affected by you, I'm willing to bet you're affected by him. Why don't I call you Baduction?" She smiled at him, inviting him to play with her. "And a hat tip to you. If your newest job is to stare at me, you've got it nailed."

He didn't know how to play, but he liked seeing her like this. Happy rather than despondent.

He shouldn't care what she felt. Caring left him vulnerable.

He scowled at her. "Stay out of trouble today."

"I will, but not because you ordered it. Because I'm a girl and girls are made of—"

"Sugar and spice," he interjected, remembering the rhyme. Boys were made of snakes and snails.

"Wrong. Girls are made of vodka and ice. The two combined increase our tolerance for masculine nonsense."

He snort-laughed. Funny girl. But the laughter died a swift death as Baden rose closer and closer to the surface, fighting with all his might.

Expression growing serious, Katarina said, "I expect you to come back unscathed."

Did *she* care about *his* well-being? That…he would allow. "I won't be harmed. I'm strong." He just wasn't strong enough to hold back Baden any longer. The warrior won the battle.

Baden shook as he returned to his normal size. He still had to bend to press his forehead against Katarina's, but he did it, so damned glad the beast hadn't hurt her—feeling guilty for allowing the fight to happen in the first place and worried over his friends' reactions.

"I'm sorry," he said, his jaw tingling from her touch.

"There you are," she replied. "My Baden."

Her eyes widened as the words echoed between them. *Her* Baden?

"Yes," he found himself saying. Agreeing.

"On your job today...maybe don't kill anyone?" She rose on her tiptoes and whispered, "If you can refrain, I'll reward you with..."

He tensed with excitement as she lowered and their gazes locked. Black flooded the gray-green. Her cheeks were flushed, her respirations quickening.

"With?" he demanded.

She licked her lips as she stared at his. "Anything you want."

Instant hard-on.

An arc of surprise passed between them...and longing. So much longing.

"I'll refrain," he said, and flashed to Downfall before he carried her straight to bed.

The club resided in the third level of the heavens. A haven for degenerates.

He pushed the beast's coup to the back of his mind—wouldn't consider the helplessness he'd just experienced.

He even pushed Katarina to the back of his mind—because he had to. If he thought about her parting words, he wouldn't last five minutes away from her. Definitely wouldn't complete his newest task.

He pushed through the crowd. The walls and floor were comprised of wispy clouds, allowing glimpses of black skies and bright stars, and yet both the walls and the floor were solid to the touch. To the left, a live band played, a group of women throwing their undergarments at the lead singer.

If only Baden's mission would be so easy.

To his right, bartenders manned a congested bar, mixing drinks and spreading good cheer. To his left, countless bodies writhed on the dance floor.

Destruction banged against his skull. *Trust no one. Hurt everyone.*

That's enough out of you.

There was only one reason he'd chosen the immortal nightclub for his meeting with Taliyah: it was owned by three Sent Ones. Merciless winged warriors who might have insight about the wreaths. Two birds, one wild stone. The warriors were currently—always—at war with Lucifer and his minions, and they'd made it their business to know the happenings in the underworld.

Baden swiped two shots of ambrosia-laced whiskey from a tray as a waiter passed him. He downed both, the taste and scent harkening back to the chase through the blazing field, but the warmth soothed him anyway.

"Hey," the waiter said. "Those are for—"

One look at Baden, and he zipped his lips, gratefully accepting the empty glasses.

Just before Baden crossed the VIP threshold, a giant of a man stepped in his path. Bulging muscles, with the mane of a lion and the flexible jaw of a bear. He was a Berserker, no question.

Baden decided to give a polite request a shot. "I'm here to speak with the Sent Ones."

"Do you have an appointment?"

"No, but I'm willing to overlook the lack and see them anyway."

The Berserker crossed massive arms over a massive chest. "They're busy, and they're not to be disturbed."

Deny us? We'll teach him the error of his ways.

We're an us now? Still on edge, Baden found himself consenting. *Just this once.*

Destruction laughed with glee as he poured dark strength straight into Baden's veins.

Like Kaia, the Berserker moved into an offensive stance, preparing to strike. Baden beat him to it, slamming a fist into the center of his chest, only corralling his strength at the last second when Katarina's voice drifted through his mind.

Anything you want.

The guy flew backward, smashed into the back wall and slid to his ass. He remained conscious, though the center of his torso was now sunken in, as if Baden had punched through skin, muscle and bone. Maybe he had. Black mist swirled over his palms before thinning and dispersing. A sight he'd encountered before. With Hades.

Baden wasn't sure what to think. At least the Berserker would heal.

Everyone in the VIP lounge stilled and quieted. Several women stared at him with sudden interest, while most of the men gaped at him with fear. They sensed a predator far more dangerous than themselves. Berserkers were usually at the top of the food chain and Baden had just taken one down with a single blow.

Destruction hungered for more.

Baden breathed in and out with purpose, determined to resist temptation.

In the far corner, two males stood. The Sent Ones. Large white and gold wings arced over their shoulders.

Though Baden had never met the pair, he knew of them. Everyone did. The one with the white hair, scarred white skin and red eyes was Xerxes. The one with the dark hair, bronzed skin and rainbow-colored eyes was Bjorn.

"You harmed our man," Xerxes told him, cracking his knuckles. "Today you die."

"I meant him no harm." Baden squared his shoulders and braced for impact. "I'm here for answers."

Behind the pair, the Berserker jumped to his feet, roaring as he healed. He sprouted five…eight more inches, grisly claws springing from the tips of his fingers.

Baden frowned, his mind suddenly buzzing with another of Destruction's memories. When he'd fought the guards at the prison, their bodies had piled up around him. He'd expanded, growing bigger than ever, his nails lengthening and sharpening into claws for the first time. Claws just…like…that.

The beast was part Berserker?

Gasps drew Baden to the present. The ends of his fingers felt as if they had been lit on fire. He looked down to see his nails *had* lengthened and sharpened into claws—like meeting the call of like? *He* was now part Berserker?

As he shook his hands, shocked by the transformation, the claws retracted.

Bjorn held out his arm, stopping both Xerxes and the

Berserker in an instant. Without glancing away from
Baden, he said, "Calm yourself, Colin, or I'll do it for you."

The warning worked, the Berserker remaining in
place.

"Look at the warrior's arms," Bjorn said to Xerxes.
"He's wearing serpentine wreaths."

Baden glanced at his biceps, where his shirtsleeves
had caught on the metal. "They're part of the reason I
wish to speak with you."

Xerxes hesitated only a moment before waving him
forward. Bjorn signaled his private bartender.

Baden strode to the shadowed corner illuminated
by candlelight. Two scantily clad women lounged on a
couch and one on a recliner, each twittering excitedly
when he came into view.

"It's Jamie freaking Fraser!"

"I know. Okay, okay, you talked me into it. I'll have
your Scottish babies."

"Take off your shirt. Or would you prefer I rip it
off you?"

Baden expected his lust to return full force. These
women offered the sex he wanted. The sex he needed.
Easy and uncomplicated. Release and relief. Except,
they weren't Katarina, and his body remained unaf-
fected.

He scowled. The identity of his lover shouldn't matter. Desire was *his* weapon, his means of governing the
beast. Craving a specific woman turned every sensation
into a weakness—gave *her* the power.

"Leave," Xerxes told the women, no hint of softness in his tone.

The twittering stopped as the three beat feet. Baden

sank into the recliner, leaving the backless couch for the Sent Ones. More room for their wings.

"Who gave you the wreaths?" Bjorn asked. "Hades or Lucifer?"

Were they the only two immortals with the power to use them? "Hades."

"So you are under his control."

"Yes." The admission was gritted, but honesty was essential. Sent Ones would taste a lie. "I can't remove the bands without removing my arms, something I'm unwilling to do. Without the bands, I'll die. Again. Only this time, death will be permanent."

A nod from both.

Getting nowhere. "How do they work?" Baden asked.

Bjorn tilted his head to the side. "Think of it this way. If you take a seed from a piece of fruit, plant and water it, the seed grows into a tree that produces fruit of its own. They are different, but they are the same."

Meaning...what? The wreaths were a seed, and the roots were now firmly planted inside him? "I have visions of another life. The wreaths used to be a person... a creature."

"You're right," Xerxes said. "The wreaths were created from Hades's heart. He removed it, burned it and forged the bands from ashes that would forever contain his essence."

What. The. Hell?

Destruction was Hades? The *memories* were Hades's?

No, no. Impossible. And yet, so many things suddenly made sense. The way Hades acted, threatening to kill him then changing his mind, almost as if he cared for Baden—because he cared for himself. The beast had known Keeley—because Hades had been engaged to her. The beast quieted in Hades's presence—because he wanted what Hades wanted.

Nothing to say? he snarled. The beast had known the truth. The beast had always known.

I am Destruction.

You are. You're also so much more. And Baden should have realized. What a fool!

"How many wreaths are out there?" he asked.

"The exact number isn't known," Bjorn said. "But my guess? Not many."

Baden didn't know if he was blessed or cursed. What would happen to Destruction when the bands were removed? The creature was bound to the metal, but not to Baden…right? Would he finally have the chance to live free of any kind of possession, as he dreamed?

Excitement…

Rage, courtesy of the beast. *I will live!*

"What about my new tattoos?" Baden demanded. "They grew from the wreaths and thicken after I kill Hades's targets."

"You should understand the insidious nature of evil better than most." Xerxes ran a dagger over his arm, creating a wound. "Right now, the injury is raw, open, unable to fight infection. It needs to scab to protect itself."

"So…?"

"Evil infects, spreads and welcomes other evil," Bjorn said.

Baden waited. The Sent One said no more. "I didn't hear an answer to my question."

"Just because you didn't hear it, doesn't mean we failed to offer it."

Pompous piece of—

A waitress arrived with a tray of ambrosia shots. After Baden knocked back three in quick succession, Bjorn waved her away.

The Sent Ones had their own troubles, he knew. Bjorn had been forced to marry to some kind of shadow queen—like Hades's shadows… *Baden's* shadows?— and she was slowly draining the life from him. Xerxes was rumored to be on the hunt for a she-beast determined to kill him.

Cheers erupted throughout the club, and someone called Taliyah's name.

She had arrived.

"Whatever happens in the war between father and son," Bjorn said, "we can't allow Lucifer to win. Our oracles have spoken. If Hades emerges as victor, the world will survive."

"If Lucifer is victor," Xerxes said, "the world as we know it will end."

Apocalypse, Destruction whispered in warning.

"You have other questions, I'm sure," Bjorn added and Baden nodded.

"But we have no other answers to offer you," Xerxes finished.

Oh, they had answers. Just no others they would share. But Baden wasn't going to push. He owed these men, and he wouldn't repay them with violence.

"Thank you for the chat," he said as he stood.

The Sent Ones stood, as well.

The red in Xerxes's eyes deepened. "Word of your association with Hades is going to spread. There'll be no stopping it, so be prepared. One day soon, Lucifer will send someone to kill you."

He already had. The prostitutes William had killed.

"I will prevail." With that, he strode off to hunt the Harpy. Not that he had to hunt for long.

She was straddling a mechanical bull in the middle of the club, her short skirt revealing every inch of her legs and a hint of the panties he needed. Pale hair danced over her shoulders as the bull bucked back and forth. She had both hands free, double-fisting shots while maintaining her position with the strength of her thighs.

The bull took an abrupt turn, presenting Baden with her back, revealing the small iridescent wings that fluttered from the slits in her pink tank top.

A beautiful woman, no question…but she didn't compare with Katarina.

The cheers died down as Taliyah leaped off the bull and landed directly in front of him.

"I hear you've got something to ask me," she said. "I'm going to let you buy me a drink. Or twelve. Yeah, definitely twelve. Our business needs to be concluded by the time the last shot is down the hatch. Clear?" She marched to the bar, her hips swaying. A mating dance. One that caused no reaction in his body.

His hands fisted as he followed behind her.

She ordered *fifteen* shots, and he tossed a gold coin at the bartender. Torin had made him a lot of money over the years.

"So? Start talking." She emptied one glass, then another.

"Give me your panties."

She'd just thrown back the fifth shot and choked on the liquid. After catching her breath, she laughed and said, "Wow. Ask nicely much? Dude. You planning on wearing them or something?"

"No." He offered no explanation.

Her amusement subsided, her eyelids slitting.

When someone bumped into her from behind, she turned so quickly Baden almost couldn't track her motions, slamming her fist into the offender's stomach. "No?" she said to Baden, not missing a beat. "That's all I get?"

Get in on the action! The leash on Destruction frayed a bit, and Baden found himself grabbing the gasping man by the throat and lifting him off his feet.

"Continue with him or with me," Taliyah said, "but not both. I'm almost done—"

The time limit on his conversation. Right. He released the male without killing him. "Hades is—"

"Hades! That's right." She licked the rim of a glass to catch a stray droplet of liquid. "You're his bitch now, forced to do his bidding."

He balked, but again he offered no explanation. The fewer details outsiders knew about him, the better.

Two more shots were emptied. "Hades and I have a wee bit of history." Another emptied glass, and this time, she trembled, but not with fear. "I'm going to guess he sent you just to mess with me. Well. I'm happy to mess with him right back." She downed yet another shot then reached under her miniskirt to pull a bright blue thong down her legs. She dangled it in front of Baden's face. "I'll give this to you—for a price."

He almost rolled his eyes. Everyone always had a price. Except the Sent Ones, he realized. And Katarina. She wanted to *give*.

Must return to her.

"Of course," he said. "Name it."

"What do I want, what do I want?" With her free hand, she tapped nails that looked as sharp as daggers against her chin. "Oh, I know! You'll deliver a message for me. Word for word."

That wouldn't end well for him, would it? "We have a deal."

Grinning, she rose on her tiptoes and whispered her message in his ear. He stiffened, sighed. No, this wouldn't end well.

"I'll tell him," Baden vowed. "Word for word."

She tossed the panties, and he caught them. Before he could thank her, she finished the last shot, and disappeared in the midst of the crowd.

Better get this over with. He flashed—

Into a bedroom with polished ebony walls and an ivory floor. The antique furniture had birds carved into the wood. There was a plush red rug, and a large canopy bed surrounded by white gauze. Hades sat at the edge, his head resting in his upraised hands.

The blind siren perched on a stool a few feet away, playing a harp and humming. The soothing sounds stroked over Baden's skin like a caress. A caress he could tolerate.

A sense of compassion struck him, surprising him. Hades—once a boy who'd been locked away and forgotten—had known more suffering than most people could ever fathom. No wonder he longed to kill anyone who posed a threat to his freedom.

The king sensed Baden's presence and jackknifed to his feet, grabbing a shirt from the nightstand. He yanked the material over his head, hiding a muscled chest tattooed with symbols Baden had never before seen.

"Leave us, Melody."

Melody. A fitting name.

The girl stood and, counting her steps, headed for the door. She smiled a mocking smile as she passed Baden.

"This hasn't been a good day." Threads of anger layered Hades's voice. "You better have what I sent you to get."

"I do." He flung the panties across the room. "I've earned my next point." He now had sixteen in total. *Tied with Pandora at last.*

Nine of his points were from kills, four from retrievals, and two from nonsense, like the fetching of the panties. But... Baden got it now. The kills took out Lucifer's major players, those who adversely affected humans. Acquiring the artifacts prevented Lucifer from using them against Hades, while the panties (and other things) amused him. Amusement kept him sane, providing light in a time of doom and gloom.

A slow smile bloomed over Hades's face as he brought the material to his nose and sniffed. "How did you get them? Tell me quick."

"I asked. In return, I promised the Harpy I would deliver a message for her."

Anticipation actually glowed through Hades's pores, creating a halo-effect around him. "Deliver it."

Baden closed his eyes and drew in a deep breath. "You are sexy, delicious and hot, but offer you my V-card? I will not. My panties get wet every time your name is called...but I'm still going to ensure...you are constantly blue-balled."

A laugh barked from Hades, one born from genuine humor. "Clever little witch."

The transformation was shocking, as if a wolf on the prowl had just transformed into a dog with a new toy. But that was the magic one woman—the right woman—

could wield over a man, wasn't it? Not that Taliyah was Hades's one.

But look at his friends. Once feral, now domesticated.

Katarina's image shimmered inside his head, her features as delicate as a butterfly's wings, and Baden's body jerked in response. He cursed. She couldn't be his one. They were too unevenly matched.

Another curse escaped him.

Mind on the task at hand. "Your son, William," he said. "He's hidden the human girl, Gilly, and we'd like to know where he—"

Hades's burst of humor vanished. "I suggest you leave. Now."

"So...no hug goodbye?" Baden meant the words as a jest...maybe.

When the king lunged for a sword, Baden said, "I'll take that as a no," and flashed to the fortress.

11

"Do us both a favor and remove your manpon."

—Strider, keeper of Defeat

The next week passed quickly. Katarina waited, a little anxious and a lot eager for Baden to call in the favor she owed him. After all, he hadn't returned bloody. But he also hadn't mentioned her reward. Had he killed on his mission? Or had he changed his mind about wanting her?

Well. She—the lowly soldier—wasn't going to worry about it anymore. Or think about him. Or yearn to kiss him…the way she'd yearned to kiss him when she'd framed his beautiful face with her hands. Nope. Nada. Nie.

She threw herself into her work. Ashlyn's kids had refused to help her, a stranger, but they often trailed after her, peeking and giggling from behind posts. She ensured Biscuit and Gravy were bathed, medicated, fed daily and given shelter, doing her best to keep her emotions on lockdown. *No love, no hurt.* And yet, true to her nature, she found herself spending extra time with the animals, determined to get them used to her presence—to maybe even crave it.

The treats she left behind after each visit had already worked wonders. Now, instead of growling when she approached, they wagged their tails and jumped around with excitement.

So precious. And they just happened to be her favorite breed: rescue. Okay, okay, they were also a mix of other breeds. The pair had short fur and large, square heads with wide, muscled chests like pit bulls. Except, in terms of body size, they were as big as full-grown Great Danes—roughly one hundred and twenty pounds—even though their (extra sharp) teeth told her they were both under four months old.

I like big mutts and I cannot lie.

Biscuit had a serious underbite. Gravy, who was mostly white, had a line of black fur over his upper lip. The most adorable mustache! The two loved to wrestle and bite fight—the canine version of *does this hurt, huh, huh, does it, well, what about this?*

Three times she'd fit them with collars, and three times they'd ripped the leather to shreds only a few minutes later. They hated the leash and bucked like rodeo bulls every time she tried to lead them.

Anytime another human...or immortal...neared them, the pair stilled and quieted. Not with fear—which was what she'd expected—but curiosity. They observed the world around them with intelligent eyes. Eyes that actually changed color with their emotions, from black to blue to green, something she'd never seen in a dog before.

The dogs became agitated only when Baden approached, and she wasn't sure why.

Her motto in the past: *if my dogs don't like you, go to hell*.

Not that Biscuit and Gravy were hers. But she knew deep in her heart Baden wasn't all bad. He couldn't be. He'd taken care of her for days...weeks. He'd bathed her—*won't think about that*—fed her, given her shelter and a closet full of clothing. More than that, he'd comforted her during the worst of her despair. Actually, he *still* comforted her.

Whenever waves of grief revisited, leaving her curled up in bed, feeling as if she were drowning, he would gather her close and pet her until she felt normal again.

Do I even know what normal is anymore?

He came and went whenever he pleased. And even when he *didn't* please; he would disappear with a scowl, the bands on his arms glowing bright red. Sometimes he returned in the same condition he left. Sometimes he returned covered in blood. *Every* time, he appeared to her first, wherever she happened to be.

The very first time, she'd offered to wash him the way he'd once washed her. He'd accepted reluctantly, as if he expected her to attack while his back was turned. The second time—and every time after—he'd handed her a rag before she could utter a single word.

Once or twice, he'd returned and paced, muttering to himself.

I'm a gentleman. Life is precious...unless the life belongs to my enemy. Everyone is my enemy. No, no, I have friends.

Pep talks, she'd soon realized. Pep talks she found adorable. He didn't *want* to hurt people, but a literal beast lived inside him and that beast craved bloodshed. Which made her impulsive offer to give him whatever he wanted quite foolish. But she couldn't bring herself to regret stepping into the fray with him. He'd been consumed by rage, and she'd desperately yearned to ease him.

But, really, she could have just sung a song to ease him. Whenever she hummed, he would drape himself across the bed and drift into a peaceful sleep.

Her junkyard dog was definitely trainable.

LGB?

Today? Pretty high. He was already pacing. She watched as he stomped through the kennel she'd built in the backyard. Biscuit and Gravy watched him, too. Without growling. Ah, what sweet progress.

He was tense, his hands curled into fists. As strong as he was, his bite would be far worse than any dog's, with real potential to damage her or worse, to kill her, but if she succeeded—*when* she succeeded—she would be helping more than Baden. She would be helping his friends. She would be helping the women he dated in the future.

A shard of jealousy razed her, which alarmed her. *I haven't done more than dream-kiss him.* Jealousy was ridiculous.

"With all your flashing around lately," she said, initiating conversation in an effort to distract them both, "have you come across my brother?"

"No." One word. No more, no less.

Had he reverted to the Baden she'd first met? Was he no longer the warrior so deeply concerned for her welfare? "With Alek out of the picture, I pray Dominik gets clean."

This time, silence greeted her.

Determined to engage him, she tried a new topic.

"Do you know Biscuit and Gravy are the same dogs we encountered in New York?"

Baden frowned but continued to pace, silent.

"Someone must have flown them to Budapest, but I can't figure out who or why."

Now he muttered, "I would know if someone was following me."

She waited for him to say more. He didn't.

Damn him, what had him so frenzied?

After she placed dinner bowls in front of the dogs, she approached him. When he failed to notice her, she stepped into his path. He drew up short, his beautiful copper gaze narrowing on her.

She wasn't afraid of him. Not anymore.

He took a step to the side, intending to move around her. Oh, no. She flattened her hands on his shoulders, keeping him in place.

"I want to know what's wrong with you," she said. "Tell me."

He snapped his teeth at her in a show of dominance. "You think you want to know my problem. You're wrong."

Her tone dry, she said, "I'm so glad you know my mind better than I do."

"Very well. I need sex." He threw the words at her as if they were weapons. "Badly."

Whoa. *Blindside!*

Heart pounding, she jerked her hands away from him. "Sex...from me?"

"Yesss." A hiss. "*Only* from you."

Only. Amazing how one little word could send pleasure soaring through her, warming her. "You told me never to touch you." Which she'd just done, she realized. *My bad.*

"I've changed my mind." His gaze dropped, lingered on her lips.

Burning her... "But you and I...we're a different species."

As if that mattered to her body. *Gimme!*

He took a step closer, invading her personal space. "We'll fit, I promise you."

Tristo hrmenych! The raspy quality of his voice, all smoke and gravel...she shivered with longing. *Must resist his allure.*

But...but...why? Before she'd committed to Peter, she'd dated around, had made out in movie theaters, cars and on couches. She'd liked kissing and touching and "riding the belt buckle," as her friends had called it. Then, after committing to Peter, she'd gifted him with her virginity. At first, he hadn't known what to do with her—he'd been just as inexperienced—and she'd left each encounter disappointed. When finally she'd gathered the courage to tell him what she wanted, he'd satisfied her well.

She missed sex. But connection...intimacy...she thought she missed those *more.*

Biscuit barked at Gravy, jolting her from her thoughts. They'd cleaned their bowls, and now wanted to play. She clasped Baden's hand to lead him out of the kennel. He jerked away, severing contact.

One action. Tons of hurt.

"I'm allowed to touch you and you want to have sex with me, but you're still disgusted by me." She stomped outside the kennel, done with him. "Well, I'm leaving.

Good riddance! Your do-what-I-say-or-else attitude was annoying, anyway."

He darted in front of her, stopping her. Breath caught in her throat as sunlight streamed over him, paying his chiseled features absolute tribute, making his bronzed skin glimmer.

So beautiful. Too beautiful.

"I'm not disgusted by you. You need me. I've come to accept it," he admitted, looking away from her. "But being skin-to-skin with another is painful for me. We'll have to proceed with cloth between us. And you'll get over your annoyance."

Another order. Of course! "First, I don't need you. Second, painful for you? How can you *proceed* without some type of contact?"

"The why could be psychological or physical. Or both. I went thousands of years without contact with another." His gaze returned to her lips, and his tongue swiped over his own, as if he could already taste her. "The how… I can imagine it. My clothing will be on but yours will be off. I'll wear gloves and sheathe my length with a condom. I'll bend you over my bed, get you wet, soaked, and kick your legs apart. I'll—"

"Enough. I—I get the picture." A little too vividly. And the image he painted wasn't exactly…unpleasant.

Perhaps he took her silence as rejection. He scrubbed a hand down his face and said, "I should just choose someone else."

The jealousy returned full force. "Do you desire *only me* or not?" she snapped.

"Only you." His pupils expanded, black spilling over copper. "Very much. You're all I think about, all I crave."

The pleasure soared again and heated, becoming a languid pulse inside her. "Then I'll allow you to take me on a date." He wasn't the best choice for her, or for any sane person, really. Also, he was part of a world she knew little about. A world where every myth and legend she'd ever heard had grown from a seed of truth. A world she wasn't sure she would ever like. But he was gloriously hot, and he made her feel something other than sad and doomed.

Once upon a time...

Their story didn't have to last long. She could train him and enjoy him for what he was—sexy, naughty and exciting.

"You will *allow* me?" He placed his hands—his big, strong hands—on her waist.

"Well." The heat of him burned through her clothing, delighting her. "Not if you're complaining, *kretén.*"

His lips quirked up at the corners. "No complaining from me, then. Only appreciation."

He drew her closer, so close her chest pressed against his, and she thought she might be reconnecting with the rambunctious girl she'd once been. The girl who loved to laugh.

Giddiness made her dizzy. "Such a good boy."

"A naughty one. When you smile you make me—" He stiffened, his eyes flickering with sparks of red.

Was the beast acting up?

Keep the interactions short and sweet. Always leave him wanting more.

"All right," she said, as if she hadn't noticed his negative reaction. "Give me an hour to prepare myself... for our mutual pleasure." She pulled from his grip— swallowed a whimper as the heat he'd imparted quickly cooled—and walked away, giving her hips an extra sway. "I'll make sure I'm worth the wait."

The sound of his ragged groan followed her into the fortress, and for the first time in forever, she did laugh.

This was going to be fun.

Baden flashed to Aleksander, who was still locked in the eight-by-eight cell made of concrete and steel. There was no door. The only way in and out was to flash.

The male was huddled in the corner, caked in mud and dried blood. His hair stuck out in dark spikes, his eyes bloodshot and narrowed on Baden, his injured arm clutched to his chest.

Baden frowned. The bones in his wrist looked as if they'd grown a full inch since yesterday, which was impossible. Humans couldn't regenerate like immortals.

"I'll never tell you where I've hidden the coin," the man spat. At least he'd stopped lying about being unable to find it.

"That's all right. One of my friends is a computer whiz. He's hacking into your bank accounts and transferring the funds to ours. By morning, that coin will be the only one you have left. Oh, and he's also finding the name and location of every girl in your *employ*. Each will be freed, and your guards will be fired. Literally."

Aleksander paled. "The last time Pandora appeared, she told me you'd taken a shine to my wife. Do you really want to leave Katarina destitute?"

Baden unveiled a smile so icy it chilled the room. He wanted the woman, and he would have her, but their date wouldn't change their future. Sex…release…and one day, goodbye. Callous of him? No. A kindness to her? Yes. Better he hit and run than allow the beast to one day decide she was a threat they couldn't afford to let live—which just might happen.

As she'd stood in front of him, the sun stroking over the dark hue of her skin, a well of tenderness had bubbled up inside him. He'd hated it as much as he'd loved it. He had to remain sharp, focused on winning his game. He had to survive the war between kings and help his friends find Pandora's box. And he had to do it all while controlling the beast.

Katarina could help with the latter, no question, but at what cost to her?

"I won't leave her destitute," he said. "When the time comes, I'll give her your fortune. She's earned it."

Aleksander hurled obscenities at him. "She's mine, demon-spawn. Mine!"

Baden battled...something dark. "I'm no longer a demon and have never been the spawn of one. I'm worse. And you can't do anything to stop me."

Far from cowed, Aleksander kicked at him. "One day, you'll regret your dealings with me."

An undeniable threat. Now he dies.

Yes. Yes. The blood they would taste...the screams they would hear...

Vibrating with anticipation, Baden closed the distance. Aleksander shrank back—bastard was cowed now, wasn't he? Too late. Baden grabbed his uninjured arm and palmed a dagger, intending to cut off his remaining hand.

Aleksander attempted to push him away. His wrist *was* longer, Baden realized, with three metacarpals already peeking through his skin like little white twigs.

There was only one way such a phenomenon was possible. He wasn't human.

Hades possessed the ability to immortalize certain humans, but then, so did several different artifacts. The coin... Baden still hadn't learned much about it, the details sparse. To use the coin was—supposedly—to force Hades to perform a boon. But what were the limits? The consequences?

"Take my other hand if you want it." Aleksander glared up at him. "You'll never take my wife."

"I already have." The *something dark* grew hot... hotter...until it burned Baden's chest, a poker pressing deep. "And if you say one more word about her, I'll teach you how to make cell-to-table dick puree." A threat he'd heard Paris make on more than one occasion.

The sharp scent of fear saturated the air. Delightful.

"Pandora," Aleksander shouted. "Pandora!"

"She promised to help you, I know." There were multiple cameras hidden throughout the space, and Torin had captured each of her flashes into the room.

He'd texted Baden every time, and Baden had joined him at the wall of monitors, waiting for her to attempt to free the human from his chains—chains that were attached to the wall with mystical bonds. They could be opened only one of two ways: a key made specifically for the lock, or the All-key, capable of opening *any* lock. A key Torin carried in his spirit.

The moment Pandora touched one of the links, she would become bound to the chains herself, unable to flash away. But she was smart, and she'd avoided all points of contact.

"Pandora!" Aleksander shouted again.

Movement at his right. Baden spun, at the same time jumping backward, barely missing Pandora's swinging sword.

They faced off, glaring at each other.

"Trying to kill me?" Baden was dressed and ready for war. Dual pistols in holsters waited at his waist. His camo pants had multiple pockets, each filled with something deadly: daggers, extra cartridges, switchblades, throwing stars and even a vial of poison. "Tsk-tsk. Hades will be displeased."

"Perhaps I meant to shave you. You're looking a little stubbly."

Well, then. Perhaps he would *shave* her, too. He pulled a switchblade, lethal silver glinting in the light cast from a single bulb hanging from the ceiling.

"This man belongs to me." She pointed to Aleksander, as if Baden needed clarification. "He's my point."

"You want him? Take him." He smiled at her. "I won't lift a finger to stop you."

She motioned to his blade. "You'll just lift a weapon, I'm guessing."

He held out his arms in a display of innocence. "I won't. You have my word."

She knew him, knew his word was as good as gold. She also knew he always planned ahead.

"Free him," she said, "or I'll take a page from your book and steal something else from you. Something new every day."

"You may try."

"Very well. Remember, you picked this path." She smirked and vanished.

Aleksander smirked as well, feeling confident now that he thought he had an ally.

Baden smiled. "Try not to scream. Actually, scream all you like. I'll enjoy it."

Baden flashed outside Torin's bedroom. He'd learned not to appear directly inside *any* room but his own. More often than not, a couple was inside having sex. Even in the living room. No one had boundaries anymore.

He knocked, his beastly strength cracking yet another door.

"If this isn't a matter of life and death," Torin called, "go away."

His friend would probably regret the qualification. "It is."

A grunt of irritation, a rustle of clothing and a patter of footsteps. Keeley opened the door, her tank top on backward, and her skirt tucked into her panties.

Oh, yes. Torin regretted.

Destruction cursed at her.

She looked Baden up and down, saying, "You've never looked better, but I've never hated you more." She flipped him off as she shouldered her way past him, muttering, "Cock blocker's not gonna like payback."

The beast tried to take over his body, to attack Torin's mate, but Baden heard Katarina's laughter down the hall and maintained strict control. What or who had amused her?

Concentrate!

Right. He strode into the bedroom as Torin buttoned his pants, forewent a shirt and plopped into a chair in front of his "command center."

"You need to tighten security," Baden told him. "Pandora threatened to steal from me. Something new every day."

"Security is already tight enough to pop a cherry. And you obviously haven't heard how busy Pandora has been. Kaia and Gwen were in town when she attacked. An attempt to hurt Strider and Sabin, I'm sure, but she had her ass handed to her and retreated." Torin typed as he spoke. "By the way. Galen came by earlier and asked me to talk to you about your old pal Distrust—"

"The demon was never my pal. And I don't want to talk about him. I need to apologize to Kaia and Gwen, to Strider and Sabin."

"Why? Strider and Sabin helped steal the box. They earned Pandora's wrath same way you did."

Still.

"*Anyway.* Distrust has possessed a woman named..." Torin scratched his head. "I've forgotten, even though Galen *just* reminded me. Whoever she is, she could use your—"

"No." He had enough on his plate. "Have you learned anything else about the coin?"

"Not really. The only people who know anything belong to Lucifer. As you can guess, I'd rather shit an actual brick than trust his associates."

On one of the screens, Baden caught a glimpse of Katarina. She stood outside Ashlyn and Maddox's room, Anya at her side. The two chatted easily, Katarina's hands waving as she spoke. An adorable trait. One she hadn't displayed before.

Adorable...and sexy as hell.

The beast snarled, but issued no command to kill. Only to...protect?

The two females strolled down the hall and parted at Baden's door, Katarina disappearing inside. Soon, he would join her for their date.

Every muscle in his body vibrated with sudden longing. *Mine...for tonight.* Perhaps tomorrow, too.

Once. Only once, Destruction said. *Maybe.*

Baden could *feel* the beast's desire for her. He wanted her with a fervency he didn't understand, but he didn't want to be weakened, and the dual desires had placed him in the middle of a desperate tug-of-war. Fight Baden, or capitulate.

Whatever he decided, Baden had already made up his mind. He would have her. He would hear her voice go raspy with passion...hear his name whispered then screamed. He would feel her inner walls clench around his shaft as he slammed into her from behind.

She's mine. Aleksander's scream echoed inside his mind.

Baden's hands fisted, the sharp tips of his claws cutting into his skin. The marriage was a sham. It shouldn't bother him on any level. But it suddenly bothered him on *every* level.

"Whoa." Torin threw a boot at him. "Get that thing away from me."

That thing—his erection. Simply because he'd thought of having Katarina at long last. The power she wielded over him already...

Running a trembling hand through his hair, he backed away from his friend. "I'm going to use your shower." He didn't wait for a reply but locked himself in the en suite to remove the sweat and grime contact with Aleksander had left behind. He also took care of his problem.

When he finished, he changed into clean clothes he gathered from Torin's closet. Even though they were a little snug.

"Where you taking your girl for the first date?" the warrior asked. He heard everything.

"Here." No reason to risk having a flashback of Hades's life in a public place, leaving him—and therefore Katarina—vulnerable. There was even less reason to put potential victims in the path of Destruction. And what if Hades summoned him? Katarina would be left on her own.

The girl was the quintessential damsel in distress.

Torin stopped typing long enough to give him *the look*. "Did I mention you suck? Females like to be romanced and you, my friend, are clearly romanerexic."

As Destruction kicked up a fuss—*I can be romantic!*—Baden muttered, "I've got to go." He stormed out of the room.

He had half an hour before the date was set to begin. He would return to Downfall. Would he still be able to flash there, without Taliyah? If not, well, he would find a way. There was always a loophole. While there, he would pick a thousand fights with the immortals, and he would exhaust the beast.

Then... Katarina would be his.

12

"When a girl says 'Go have fun,' do *not* go have fun. Abort mission!"

—Scarlet, keeper of Nightmares

I think I'm going to train a beast so evil his name *is Destruction?*

I've lost my mind. That's the only explanation.

As a hard knock echoed through the bedroom, Katarina smoothed trembling hands over the dress the beautiful Anya had given her—aka *a sure thing*—and remembered the goddess's sage advice.

You gotta talk less and bang more. Don't be afraid to withhold sex as punishment. And don't be reminding him of all that shitty stuff he did. Seriously. Hide nothing, but make sure you keep all your secrets. Never lie. If you want to have a little fun, threaten to leave, then—surprise—don't leave. Oh, and most important, if he messes up, never let him forget it.

Did the woman know how many times she'd contradicted herself?

Another knock, and Katarina's heart performed a series of flips. There was no reason to be nervous. If the date failed, the date failed. No harm, no foul.

Chin high, she opened the door. Baden leaned against the frame, and oh, wow, one look at him made her drunk with desire, her veins fizzing as if filled with champagne.

He's going to be mine.

He'd brushed his red hair from his face and fit his big, muscled body in a black T-shirt and biker leathers.

Sweet...carnal...perfection.

He had a handful of cuts on his brow and jaw, and his knuckles were bruised, but the injuries only added to the bad-boy appeal.

She wanted everything he had to give. His kiss, his touch, his body sliding into hers.

The breathtaking desires...depressed her. She was moving on with her life while her dogs rotted in their graves.

A wave of grief...a hollow ache.

Baden sensed the change in her and drew her against him, his uncompromising strength enveloping her. "I've got you, Rina. I'm here."

She basked in the comfort he gave so easily, and the ache eventually vanished.

Great! My "weakness" is showing. She pulled back, embarrassed, and licked her lips. *Let's get this date on track.* "I'm going to be completely honest with you. I look amazing. But I'm already wanting to *127 Hours* my feet. These heels are mountains!"

He barked out a laugh, the sound so rusty she knew he hadn't made it often. "Aren't you supposed to compliment *me*?"

"No way. Ladies first."

His gaze raked over her slowly, heating, his lids growing heavy. "*I'm* going to be completely honest with *you*. I don't deserve a compliment. I'm unworthy of your exquisite beauty."

What a compliment! The ache returned, but this one was different, hot and glorious...throbbing. Peter had praised her often, but she'd taken every "Looking at you is the reason I exist" for granted. Never again.

"Thank you." *I won't fall into his arms before dinner.* Well, not again. "And Baden...you deserve a *thousand* compliments. You are a feast for my eyes, and no other man can compare."

Because he wasn't a man, she reminded herself. He was immortal, and life and death meant different things to them. And that was okay. They weren't trying to forge a forever-after bond here. They were temporary.

At this stage in her mortal existence, a little fun was all she wanted, all she needed.

His amusement drained fast and sure.

"What's wrong?" she asked, unsure where she'd gone wrong.

"You think me beautiful."

The problem? "I do."

"The beauty is only on the outside."

"That's not true. I see beauty inside you, too."

He searched her features, as if he couldn't quite believe her claim but could think of no way to refute her. With a sigh, he held out a gloved hand. She craved skin-to-skin contact more than water or wine to drink, but she kept her disappointment in check and twined her fingers with his.

Contact hurt him, he'd said, but he wasn't sure if the problem was mental or physical. Her guess? Physical. Sometimes, when a dog spent the bulk of his life chained up outside with very little human contact—*see Katarina turn into a momma bear*—his fur became overly sensitized.

If she was right, Baden *needed* contact. It was the only way to desensitize him. But she couldn't push for too much too fast. They had to take this one step at a time.

As he ushered her down the hall, she said, "What do immortals do on dates?"

"I don't know, but this immortal is having a candlelit meal with his favorite human." With a tug, he pressed her against the wall, eating up her personal space, his warm breath fanning over her brow. "Unless you'd rather do something else?" His coppery eyes devoured her...dared her...

A new cascade of shivers had an avalanche effect, growing stronger and hotter as they tumbled through her. The throbbing between her legs returned and amplified, her nipples beading, pressing against her bra, desperate for contact. For him.

Despite her desire to pull him closer, she flattened her palms against his pecs to hold him at a distance. "You really think I'm that easy?"

"If I say I hope so...?"

"Your honesty will impress me...but it won't sway me. Let's eat."

He leaned closer, traced his tongue over the seam of her lips. "What if I want to eat *you*?"

Oh, sweet heaven. "I'm not on the menu." More shivers, accompanied by tingles. "Yet."

"That's too bad, *krásavica*." He rubbed a very impressive erection between her legs. "Too bad, indeed."

A whimper escaped her. "I think you need to work on your Slovak. *Krásavica* means *glamour girl*." Fashion wasn't her thing. Never had been, never would be.

"I know. Glamour girls are lovely...charming."

An-n-nd there went her pleasure. "Basically another word for *useless*." He'd never see her any other way, would he? "I have a name. I prefer it." She pushed at him, and he frowned.

"I meant no insult. In a life as ugly as mine, beauty isn't useless. Beauty is priceless."

Guilt flared in the pit of her stomach. Perhaps she'd been a *little* hard on him for his choice of designations. "I'm sorry for giving you attitude."

"Don't be. I happen to like your attitude." He led her down a flight of steps and into the kitchen where he'd set up the candlelit dinner for two. The scent of seafood, butter and yeast filled the air, making her mouth water.

"Did you cook this?" No, impossible, she thought as soon as the question left her. She'd only given him an hour. "I bet you sent one of the girls to a nearby restaurant."

"Wrong on both counts. I had Lucien—he's the keeper of Death—"

"I know. I've met him. Even wore his T-shirt." He seemed to be the most levelheaded of the bunch. He loved rules, strove for a peaceful resolution whenever his friends argued and, the best, he always remained gentle with Anya, his fiancée; he'd earned Katarina's respect.

"Lucien can flash. What you and I did the day I took you to Aleksander, moving from one location to another with only a thought. He called in an order and picked it up." Baden held out a chair for her. "In Paris."

Impressive. She sat, asking, "Why didn't *you* pick it up? You can flash."

He settled in the seat next to her, their thighs brushing together. "I can only flash to specific people. And apparently any place I consider home."

People like Aleksander. So… Baden's victims?

A gloved finger stroked the line of her jaw. "You just flinched. Why?"

"Your intentions toward Alek," she said, opting for honesty. *Hide nothing.*

A vein throbbed in the center of Baden's forehead. "If you're planning to ask me to release him, don't. He won't leave the fortress alive."

On one hand, yay! No more crazy, cruel Alek terrorizing the world. On the other hand… "Cold-blooded murder isn't an acceptable solution to anything. And I don't want him released." *Don't want you committing a dark deed, sending you deeper into your turmoil.* "I want an annulment…and maybe for you to leave him locked up for the rest of his natural life. As long as there's breath, there's hope."

"He isn't human, which means he'll live—"

"What!" Not human? When did *that* happen? "He's immortal?"

Baden frowned. "The beast is pawing at my head… I think Aleksander is merely half immortal, that he'll live longer than you but not forever. Now." He poured her a glass of red wine. "I don't want to talk about him."

Such a normal action from a man who wasn't normal. "News flash. Your wants aren't more important than mine."

He searched her eyes before he nodded. "You're right. Now I'm the one who's sorry. Forgiven?"

How could she deny him when he hadn't denied her? "Forgiven," she said with a little smile.

As she sipped and moaned at the richness of the wine, he removed the lids from the platters of food. "Do you like seafood?"

"Love it." Pretending to be a lady—only taking one small bite at a time—wasn't as difficult as she would have guessed. With Baden's attention fixed on her, watching her every move, her stomach twisted. The rest of her continued to *ache*.

"You look uncomfortable," he said, almost sounding…smug.

"I am." *Play a* little *hard to get.*

Actually, why bother? It had been too long since she'd experienced any kind of pleasure. If a night with Baden meant forgetting the past six months, if only for a little while, well, sign her up for a little some-some *tonight*.

"How, exactly, did you meet Aleksander?" He growled the name, as if it scraped his tongue.

If Baden were a dog, he would have barked at her, too. Maybe even nipped her. He would have been labeled aggressive, but as she knew, aggressive wasn't synonymous with cruel. A growl was merely a warning: dark emotions were escalating.

If fear was the culprit, she knew to create distance while remaining within eyesight. But that wasn't the case here. Baden had no concept of fear. He was angry—at her? Or her circumstances?

For a man who'd once claimed her marital status meant nothing, well, that would be big. Huge.

"I thought you didn't want to discuss him?" Studying his features, she added, "My husband, I mean."

He bared his teeth in a scowl. "I didn't. Now I do."

And what Baden wanted, Baden got.

She reached out and traced her fingers down his gloved arm. The action served a dual purpose. One, it helped get him used to her touch without paining him, and two, it reminded him she was here with him, not Alek, hopefully soothing the worst of his anger.

He stared down at her hand with confusion...and longing?

Oh, yes, and it nearly undid her. She continued stroking him, saying, "He wanted to buy home protection dogs from me. He, meaning my husband."

Baden's scowl deepened.

Stroke, stroke. "Then, while I had him within my clutches, I seduced him for his money and power." *Don't remind him of his shitty behavior. Oops.*

Baden's copper gaze narrowed on her. "Do you want me to kill him *now*?"

"No." *Stroke, stroke, stroke.* "I'm just reminding you of your assumptions about me."

He pushed out a breath, his shoulders turning in the slightest bit. "My apologies. I know you better now, and know you only married him to save your pets."

As another wave of grief crashed over her, she pulled her arms close to her middle, ending all contact. "But I failed."

He leaned over to place a gentle kiss on her lips, and his cheek brushed hers. He grimaced. To her disappointment, he retreated.

"When I refused to sell Alek a dog," she said, "he asked me to dinner. I said no, and he made certain my brother acquired a taste for heroin, so that, when Alek told him to poison Midnight, the oldest member of my pack, Dominik obeyed." Her chin trembled, but as usual there was no burn of tears.

"Your own brother betrayed you?" Baden's fork bent.

She fought a growing sense of emptiness. Where was Dominik now? "In an effort to save my other three dogs, I found them new homes. Alek tracked them, again with my brother's help, and stole them, hid them. He showed me pictures, said I could have them back after the wedding. I—" Hurt too much, and couldn't do this. "Let's change the subject, okay?"

He set down the ruined fork and shifted, his knee grazing hers. "Why do you never cry?"

He wasn't the first to notice, but he was the first to ask. "I cried while my mother was sick. After she died, I just…couldn't. I was tapped out, I guess."

"She suffered?"

"Very much."

"So you were relieved her suffering had finally come to an end. And guilty that you were relieved."

"Yes." An insightful observation for a self-proclaimed brute. "How did you know?"

The guilt she'd glimpsed every so often tightened his features. "When I was beheaded, I wasn't taken by surprise. I could have ducked. I could have fought, but I didn't. I remained unmoving. I…in essence…committed suicide in hopes of saving my friends from Distrust."

Judging by the conversations she'd overheard in the fortress, she knew those friends suspected he'd wanted to die, though he'd never confirmed or denied it. And yet, here and now, he trusted Katarina to keep his secret and not hold the outcome against him.

Her heart swelled. "Maybe you did it for yourself,

too? To finally know peace." Was that the true source of his guilt?

A stiff nod.

Lightbulb! No wonder he hated weakness. His greatest loss and regret had been born in the moment he'd stopped fighting.

"You're a changed man," she said. "What you did, you would never do again. You grew and you learned." And now, they both deserved a break from their pasts.

She plucked at the collar of his shirt and leaned closer to him, as if she planned to offer him a treat...a kiss. As he tensed, readying for the press of her lips, she released him and leaned away.

Disappointment darkened his features, and she almost laughed. Just like that, she felt buoyant, even... mischievous?

"I'm trying to decide..." she said. Oh, yes. Mischievous.

"Between?" The word was gnashed.

Her voice dropped to a raspy purr. "Between taking what I want, and making you come get it."

He looked at her as if she'd just fallen from heaven. His big hand settled on her hip and with a single tug, he pulled her halfway onto his lap, leaving her no choice but to straddle his thighs.

"I'll come get it," he said and nipped at her chin.

Panties? Suddenly drenched.

"Perhaps I'll reward you for your initiative." She cupped him between his legs...and oh, sweet heaven, he was hard. Bigger than she'd realized. Thicker, too. Longer and harder. "Perhaps not," she said, removing her hand. "Are you pained?"

"Yes. But ask me if I care."

She didn't want him pained. But she didn't want to end their play, either. "Do I owe you any other rewards?"

"You do. Anything I want." He slid her down his thighs, until she was perched on his knees. Then he pulled her back, rubbing her core against him.

She shivered, barely able to gasp out, "What do you want?"

"For you to come on me."

Darling man. "That can be arranged…" She arched her hips, once, twice, grinding on him. Moaning, she grabbed hold of his shoulders to hang on and enjoy the ride.

He gripped her hips and forced her to slow down, agonizing her, and…and…there!

Her mind hazed with the intensity of the pleasure. "This is *so good*! Don't stop. Please, Baden, don't stop."

He didn't stop. As she planted her feet on the floor and pressed down as hard, as hard as she could, he sucked in a breath.

"I like this," she whispered. "I think I might keep you."

He stiffened, then stilled. "You know this can't go anywhere." Every word emerged more ragged than the last, his hold on her tightening, almost bruising. "Yes?"

"Of course. I meant I'd keep you for a little while." His need to explain was a bit insulting, and she found herself adding, "You realize I'm only using you as a distraction from my troubles, yes?"

His grip tightened further, definitely bruising her. What? He didn't appreciate her honesty? He wanted to be the only one who considered their arrangement temporary?

Men!

"We're too different," she said, so desperate to move she followed up the statement with a whimper. "Now, enough—"

"Because I'm immortal?"

"And because you're a killer." She nibbled on her bottom lip, the fire inside her cooling. Stroking his arms again, she said, "What's the beast want right this very second?"

"To fuck you and fight, in that order."

Harsh words, harsher tone. Did he hope to scare her? Or prepare her? "Fight…me?"

"Not you."

Good. "You're not going to hurt me," she told him.

"*I'm* not," he agreed. "Never."

"But the beast might do so unintentionally?" *Stroke, stroke, stroke.* "Maybe we need to distract him. Or maybe he just needs to get to know me before he fucks me. That way, he'll only want to hold me afterward."

Baden suddenly radiated pure aggression. Liked a girl with a dirty mouth, did he?

"What do you want to try first?" She placed her mouth at his ear and blew gently. "Distraction? Or getting to know me better?"

"Let's just get to the fucking," he all but yelled—and she was almost certain she heard two distinct voices.

Her muscles clenched with eagerness. She actually *liked* his—their?—forcefulness?

She ran her fingers through the silken strands of his hair before taking his gloved hands and placing them on her breasts. "All right, but only if you name three things you really, really like about me."

His pupils flared. "You're beautiful. I believe I mentioned this."

"Yes, but thousands—millions—of others are more so."

"No one is more so." He stared at her beading nipples as he kneaded her. "You have the singular ability to make me laugh."

Better. Major points for that one. "What else?"

Outside, one of the dogs barked, then the other. Angry, someone's-going-to-get-eaten barks. Katarina stiffened, her hands falling to her sides.

"I have one other thing to tell you." Baden grabbed her wrists and threaded her fingers into his hair before cupping her breasts once again.

I'm not going to get attached to the dogs, remember? I'm going to keep my distance and preserve—

Another bark.

"That will have to wait." She jumped to shaky legs, ending the sensual play. "Something's wrong with the pups." She ran to the left—argh! The door led to a pantry closet. She had yet to learn the layout of the house.

"Katarina—"

"Pandora is here," a voice said over the speakers. A voice she recognized. It belonged to the white-haired warrior named Torin.

Pandora... "Your enemy-friend?" she asked.

"Mostly enemy now. Stay here." Baden leaped up and, with his hands on her waist, placed her on the table. Then, he sprinted away.

Stay here? Please. Katarina followed him, as close as his shadow.

"Go back," he spat, racing through hallways.

"Not a chance. And just so you know, if this dating

thing is going to work with us, you *must* stop ordering me around."

He pushed past the outer door. Stubborn to the bone, determined, she remained hot on his heels.

Sunlight. Summer heat. The chirp of crickets and the buzz of locusts. The scent of pine. Details hit her, painting a scene that should have delighted her. But the kennel loomed ahead and the black-haired bitch from the hotel—Miss Headbutt—held Gravy in her arms. The big pup struggled for freedom while Biscuit, who was still in the kennel, banged at the bars in an effort to reach his brother.

Pandora smiled as Baden roared her name.

"Not another step," she said, placing a blade at the dog's throat.

Katarina froze, horror flooding her. *I'm helpless. Again. Supposed to sit back and do nothing while an innocent animal is endangered.* "No! I won't let you do this." She jolted into motion. "Let Gravy go!"

Baden grabbed her wrist, preventing her from making any progress. Though she fought for release, she remained bound, the warrior far too strong to incapacitate.

"Give me Aleksander," Pandora said, "and I'll give you the dog."

"An unacceptable trade. I'd rather you leave with this." The words were pure evil—and they were spoken while Baden threw a dagger.

A second later, Pandora reeled back, the dog dropping from her arms, the blade buried hilt-deep in her eye.

13

"That's an excellent point. Now, if I may present
my rebuttal. Go fuck yourself."

—Reyes, keeper of Pain

One second Baden had control of his temper, the next
Destruction—utterly—ruled him. And yet, somehow,
his thoughts remained his own, as if he and the beast
were sharing his mind. No longer two separate beings
but someone new.

Someone extremely pissed off.

His body grew...and grew...his skin stretching tight
over enlarged muscles and elongated bones. An animalistic roar split his lips as his vision tunneled, a red haze
spotlighting Pandora.

She'd threatened him. Threatened his woman and his
dogs. She would pay in blood. The rules be damned.

The tips of his fingers burned, his claws sharpening.
As he stomped toward her, she yanked out the dagger.
A black river poured down her face. She stood to unsteady legs. He'd seen her in worse condition. Now he
would see her dead.

Fangs extended past her bottom lip. She raced toward him, and they met in the middle, a tangle of fury. As they sliced and bit at each other like wild animals, they tumbled into the kennel with so much force the walls rattled and fell.

With a roar, he grabbed her by the hair and tossed her into a nearby BBQ. She rent the metal grill in two, clouds of charcoal forming around her. She hurled a larger shard at him. He plucked the piece from his chest as she raced over—shoved him into an outer wall of the fortress. Stone cracked, and dust plumed.

"I've got you." Katarina's gentle voice cut through his red haze, and though she spoke to the pups, he took comfort in it. "I won't let anything happen to you."

A stray thought: *I like her maternal instincts.*

He had to remember to tell her, wanted so badly to pick up where they'd left off.

Pandora focused on her, the bloody dagger still clutched in her hand. Baden could almost hear the being in her mind: *Kill the girl, she's a threat.*

Panting now, Baden stopped in his tracks. Katarina was crouched in front of the dogs and crab-walking backwards, keeping the pair behind her, her body acting as their shield. A courageous act.

Foolish girl! She could be hurt.

He flashed in front of her and swung a meaty fist into Pandora's jaw.

Two other warriors arrived on the scene.

"What do you want us to do?" Maddox called. "Your wish, my command."

In unison, Baden and Pandora focused on him.

Demon. Threat.

Friend. He's my friend.

The worst kind of danger!

Body moving of its own accord, Baden approached Maddox, Pandora keeping pace at his side.

The warrior frowned at him. "What are you doing?"

"Kill," Pandora said.

"Good idea. Don't mind if I do." Anya, the second intruder, jumped up, kicking Baden with enough force to rattle his brain against his skull.

Goddess, anarchy, threat. Friend!

How better to lure us into a trap...

Next she plowed into Pandora. The two hit the ground, Pandora attempting to stab her as they rolled.

"Help the others, Baden." Katarina, still using that gentle tone. "Yes? Don't hurt them. They need you."

His attention switched to her; the dogs stepped to her side and growled at him. To warn him away? *No one keeps me away from her!* He snapped his teeth at the animals.

"Maddox, a little help, please." Anya swung at Pandora, only to be blocked.

Pandora laughed as she crushed Anya's knuckles in her grip.

Maddox launched his body in front of the goddess, taking a punch meant for her. His jaw snapped out of alignment.

Kill! Destruction focused on Maddox.

No. Baden dove, managing to twist midair, aiming for Pandora instead. They rolled down a hill. Before they came to a stop, she sank a dagger into his side. Jab, jab. His kidney received the bulk of abuse, and if he'd been human, he would have bled out then and there. Scowling, he wrapped a hand around her neck and the other around her wrist, holding her in place while cutting off her air supply.

Does she even need to breathe?

The need had slowly come back to him. Perhaps the same was true of her. He increased the ferocity of his hold.

She struggled against him, clawing at his arms, shredding his skin.

Boom!

The ground vibrated, a blast of heat blustering over him. He would have fallen if he hadn't already been on his knees.

"Bomb!" Anya shouted.

Pandora's doing?

Maddox bellowed the names of his family members as he took off in a mad sprint, Anya right on his heels.

"How many did you set?" Baden demanded of Pandora.

"Not…me."

"Baden!" Katarina cried. "Help me!" He heard pain. Had she been hurt? "Please."

He broke Pandora's neck before leaping to his feet and climbing the hill. She wasn't dead, wasn't even forced into unconsciousness. Her narrowed gaze followed him while her body could not. He found Katarina on the ground, a long wooden beam pinning her leg and Biscuit's hips. She and Gravy worked furiously to lift the beam, but neither was strong enough.

Boom!

Another blast of heat threw Baden across the yard. He rose quickly, closing the distance once again, ripping away the beam with a swipe of his arm. "Can you walk?" Blood leaked from a wound hidden underneath her skirt as he helped her stand.

She should have cried.

She didn't cry, and it almost broke him. Nothing should be denied to her, not even tears.

"I think so," she said, her voice trembling. Streaks of dirt coated her cheeks. "What's happening?"

"Up there!" Pandora shouted.

If not for the soul-curdling screech that erupted from the sky, Baden would have ignored her. His gaze shot up, quickly finding a hideous winged creature hovering above the fortress, smoke wafting all around him. He had crimson skin, two thick horns protruding from his scalp. Sharp yellow claws extended from his hands and feet, and a smaller horn protruded from each of his heels. He wore a flesh-colored loincloth. Leathered *human* flesh?

With an evil grin, the creature held out his hand. A ball of fire grew over his palm, the flames a mix of black and red. He aimed at Baden.

All Baden could do was grab Katarina and the dogs and flash to the holding cell where Aleksander remained, before the three were hit. The room was untouched by the violence that had taken place above-ground, the bastard still chained to the wall. He would be unable to reach Katarina.

"As long as you stay on this side of the cell, he can't hurt you," Baden told her. Destruction banged against his skull, enraged, ready to return topside and kill. "Patch your thigh and stay here." Not that she could leave without him. "Do *not* get near the man."

Boom!

The walls rattled, and dust filled the air.

"Don't leave me here, Baden. I—"

No time to argue. He flashed to the fortress. Or, what remained of it. Amidst the rubble, he caught sight of a fine-boned hand, fingernails painted pink. Ignoring the beast's desire to hunt the new enemy, he rushed over and dug through stone and debris. Strawberry-blond hair finally came into view and his stomach sank. Gwen—Sabin's mate. Her eyes were cloudy, her chest motionless. Soot and blood caked her cheeks.

Baden freed her, wondering if he would find the keeper of Doubt nearby, dead. As he pressed two fingers into Gwen's neck to check for a pulse—*be alive, please be alive*—the bands on his arms heated. No. No! Not now. But he was helpless to stop the pull and dematerialized…reappearing in Hades's throne room, Pandora beside him.

"Send me back," he commanded, trying to flash and failing. "Right now."

Hades stood at a long rectangular table, the four kings surrounding him in a show of support.

The Iron Fist was shirtless, revealing tattoos similar to Hades's. Strange and…alive? Those markings *moved*, slithering over his skin. He had long, wavy black hair, a thick beard shadowing his jaw.

The warrior with a slight bluish tint to his skin, eyes surrounded by black paint—surely he hadn't been born with such coloring—and staple-like piercings that stretched the length of his eyebrows, laughed. "Your puppet thinks he's in charge. How adorable." He had a slight accent. What he didn't have? Hades's essence.

Destruction snarled with hatred.

Baden leaped at him and threw a punch, the strength of an army in his arm; he could feel it, the bands so hot they blistered his skin. The male merely stumbled back a step and worked his jaw.

"Not bad."

"I told you he was strong," Hades said, sounding like a proud papa.

"But he's not overly bright." The new voice came from behind him, warm breath fanning his neck just before he was lifted over the head of the Iron Fist—*must have flashed behind me*—and tossed across the room. "Perhaps the blow will knock some sense into him."

Bones shattered, pain a burst of sensation, but he didn't care. He stood and limped over. *Threat. Will kill.*

Once again Pandora kept pace beside him. She still had only one good eye and it was locked on the male responsible for Baden's unplanned flight. "I'm allowed to hurt him." She wasn't exactly steady on her feet, either, but at least they had a common enemy in sight. "You're not."

"Enough," Hades said, looking bored.

Baden and Pandora froze, their limbs locking in place.

"Send me back," Baden repeated, his rancor echoing from the walls.

"This is the thanks I get? I brought you here to warn you. Lucifer has sent an assassin to destroy you. His name is…something. I forget because I don't really care. He'll use—"

"We know," Baden and Pandora shouted in unison.

"He's at the fortress," Baden added. "Which might have already fallen."

"Well, then." Hades stood and stepped toward them. "To defeat such a warrior, you're going to need a boost." He touched their bands, the heat cranking up a thousand degrees.

Baden roared as his knees buckled. Destruction

roared, as well, but it wasn't only a new flood of pain he felt. Power exploded inside him. So much power.

"The one to defeat the assassin," Hades said with a smile, "will receive five bonus points. Go."

Baden wasted no time; he flashed home. Pandora appeared beside him, equally determined to win those points.

Truce over. "Mine." He picked her up and launched her across the rubble.

Drunk on the power, Destruction quickly worked himself into a maddened frenzy. *Killkillkill. Never stop. Raze the world!*

Baden's hands fisted of their own accord. He would hurt anyone foolish enough to get in his way.

Yes, yes. He focused on the assassin, who had been grounded a few yards away, his wings bent at an odd angle. Smoke thickened the air, the black tendrils beautifully macabre as they curled toward the clouds like ribbons, but Baden had no trouble identifying the warriors currently engaged in battle with his target. Paris, Sabin, Maddox and Torin. They swung swords, fired guns, and threw punches and daggers, inflicting damage but not death.

KILL!

Baden could suddenly *taste* the desire to end life. His blood was hot and only growing hotter, even as the bands cooled.

"Mine," he said and took a step, just a step, but the next thing he knew, he was standing in front of his target. Maddox's punch landed on the back of his head, but he barely felt the blow that would have killed a weaker man.

The assassin grinned, revealing his lack of a tongue.

Not to mention tusks as yellow as his claws. He slammed a fireball into Baden's face—and Baden loved it. The flames only empowered him, bonding with whatever juice Hades had given him, his body acting as a conduit. And a syphon.

The assassin's grin waned, and he stumbled backward.

Baden tracked him, punching a fist through his breastbone and ripping out his heart. That. Easily.

Pandora appeared behind the creature. She swung her sword, hacking off his head. The head flew like a football. The body flopped to the ground like a wet noodle, blood spurting out, quickly creating a pool.

One down, many more to go. His enemies were weakened from the battle. *Strike now!*

Shhh. You don't need to kill anyone. I'll keep you safe.

Katarina's voice drifted through his head, soothing Destruction, and Baden frowned. She wasn't here, and she'd never said those words to him. She also wasn't strong enough to guard him.

"You okay, man?" Sabin asked, patting his shoulder.

Calm. Steady. Baden dropped the rotted organ, saying, "How's Gwen? The others?"

Agony darkened the warrior's eyes. "Lucien flashed her to a safe house, and as soon as Cameo woke Keeley, she used the last of her strength to relocate the others. Everyone but Galen is accounted for. If he's here, he's buried in the rubble."

"He's not here. He's been gone for hours." Torin scrubbed a hand down his face, leaving streaks of crimson behind. "Our piece of shit attacker knew to take Keeley out first so that she would be unable to aid us. He purposely bombed our bedroom before hitting the rest of the fortress."

"Everyone is…"

Sabin gave a stiff nod. "Alive, yes. Stable? No."

Baden locked on Pandora, who watched his friends with murder in her eyes. "You," he spat. "Had you not attacked my dogs, we wouldn't have been distracted."

They were in each other's faces a moment later.

"You want a go at me?" she snarled. "Huh?"

"You mean *another* go. How's your vision. Twenty-shitty?"

She screeched and drew back her fist. Maddox got between them and pushed them apart. "Leave," he told her. "Now. Or Baden won't be the only one beating on you."

She opened her mouth to protest.

Maddox said, "I'm giving you this chance because we did you wrong when we stole the box—because *I* did you wrong after my possession—but I won't give you another one."

"You're not going to win this fight," Sabin told her. "We're too keyed up, and you're too injured."

They didn't know about the extra juice Hades had given her. She *might* be able to take them. But weaving doubt was Sabin's business and business was good. She paled and vanished.

Baden scanned the devastation around him—there would be no salvaging the place. Guilt rose. "I'm responsible for this. I never should have returned, never should have moved in."

"Don't talk crazy." Torin kicked a piece of wood out of his way. "Let's retrieve what we can while we await Lucien's return. We're better together, and that's final."

"It's good to see you…wife."

Katarina hissed at the man who'd brought her so

much pain and misery. "You aren't my husband. You were my blackmailer and my brother's supplier. Now you're my dogs' murderer."

"You can buy more dogs. Many more. In fact, it looks like you've already begun."

Panchart! The hate she'd managed to bury welled up, nearly drowning her as surely as her grief. He deserved to suffer, and yet he looked perfectly content. The chain wrapped around his waist was the only indication he wasn't there of his own free will.

"Did the redhead buy you those mutts?" The corner of his eye twitched. "You should return to sender. You deserve dogs with a pedigree a mile long."

The dogs sat beside her, the fur on their backs raised, their gazes glued to Alek. As well behaved as dogs she'd worked with for months.

"Baden is none of your concern. Nor am I. Nor are the dogs." She ripped the hem from her dress and wrapped the material around her thigh to stanch the flow of blood. "And pedigree says nothing about worth."

Alek glared at her. "Have you fucked him?"

Was the blunt question meant to intimidate her? "I could work my way through an army and *still* it wouldn't be a concern of yours."

"Don't kid yourself. You are my concern, because you *are* mine. My wife…and my property."

The dogs took offense to his tone, jumping up and emitting a low warning growl.

Knowing better than to startle an angry animal with an unsolicited touch, she began to hum. They relaxed and settled on their haunches.

The ceiling shook, more dust raining down. Where was Baden? Was he okay?

"I suggest you play nice, wife." Alek attempted to scoot closer to her, but the chain stopped him. "Soon I'll use the coin to dethrone Hades and take his place in the underworld. I'll be a king."

A king. Of the underworld. Aka, of evil. On paper, it was actually the perfect job for him. "That's what the coin does? Buys you a kingdom?"

"It forces Hades to grant my wish, whatever that wish might be."

"How did you get it?"

He hesitated only a moment before replying. "A gift from my mother."

"You have a mother? Aw, is she proud of her murderous little sociopath?"

"She's dead. I blame my father." He smiled with a touch of mania. "But Papa got his in the end. I made sure of it. And if you want to keep your pretty tongue, you won't speak of my mother again."

The dogs barked, but remained in place.

Tongue removal must be all the rage among evil overlords. She'd noticed the winged devil had lacked one.

"Is my brother alive or did you kill him, too?" she asked, facing the wall to press her hands against the cold stone. There had to be a way out. Not that she doubted her safety. But the women and children might need her and the dogs.

"After the massacre at the chapel, I sent Dominik to my country estate. I won't harm him…as long as you treat me with the deference I deserve."

This. This would have become her life if Baden hadn't showed up. Threats and coercion. She owed the warrior a debt of gratitude.

She managed to extract an already loosened stone.

"You think to leave me?" Alek rattled the chain as he tried to stand. "No. You will stay. Do you hear me? You will stay!"

She turned and lobbed the stone at him, only to gasp. His eyes...they were lit up with sparks of red.

Baden was right. Alek *wasn't* human.

How? How was that possible? How had she not known?

"When I'm king of Hades's realm," Alek said, his tone low and silky now, "you will be my queen. Don't you want to be my queen, *princezná*?"

"I'd rather be a servant for a good king than the queen of a bad one."

"So...yes?"

"Hard no." But...

Katarina drew in a breath, slowly released it. Right now, she was part of Baden's world. He admired strength, and she'd often claimed to be strong. It was time to prove it.

If she couldn't escape, she might as well go on an information hunt.

"Where's the coin now?" she asked and winced. Too much too fast.

Another manic smile bloomed. "You can search the world, but you'll never find it."

He was so confident. Search the world...

So, where else could she search, if not the world? The *under*world he'd mentioned?

No. Not likely. He wouldn't trust the coin with anyone else. Not if it could do what he thought. He wouldn't want it far from his reach. "As much as I hate you, I don't want to be a prisoner, either," she said. *Can you relate, kretén?* Blanking her expression, she said, "If I help free you, you must vow to take me with you. And let my brother go."

His eyes narrowed on her, but he nodded. "So be it."

Such easy capitulation? Liar!

She stood and took a step toward him, then pretended to rethink her decision and edged back. As he tensed, she took another step forward. "*How* am I to free you?" she asked, as if nervous.

"Pick the lock on the chains like you picked the lock on your bedroom door." He practically vibrated with eagerness. "I can do the rest."

Another step brought her closer to him. "In other words, I do the grunt work for little reward. No! I want the coin, too."

Look at me. A pretend gold digger deluxe. Baden would be pleased.

"I'll share it with you," he said as anger clearly stirred inside him.

Another lie. "How do I know you really have it?"

"You'll just have to trust me."

She shook her head, adamant. "After what you did to my dogs? No. I don't trust you." There would be no bluffing her way past that particular truth. "You need to prove its existence."

"I have it, I swear." The edge of his voice sharpened to a blade-point. "That's all you need to know."

"Sorry, *husband*, but I have to see it."

His lips peeled back from his teeth in a scowl he'd only ever turned on employees who'd wronged him. "Free me," he commanded, "and then I'll show it to you."

Remaining at a distance, she scanned the chains. "The lock looks complicated. If it were easy to pick, you would have found a way already. Maybe I'm not skilled enough…" According to Baden, she wasn't skilled enough to do anything.

My bitterness is showing. Mind on the task at hand.

"The key," he said. "Find the key."

"How? Baden watches my every move. What if you used the coin? You could become king, as planned, and summon an entire army to free you." If Alek bought this, well, he was even crazier than he looked. "Tell me where it is. I'll convince Baden to flash me to its location, and hide it on my person before he finds it. He'll never know."

Alek kicked out his leg, swiping nothing but air. His sanity was unraveling. "Whore! You're planning to use it for yourself."

She petted the dogs behind the ears before they had time to react, and lifted her chin. "I'm afraid, weak. Would never approach Hades without you." Surely he'd buy *that*. "But I can't risk Baden's ire. He's a cruel man." She forced a shudder. "Very dangerous."

Alek huffed and puffed. He managed to smooth his features, though he couldn't hide the furious gleam in his eyes. "You're a woman. I'm sure you can figure out a way to distract him from his anger."

Ready for her to whore already, even though he'd used the word derogatorily only a moment before?

Panchart! "All right," she said. "I'll put my life in harm's way and seduce Baden…if you prove the coin's existence."

Alek stared behind her and paled.

Uh-oh. Trouble.

"You've made a grave mistake, *nevesta*," Baden said from behind her, his voice layered, as if the beast spoke *with* him. "Grave, indeed."

14

"There are three ways to look at the glass. Half empty, half full, and why are you eyeing my glass, bitch?"

—Gwendolyn the Timid, Harpy from Clan Skyhawk

A warm, salty breeze caressed Gillian's skin. She lounged in a cushioned chair on William's private beach, a wispy white canopy above her. The sun was in the process of setting, painting the sky with brilliant shades of pink, purple and gold. Only inches away, crystal-clear water lapped at white sand, leaving foam in its wake. So close yet so far.

The only thing that disrupted the beauty of the land? The eight guards dressed in black and armed to the max. They stood a few yards away from her, forming an octagon around her.

William had left to do…she had no idea what. His father had appeared and said, "There's trouble."

Poor Liam. Pulled in too many directions. She was only making things worse.

The two had left soon after, but not before William had carried her out here, wanting her to have sun and fresh air, hoping it would invigorate her.

Hate to break it to you, Liam, but this experiment is a fail.

She was as weak as before, but now she was angry. She deserved an answer to the question she'd lobbed at him as if it were an H-bomb: *What is* morte ad vitam?

The most he'd told her? "You're changing, poppet."

She knew that, but dang it. This was her life…and her death.

A whimper escaped her. *Not ready to die.*

"Do you need anything, Miss Bradshaw?" one of the guards asked. The men were over-the-top formal with her because William had threatened to castrate anyone who offended her.

Only her Liam!

"No, thank you," she managed to croak. *Not from you.*

A second later, a *thud* rang out.

She barely had the strength to turn her head, but caught sight of two guards, now prone in the sand and motionless. Three others rushed toward them, guns drawn, but they were met by an invisible wall and crumpled to the ground, as well. The remaining three decided to close in and surround her. Only, one at a time, they ended up on their backs.

Puck sidled up to her side, as calm as the ocean, making her gasp. He wore another loincloth, this one braided locks of hair. His furred legs were less startling than before and oddly attractive.

The invalid and the beast.

"Did you kill them?" she demanded, hating the whisperlike quality of her voice.

"Would you like me to deliver a lethal blow?" He sat beside her chair and stared out at the water. "I merely put them down for a nap, but I can slit their throats, no problem. Just say the word."

"N-no. Please. No."

"Very well, then." He said no more, and her panic slowly receded.

The muted rays of the sun reached out to stroke him, creating a halo effect. Which was odd, considering he had horns. Part angel…part demon. Part goat, she added, remembering his legs. All warrior. The razor blades woven into his dark hair glinted in the light.

"Why are you here? I can't aid you," she said, remembering his parting words the last time he'd showed up.

He hiked his big shoulders in a shrug. "I was told your situation is so sad, I'll come to care."

"Who told you *that*?" William? Not likely. Closed-mouthed tyrant! "And why do you want to care?" Her mind, fogged though it was, answered the question before he could reply. He was possessed by Indifference, and the demon probably always wiped away his emotions before he had a chance to feel them. There was always a consequence to demon possession. "*Do* you care?"

He thought for a moment, sighed. "Not even a little."

Well, *she* suddenly experienced envy. To no longer be affected by her past? To no longer be bothered by nightmares and fear? A priceless gift. "Do you ever feel *anything*?"

"Only very rarely, and then…" His voice trailed off, and he shrugged again.

"Lucky," she muttered.

"Lucky? Lass, I could set you on fire, watch you burn

and as you scream in agony I'd only be interested in the warmth of the flames on a chilly night."

"Okay, maybe lucky was too strong a word." She nibbled on her bottom lip, watching him through the shield of her lashes. "*Are* you going to set me on fire?"

"No. I left my matches at home."

So comforting. And yet, for the first time since the illness had struck her, she wanted to smile.

They sat in silence for several minutes, her gaze constantly returning to him, her interest in him growing. He really was a beautiful man and though—to her—all immortals usually looked the same age, this one actually appeared younger. Why?

A cool, salty breeze washed over her fevered skin, and she shivered. He immediately removed his shirt and draped the material over her. Her gaze dropped to his chest and…oh, wow. He had muscle stacked upon muscle, unlike her stepfather and stepbrothers, who were—

Breathing became a little more difficult as her airway constricted. She turned her head away from Puck, searching for a distraction. Her nose brushed against the soft cotton of his shirt and her mind enjoyed a blissful vacation. Nothing had ever smelled this wonderful. All that peat smoke and lavender infused the cloth. And his heat! The rays of the sun had left her cold, but his shirt gave her a toasty high.

"Thank you," she muttered, feeling like a kitten that had just found the cream.

"You're welcome."

They lapsed into another round of silence. If this kept up, he might leave. She didn't want him to leave.

Just don't want to be alone. That's all.

She racked her brain for a conversation starter. The

best she could come up with? "So, uh, how did you go invisible?"

"I didn't. I simply moved too quickly for you—or them—to track."

He answered her so readily, without a single moment of hesitation. That was new. William often spoke in riddles, and the warriors in Budapest always sidestepped her questions, as if they feared revealing too much to a human.

Maybe Puck would answer *the* question. "What is *morte ad vitam*?"

He arched a brow at her. "Is that what's wrong with you?"

"Yes. All the doctors agree." Her mouth dried as he frowned. "What does it mean?"

"Your body is trying to evolve, to become immortal, but it isn't strong enough."

What! No, no, no. Impossible. She was human, born and bred. She would always be human.

"The only possible chance for your survival," he said, "is for you to bond with an immortal, linking your life force to his. But even that isn't a guarantee. You could drain his strength and make him human."

Bond…as in marry. What William refused to do with her or anyone. Good thing, too.

Marriage meant wifely duties. Like having sex. She would much rather wear a chastity belt for the rest of eternity.

William probably didn't want to go that route because of his curse. Or he knew something she didn't. Several of the Lords had bonded to their mates, and there *had* been consequences. The couples' lives were now forever tied for the good, the bad and the oh, so sad. If one died, the other would soon follow.

"Well, that sucks." She would rather die today—this second!—than place William in a moment of unnecessary danger. "How much time do I have before I..."

"Considering the condition you're in now, I'd say another week, maybe two."

Fourteen days at most. "I'll never get to do the things on my bucket list. If I had a bucket list, I mean."

"Perhaps you should make one. I can help."

Her brow furrowed with confusion. "Why would you want to help?"

"You could use a distraction, and I could use a new goal. The woman I wanted didn't want me back, so we parted ways. Now..." He shrugged.

"Women are goals to you?"

"Why not? My goals keep me from sitting on a couch, watching soap operas all day and eating old pizza."

"But if you don't feel anything, how do you know when you want a woman?"

"I rarely feel emotion, but I often feel desire. The two aren't mutually exclusive, lass."

"That's true." She smiled her saddest smile at him. "I feel all kinds of emotion, but never desire."

A spark of curiosity lit his expression. "You are of age, yes?"

Dreading where he was going with this line of questioning, she gave a hesitant, "I'm a legal adult, yes." Finally.

"And you've never desired a man?"

She stared at the water as the sun disappeared on the horizon. Shadows fell over her hideaway, the torches burning atop a wealth of poles circling her providing the only light. She inhaled and exhaled slowly, precisely, fighting the rise of shame and hate and horror that always found a way to the surface of her heart whenever this topic came up.

"Ah. I understand. Someone hurt you." He said it so matter-of-factly.

Her hackles rose. "I don't want to talk about it. Change the subject or leave." Well, well. The burst of anger had come with a side of strength. One she hadn't experienced since this whole thing had kicked off.

He didn't change the subject and he didn't leave. "I will kill the male responsible. Just tell me his name."

"Names. Plural," she snapped, then pressed her lips together. She was confident William had already killed them. Having lived with the Lords as long as she had, she'd sometimes looked up the names of her tormentors— a compulsion she despised. One day she'd discovered a police report about their horrific murders. Though no bodies had been found, their blood and...other things had been splattered all over the walls and floor of the very house where she'd suffered. The case remained unsolved.

When she'd questioned William, he'd hurriedly distracted her with a new video game, as if he feared her reaction. Except he never feared anything!

But *she* feared her reaction. Gratitude struck her as inappropriate, but then, so did anger.

"One man or one hundred. It makes no difference to me," Puck said, still so matter-of-fact.

"Thanks for the offer, but they're already dead."

He nodded. "William must have taken care of them."

"Are you on friendly terms with William?" she asked.

"I know of him and I'm sure he knows of me, but we've never officially met."

"If you want to be his friend, sneaking around his property isn't—"

"I don't want to be his friend. He can hate me. I don't care one way or the other."

"That's unwise. If you aren't his friend, you're his enemy. His enemies die. Painfully." A fact she'd had to accept about him. He was what he was, and there was no changing him. Not that she wanted to change him. Why mess with perfection?

Puck smiled at her, for a moment he was almost... adorable? "My enemies die gratefully, glad to finally escape me."

She rolled her eyes. "You immortals and your blood feuds."

"Don't you mean *us* immortals?"

A pang of longing—*I want to live.* One she ignored. "I'm going to die, remember? Before the transformation is complete." *So* weird to say! "And I don't want to think up a bucket list." She'd have to pick things she could do from her sickbed, and how sad was *that*?

"You will die, yes." He threw a pebble into the water. "I could marry you, I suppose. Save you."

She gaped at him. "Are you actually *proposing* to me?"

"Yes. No. I don't want to marry you, but I don't *not* want to marry you. It's just something to do. Something with the potential to be mutually beneficial."

I can live! Maybe. Or she could kill him.

All right, let's say she married him and she survived the transformation. What then? They would be man and wife. He would want to do things to her body, just as she dreaded. Bile churned, her stomach threatening to rebel. "Aren't you worried I'll make you mortal?"

"I'm the dominant. My life force would overpower yours, no question."

He sounded so sure, and part of her was tempted. *I can be saved!* But…was her life worth the trouble that would follow such a bond? "Thank you for the kind offer non-offer, but I'm going to pass."

"Because of my horns?"

"No." Those were oddly…cool, she thought now. And maybe just a little sexy.

Sexy? *Nothing* was sexy to her.

He deserved the truth. "You would want to have… you know."

"Sex?"

Her cheeks heated as she nodded.

"You are correct," he said. "I would."

"Well, I wouldn't. Ever."

"You think that now, but I would change your mind." He threw another pebble into the water. "Not that I would force you. I wouldn't. That's one of the rules I live by. I would wait for you to want it."

"I'm telling you, no matter how skilled you think you are, you'd have to wait forever."

He snorted. "I'd have you in my bed within the month, guaranteed."

Her heart skipped a beat, something warm pouring through her veins. Something she'd never experienced before.

His head tilted to the side and his ear—his pointed ear!—twitched. "William has returned. He'll be here in five…four…three…"

"You should go," she whispered, worry thundering inside her chest. "Please."

"One."

William sailed through the double doors leading to and from the home's living room. He crouched beside her and frowned. "Are you all right, poppet? The guards—"

"I'm fine," she rushed out, turning to gaze at—Puck was gone. Just gone. And William had no idea, otherwise he would've focused on the intruder first. She breathed a sigh of relief. A fight wasn't something she wanted to witness, especially since she could do nothing to help either—no. Scratch that. Help William. Only William. Of course.

He came first.

"What happened to the men?" He studied their sleeping forms, and she had the distinct feeling each man would be dead by morning—or wish he were dead.

"*Someone* happened to them." *I have to tell him, don't I?* "A man. Puck. He came here and moved so quickly I couldn't even see him. The guards were no match for his speed and strength."

William stood so fast she would bet he'd given himself whiplash. In both of his hands a dagger glinted in the firelight. "Puck. The keeper of Indifference. He's sworn vengeance on Torin for trapping him in another realm. How did he escape?"

Puck had failed to mention anything about that. And really, Gillian couldn't imagine him caring enough to exact vengeance against anyone. "How do you know what he's sworn if you've never met him?"

"My spies. They are everywhere, poppet."

"Or Torin told you," she said drily.

"Did Puck say anything to you? Did the bastard do anything to you?" Antipathy dripped from every word.

"He told me about *morte ad vitam*." As William cursed, she added, "You won't hurt him for it. And you won't kill him. Or pay someone else to kill him." A girl had to cover all her bases. "I should have heard the truth from you, but I didn't, so he kindly offered to help."

"Offered. To. Help. How?" The last was spit into the darkness as William noticed the shirt draped over her.

On dangerous ground. Proceed carefully. "Promise me first," she said. "Please."

He remained silent as he ripped the shirt from her and tossed it into the water. She swallowed a whimper.

William scooped her up and carried her inside the house. She'd seen so little of the place. Only the path to her bedroom, really. A massive living room with sections of walls and ceiling strategically cut away to maximize daylight and ocean views. Floor-to-ceiling frosted glass windows welcomed nature inside while maintaining a sense of privacy.

A white couch curved into a half-moon, and two lounge chairs—also in white—offered a place to stretch out and relax in front of a stone fireplace with a lion carved on each side. The coffee table looked to be made of recycled wood he'd found on the beach.

"The verdict?" William asked, noticing her scrutiny.

"Clean, classic and yet homey, with touches of the ornate," she said. "So, not really you." He was extraordinary, unique and wicked. "How long have you owned the place?"

"Since the day we arrived, and I...relocated the owner."

What! "Liam, you can't just—"

"I can, and I did. Might is my right." He climbed the winding staircase with ease and entered the first bedroom on the right. The walls were yellow and the comforter on the bed light blue. Reminded her of sunshine and morning sky. The nightstand had sailboat steering wheels for legs, lending a touch of novelty.

He eased her onto the mattress and tucked the covers around her. "Are you thirsty? Hungry?"

He considered Puck a closed subject, didn't he? Frustrating man. "I can't in good conscience allow you to—"

"Your conscience doesn't need to bear anything. Mine alone will carry the burden."

"That's a problem. You don't actually have a conscience."

"Perhaps I'll acquire one." He arched a brow. "How much do you think they're sold for nowadays?"

What was wrong with the men in her life?

"Are you thirsty?" he asked again.

"No," she grumbled. "And, just so you know, I'm not going to marry you."

He was as taut as a drum as he sat beside her. "I don't remember asking, poppet."

"I know you haven't asked, just as I know you *won't* ask. This way, when I'm gone, you won't waste time feeling guilty, wondering if you *should* have asked."

"You're not going to die," he said softly, menacingly. "I won't let you."

There were some things not even William the Ever Randy could stop from happening.

She gathered what strength she could to reach out and clasp his hand. "I love you, Liam. When I had nothing and no one, you gave me friendship and joy, and I will be forever grateful to you."

His eyes narrowed to tiny slits. "Stop talking as if this is the end for you."

She offered him the same sad smile she'd given Puck—where had he gone? What was he doing? And why did she care about a man who cared about nothing? "You have faults. A lot of faults. But you're a wonderful man."

The ticking stopped. He even looked as if he'd stopped breathing. "This wonderful man will find a way to save you. I'm working every day, every hour, every minute. Now get some rest." With that, he stomped from the room, slamming the door behind him.

The sad thing? Gillian stared at the balcony, waiting—hoping—Puck would appear. One minute bled into ten, but he never showed. Disappointment zapped the rest of her strength, and she closed her eyes.

As she drifted off, she thought she smelled peat smoke and lavender...thought she heard a deep voice whisper, "Sleep, lass. I'll make sure you're safe."

15

"Always believe a woman who says she's innocent. Your trust in her will *never* come back to bite you in the ass."

—Gideon, keeper of Lies

A thousand new memories filled Baden's head. Destruction's memories. *Hades's* memories. They took over, consumed, causing the beast to foam at the mouth. He wanted to rip Katarina to shreds. She had betrayed him just as royally as his mother.

As a child, Jezebel had strapped him to a rack. His every joint had been pulled out of socket, his muscles torn. Mother Dearest had also hung his intestines from a spit, roasting them while she ate his liver—straight from the source. She'd laughed and poured buckets of demonic insects over him. The little critters had crawled inside his mouth, down his throat, in and out *every* orifice.

When she'd failed to kill him—the one prophesied to destroy her—she'd sold him to one of the kings of the underworld. The male had controlled a pack of hellhounds. Not through bonding. The hounds had to be willing for that. But through threats. *Do what I tell you, or watch as I kill your mate.*

Upon his order, they'd tracked Hades...ripped him apart.

So much pain...so much agony. Of the body and of the soul. He'd loved his mother, but he'd hated her, too.

And now, Katarina thought she had the wits to trick him? The courage to betray him? She thought she could free her piece-of-shit husband and leave him?

Destruction roared with a rage he'd carried all these centuries, the emotion leaking into Baden. Power before sentiment. The weak always sought a protector. *Any* protector. It was just a fact of life.

Some part of Baden defended Katarina. Her mind was well-honed; she was intelligent and crafty. She could survive the world without him—without Aleksander—and even thrive.

The thought...couldn't be correct. She needed a strong man to save her. She would always need a strong man to save her.

She raised her chin, her gray-green eyes crackling with fury of her own, daring him to speak against her.

In the revelation of her deceit, she dared challenge him?

Maybe her mind wasn't so well-honed, after all. She purposely incited his worst.

Calm. Steady. Baden placed Biscuit in her arms and scooped up Gravy. With his free arm, he yanked his betrayer against him. Chest to chest. She gasped in surprise...perhaps in fear.

Baden and Destruction cursed her in unison. *A treacherous bitch shouldn't feel this good.*

Aleksander lunged at him with all the slack the chain

allowed. His mistake. Baden booted him in the face, nearly snapping his neck.

Far from satisfied, he flashed just outside the safe house, where Keeley and Lucien had flashed the others. The temporary home was a shack on the outside, but was a tricked-out arsenal/makeshift hospital on the inside. He released Katarina in a hurry, as if she were toxic waste—because she was—and placed the dog at her feet.

Baden expected her to grab hold of his arm and cling, to sob and make excuses for her behavior.

You misunderstood...

I was so scared, so confused, but now I'm back on track.

I would never betray you. I crave you too intensely.

She merely flipped her hair over her shoulder and sneered at him. "You don't need Distrust to be a suspicious, unreasonable *kretén*, eh?"

"How am I unreasonable, *zvodkyne*?" Seductress. *Tell me. Please.* "Your own words condemn you."

"You're right. Now go away." She dismissed him with a regal wave. "You only hear, but you do not listen."

"What does that even mean?" he demanded.

The hinges on the front door creaked; Sienna stepped onto the porch, ending the conversation. One of her enormous black wings was bent at an odd angle, and she had stitches on her forehead.

A serene expression overtook her features as she approached. Her demon, Wrath, sensed the strife between them and ate it up, a fact that irritated both Baden and the beast.

"Thought you might need these," she said, holding out two collars and leashes.

"Thank you. *You* are kind and understanding." The dogs bucked as Katarina anchored the straps of leather in place. But when she began to hum, they settled, suddenly docile.

Baden scowled. She'd once subdued him just as easily. Never again!

"You're, uh, welcome?" Sienna said and returned to the house with only a single backward glance.

When Katarina attempted to follow the girl, Baden latched onto her wrist. "The attack we just faced was a hired hit. I'm a wanted man." The anger in his voice would have caused anyone else to run, but not the human. Never the human. Foolish girl. Foolish *Baden.* Why did he admire her so? "Hades has two sons. William, whom you've met, and Lucifer, who is ultimate darkness with no hint of light. He'll steal from anyone, kill anyone and destroy anything. He wants me dead. He wants all my allies dead. You need my protection, and you'd do well to remember that."

"Lucifer...as in the devil? The original fallen angel? The one who bargains and cajoles and tricks, damning souls?"

"The very one."

"Well, I have nothing to fear. I'm not your ally. Screw your protection, and screw you." Chin lifting another notch, she wrenched free of his clasp and marched into the house, the dogs trotting behind her.

Baden trailed after her, too, catching up in a living room furnished like any other. A couch, two chairs and a coffee table. He gritted out, "Does your leg need further tending?"

"No. There's a small cut, nothing more."

He wanted to see it, to assure himself it wasn't deeper than she realized, but he bit his tongue. Her hurts were not his problem. Not anymore. "If you value your life, you'll stay here and you'll stay quiet." He would deal with her treachery after he'd seen to his friends. Men and women who would *never* betray him.

"I can help—" she began.

"But you won't. I don't trust you."

"Fine. We'll stay away from the action." She plopped onto the couch and patted the spots beside her. The dogs jumped up and sat. "Not because you ordered it, but because my sweethearts need time to calm."

Caters to the dogs, but not to me.

Baden stomped through a doorway to the right, entering a small greenhouse where Keeley lay in a pile of dirt. The enclosure was warm and moist, the air scented with roses. Her flesh was in the process of sewing itself back together.

Torin crouched beside her, drifting his fingers through her pink hair. He was chalk white, his features ravaged. "I love you, princess. I *need* you to heal. Just like before. Just like *every* time before. You can do it. You can do anything."

Behind the pair, Paris and Amun shoveled more dirt into a wheelbarrow. To dump on Keeley?

"How can I help?" Baden's mouth dried. What his friends felt for their women…it was foreign to him, and yet an undeniable spark of longing lit him up inside. To have someone of his own…

Torin's emerald gaze flipped up, glassed by unshed tears. "You can't. I've got her, and she's got her dirt."

As a Curator—once a spirit of light, tasked with the

safekeeping of the planet—she was bound to the earth and its seasons.

Baden scoured a hand down his face. "I'm sorry. I know you think we're better together, but I should have left the fortress weeks ago. My connection to Hades put everyone in the middle of his war with Lucifer. William warned me, told me I would bring nothing but harm."

"William isn't the be all and end all," Paris said. "No matter what happens, you belong with us. And we were on Hades's side, anyway. Lucy would have come for us sooner or later."

"Now, at least, we know beyond a doubt we're on the right side," Torin said.

Yes. While Baden had already lost his grudge against Hades—for the most part—he'd still resented some of the man's darker tasks. No longer. Now he would do everything with a sense of urgency and eagerness.

Lucifer would pay for what had happened this day. He would pay greatly. His utmost weakness was the Morning Star, the main reason he wanted to possess it. The death of the Lords was just a bonus.

For Baden, finding it had never been more important.

"Shout for me if anything changes." He strode through another door, entering the medical ward, where the others had congregated.

Ashlyn reclined on a gurney, a gash on her cheek. Most likely it would scar. The twins were clutched to her chest, both covered with bumps and bruises.

Gwen was conscious, now sucking on Sabin's carotid as if it was a juice box. Harpies, like vampires, needed blood to heal; Sabin's must have been potent, because it had already worked magic. His wife's cheeks were bright with color.

Scarlet, the keeper of Nightmares and Gideon's pregnant wife, had her left leg propped on a mound of pillows. She had a compound fracture, her tibia peeking through her skin, blood seeping from the wound.

Gideon was beside the bed, hunched over and vomiting into a bucket.

He must have spoken a word of truth sometime during the chaos, allowing the demon to sicken him.

Evil always pounced on the chance to hurt—even with its host.

The blue-haired warrior wiped his mouth with a shaky hand and kicked the barf bucket a few feet away. "Not sorry," he rasped to his wife. "Love seeing you like this." He had a gash that stretched from his hairline to his jaw, cutting through one of his eyes and practically splitting his nose in two.

"I've had worse," she told him. "And don't take this the wrong way, darling, but you're hideous. Go lie down. Lucien and Anya are the doctors du jour and they can—"

Gideon gave an adamant shake of his head. "Yeah, you're fine. I'm leaving."

"I can set her leg," Baden interjected. "I have field training." He'd had to doctor himself in the realm of the dead. "I can help." He *needed* to help.

Relief bathed Gideon's features. "No way and no thanks."

Baden gathered everything he required and got to work. Scarlet refused an ambrosia-laced whiskey for the sake of the baby. A mother's love was something Baden had never known. Not in life, and certainly not in the beast's memory.

Gideon held Scarlet's hand while Baden fit the bones

back together, but it wasn't until he stitched the wound closed that Scarlet began to snarl at him, the pain too much to bear.

Between one blink and the next, he saw spiders crawling all over the room. An illusion brought about by her demon. The bastard specialized in bringing people's worst fears to life. Today, the fear happened to spring from Gideon, who stumbled backward, patting at his arms and cursing.

The spiders avoided Baden altogether, as if *they* feared *him*.

"This game is fun," Gideon bellowed.

"Sorry, so sorry." Scarlet closed her eyes, her brow furrowing, and the illusion began to recede.

When Baden finished his task, the woman sagged against the mattress with a sigh of relief.

"No thanks, man." Gideon patted his shoulder, the contact irritating Baden's skin, despite the shirt he wore. He turned to his wife. "I hate you. I hate you so much."

"I hate you, too."

A tender, poignant moment between two people who would die for each other.

A pang in his chest, Baden washed his hands and checked on the other patients. Most were already patched up and on the mend.

Strike now. No resistance means total victory.

Threaten them again and I'll find a way to end you.

The beast sputtered, surprised and…hurt?

A guy could only take so much. Baden had been pushed past his limit. He—everyone—had been unprepared for the battle today, and it was his fault. He'd known Lucifer would send someone after him. He'd been warned. But he'd foolishly thought he could handle it. *Bastard will have to get through me.* Well, the bastard had. Quite easily.

Lucifer would send another assassin, and soon.

As Hades's trusted enforcer, Baden was a greater hazard to Lucifer than his friends. He would leave, hopefully removing the target on them, giving them time to heal from their injuries.

He would take Katarina with him, despite the danger. If ever she helped Aleksander, hurting the men, women and children Baden adored…

His friends would protest his decision. Loudly. Look how Torin and Paris had reacted at the mere thought of his departure.

At the very least, the warriors would insist someone go with him. Only Cameo and Galen were mate-free, which meant they were the only two Baden would willingly accept, but he didn't want to put Cameo at unnecessary risk. Galen—Baden shrugged. He would put the warrior at unnecessary risk, no problem. There were ways to ensure the deceitful prick remained faithful.

He searched the makeshift triage area and found Galen leaning against the far wall, studying the occupants with a bored expression.

As the keeper of Jealousy and False Hope, Galen tended to cause trouble everywhere he went. Had he known the assassin was on the way and *that's* why he'd left the fortress hours earlier?

Betrayer!

Destruction drove Baden straight to the male. He wrapped a hand around Galen's throat, lifting him off his feet.

Smiling—smiling?—Galen swung up his legs around Baden's neck. The position bent his arms in ways they weren't supposed to bend, forcing his grip to loosen, and though Galen's wings had been cut off months ago, they were now growing back and big enough to anchor him—he hovered in the air while Baden stumbled back.

Galen maneuvered his feet to Baden's shoulders and pushed, increasing the distance between them. Baden could no longer maintain any kind of grip or even his balance. He released Galen, who dropped to the floor in a crouch.

Blue eyes peered through hanks of pale hair, his grin only growing wider. "Want to talk about your problem or continue your ass-whooping?"

"Where were you during the attack?" Baden demanded.

A flicker of unease, quickly hidden. "Out."

Out? "Doing what?"

"My thang."

"And what is your *thang*?"

"Something that's not your business," Galen replied.

"Everything that endangers my friends is my business."

"Really?" One golden brow arched. "Did you feel the same four thousand years ago, when you allowed my man to take your head?"

The words were a dagger to the chest. Galen had once been leader of the Hunters, a faction of humans determined to rid the world of "evil" immortals. Humans who hadn't realized an immortal led them.

"Did you aid Lucifer's assassin?" Baden demanded.

"Fuck you. I may be rotten to the core, but I'm not stupid."

"That's not an answer."

"Good, because it wasn't meant to be."

"I don't trust you. I'll *never* trust you."

With an exaggerated frown, Galen placed a hand over his heart. "Am I crying? I'm certain I'm crying."

Destruction snarled.

"Months ago you told us Cronus locked you up in the Realm of Blood and Tears. Guess what?" Baden spread his arms. "Cronus was dead at the time of your incarceration."

"So?"

"So. You've been caught in a lie."

"Or what you think is a lie." Defiant, Galen said, "I don't know how, but Cronus *was* the one who locked me up. The other possessed warriors, too. Cameron, Winter and Puck. Ask Keeley."

"I can't ask her. She's too busy fighting for her life."

Concern caused lines of tension to branch from the warrior's eyes, as if he truly cared. "For all we know, Cronus has a twin."

"And this is the first we're hearing about him? No."

"An alternate reality? Time travel? Anything's possible."

"You won't convince me—"

Delighted feminine laughter stopped him cold. Or hot. Baden turned to see Katarina squatting beside Ashlyn's bed, shaking hands with Biscuit. She'd taught the stray a trick already?

Beautiful, cunning bitch. She'd probably lied about the death of her dogs in a bid for sympathy.

Could she really fake that kind of pain?

The children cheered. Completely won over.

Like I once was. So gullible…

"You should work on that," Galen said, his tone dry.

"Staring at your girl like a creeper will only get you a restraining order. And maybe a blade across your carotid. Because yes, I could have killed you five times over since you started watching her." He hiked his wide shoulders in a shrug. "Who knows? I still might."

"She's not my girl," he muttered.

"Out of everything I said, *that's* what you focus on?" Galen rolled his eyes. "You're worse off than I thought. As bad as the rest of them."

Maybe, because Baden continued to watch her, unable to look away, his gaze held captive. There was no denying the desire he still felt for her. Fool! He wanted her in his arms, and in his bed. And he would have her, he decided. He didn't have to trust her to enjoy her delectable little body.

First things first. Finding a new home base and convincing Galen to join him. With the right incentive, the prick might even guard Katarina whenever Baden had a new mission.

If he betrays me...

I'll make sure the incentive properly motivates him to behave.

Baden thought for a moment, nodded with cold determination. He knew just the thing.

Katarina avoided Baden's general direction as she checked on the people who'd checked on her while she'd mourned her dogs. Some had fared better than others, but wow. Immortals could be wounded just as badly as humans. Who knew?

"I recognize the look in Baden's eyes." Maddox had parked himself on his wife's gurney, his daughter curled on his lap, his son stretched out beside Ashlyn. "He's leaving us again."

Katarina's heart kicked into a too-swift rhythm. As she petted the dogs, she told the warrior, "If he wants to go, don't try to keep him here."

Maddox focused on her, and she would have sworn a faint skeletal mask covered his features. "Who are you to him? To us? You calmed him *once*. You don't have a say in how we treat him."

Ouch. Way to put her in her place.

Ashlyn batted at his arm. "Rude!"

"You didn't marry me for my kind demeanor," Maddox told her, nipping at her fingers.

Katarina flipped her hair over her shoulder. "I don't have to be anyone to Baden—or to you—to know steel bars aren't the only thing capable of creating a cage. You love Baden, and you don't want him to resent you. Therefore, you have to let him go."

She had to let him go, too. She was ninety percent certain he would drop her off somewhere as soon as he finished here, and one hundred percent certain she was ready to return to her old life. Baden had heard her pledge to Alek and now believed she was a power-hungry whore. It hurt. It hurt bad. The man who'd held her in his arms and comforted her, who'd placed her on his lap and pleasured her, hadn't given her the benefit of the doubt. He hadn't even asked for her side of the story. Or, more accurately, ordered her to tell it. Now, she wasn't going to explain a damn thing. Let him think the worst.

Thank the good Lord she hadn't slept with him! Any man who thought he was right all day every day and overlooked her wishes wasn't worthy of her attention.

And yet, she was disappointed she wouldn't have an

opportunity to train him, certain she still wanted him but didn't want to want him, saddened she wouldn't have the chance to desensitize his skin and gutted that she wouldn't see him again. Well, his loss! She would have rocked his world.

"She's someone special to him," Ashlyn said, "and you know it. We *all* know it. She has a say."

Before this, Katarina *might* have been someone special. At least as a possible lover. Now they would never know. "No, Maddox is right. I don't have a say with Baden. And I don't want one. I'm going home. I'm going to miss you. I'm going to miss you all." The ladies of the house were total sweethearts.

She wondered if she could keep them after the breakup. Baden could keep the men.

"Stay in touch," she added, giving Ashlyn's foot a gentle squeeze. "If you look up my name, you'll find me." To the kids, she said, "I'm taking the dogs with me. You can visit—"

"You'll take the dogs over your dead body," Urban snapped.

"Yeah." Little Ever nodded, her golden curls bobbing at her temples. "Your dead body."

"Children." Ashlyn sighed. "What have I told you about intimidating others?"

"Make sure the situation really is life or death first," Urban grumbled.

"That's right."

Katarina fought a grin—until she felt a familiar heat press against her backside. She stiffened, Baden's scent teasing her nose, her nerve endings suddenly buzzing with sensation...with the need for more.

I'm furious with him. I shouldn't crave him.

"I've spoken to Galen," he announced to one and all. "He and I are leaving. For the safety of everyone I love," he added as protests rang out.

"Not this again," Lucien said.

"You need us," Sabin said, "and we need you, too."

Reyes, the keeper of Pain, glared at him. "We're part of the war whether you're with us or not."

Baden remained unmoved. "You need time to heal, and I'm going to get it for you by keeping Lucifer busy, unable to spare a soldier to hunt you. I can flash into the underworld. You can't. Even Lucien is blocked." Amid the strained pause that followed his words, he said, "I know I don't have the right to ask you to let me go—to accept this—but I'm asking, anyway. For me… for your women."

Gradually, the warriors got on board. As stubborn as he was, they must have accepted what Katarina had known from the beginning. He would move heaven and earth to get his way.

He whispered in her ear, "You, *krásavica*, won't be going home. You'll be coming with me."

What! His arm snaked around her waist, a hard band of heat and strength. A pleasure as much as a pain. "You are so wrong it's laughable. I *am* going home." And finally starting over.

"I once said I'd take you anywhere. But you picked me. Now you'll face the consequences of your decision."

She stiffened. "So I'm to be your captive again?"

"If that's the way you want to play it."

"I don't want to play with you *at all*."

"Well, I can't have you running around, trying to help your precious *husband*, now, can I?"

"You're an *idiot*. You know that, yes? If you lock me

away, I'll… I'll…" What? She couldn't rail at him for his violent ways one day, and threaten him with bloodshed the next.

Maddox jumped to his feet, red flickering in his gaze, reminding her of Alek and Baden at their worst. "You court Violence."

Baden swung her behind him and pointed a finger at the man. "She's mine. No one else will touch her. Or terrorize her. Or even look at her."

First, he'd accused her of wrongdoing. Now he defended her? Confusing man!

As soon as Maddox backed down, Baden turned toward her. Glaring, he said quietly, "I might be an idiot, but you still desire me, so what does that make you?"

"I don't—"

He bent down and grazed her earlobe with his teeth. "Your blood is rushing so fast I can hear it. Your nipples just hardened and the scent you're giving off…" He trailed his nose along her neck, inhaling deeply, perhaps forgetting the pain he felt at skin-to-skin contact. "Delicious."

Shivers betrayed her, arousal drenching her panties. "We shouldn't be having this conversation here." With witnesses. Or at all!

"Agreed." To the others, he said, "I'll text you often."

The room disappeared, a new one taking its place. The walls were papered in lace and velvet, and portraits of a gorgeous blond—Galen—with massive wings hung here…there…everywhere. The warrior must have lost those white-feathered beauties at some point; they were basically nubs now. The furniture was a mix of polished wood, ivory and wrought iron while plush carpets led to a spectacular fireplace made of sapphire-veined marble;

cherubs were carved along both sides, framing panels of stained glass.

Her new gilded cage?

She wrenched from Baden's embrace. "How dare you leave my dogs—"

"They are yours now?" He strode to the wet bar and poured himself four fingers of what looked to be whiskey yet smelled much sweeter. "How quickly my female changes her mind."

The dogs *were* hers. The way they'd stayed by her side during and after Pandora's attack…the way they'd let Alek know in no uncertain terms they would defend her with their lives… Yeah, they were hers. And she was theirs. *Not* Baden's, as he'd so baldly stated.

"I'll fight you every day, *every minute*, until they're returned to—"

"Sheath your claws, vixen. Galen is bringing the dogs."

Oh. "If he hurts them—"

"He won't. He's been warned." Baden poured himself another drink, drained the contents. He faced her, his eyelids hooded, his lashes practically fused together. "We need to get something settled between us."

Here we go. He would rail at her for her supposed betrayal. And okay, yes, what he'd heard was damning. Still! He should know her better. "If you insult me…"

"You'll what?" he asked with no small amount of malevolence.

"I'll take the possibility of sex off the table." Wait. *I thought I already had.*

He went hard as stone, and not in the good way. "Sex stays on the table either way."

Oh, really? "Are you planning to force me?"

"Like I'd have to. You look ready to force *me*."

Stupid nipples! They were still beaded, eager for him.

She perched on the edge of the coffee table. The position put her at a disadvantage, something she would never allow while training a new dog, but Baden was a unique breed. By placing herself in the perceived weaker position, he might stop doing the offensive-defensive parry and start listening to what she had to say.

"Did you know the coin can buy a royal title in the underworld?" she asked. "Actually, it forces Hades to grant the owner's wish, whatever it is."

He'd been in the process of pouring himself another drink, but slowly turned to meet her gaze. "How do you know that?"

"Alek, of course."

He grazed his tongue over an incisor. "The male can't be trusted and neither can you."

"You are so right. I'm out to destroy you." She gave her nails a little buff. "Have been from the beginning. It's why I practically *begged* you to kidnap me from my own wedding."

He continued as if she hadn't spoken. "In this case, however, you both speak true."

She continued as if *he* hadn't spoken, fluffing her hair. "Alek has vowed to make me a queen. Every girl dreams of being a queen."

Baden stepped toward her…stopped. "Do not say the bastard's name ever again."

"Or?" she prompted, challenging him *and* the beast. *Bring it!* This girl was ready to reach the next level.

As he took another step toward her, his hands fisted. "Why aren't you begging for my forgiveness? Or mercy?"

She laughed without humor. "I have nothing to apologize for. I did nothing wrong. And I doubt you're capable of mercy."

"Your betrayal—"

"Who did I betray? Alek is—"

Baden roared, "That name."

"You had your turn to speak. Now it's mine." Provoking this man was a gamble. With her life! This could backfire and get her bitten. Literally!

But without risk, there was no potential for reward.

"You aren't my husband," she added, "so my loyalty shouldn't belong to you. It should belong to Alek." The very idea disgusted her, but she had a point to make. She smiled sweetly. "Don't you agree?"

16

"When I flip you off, run. I've just told you how many seconds you have left to live."

—Maddox, keeper of Violence

Rage mixed with possessiveness and lust, heating Baden from head to toe. *Steaming* him. He closed in on Katarina at last, dropped to his knees and cupped hers, spreading her legs with a single push. She watched him, wide eyes sparkling, but she didn't protest as he moved between her thighs. Her breath caught as he leaned in, flattening his palms on the coffee table to cage her with his strength.

"What are you doing?" she asked softly. Tremors rocked her sweet little body.

Behind her, sunlight streamed through an oversize oval window, illuminating the dust motes dancing between them.

She was married. A fact he liked less and less. She had used him. At the moment, he didn't care. He wanted to mark her. Had to prove she belonged to him, and only to him.

"Your loyalty is to me," he said. As he inhaled, she

exhaled; as she inhaled, he exhaled; they were breathing each other's breaths. "You need me to survive in this world. To protect you and our dogs."

"I soooo don't need—"

"Oh, but you do." He slowly dragged his tongue between the seam of her lips. *Liiiick.* Tasting her sweetness, savoring it.

She gasped his name, jerking as if hit by a bolt of white-lightning. "I'm not doing this. Not with you."

"You are. You want more, *krásavica*, so let me give you more."

"You don't like me anymore."

"I don't think you like me anymore, either. Does it really matter?" He still burned for her. "I want you."

She leaned toward him, melting, only to catch herself. She *cursed* his name and plucked at the collar of his shirt. "You're too old for me. *Way* too old."

"Age didn't bother you earlier, when you were grinding on my thighs." As she sputtered for a response, he added, "You're too weak for me, but I got over it."

"I'm not too— You know what? It doesn't matter. You were a temporary distraction then and you're a temporary distraction now. Despite our unsuitability, you can still give me an orgasm. One I deserve after putting up with you."

He knew they were temporary, but her blasé attitude was far from appreciated. However, admonishing her would have been counterproductive to his goal: getting her into his arms, achieving the ultimate satisfaction.

She tangled her fingers in his hair. "No grimace or hiss? Someone is making progress. And it's me!"

He loved the way she moved her lips. His mind in a

fog of dizzying desire, he couldn't process her words. "Meaning?"

"Meaning I think I can desensitize you. Now. You better give me the pleasure you promised me before I change my mind about this."

There would be no changing her mind. He scowled even as he traced his tongue over her lips. This time, *her* tongue emerged to greet him. Flames of arousal spread through him, a blistering wildfire that couldn't be stopped. There was pain, but it didn't compare to his need.

The beast protested. *She's our betrayer. She means to harm...means to...*

She moaned, as if she was delighted by his taste the way he was delighted with hers. Mint and whipped cream. Clean, rich and decadent. Addictive. *She's dessert.*

I—want—more.

More. Yes. Baden ate at her lips as he anchored her arms behind her back, forcing her spine to arch and her breasts to smash into his chest.

"Keep your hands like this," he commanded. To ease his pain, yes, but also to keep her vulnerable and unable to act against him while he was distracted.

"I will...as long as you make it worth my while."

The rasp of her voice awoke an urge he'd never known—take and give *everything.*

Her breasts rubbed against him and, despite the shirt he wore, the friction was both a pain and an ever-increasing pleasure. He'd never held such a bounty of femininity.

Will have her. Finally.

He wasn't sure whether the thoughts originated in his mind or the beast's, wasn't even sure it mattered anymore. The tether to his control slipped. He deepened the kiss, ravaging her mouth; his tongue plunged in and out, thrusting against hers in a mimic of sex. She released a chorus of delicious moans—sounds of surrender—and he swallowed every single one.

Mine! Pin her fully—take everything!

He fought the desires. He would be gentle, or he would leave. When he leaned back far enough to cup and knead her breasts, she followed him, softening against him.

"I made it clear I'm only using you for an orgasm, yes?" She panted the slightest bit. "As soon as I get it, I'll be done with you."

A denial nearly burst free, but he forced a laugh instead. "Maybe I'll take my own orgasm and leave you desperate. Or make you beg for yours."

She winced and gave him a pitying look. "As if I'd care. This gold digger would simply turn to someone else."

There was no stopping his denial this time. "I'll kill any man foolish enough to touch what belongs to me." He dove in for another kiss, needing to halt the conversation—needing her. A brutal clash of lips, tongue and teeth, and in that moment, he lived for her. All of her. Only her.

"Wait. I need better access to you." She gave him a push then stared at his chest, as if willing his shirt to burn away. "Help me stand."

She'd broken his command, but he obeyed her without protest, straightening and drawing her to her feet; the kiss never paused. She backed him into a chair. When he fell into a sitting position, she climbed onto his lap and straddled him. A power play, putting her on top. Only an illusion of control. No matter the position, he would always possess the power—and he would prove it.

He gripped her hips and ground her core against his throbbing erection, setting a frenzied pace, driving them both to the edge of madness. *Want what's mine... need...now.* On their date, she'd been the one to speed things up, and he'd been the one to slow everything down. Now, this moment, he couldn't move fast enough.

More! Give me!

"Feels so good, *pekný.*" She took him by the wrists and moved his hands to the arms of the chair. A recliner. "But today there's no reason to hurry." She bit his lower lip, drawing it through her teeth. With another push, she changed the angle of his body, forcing him to lie back. Then, oh *then*, she began to rub against him of her own accord, slow, so agonizingly slow. "You can enjoy me while you've got me."

Another reference to her departure. He squeezed the arms of the chair and the wood cracked. "You need me," he reminded her. "And not just for this."

"I don't."

He offered no other rebuke, his every nerve ending electrified, his desire for her only escalating. Instead, he lunged forward and sank his teeth in the cord that stretched from her neck to shoulder. Finally leaving his mark.

She shuddered against him, gasping his name with breathless wonder. Then she rotated her hips, gradually increasing the pressure. Press...retreat...press... retreat. Agonizing him.

"Do you like this?"

"Love...it." As his inhalations quickened, he stared up at her face, enraptured. Her features were luminous, her eyelids heavy, her lips soft and pink, slightly swollen from his kisses. A flush brightened her cheeks, and her dark curls tumbled past her shoulders in well-loved tangles.

He reached up and fisted the strands. "Let me keep and protect you until Hades's war is over."

She stilled, her nails digging into his shoulders. "You keep reminding me how weak I am."

"Because you need me." Within a few short seconds, the lack of pressure and movement proved excruciating. Sweat beaded on his brow. "I'm strong."

"You're also stubborn. But how about this, hmm? I'll let you pleasure me, and I might even stick around for a while, but you'll keep your thoughts on strength and weakness to yourself." She teased him with a feather-light stroke, her core brushing his erection. "Say yes, and we'll get back to business. I'm wet. Shall I prove it?"

"Yes. Yes!"

She stood and pulled her dress over her head. Her bra and panties were blue—and the panties had a definite wet spot in the center. He groaned as he drank in the rest of her. Drank his fill. The long, endless legs so wonderfully dark, her injury hidden by a bandage. The flare of her hips created a heart. The indention of her stomach…the lacy bra couldn't shield the crest of her nipples.

She was purely female, and he wanted her all over him.

He crooked his finger at her. "Return to me."

"How about another bargain?" She placed a knee on each side of him, goose bumps erupting over her flesh. "I'll stay right here…if you'll put your fingers inside me."

Agonizing? No longer. She—was—*killing*—him.

A definite threat to his survival, but he was certain he and Destruction would go with a smile.

The urge to rip his gloves off with his teeth bombarded him. He would slay an entire army for the chance to feel her silken heat. But he couldn't risk it. This was only his second encounter with pleasure in centuries. If he spoiled it with a flood of unnecessary pain...

"I agree to your terms." A sense of urgency drove him as he tunneled his fingers under her panties. Even with the leather he could feel her slickness—she was soaked—and the sweet burn of her feminine heat. He thrust a single digit in, going deep, her inner walls clamping on him.

Moaning, she plumped her breasts and pinched her nipples. For his enjoyment, and her own. Such an uninhibited reaction delighted him.

Slowly, he fed her a second finger, stretching her. So tight! So perfect.

She groaned a sound of desperate hunger. "Feels good."

Good. Yes. But they could do better. "Ride my fingers." His jaw was clenched so firmly he almost couldn't get the words out. Somehow, she'd completely stripped him of his humanity, turning him into an animal with only one goal: climax.

Or a beast.

"Like this?" Up she rose...down she slid. "Mmm, I hope so. That's *amazing*."

"Yes, just like that." He used his thumb to circle the heart of her. "You're squeezing me, scalding me." *Ruining me for anyone else.*

She tilted his head, giving herself an unobstructed path to his lips; she traced her tongue along the edge of his mouth. "I want my hand around you. Let me?"

Yes! He still couldn't risk skin-to-skin, so he would wear a condom. Where were the condoms? No time to search. He'd have to let her go, and he couldn't let her go. "Keep your hand outside my underwear."

"I will...if you'll kiss me harder."

"Always bargain like this." He slammed his mouth against hers, drawing a moan from her, and she unzipped his pants. "Never stop."

He hissed as she wrapped her fingers around his shaft. Up...down...she stroked him while continuing to move on his fingers. Yes, oh yes. This! This made him lose his ever-loving mind. The friction sparked new wildfires, until everything but arousal had burned off him. He pushed his tiptoes into the floor to raise his thighs and force her to lean against his chest to maintain balance.

He thrust his fingers deep, deep, deeper inside her.

"Yes! So close," she rasped, her hips arching to chase his circling thumb.

He pressed against her bundle of nerves, and she shouted her pleasure to the ceiling, coming, coming so hard, her inner walls clenching on him, as if to ensure he stayed right where he was. She bucked against his fingers, once, twice, three times, her nails cutting into his shoulders.

When her forehead rested on his shoulder, she gasped out, "Needed that. Thank you." Panting, she squeezed the base of his shaft. "Now let's take care of you."

He trembled as he arched a brow. "Sweet, Rina. What makes you think I'm done with *you*?"

Katarina buzzed with satisfaction and anticipation. Baden's fingers were still inside her, still revving her engine despite her climax. She was hot, and she was achy—one taste had only made her hungrier for this dark and dangerous man.

She gave the base of his erection another squeeze. He was so big, thick and long, and harder than a police baton. "Am I hurting you?"

"Hurts *good.*"

Desensitizing him already? Or was the condition mental—a manifestation of his detachment from the world?

Figure it out later. Enjoy! With a moan, she arched her back, presenting him with her cleavage.

"Does my *krásavica* want her nipples sucked?"

His glamour girl? He kept claiming her...

"I do," she said. His eyes were almost completely black, his pupils overshadowing his irises. Fine lines bracketed his mouth. How intense was his need to come? "Very badly."

With his free hand, he jerked at the center clasp of her bra, freeing her breasts. Cool air kissed her skin, propelling her need ever higher.

He licked his lips, as if he could already taste her. "Your little nipples are desperate for me, aren't they?"

"Desperate...aching." She gripped the top of the chair with one hand, still holding on to his shaft with the other—*never going to let go.* She slanted forward, placing one of her nipples at his mouth. An offering.

An offering he accepted. His tongue emerged, taunting the needy bud. First hard and fast, then slow and easy. The ache between her legs only worsened. Or got better. She soaked his glove and even her panties. How naughty that was. He was fully dressed while she wore a thin scrap of cloth he'd easily moved aside.

He suckled on her, incredible, world-shaking pleasure consuming her. Soon, remaining still was no longer an option. She began to ride his fingers all over again, arching forward, back, forward again.

As he switched his attention to her other nipple, he rasped, "You are made of ambrosia, surely."

Always so complimentary. She might never get enough of him.

She pumped her hand up and down his shaft, his breathing becoming shallow. The faster she moved, the more curses that left him. Soon, a fine sheen of perspiration glossed his skin. He was close.

She ran his earlobe between her teeth. "Maybe one day, if you behave, I'll take your cock in my mouth and suck you dry. Would you like that?"

He grunted a response, his thumb returning to work her feverishly. Pleasure fogged her mind, such intense pleasure; she reached a point of no return for the second time. The house could have crumbled. An army could have marched inside. The world could have ended, and she wouldn't have cared. Only satisfaction mattered. Hers…and surprisingly enough, his.

Need more.

"Take your fingers out of me," she commanded. For once, she would be the one issuing orders.

Not that he heeded her. He only surged those fingers deeper.

She almost couldn't bring herself to utter her next words. "I want to feel you come against me."

His fingers slid out a second later. She groaned at the emptiness he left behind, but pressed herself against his erection and rubbed…rubbed…

His gaze hot on hers, he brought his fingers to his

mouth and hungrily licked away her desire. The sight…
the very *thought* that he was taking a part of her inside
himself…the sweetest part…she flew over the edge,
rubbing him harder, rubbing him faster, using her core
to kindle his climax and stoke her own. Suddenly he
roared her name.

He cupped her ass, his fingers digging into her giving flesh, and jetted into his underwear, wetting the
material and her hand. She'd feel him tomorrow—and
she'd love it.

She collapsed against him, utterly spent, her breathing as labored as his, her mind reeling. They hadn't had
sex, and yet he'd made her come twice.

This man…oh, this man. He affected her.

"Off," he said, surprising her. When she failed to
move fast enough for his liking, he stood, ensuring she
slid off his lap.

Her legs were the consistency of jelly, and it required
a conscious effort to remain on her feet as she stumbled
away from him.

"Get dressed," he said, looking anywhere but at her.

"I will, but only because I *want* to dress." A pang of
hurt, but really, had she expected anything different?
He didn't like or respect her. As if he'd really want to
cuddle with her now.

You need me, he loved to tell her. The implication?
He didn't need *her*.

Anger overtook the hurt. "Well, well. Look who's in
a rush to change his underpants. You unloaded a bucket's worth of batter, didn't you?"

He tossed her discarded garments at her, silent. Motions jerky, she covered her nakedness; her efforts to
hide her trembling were wasted.

"Just so you know, you had a great start but a de-plorable finish," she muttered, smoothing the material in place.

"You enjoyed yourself," he snapped.

"And so did you. So what's your problem?"

"Maybe all the contact pained me more than I ad-mitted."

Maybe...wasn't really an answer. The single word removed both truth and lie from the sentence. What didn't he want her to know? "Maybe you're beginning to have feelings for me, and you don't like it." The taunt echoed in her mind, and her eyes widened. Her feelings toward him had certainly softened, so why couldn't his have softened toward her?

"You should pray that doesn't happen," he said qui-etly, menacingly. "I'm dangerous."

Not to me. Even when he'd thought she'd betrayed him, he'd offered her pleasure rather than punishment.

He added, "There's darkness inside me, and it's only growing. I have no light."

"Well, guess what? There's light inside me, and when darkness and light go head to head, darkness runs and light saves the day."

He frowned at her. "You think you can save me?"

"Don't be silly. One person can never save another. Not in the true sense of the word. We all make our own choices. I'm just saying I'm willing to share with you."

His frown intensified, but he remained silent.

"A demon once inhabited you," she said, "but you kept your wits until the end and overcame him. Right? Mind over matter. Now you can do the same with the beast."

"You make it sound easy, yet you have no idea the battle—"

"Oh, I know it's a battle. Your own mind is often your fiercest opponent." Her smile held an edge of sadness. "When I lost Peter—"

"Peter?" The name lashed from him. "Who is Peter?"

"My fiancé. Before Alek."

Baden relaxed, but only slightly. "Who broke things off?"

An invisible hand wrapped around her heart and squeezed. "Neither of us. Alek killed him."

He softened. "I'm sorry."

"Thank you. The point is, I wanted to wallow in my sorrow, but I didn't. I couldn't because my dogs needed me."

"Dogs Aleksander later took from you."

Her chin quivered as she nodded. "You saw what happened when I *did* wallow."

"I also saw what happened when you stopped."

"I had to change the direction of my thoughts. Instead of lamenting about what I lost, I had to focus on what I had left. My emotions soon followed my mind. The same can happen for you."

He pondered her words and for a moment, she thought she had him. Then he scoffed at her. "Our situations are different. You weren't influenced by an outside force."

"And you are. Boohoo for you." She twisted her fists under her eyes to mimic tears. "Guess you're not strong enough to overcome." A challenge. A clear taunt. "I was."

He took a forbidding step toward her. "You need—"

"Don't say it." She raised her chin, stood her ground.

I am the alpha dog. I am pack leader. "If you don't like what I'm saying, refute it, but don't you dare insult me. Or order me to feel a certain way."

He halted, his hands clenching and unclenching. *Good boy.* He'd calmed on his own, with no real prompting from her.

His training would be easier than she'd suspected. Beauty would totally tame her beast, yo. She just had to concentrate and stop losing herself in the vast expanse of his sexiness.

Thought I planned to leave him sooner rather than later.

Well, plans changed. Again.

The door burst open, and a scowling Galen stomped inside the room. He held a leash in each hand, Biscuit and Gravy bucking at the ends. "Special delivery. Enjoy. Or not. Yeah, probably not."

Happiness sprouted. He dropped the leashes, and the dogs bounded toward her. She crouched, welcoming them with open arms. They licked her face as she petted and praised them. Most trainers discouraged licking, but she'd always enjoyed the show of canine affection. Dogs spoke a different language than humans, and licking said, "I love you."

"What's that stain on your pants?" Galen asked Baden, obviously trying not to laugh. "What were you crazy kids doing while I was away? Shall I venture a guess?"

She pressed her lips together to stop a laugh of her own.

Baden murmured curses under his breath. "Katarina, you've seen Galen around, I'm sure. He's the keeper of

Jealousy and False Hope. He owns this home, which is located in another realm."

She'd seen Galen around, yes, but they'd never actually spoken. She'd noticed most of the warriors avoided him. "Another realm?" she asked.

A nod. "You can trust the male with your life, but nothing else."

Galen lost his amusement in a hurry. "The murderous beast-man likes to cast stones. Excellent. We should probably start a dodgeball team. Or like the Harpies, a dodge-*boulder* team."

"I need to leave before I do something I'm not sure I'll regret." Baden stomped out of the room, Katarina's mirth dying, too.

Her gaze landed on Galen. His prettiness was almost hypnotic, but in a scary serial killer kind of way. "What did he mean, another realm?"

"Think of it as another world. Because it is."

Immortals…other worlds…what else did she not know about? "Why the animosity between you two?"

He ignored her, saying, "I'm supposed to keep you safe any time Baden is off on one of his missions for Hades, but I won't hesitate to gut you if I think you're a danger to him."

Biscuit prowled toward him, growling, until she called the pup back to her side.

"You love Baden?" she asked.

Galen shrugged. "I love myself, and I need him. You, little girl, aren't that lucky."

17

"I wish I was kissing you instead of missing you."

—Aeron, former keeper of Wrath

Baden stripped out of his soiled clothing, glanced at the unlit hearth and decided burning every stitch was a sound plan. He threw a blazing match in the center, then the clothes, watching the fabric smolder. The garments would only serve as a reminder of Katarina and the way he'd come like a wee lad being handled for the first time. Humiliating, but also…worth it? He climbed into the steaming shower.

Hot water pounded against his face and shoulders, droplets trickling down his chest; even without the clothes, his mind returned to Katarina. The pleasure she'd given him…he'd never experienced its like. He'd wanted her so badly he would have done anything she'd asked, given her anything she desired. He would have *died* for her.

She'd had power over him—over both of them—and yet Destruction had been willing to kill for her. Her, not himself. As if her enemies mattered more than his.

As if every foe needed to be taught the error of turning his sights on the human.

Damn it, she still had power over them!

Having more of her was no longer optional, was now a necessity. Her taste. Her purrs. Her groans and moans, and the breathless way she uttered his name— or shouted it. Her hand, fisting his length just right. Her passion unleashed, pure wicked indulgence, as she ground herself on his fingers.

He banged a fist against the tile. What the hell was he going to do about her?

With some of his pent-up lust at last assuaged, his head was clearer than usual, the beast quiet. Baden was able to replay the damning words he'd overheard Katarina say to Aleksander.

I'll put my life in harm's way and seduce Baden...if you prove the coin's existence.

The man had killed her dogs; she hated him with the heat of a thousand suns. Would she truly free him, simply to become a queen of the underworld? Not a chance. So she must have had a very good reason for making such a promise.

A sudden suspicion drifted through his mind. Had she hoped to find the coin for *Baden?*

Yes. Absolutely. No question. He cursed his quick temper, cursed his paranoia. He owed her an apology. Not that words would be enough to fix the problems he'd caused.

As he shut off the water, the bands began to broil his biceps. A soft red glow filled the stall. He hurriedly reached for a towel...only to dematerialize without it. He reappeared in Hades's throne room, wet and naked, weaponless.

The scent of smoke and the sounds of distant, discordant screams registered as he performed a quick scan. No one stood within striking distance, but the guards lined up against the far wall leered at him. He glared, daring them to say a word.

"For the sake of my eyes, dress," Hades commanded, drawing his attention. He materialized atop his ghoulish throne, his body encased in a three-piece suit.

Baden held out his arms, all *feast your eyes, asshole*. "Someone should have told me it was business-formal Friday."

"Pippin!"

The old, robed man stepped from a puff of black smoke. "Yes, sire."

"It's makeover Monday. Give Baden a new look."

"Yes, sire." Pippin chiseled a pebble from the edge of his tablet.

Hades. Flames. Ashes.

Those ashes adhered to Baden's skin, as if glued, swiftly morphing into black leather pants with a multitude of zippers and a cotton T-shirt. Both were a perfect fit.

Baden wanted one of those tablets.

"Much better." Hades drummed his nails against the arms of the throne. "Update me on your search for the coin."

"Aleksander has proven more stubborn than I anticipated."

"And the other tasks on your list?"

"Nearly completed."

"Then you'll be pleased to know I have a new job for you."

One of Destruction's memories fought its way to

the forefront of his mind. His mother, the dark-haired beauty who'd feasted on his liver, sat upon a throne. *That* throne. Hades's. She cringed at his approach, her sharp claws digging into the arms as she fought to rise—but she *couldn't*. He held her in place with a power she couldn't overcome. Shadows, all his beautiful shadows, swirled around her, hissing at her.

"—listening to me?" Hades snapped.

The male had suffered greatly at her hands, and he'd killed her for it. Killed his own mother. Mercilessly.

There was no line he would not cross when betrayed. *Focus!* "I'm listening, yes." Now.

"I want this artifact in my possession by the end of the day." He clapped his hands and Pippin placed a new stone on his palm.

Flames. Ash. Baden breathed deeply, inhaling every particle. The artifact—a necklace—was known as the *cœur de la terre*. Two hundred carats of mystical blue coral. Exquisite, or so women claimed, but mostly desired for its supernatural properties. With it, a male or female of any race, even human, could live and breathe underwater with the Mers.

The current owner: Poseidon's mistress, a delicate-looking forest nymph.

"Just one minor issue with this mission. Hardly bears mentioning," Hades said with a wave. "If you succeed, the water king will lose his favorite concubine, and he'll send assassins to kill you."

Wonderful. "He won't be the first or the last. I'll handle him."

Hades glanced at his manservant. "See, Pippin. I'm not being needlessly cruel. Baden welcomes the challenge."

"Yes, sire."

To Baden, Hades said, "Handle the water king, but don't kill him. If the concubine has to die, she has to die. And remember, what you do, you do for the greater good."

The greater good. Victory. The protection of his friends...of Katarina.

"I'll acquire the necklace." The qualification—*by the end of the day*—allowed him to launch a strike against Lucifer first. He was already in the underworld, so why not?

"Stop. I know that look," Hades said with a frown. "What are you planning? Tell me true."

The answer left him, pulled out by the power of the king's command.

Hades thought for a moment, nodded. "Very well. I'll even aid you. Pippin, if you please..."

Another piece of the tablet provided a map of the nine underworld realms and the ability to flash anywhere within them. The only location forbidden to him was inside Lucifer's palace, the walls mystically blocked.

But there were ways around that. Or there would be by the time he finished.

When a weight pulled at the waist of his pants, he looked down. A grenade hung from every belt loop. He grinned. Here was the way.

Like for like. Lucifer destroyed his home, now Baden would destroy his.

He flashed to the outskirts of the male's palace. A towering monstrosity built from blood and bones. The surrounding moat was a mix of acid and the tears of the damned. Above, dragons flew through a sky of smoke and fire.

The scent of sulfur and brimstone pervaded, blending with the fetid stench of death. A thousand screams of pain and fear created a gruesome soundtrack—far worse than anything he'd ever heard in Hades's domain.

Armed guards patrolled the palace parapet. They spotted him and activated a shrill alarm. Baden lobbed a grenade. *Boom!* As the parapet crumbled in a burst of fire and debris, he flashed to the other side of the palace and lobbed a second grenade. He continued the assault until his belt loops were empty. Took a total of ten minutes, but during that time more than one guard managed to pinpoint his location. They pitched spears in his direction while others pitched spears everywhere else so that, when he flashed to a new location, one of those spears would find and gouge him.

Which it did.

On impact, he lost the ability to flash, was pinioned by an invisible barrier, Destruction roaring. Every guard focused on him then, throwing more spears. Just before the avalanche reached him, the beast was able to free him from the immobility.

He flashed again, intending to grab a handful of discarded spears, but he reappeared atop a steel trap—one made for flashers. Metal teeth snapped closed around his ankle, preventing him from dematerializing. The lines that marked every kill he'd made for Hades began to burn and blister, as if the beast breathed fire on them from the inside. Smoke actually rose from his skin, soon forming a wall around him.

Not smoke, he realized, but the creatures that had once lived inside his victims.

Shock clouted him in the chest. He'd witnessed the rise of shadows from Hades, had even seen a hint of the shadows when he'd dealt with the Berserker, but he'd never expected this.

An army took shape around him.

What the hell was he supposed to do? The humans who'd once hosted the creatures hadn't known how to utilize them, Hades had said. Baden had no idea how to utilize them, either…and yet they were…helping him?

They *were*. The creatures separated from him, though an invisible tether kept them bound to his soul, preventing them from going too far. They stopped every weapon tossed his way—even a grenade. As fire blazed around him, unable to touch him, he reeled. Within seconds, the shadows were able to eat through the metal clamp, freeing him.

Be ready, Destruction said.

The very moment the shadows reabsorbed in his arms, Baden flashed home…but the fire leaped at him and he ended up taking multiple embers with him. They kindled on the carpet and curtains in the sitting room. He rushed to stomp them out before they could spread. When he finished, smoke filled the room. True smoke.

He wasn't going to think about the shadows, or what they were capable of doing. Not now. He had too much to do.

Where was Katarina?

He stalked through the home. A stronghold in a desert realm where no one else would ever dare venture. The only patch of grass was located in a gated oasis found in the backyard. When wheeling and dealing with Galen, he'd insisted on a place for the dogs to run and play. Because. Just because. Galen had delivered, in his own unique way. Other than the palace and the oasis, the realm offered mile after mile of glaring sun, burning rocks, and black sand dunes.

Welcome to the Realm of the Forgotten.

To enter, you needed a key. Only Baden and Galen had one.

The longer he stayed here, the more likely his memory was to fade from the minds of everyone he'd ever met. A calculated risk. He didn't want Hades to forget him. More missions meant more points.

In return for the key, Baden had to arrange a date between Galen and Legion. Or Honey. Or whatever the demon-girl-turned-human called herself these days.

Aeron loved her like a daughter. After the terrible abuse she'd suffered in hell, the male had done everything in his power to heal her mind as well as her body. While he'd had no trouble with the latter, he'd had no luck with the former. She suffered still. Maybe Galen was the answer. He and the girl had history.

Muted voices drew Baden around a corner and into a spacious kitchen with top-of-the-line appliances and white quartz countertops. His woman—his sweetest torment—came into view, and his body hardened, readied for her.

Had my fingers inside her. Want them there again.

She'd taken a shower and changed her clothes. A pink tank top and faded jeans made her look feminine and delicate—but he wanted her naked.

She placed bowls of food and water in front of the dogs while talking to—

The name clicked, and he realized why he'd once forgotten it. Fox, the new keeper of Distrust. She'd been here all along.

Stay away from Fox.

Words William had once said to him. Why?

Galen's right-hand woman—back when he'd led the Hunters—had black hair, blue-gold eyes and angular features. She was slender but obviously tough. The kind of woman Baden had always found most attractive, and yet she couldn't compare to the delicate Katarina.

"—he like?" Fox asked. With Distrust as her companion, she must be in a state of mental anguish at all hours of the day and night.

"Stubborn," Katarina said. "Aggravating. Distrustful—"

"That, I can understand."

He—as in me?

Baden pressed his tongue to the roof of his mouth.

But Katarina wasn't done. "Infuriating. Annoying." A heavy sigh. "Witty, sexy and protective. Too protective!"

She thinks I'm sexy.

Galen sat at the table in the corner, sharpening a blade. Their gazes met, and the male shrugged, all *Women!*

"You failed to mention someone else lived here," Baden remarked.

The girls jolted, facing him in unison. Katarina's jaw dropped.

"You're covered in char," she said.

"I am." He looked away from her, his gaze colliding with Fox, a sense of effervescence between them.

Longing? For her? No. Never. Had to be for Distrust. But Baden wanted nothing to do with the fiend. He wouldn't miss a cancer that had been cut from his body, or any other disease he'd shed.

Except, at times, the demon had been his only source of companionship. Even with the other warriors around him, he'd often felt isolated.

But feelings weren't always accurate, were they?

Smoke began to waft from Fox's dark hair, the strands becoming flames. The demon was enraged? Because of him?

"Whoa," Katarina said to her. "What's happening to you?"

Fox rubbed her temples, the flames dying. "Sorry. Still learning control."

Galen smiled at Baden. "Would you believe I forgot about my dear Foxy Roxy?"

No, but he wasn't going to bust a nut about it. "I need weapons. The best you have."

Katarina glared at him. "Are you *ignoring* me?"

"No." A short but accurate response.

She pursed her beautiful lips.

Fox waved at him. "Nice to meet you. I guess."

His gaze returned to her, Destruction pawing at his mind.

She'll turn on us the way you almost turned against your friends. Kill her now.

Cold-blooded murder will never be okay. Katarina's voice echoed inside his head.

Galen stood, saying, "You want weapons, I have weapons. This way."

Baden followed him down a long hallway.

Katarina raced to keep pace beside him. "Why do you look like you caught fire? And why do you need weapons?"

"I'm at war. And I've been given another task."

"Is the new task super dangerous?"

"Of course. Why? Are you going to insist on accompanying me?" He opened his mouth to remind her of her weakness and his strength, how she needed him but he would never need anyone, only to recall her threat to leave him.

*Perhaps I need…*her?

"Uh—no," she said, disappointing him. "You have a job, and I have a job. The care and feeding of my new pets."

"Don't you care whether I live or die? Shouldn't you want to watch my back?"

With a snort, she patted his arm. The skin-to-skin contact was paired with a lance of pain. He sucked in a breath, and she jerked her hand away. And yet, without her touch, he only felt a keen sense of disappointment.

Galen stopped inside a bedroom he'd turned into a warrior's wet dream. Shelves lined the walls, and guns of every caliber, swords, daggers, grenade launchers, flamethrowers, and so much more filled the shelves.

"You'll want to change." With the press of a button, a closet opened, revealing an array of garments. Galen selected a black T-shirt and tossed it at Baden. "There are slits in the back for wings. You can use them to hide a pair of swords."

Baden made the exchange. "I'll also need a phone."

Galen dug one out of his pocket and tossed it, too. As he stomped from the room, he muttered, "The former leader of the Hunters is now reduced to babysitting. FYI, this wasn't part of my life plan."

Baden texted Torin: reached new place am fine you guys still good.

No typos. A first for him.

Before he pressed Send, Katarina read the screen and said, "Don't forget to add LMDO."

He searched his mental files, but couldn't place the acronym. "Why?"

"LMDO. Laughing my dentures out. You know, because you're so old."

He glared at her and pressed Send so hard the phone cracked. "Do you need another reminder that my age doesn't matter?" He stuffed the device in his pocket. *When can I fill her with my fingers again?*

Next time, he wasn't going to wear gloves. He could tolerate the pain in order to receive the pleasure. And there *would* be pleasure. The heat and wet of her...the tightness, her inner walls clinging to him...

She pretended not to hear him. "Or maybe you should have used BFF so BTW. Best friend fell so bring the wheelchair."

Destruction...laughed? The sound, whatever it was, should be labeled *cats being murdered.*

"You're more angry with me now than before, when I accused you of betrayal—for which I'm deeply sorry," Baden remarked. "Why?"

A blush stained her cheeks, intriguing—and delighting—him. How low did it go? "I'm always angry with you. You've insulted me numerous times, and now I discover you're holding *another* woman hostage."

"She's not my hostage, and I was wrong to insult you. I will beg your forgiveness later tonight. On my knees. While you sit before me."

She shivered, then she gaped at him. "Wait. Let's backtrack. Did you, a male, just admit to wrongdoing?"

"Surely not," he quipped. "Such an unprecedented event would be marked by a chorus of singing angels."

She grinned at him, but her amusement faded fast. "I saw the way you looked at her."

The darkness of her tone…was she *jealous*?

If possible, he would have grabbed Destruction's arm and held it in the air. They were champions who'd just won a mighty battle.

"How did I look at her?" He sifted through the weapons, selecting two daggers, a semiautomatic and three extra clips.

"Like you're looking at those weapons," she said, a little shrill. "As if they're the answer to all your problems."

"She carries a part of my past. But I'll only be handling the weapons, not Fox. My desire isn't for her."

The pulse at the base of Katarina's neck fluttered. "Who is your desire for, then?"

He closed the distance between them, his gaze hot on her. Rather than answering her question, however, he said, "Don't pick a fight with her while I'm gone."

Anger crackled from her. "Do this. Don't do that. Bastard! I will do what I—"

"If she were to hurt you, I'd have to kill her, and then the demon would roam free or perhaps even try to inhabit me again."

"Oh. Well. When you have such a valid reason…" Katarina melted against him and reached up to toy with the ends of his hair. "Besides, I'm too sweet to pick a fight with anyone."

"You definitely *taste* sweet."

A slow smile. "Am I a triple-X-rated porno in your mouth?"

"No, you're better." Far better. Finally, he told her what she wanted to know. "You are the one I desire."

Beaming at him, she said, "Why don't you remind me about my affection for *your* mouth, hmm?"

Denying her wasn't a possibility. He dove down for a swift kiss, meaning to roll his tongue against hers once…maybe twice…but found himself backing her against the wall and feasting. He clasped her ass and hefted her off her feet, forcing her to wrap her legs around his waist. He ground his erection at the apex of her thighs, drawing a ragged gasp of need from her.

"I'm remembering a lot of other things, too." She purred as she arched to meet him thrust for wanton thrust. "Like the way your body makes mine feel. Hot and achy…needy."

If he didn't leave now, he wouldn't leave at all. *Get the necklace, gain a point, finally have Katarina.*

He wrenched away, leaving them both panting.

"Be naked when I return." His tone—as hard as his shaft—offered no room for argument.

Shivers rocked her, but she maintained a bored expression as she said, "Ask nicely."

For this, he would beg. "Be naked…please."

"And deny you the privilege of undressing me? No! I'll be fully clothed and you'll thank me for it."

Must have her now.

Yes—no! Must leave. Task first, woman second.

For the first time, his priorities seemed…off.

"I won't be gone for long." He palmed a dagger and a semiautomatic and flashed directly to the forest nymph…who was at a cocktail party. Water surrounded a clear dome, but the dome itself was dry. Crowds of immortals filled the space, like sardines in a can, each decked out in formal attire, the women in gowns and the men in tuxes.

Baden was seriously underdressed. And Destruction wasn't happy, closed in by vampires, shifters, sirens, Harpies, Fae, Goblins, Gorgons, witches, even a Cyclops.

Calm. Steady.

A waiter passed with a tray of what looked to be Jell-O shots. Odd, considering the decor and the attire.

His ears twitched as a familiar "whoo hoo" rang out. Tense, he pushed his way through the masses, hissing anytime someone brushed against him. He passed towering marble columns chiseled to resemble Poseidon and came upon the nymph—who teetered on her feet beside Taliyah. The two were doing shots and sucking limes.

Behind them stretched a dais where Poseidon watched their antics from a throne made of coral. Baden knew the male spent half of each year in the water and the other half on land, weakened because of some kind of curse—but then, wasn't every man's downfall because of a curse? This was a land/legs month.

His attention remained fixed on the nymph, his features set ablaze with unfulfilled desire.

"This time," Taliyah said, her words slurred, "we'll do the shots while I'm you and you're me. Quick, let's switch clothes and jewelry."

Baden tensed. She was here to steal the necklace, too, wasn't she?

As if she was completely aware of her surroundings—and Baden's presence—she peered over at him and winked.

"Dude! That's the best idea ever!" The nymph reached for the clasp at her nape.

Poseidon jumped up and roared, "Don't you dare."

Many of the guests flinched.

Taliyah scowled, but quickly schooled her features to reveal only mild disappointment. "Now our shots won't taste as good."

"I know, right!" The nymph gave the sea king a thumbs-down.

Everyone leaped out of his way as he stormed to her side. He clasped her arm, and two men—guards, by the look of them—closed in. "Take her to her quarters. Remain outside her door. No one enters, no one leaves."

"Boo hiss," she called as she was "helped" away. "The party was just getting interesting."

Baden shared a last look with Taliyah—a glare—before sinking deep into the crowd to keep from drawing Poseidon's notice.

"Oh, look at you, a juicy slice of man meat." A redheaded Harpy petted Baden's arm, making him glower. He jerked away from her, only to bump into another Harpy. This one was black and extraordinarily pretty with amber eyes and pouty red lips. *Know her...*

Her identity clicked. She was Neeka the Unwanted. Taliyah's best friend. Once a captive of the Phoenix.

Her claws dug into his arm and though she smiled up at him, an aura of spite surrounded her. "The necklace is ours. Leave or bleed. Your choice."

Baden grabbed her by the neck and squeezed before he'd even realized he'd moved. *Damn it, beast!* He released her just as quickly.

She flipped him off, unperturbed. "Nice knowing you, warrior."

Alongside the redhead and Taliyah, she vanished in the crowd. Baden strode down the path the guards had used, cataloging all possible threats rather than flashing. When he reached a separate hallway, he spied one of those guards behind a potted plant, unconscious. The girls worked fast. Noted.

He came to another fallen guard in front of a locked door, and knew he'd reached his destination. Wasting no more time, he flashed inside the room. A bedroom. The walls were painted sky-blue, with potted plants and flowers hanging in every direction. The three Harpies—Taliyah, Neeka and the redhead—enclosed the nymph in a circle. She fought like a trained assassin, not nearly as drunk as she'd appeared. Not drunk at all, actually. The four women clashed in a tangle of punching arms, cutting claws and kicking legs. They moved so rapidly he had to concentrate to pick up their individual movements.

A flash of memory. One of his own. Sitting beside Paris, eating popcorn and watching immortal females "cat fight" just for a chance to date the male.

Grunts and groans quickly brought him back to reality. A spray of blood. A tooth flew through the air like a discarded piece of candy.

Baden used furniture to blockade the door.

"Give me the necklace," Taliyah commanded.

"You don't need it, bitch," the nymph piped up.

"Neither do you, whore." Neeka punted her in the stomach. "You're about to die."

"I've been assured I'm not dying for another year, at least!" The nymph again. "You have no idea what I've had to endure. I'd *rather* die than give it up."

"Well, I'm here to oblige you." The redhead offered an aloof grin as she slashed with fingers tipped by metal claws. Unable to grow real ones? "It's to be the next prize at the Harpy Games."

The nymph was good, but she couldn't hold out against three highly skilled Harpies much longer. Not many could.

Destruction longed to dance in their blood, but even he recognized the unlikelihood of emerging unscathed.

He flashed to the center of the circle, an advocate for the nymph, taking the next blows in her place. Claws to the neck. A fist to the kidney. A boot to the stomach.

Sharp lances of pain were merely kindling for fury. It sparked. It grew and spread. It consumed him. He aimed his semiautomatic, quickly putting a bullet between the redhead's eyes.

She'd wake up...in a few days.

He focused on Taliyah and fired off another shot. Expecting it, she dove out of the way.

Claws sprouted from the ends of his fingers, and he lost his grip on the weapon. A weapon he didn't actually need.

The shadows were rising...

Neeka yanked Taliyah toward the door as Destruction fed Baden a stream of information. The shadows were the offspring of Corruption. If left unchecked, their darkness would infect a host, directing his—or her—thoughts and actions.

With a single touch, that darkness—like a virus— would infect these Harpies, too, and begin to direct *their* thoughts and actions.

The wreaths, like armor, kept Baden immune.

The Harpies grabbed the redhead and dragged her out of range. The shadows watched and writhed, eager for combat.

Taliyah glared at him. "I want that necklace, Red."

"Hades will have it within the hour. If you ask nicely, perhaps he'll gift it to you."

"You're not understanding me. Give it to him, and I'll make you regret it. A lot."

He had many regrets. He didn't think this would be one of them.

The shadows hissed, and even moved toward her. She hauled her comrades into the hall and kicked the door shut. The last thing he saw was her scowl.

The shadows returned to their marks.

A glass vase crashed into his head. As the pieces tinkled to the floor, he spun to glare at the nymph. Her eyes widened with horror when he remained standing.

He showed her the semiautomatic then the dagger. "One way or another, I'm leaving with the necklace. Let's do this the easy way. Hand it over."

Clearly, the line he walked between good and evil had thinned more with every task. He'd thought he'd maintained a strict code: no killing women or innocents, ever. She was both, and still he'd threatened her.

At least he'd offered her an out.

What would Katarina do?

Anger contorted the nymph's features, only to evaporate like morning dew. She smiled and batted her lashes at him. "Why don't you steal my virtue instead? You'll enjoy it more, I promise."

An offer to slake his need and clear his head, but he wasn't the least bit tempted. He wanted the human. Wanted his hands on her, and only her. Wanted her hands on him, and only him. Wanted nothing between them. No clothes, no pain. If he couldn't have the latter, he would settle for the former.

Somehow, she'd bewitched him.

In this situation, she would charm her way to triumph. The problem was, he lacked any sort of charisma. What he did have? The truth.

"Give me the necklace. I don't want to hurt you, but I will if I must."

"Or you could walk away," the nymph said.

"Last chance." He gave both weapons a shake. "My woman will reward me for allowing you to live. I want my reward. But if I fail to give the necklace to Hades, I'll be punished and another warrior will be sent to you."

"I'll hide before—"

"Wouldn't matter. Pandora would find you."

"Pandora?" The nymph shuddered, her cheeks paling. "Here. Take the necklace and go!"

18

"The definition of marriage? When a woman adopts an overgrown man-child who cannot be handled by his parents any longer."

—Olivia, fallen Sent One

Katarina: 0. Baden: 1.

Potrebujem pomoc—I need help.

Katarina had forgotten her desire to train Baden the instant he'd looked at Fox with yearning—yearning for a woman who wasn't "weak." Her pride had taken a serious beating.

When his expression had projected anger immediately after, she'd deduced the truth. The yearning had stemmed from camaraderie rather than sensuality. As if he'd seen an old friend after years apart, and both looks had been directed at Distrust.

He hated the demon and rightly so...but perhaps he missed the companionship. Right now, he trusted himself around so few people. With good reason! Hades was doing his best to turn him into a prized pit bull, a fighter whose only instinct was to attack.

Well, too bad for Hades. Pit bulls were actually gentle giants. When raised right, they were sweethearts through and through.

Time to up her game, Katarina thought. And she had a plan. A trial by fire. Or rather, a trial by touch.

Touch was the greatest tool in her arsenal. While Baden used guns and knives to convey a message, she used her hands. Skin-to-fur—or skin-to-skin contact created a bond between two creatures—uh, people. Touch said *you are not alone.* Touch said *I'm here for you.*

And really, she just wanted to get her hands on him again.

Biscuit and Gravy nipped at her pockets as she led them to the bedroom she'd claimed as her own. A decadent affair with vibrant gold curtains, portraits of kings and queens hung throughout, and hand-carved furniture. She'd just finished baking sugar-free dog cookies, the plastic bags in her pockets stuffed with the crumbles.

"Sit," she said, and after each dog obeyed, she passed out treats.

Before offering another, she asked the boys to shake her hand. "Good job, guys."

They devoured the next round, and she thought she might burst with love. Why had she tried so diligently to guard against the pain of another loss? Humans needed love to survive. Love was sustenance. Love was life. The more she poured into others, the more others could pour into her.

Biscuit licked her hand. Gravy hopped around like a bunny as he tried to bite his brother's tail, intending to use it as a chew toy. A friendly bout of wrestling broke out. The two exuded more happiness every day, not to mention a more playful spirit and confident outlook.

She'd begun to think they'd make excellent guard

dogs. *Schutzhund* training worked best with puppies that were calm and confident from the start, who'd been socialized early so that nothing startled them. Not that nervous, unsure dogs couldn't be trained, but it was often the same as giving a fully-loaded assault rifle to a frightened man whose finger twitched every time he spotted his own shadow. Also, nervous dogs tended to have selective hearing and often ignored their handler's commands, biting anyone, even their handler, out of fear for their own safety, not out of a desire to protect.

Biscuit and Gravy probably hadn't been socialized and might even have a history of abuse, judging by the way they reacted to strangers, but they definitely had the necessary confidence. They also had a high prey drive, which was another essential. The need to find, pursue and capture food. Or, one day, bad guys.

The two had already excelled at basic obedience training, and though she'd only just begun teaching them to track—toys, treats, and one day, if she decided to take them to the next level, drugs—they'd proven adept at that, too, with a keen sense of smell. Next would come bite work, which would begin as a game.

In fact, she made everything a game from start to finish. The heavy, padded sleeve she gave them—a prelude to going after a living being—was used as a chew toy. They played tug-of-war with it, driving their excitement level higher and higher. The goal was never to hurt but to hang on to the toy until she told them to release it.

The key? Redirect their aggression. And love them. Always love them.

So many people who'd paid for her services had asked how she worked such miracles with dogs. Her answer was twofold. One, she picked her pups from shelters. Adopt don't shop! Shelter dogs knew a home was a gift. And two, affection gave birth to protection. It was as simple as that.

Her other dogs, the ones she'd rescued from fighting rings, had needed more affection and reassurance than these two. Even more time. Time that had been as mentally and emotionally exhausting as it had been exhilarating. Another reason she'd had to remain strong after her mother's death.

Without strength, we have nothing.

She'd had something to give.

"I'm going to take care of you," she whispered. "And I'm going to give you the life you deserve."

They stopped wrestling and peered at her with adoration, as if they'd understood her words. She thought they might be trying to tell her *We're going to take care of you, too.*

They shared a look of…anticipation? Gravy's head tilted to the side. Biscuit nodded. In unison, they closed in on her. Each nuzzled one of her wrists, and when she tried to turn her hand to pet them, each flashed a pair of fangs—*fangs?!*—and chomped deep into her vein.

A torrent of pain! Yelping, she tried to yank free, but the two only clamped on harder. At least the pain faded, replaced by a warm rush of—

Tristo hrmenych! Was she high? She'd always eschewed drugs, but this fit her brother's description perfectly—vertigo, a feeling of lightness, as if she could float away like a balloon, a sense of ecstasy, all right in her world. Shit! What was happening to her?

The dogs released her at last, and she toppled over. Her limbs shook, her bones vibrating. Each of her organs caught fire; the blaze consumed her, sweat soon drenching her. She was dying. She had to be dying. She—

Fingers snapped in front of her face. She blinked open her eyes to find out she was seated rather than prone. Even more confusing, the pain had left her completely, her skin and clothing dry with no hint of perspiration. The only sign something had happened was the metallic taste in her mouth. Had she bitten her tongue? No, there were no sores on it.

Galen crouched in front of her, his expression concerned. "Want to tell me what's wrong with you? You've been sitting here for at least five minutes, grunting and groaning zombie-style."

But...but...only a few seconds had passed. Right? "I'm fine." Her throat burned, as if she hadn't used it for days, maybe weeks. She shook her head to scatter any lingering hints of lightness.

Biscuit and Gravy were seated at her side, calmly watching the warrior. For one crazy moment, Katarina imagined she felt their dislike for the man—stranger!— and their unbending determination to protect their *silly human*.

Frowning, Katarina held up her arms, turning her hands in the light. Her wrists were normal. There was no evidence of a wound, not even a bruise. She'd *imagined* the bite?

"I'm fine," she repeated. "Really." Maybe she'd fallen asleep and dreamed the bite. Or hallucinated? Totally possible. She was semi-dating an immortal warrior. Weirder stuff happened every day. "What are you doing here?"

"I fixed lunch. My specialty. Ham sandwiches."

Lunch? She hadn't missed minutes, but *hours*.

"Thanks, but I'm not hungry." Her stomach was too busy twisting into thousands of little knots.

"All right." Galen stood with fluid grace. "I'll put one in the fridge in case you change your mind. If I get hungry later, well, every man for himself. You had your chance."

"You are too kind."

"I know. And now that I've buttered you up..."

The meaning of the phrase eluded her. Buttered up? "Are you hitting on me?"

Galen wiggled his brows at her. "You wish. I'm hoping to convince you to talk to Baden about helping Fox deal with Distrust."

"She's having problems?"

"Only every day."

Compassion stirred, but so did the memory of Katarina's introduction to Galen. He'd threatened her. She said, "If you call me your sweet doodlepop from now on, I will consider thinking about maybe mentioning the woman to Baden."

He grinned at her. "I hope you're this way with the redhead...doodlepop." He saluted her before exiting the room, sealing her inside with the dogs.

For the next several hours, she busied herself with the rest of the day's training, determined not to think about what happened. Or what hadn't happened. Whatever! When one of the boys began to pee or poop, she barked out a firm command to stop and escorted the two outside, offering a reward whenever they finished their business in the grass.

The house—palace—had a million rooms, every corner offering a new hallway to lose yourself, so she always stuck to the same path. A straight shot downstairs, through the kitchen, the laundry room and finally a sunroom. The backyard was fenced by a tall wall made of gold, steel and iron. The grass, bushes and array of flowers were perfectly manicured, and a myriad of trees provided shade from a glaring sun.

When training ended, she stayed outside, letting the boys run wild as she created a mental shopping list. Doggy door, organic food, tags for the collars, stronger leashes, urine neutralizer spray and toys.

—*Toys*—

The unfamiliar voice registered, along with the fact that the word had been spoken in a language she'd never learned or even heard before, and yet she'd understood it. Brows knitting together, she spun in a circle. No one stood around her.

But both dogs stiffened.

—*Demon girl comes*—

Again, the unfamiliar voice took her by surprise. This time, however, she realized the words had been spoken *inside* her head. But they didn't originate with her and the only other beings with her… She looked at the dogs. No, no. Impossible…yes?

The dogs scurried in front of her as she pivoted. Biscuit growled at Fox, who opened the door and leaned against the frame, and Katarina actually *felt* his burst of anger. *This is weirder than weird.*

"You're good with them," Fox said.

"I love them," she replied. It was as simple as that.

Both Biscuit and Gravy smiled up at her, as if they'd understood her words. Did they?

Fox rubbed her temple. "Do you love Baden? Wait. You know what? Never mind. Don't answer that. I won't believe you." She laughed, the amusement tinged with bitterness. "The demon, you know."

Katarina petted the boys behind their ears. "It comes with a heaping side of paranoia, does it?"

"If you knew the number of conspiracy theories I have running through my head at any given time…"

"Are you hoping Baden will take the demon back?" Because, even if he agreed to it, Katarina would fight tooth and nail to stop the repossession. The man had enough to deal with already.

"Yes. No. I don't know. I don't know *anything* anymore."

Compassion welled a second time. More than before. Katarina couldn't do much to help the girl, but she could offer a distraction. "Since you're here, I could use your help gathering a few supplies for the dogs."

"Give me a list, and I'll round up everything personally."

"Wonderful." She voiced everything she wanted. "But, uh, I also need a few personal items." To begin her seduction—training—of Baden. "Like a masseuse."

"Not a problem. I have one on staff."

Even better. "Does he…she?…have a portable table?"

"He. And yes."

A male. The best-case scenario. "I also need lingerie. A lot of lingerie, and make sure it's super slutty. Something you'd imagine a prostitute would wear. High class! No, scratch that. Low class. Oh, and I need toiletries. Preferably vanilla scented. And condoms. A lot of condoms. Those don't need to smell like vanilla. A swimsuit—do you have a pool? Never mind, doesn't matter. A string bikini. Shouldn't you be writing these down?"

—*We fetch for you?*—

An-n-nd there was the unfamiliar voice, louder and

clearer than before. She peered down at the dogs. Both stared at her expectantly, waiting for her response.

They were speaking to her, weren't they?

Such a daft thought and yet, the suspicion niggled at her.

"No," she told them, just in case. "No need to fetch."

They sighed with disappointment.

"You converse with your dogs?" Fox asked, frowning.

"You don't?"

The woman smoothed her dark hair from her cheek while giving Katarina the dreaded side-eye. "I'll have the items delivered to you by the end of the day."

"Or sooner." Baden could return at any moment. "Like, say, within the next two hours sooner."

"I'll do what I can. Just...don't hurt the warrior. If you do—"

"I won't."

"But if you do—"

"I really won't. I...like him."

"—I'll kill you," Fox finished.

As the dogs growled at her, she turned on her heel and strode off.

Katarina kneeled to pet and praise her students. They'd sensed a threat and reacted, remaining calm, staying by her side. Now they wagged their tails and kissed her liberally.

This world she found herself in was different than any she'd ever known, but this, these dogs, they were her norm. And Baden...he was just hers. For now.

Baden flashed to Hades. The king sat upon his throne, dictating instructions to Pippin, who stood beside him, chiseling in the stone tablet.

"—head removed, limbs severed, chest opened and—" Noticing Baden, Hades changed course. "Well?"

Baden tossed the *cœur de la terre* at him. "Another point."

"Excellent." Hades anchored the chain around his wrist, regarding Baden with something akin to anger. "Did you hurt the Harpies?"

"No. There was no need."

Hades relaxed, but only slightly. "Every detail. Now."

The story spilled from him, ending with the shadows chasing the Harpies away.

"The shadows...they are minions of Corruption, yes?" A demon High Lord with the ability to mate with any willing human spirit. He derived pleasure only when he ruined a good person.

Hades worked two fingers over his stubbly jaw, as if debating his next words. "They are, their evil conceived inside the human heart."

Destruction had gotten it right. And now, without the heat of battle, he was...not pleased. He bore the seed of Corruption in his flesh.

"Why so grim?" Hades asked. "The wreaths make you immune to their particular brand of feeding. They only wish to protect you, their host. And to consume your enemies, of course."

True—for now. But Corruption, like any evil, would one day turn on its host. That was a guarantee. "What happens when I win your game and the wreaths are removed?"

An enigmatic smile. "You still won't have to worry."

Because he wouldn't survive the removal?

No. He and Hades shared a bond, and neither of

them could deny it. The answer, whatever it was, simply wasn't clear to him yet.

"Pippin." Hades brushed a piece of lint from his knee. "Did I decide to punish or forgive my charges for breaking the rules and fighting with each other?"

"Forgive, sire."

Hades's shoulders rolled in with disappointment. "Very well. I never refute my own decisions."

"Except for the ones you refute, sire."

"This is true. You get me, Pippin. It's why I haven't fired you today."

"We still have several hours to go, sire."

Baden butted in, saying, "Give me another task."

Hades regarded him for a moment. "So eager to defeat Pandora?"

"So eager to defeat Lucifer."

Approval glinted in the king's black eyes. "We're closer to victory every day." With a flick of his fingers, he waved Baden away. "Go now. Rest while you can."

There was no rest for the wicked. He had another piece of business to attend to—severing Katarina's tie to Aleksander at long last.

Baden wouldn't kill him. Katarina wanted the male locked away forever, and so he would be locked away forever. In return for sparing Aleksander's life, Baden would insist the male disavow her, in effect divorcing her. In their world, it would be enough, a man's word his bond.

He flashed to the dungeon beneath the fortress in Budapest and—

Both the man and chains were missing.

Damn it! The bastard hadn't been freed with the All-key. Torin would never betray him. Baden knew that with every fiber of his being, which shamed him as he remembered the times he *hadn't* trusted Torin and the others. Times he would remember when he looked at Fox, he was sure, and considered the ramifications of hosting Distrust. The darkest days of his life. So dark he'd preferred death.

Now he had the bands, and the shadows, making him even more dangerous than before. And yet, he had no desire to end his life. He would fight for what he wanted.

He would fight for *Katarina*. Right now, she was his one bright light. He'd spoken true: he couldn't lose her.

But she was still married, a tie he wouldn't be breaking as soon as he'd expected. Fury… Someone must have found the key to the chains in the rubble of the fortress. Someone with the ability to flash…or even just the ability to flash to Aleksander specifically.

Pandora! Her name was a scourge inside his mind; Destruction roared.

She would pay. Baden, too, possessed the ability to flash to Aleksander, which meant he'd just missed the male's escape; otherwise he would have ended up somewhere else. He palmed a dagger in each hand and flashed—

To the center of a busy highway. A horn blasted, a truck seconds from hitting him. Bitch was trying to get him killed without breaking the rules. He flashed as the vehicle clipped his arm, ending up spinning to a stop inside a woman's locker room.

Half-dressed females who were already worked up about Pandora and Aleksander gasped and screamed and threw towels and shoes at him. He flashed again, this time appearing in a graffiti-ridden alley.

A series of *pops* rang out…until a *click, click* signaled an empty clip. He ducked, one of the bullets managing to graze his collarbone. Another memory he hadn't lived knocked on the door of his mind, but this time, he had no problem ignoring it, his will growing stronger.

As he straightened, his gaze locked on Pandora. The eye he'd daggered was still in the process of healing. The more vulnerable parts of the body required more time. But at least she was regenerating, despite being a spirit.

Growing new limbs might be possible. But only with the bands?

She wore a black tank, revealing the marks of Corruption on her arm.

In terms of humans they'd killed, they were even. Baden had six other points, not counting the points they shared for killing Lucifer's minion. How many others did *she* have? And why did he feel no desire to slay her, despite her actions this day?

"Hello, Baden." She flashed her teeth in a parody of a grin, reloaded and took aim. Aleksander was anchored to her waist, a rope tied to the end of the chain and wrapped around her wrist. A handicap. Perfect. "Your little trap failed, as you can see. I found the key in the rubble."

"You have something that belongs to me," Baden said as Destruction snarled.

"He's mine!"

Baden launched a dagger, aiming for the rope.

Pandora must have thought he meant to kill the bastard rather than allow her to leave with him because she leaped, taking the hit in her thigh. She cringed, lifting her semiautomatic and firing off two more shots.

The bullets slammed into his torso, shredding his stomach. He leaked black goo and hemorrhaged strength.

"If he's dead, he can't tell us where to find the coin." She kept her gun trained on Baden, her arm trembling as she leaked her own river of black.

Could she not bring herself to injure him further? She must feel the connection, too.

"He'll never tell us," Baden said. "And the coin isn't why I want him." He addressed the male. "Voice your divorce from Katarina."

"Never," Aleksander vowed.

Thinks to deny me?

Rage…

"The girl again." Pandora shook her head with disgust. "Only the coin matters. It will force Hades to grant my greatest wish."

Her certainty… "I know that, but how do you?"

"You're not the only one with friends, Baddy Boy."

His head canted to the side as he studied her. "You plan to use the coin to buy the kingdom for yourself, do you not?"

"Yes! Don't you?"

"No." But at least she was honest. "You've never been possessed. You don't know the horrors of living with a demon."

"I'm host to shadows and a being with memories I've never lived. I can handle demons."

Wrong. You didn't handle demons. You starved them.

"Besides, an army is an army," she added. "I'll never be helpless again!"

A sentiment he shared. To a point. "There are other ways. *Pandy*."

She gave a violent shake of her head. "Leave now, and live. Stay, and we'll fight to your next death."

Destruction ran his hooves through his mind, ready to charge her. A threat was a threat, no matter the connection.

Katarina would disagree. *As long as there's breath, there's hope.*

"Do you truly want to forfeit freedom from the bands?" Hades could forgive a few bumps and bruises, but not a murder.

Eyes wild, she said, "The coin will buy my kingdom *and* my freedom. Perhaps I'll spare you today and take you as my slave tomorrow."

That was her grand plan? "You think Hades doesn't already have kings under his control? I've seen them. You've seen them." The warriors who'd tossed him across the throne room as if he were as light as a feather. "You might have a kingdom, but you sure as shit won't have your freedom."

"I will." How desperate she sounded. "I can't go on like this."

Compassion nicked him, an emotion he'd rarely felt for this woman. He blamed Katarina. Her softer side must have rubbed off on him.

Aleksander smirked at him over Pandora's shoulder, and the beast *bang, banged* against Baden's skull in an effort to reach the male.

His temples throbbed. *Focus.* "I won't let you—"

"Give me one night with him, and I'll vow never to harm your human."

Pandora's words shut down his threat and even quieted Destruction. She'd just offered the one thing he couldn't refuse. "I'll give you one night." A calculated risk. If she found the coin, she would gain another point. And even if she failed, the male would be away from Baden's strict control.

"Tomorrow," he added, "I *will* come for him."

"Deal. But if you come for him early, ambushing me, I'll turn my sights to the girl."

"And I'll ensure you remain an armless, legless husk."

She snorted. "I like the thought of you in a cage of my own making. Perhaps I'll spend the entire night creating traps for you."

He smiled at her, pure challenge. "I'd be disappointed if you didn't."

"Until tomorrow then." She vanished with Aleksander, who was still smirking. Fool. He thought because Pandora was a woman she would be easier to escape and less of a danger. Baden knew her well. She hurt her victims in ways that would haunt them for the rest of their days. The nymph had known it, and soon Aleksander would, too.

Return to Katarina. Stake a claim.

His smile turned to pure seduction as he flashed home.

19

"The bow chicka wow wow is a powerful thing.
Use it or lose it."

—Danika, the All-seeing Eye

Katarina walked through her bedroom while running
through her mental checklist. Overhead light and all
lamps disabled. Check. Candles scented with vanilla
and lavender placed throughout and lit. Check. The
massage table set up and draped with a heated blanket.
Check. Her body cleaned with vanilla soap and covered
only by a cashmere robe. Check and mate.

The dogs slept peacefully in the bathroom. The masseuse was on standby, awaiting her call. All she lacked
was Baden. Where was he?

She sat in the chair by the crackling hearth, loung-
ing to appear sexy. But an hour later, she was on her
feet, pacing, being sure to sway her hips. Just in case.
If Baden stayed out all night, she'd…she'd…argh! She'd
go to bed frustrated. And as payback, she would ensure
he went to bed frustrated for a week. *Whimper*. Negative reinforcement would hurt them both.

Sighing, she strode to the window and stared out.

One minute ticked into another, dark thoughts drifting through her mind, ruining her sensual mood. Here she was, determined to seduce Baden, while her brother... what? He was out there somewhere, probably high as a kite. Or maybe he'd overdosed and would never have a chance to get clean.

Why do I even care?

She sighed, the answer already clear. Dominik was the only family she had left and family—for good or for ill—was bonded. Always and forever.

"Katarina."

Baden's growly voice jolted her, a cascade of shivers warming her. Trembling, she turned to face the object of her fascination—the only person capable of distracting her from her troubles simply by saying her name.

As usual, the beautiful man stole her breath. He'd showered. His hair was damp, the strands a darker red, almost brown. He wore a black shirt and camo pants that were tucked into combat boots. His gloves were firmly in place.

"You were sad. Why?"

"I worried about my brother."

"You will stop...please. He caused you pain. He shouldn't have the privilege of being part of your life."

Well. Baden was learning to request rather than demand. In his own way, yes, but progress was progress. And oh, the way he complimented her...she would never tire of it.

As he looked her over, taking in her scantily clad body, his chiseled features drew taut with tension. A tension so fierce it thickened the air around him, sizzling with electric energy.

"I like the robe," he said. "Now take it off."

Oh. Wow. Okay. If she'd been wearing panties, they would have become soaked in an instant. Apparently there were times she *liked* his commands. Still she replied, "Ask nicely." Consistency was a key to successful training.

"Will you please take it off?"

She smiled at him, proud of him. "I will, yes. For my massage."

Baden wanted her, clearly intended to have her, but he planned for it to happen without skin-to-skin contact. Absolutely unacceptable. Reach for the stars first, and if you must, settle for the flowers second.

"Massage?" he asked, intrigued.

"A *desperately needed* massage. I'm sore from recent...vigorous pursuits." Her trembling only increased as she picked up the phone. The intercom system allowed her to connect to any room in the house but nowhere outside. Struck her as odd, but she wasn't going to sweat it. She stamped the proper code for the servants' quarters and when greeted, asked to speak with Fox's masseuse.

When he came onto the line, she said, "I'm ready."

Baden crossed his arms over his chest. Arms she hoped to have wrapped around her very soon. "A massage. From a woman."

She laughed as if enchanted. "Don't be ridiculous." With a tilt of her chin, she motioned to the chair she'd pushed to the side of the portable table, a location that would grant him an unobstructed view of the proceedings. "Sit."

His arms lowered, one of his hands resting on the hilt of a dagger. "A male?"

"Yes. I like deep tissue, and as you so enjoy pointing out, men are oh, so much stronger." She fluttered her eyelashes for good measure.

"Not always," he grated. "Women can be—"

"But don't worry, *naivka*," she interjected. "I'm going to let you watch." *And you have no idea what you're in for.*

"I'll do it. I'll massage you." His hard tone dared her to challenge him. "I'm stronger than any human."

She pouted at him while trying not to giggle like a schoolgirl. "Touch pains you, and tonight I only want to pleasure you."

His nostrils flared as he inhaled sharply. "I'm wearing gloves. I won't be pained."

Oh, how very eager he sounded now. "Okay, let me rephrase. I want flesh on my flesh. It's warmer...deliciouser."

A muscle jumped underneath his eye. "*Deliciouser* is not a word."

"Please excuse my poor English. Excitement has muddled my poor little girl brain." She sashayed to him and led him to the chair. "Now, if you'd be so kind as to sit..."

He didn't. She pushed, and he fell into place, glaring at her. "I don't like this."

That's crystal clear, darling. "Is the beast demanding a fresh kill?"

"Yes! And he's very determined."

"Well. Whatever you do," she said, leaning down to press her lips against his ear. "Do no harm to the human. I repeat, do no harm to the human."

He gripped the arms of the chair. "I can't make any promises."

She straightened, saying with a firm tone, "You'll make this particular promise, or I won't let you watch."

Oh, oh. He *reeeally* didn't like that. Red glinted in his eyes and when next he spoke, he spoke with two voices, both layered with fury and…possession? "You think you can force me to leave, sweet Rina?"

"No." *Proceed carefully.* They were entering dangerous territory. "But I can certainly move to another room."

"And I can follow. No door will keep me from you. No wall, either. To reach the one I want, I'll remove any barrier, tolerate no obstacles."

Scary hot words, scary hot man. "Well, I can deny you access to my playland." To be sure he understood her meaning, she ran her hands down the curves of her body. "And there's nothing you'll be able to do about *that*."

A moment passed in tense silence.

Finally, he offered a stiff nod and said, "I won't kill the human."

Almost too easy. She swallowed a laugh. "You won't hurt him, either."

He ran his tongue over his teeth. "I won't hurt him."

"And you'll talk to Fox, help her out. I kinda like her." When the woman wasn't dipping a toe in the pool of paranoia, that is.

"Yes," he said with bite. "I'll help her."

Such a good boy, and good boys deserved a reward. Katarina took his gloved hand and cupped it over her breast; her nipple *throbbed* for his attention. He moaned, palming his massive erection with his other hand.

"See what you do to me, Rina."

"If only you could feel what you do to me, warrior…"

Another moan as he kneaded her.

A soft knock sounded at the door. Baden stiffened, and she twittered with glee. She released him—every feminine part of her screamed for every masculine part of him—to skip to the door. *Let the games begin.*

Seeing the masseuse for the first time stunned her. He was fully human, like her, and young, probably in his mid-twenties, with straight brown hair pulled back in a man-bun and dark eyes framed by long lashes. He displayed no telltale vulnerabilities, his physique matching the voice she'd heard over the phone: strong. Obviously he worked out. Not that a lifetime in a gym would make him an even match for, say, a male like Baden.

Pride coursed through her. *That's* my *man.*

"Come in. Please." She stepped aside.

"Thank you. I'm Thomas, by the way." He entered with a basket of oils, stumbling over his own foot when he spotted big, intense Baden in the chair.

"Don't worry," she said. "The warrior has promised not to harm or kill you."

Thomas paled. "That's…comforting?"

Baden merely glared at him.

"*Very* comforting. Now. Be a dear," she said, her eyes locked on Baden, "and turn away. Also close your eyes while I undress and get situated on the table."

"Of course." He obeyed swiftly, and not just because he feared Baden's reaction. Fox had told her about saving him from a horde of vampires years before—vampires!—and how he'd been completely devoted to her ever since, serving her and her guests to the best of his ability.

Katarina untied the belt at her waist, Baden going still with sublime attentiveness, as if she were the only

other person on the planet; he didn't even seem to be
breathing. She shrugged out of the robe, the material
pooling at her feet, every inch of her suddenly revealed.

Flipping her hair over her shoulder, she allowed him
to look his fill. She wasn't shy. Why pretend?

He gripped the arms of the chair. "You are…"

Cool air teased her distended nipples while the heat
of his gaze dampened her core. She traced a fingertip
from sternum to navel then turned, presenting her ass.
"I am?"

"Katarina." A husky plea. "You are exquisite. My
every fantasy made flesh."

Oh, the things he says, the things he makes me feel!
"And this is only the beginning…" she said, forgetting
for a moment that they had an audience. She climbed
onto the table and covered her lower half with the blanket. "I'm ready."

Thomas rifled through the oils, selecting the one he
wanted before discarding the others.

"Let me know if I press too firmly or lightly," he
said, rubbing the oil over his hands. The scent of lavender wafted from him as he reached for her.

When a growl parted Baden's lips, Thomas hesitated.

"Baden," she said. "Behave or this stops."

He quieted straightaway.

Well, well. He didn't like another man handling her,
but he sure did enjoy the show.

Thomas got to work, digging his fingers into the sore
muscles in her back. She hadn't lied to Baden. Vigorous
activities had left her sore. Besides, hanging out with
immortals could be stressful.

His scrutiny of her face intensified with every new
touch. Judging her expressions?

"Harder," she said, and Thomas complied, drawing a moan from her. Her attention remained fixed on Baden, whose features were stark with desire, blistering sensuality and simmering jealousy.

He had a hard-on the size of a battering ram, and he wasn't even trying to hide it. His muscles were clearly knotted; he needed a massage of his own.

Must get my hands on him. Soon...

One minute bled into another. His tension skyrocketed to new high after new high, making the air ever thicker. She thought she would have to swim to reach him.

Drowning...

She imagined the hands on her belonged to Baden... stroking her skin...and it wasn't long before she was so desperately aroused she was mewling.

"Leave us," Baden barked. "Now. For your own safety, never return."

Thomas didn't bother gathering his supplies. He darted to the door. The exit sealed shut with a soft *snick*.

Katarina didn't wait for an order—Baden wasn't in charge today—but stood to shaky legs. "I'm going to assume your rudeness stems from your own soreness and that you need a turn on the table. Come."

"No. You come." He crooked his finger at her, and she knew what he had planned. A repeat of what they'd done before. At least to kick things off. And she was tempted, so very very tempted.

Having his gloved fingers inside her had been good, but she wanted great.

Eye on the prize. Give me skin-to-skin or give me nothing.

"No, *pekný*. I'm staying right here. But you...you're

taking off your clothes and climbing onto the table. The sooner you do, the sooner I get my hands on you."

His pupils flared with a new infusion of lust. "You're going to touch me?"

"Oh, yes. The pain might very well be temporary. A sensitivity you developed as a spirit unable to make contact with another. If so, we'll desensitize you. You can already withstand more than before, yes?"

"Yes." The longing he projected...but still he hesitated. "I've wanted this, imagined it. I shouldn't risk harming you with my strength. I shouldn't relax my guard, allowing myself to be vulnerable..."

"But..."

"But I will trust myself to be gentle. And I will trust you not to betray me. Because I need you more than I've ever needed anything. Even a second life."

As his words rocked her, he stood. The sheer sensuality of the movement made her ache a thousand times worse. A flash-fever in her veins.

He pulled his shirt over his head, revealing a wide chest packed with muscle and sinew, bronzed skin she would forever drool over, and the butterfly tattoo she hoped to trace with her tongue.

One day I'm going to devour this man.

He tugged off the gloves, the black lines on his arms a bleak reminder of the violent life he'd lived—a life she wanted to soothe. She'd noticed those lines deepened in color every time he returned from one of Hades's tasks, knew they represented a death he'd dished.

Once upon a time, a thought like that would have freaked her out. She and Baden were too different. Now? Bring on the new story, the new ending, because she was thoroughly enjoying this new beginning. His kindness and concern had built a bridge across the vast gulf dividing them.

He shed his boots, his pants, then his boxer briefs, finally leaving him completely bare, and oh, *he* was the exquisite one. He was absolute perfection. A thousand other words described him, but none actually did him justice.

His shaft…she almost couldn't believe she'd had her hand wrapped around it. It was big. Too big…but the ride to the finish line would be *fun*.

"You're staring, *krásavica*." His fingers enfolded the wide base and stroked up. "Do you like this? Want it?"

Eye on the prize. Well, the *other* prize. "I do. So let's do what's necessary to ensure I get it."

He approached her, stopping when they were a whisper away. His delicious scent teased her: *lick me, bite me, never stop.* His heat taunted her: *I have what you so desperately crave.*

A single deep breath would rub her nipples against his chest, creating a crucial friction…and her resistance would crumble.

Biting her lower lip, she motioned to the table. He climbed on top and stretched out on his back, facing her.

Naughty boy. "Want to watch me, do you?"

"Always," he rasped, unabashed.

She selected a bottle of vanilla-scented oil and moistened her hands. Pressing her hip against the side of the table, she held her fingers just over his chest without actually touching him, letting his anticipation build until he vibrated.

Now. She traced a fingertip lightly down his sternum, and he inhaled sharply.

"Painful?" she asked.

"Yes."

Expected. For now. "Tell me if it worsens." She traced her fingertip along the same path, again and again, always gentle, the oil leaving a glistening trail.

After a while, the furrow faded from his brow. His frown eased.

"Just as bad as before?" she asked, turning her attention to his butterfly tattoo.

This time, he hesitated. "Yes?"

A question. Definite progress.

The new ground she conquered caused his furrowed brow and frown to return with a vengeance. Thankfully, prolonged contact eased him, just as before. By the time she'd covered his entire chest, he'd stopped stiffening altogether and arched into every caress.

Keep it short and sweet! Always end on a positive note.

Though she trembled, thinking she might die of want, she concluded the session while both of them were eager for more. He protested. He protested loudly. Only her promise to start again first thing in the morning pacified him.

But the night proved torturous. A night they spent in different bedrooms. If they were together…

At dawn, she lumbered to the bathroom and took a shower. The water only reminded her of the heat and softness of Baden's skin. *Need to get my hands on him again.*

She pulled on the cashmere robe. A naked Baden waited for her outside the door. He was hard, and he was fierce. Silent, he drew her to the table, stretched atop it, and waited.

Game, set, match.

"You're ready?" Her trembles returned as she moistened her hands with the vanilla-scented oil.

"Beyond."

With the first stroke, he groaned a sound of ragged desperation. With the second, he stiffened. With the third, he…relaxed?

She worked her way down, drawing closer and closer to his shaft, the object of her captivation.

Was he truly ready for more?

Shouldn't rush, just because I'm starved for him. She changed paths, heading up, up; she circled one of his nipples, then the other. He cursed, even as the little brown buds tightened for her.

"Think they can tolerate the feel of my mouth?" Wisps of desire infused her voice. There was no hiding her need. Right now this man *owned* her.

"Think I don't care if they can or not. I want your mouth." Agony and pleasure pulsed from him, a potent black magic that intoxicated her. "Give it to me. Please."

The ache between her legs…too much! But she lowered her head, anyway and flicked her tongue over his nipples. When his moans became harsh demands, she began to suck.

"Katarina." He reached for his erection, as if to stroke it.

"No." She grabbed his wrist, stopping him. "That's mine. I won't share."

His gaze implored her. "Then do something with it. No walking away this time."

She would do something, yes…but not just yet. If she did too much too fast, his agony might completely overshadow his pleasure.

"No walking away," she agreed.

He gripped the edge of the table, his knuckles white as she slid her fingers down, down the ropes of his stomach. Her mouth followed. She dabbled at his navel, tracing her tongue around the edges before caressing and kissing his thigh, teasing him.

When he jerked his leg away from her, she paused, concerned. "Do you need a break?"

"No!" A bead of sweat trickled down his temple, catching in his hair. "Keep going. *Please.*"

Distract. "What did you think of me," she said and licked his hip bone, "the day we met. I know I looked hideous. I remember your disgust."

"The disgust wasn't directed at you but me. I wanted you with a desire I didn't yet understand. I never intended to take you with me, but I couldn't leave you behind. I wasn't strong enough."

The admission did funny things to her insides. "I thought you were there to rescue me, and for once I didn't care about being a damsel in distress. Now I know you *did* rescue me…and that you're one of the best things to ever happen to me."

Pride glinted in his copper eyes. Pride and pleasure. "I'll protect you," he said, the words heavy, as if weighted with a vow. "I'll always protect you."

"And I'll protect you."

But he wasn't done. "You can rely on me, Rina. I'll take care of you."

As lovely as the sentiment was, she didn't want to rely on him. It would create an imbalance in an already imbalanced relationship. When one person always gave and the other always took, the scales never evened out.

Now wasn't the time to tackle such a serious issue, however. "How does your body feel?"

"Ready. I want you. I need you. Take me in your mouth or take me in your body. *Just take me.*"

Ecstasy…agony of her own…both unfurled deep, deep inside her. Perhaps she and Baden weren't so imbalanced, after all. The powerful warrior was willing to *beg* for her. "Are you in pain?"

"Yes, but it's different now. Better and worse at the same time." He bolted to his feet. "I will have you," he all but growled. He hooked his fingers on the lapels of her robe and gave a little push.

The material floated to the floor, leaving her naked. His gaze stroked over her from head to toe, both reverent and ablaze with lust, making her shiver, the intensity of his need feeding her own.

"Yes, you will have me." She brushed her fingertips over his nipples, an urge to bite and scratch him—to leave no part of his body unmarked by her passion—assailing her. Astonishing her. She'd never before experienced such animalistic urges, but damn if she didn't *like* them. "How do you want me?"

"In every way." He gripped her by the waist, carried her to the bed and tossed her atop the mattress. As she bounced, he placed his knees on the edge and crawled toward her. "Spread your legs."

She smiled at him, slow and seductive. "Are you saying it's on till dawn, *pekný?*"

"I'm saying I'm finally taking what's mine."

20

"The only reason a woman should kick her man
out of bed is to make love to him on the floor."

—Amun, keeper of Secrets

Baden rose to his knees. Katarina was, without a
doubt, the most erotic female in creation. With her
naked body angled toward him, she leaned back on
her elbows, thrusting up her breasts and drawing his
attention to the dusky crests in the center.

Destruction purred his approval, issuing no demands. He wanted what Baden wanted. Perhaps even
needed it.

Unable to resist her magnetic allure, he traced his
gaze down the flat plane of her stomach to the tiny
thatch of dark curls already wet with arousal. As commanded, she parted her mile-long legs and bent them
at the knees, placing her feet outside his thighs, offering a full-frontal view of his new paradise.

"Do you like this? Want it?" The husky quality of
her voice as she parroted his words back to him…she
knew the power she wielded over him and reveled in it.

He couldn't fault her. His shaft, already throbbing

with want, wept at the tip. "*Like* is too mild a word."
He trembled. He ached. And he no longer cared about
the pain of skin-to-skin contact. The pain of *not* having
his hands on this woman had already proven far worse.
He'd tossed and turned last night, a man haunted.

"I have to taste you." He sounded drugged, his words
slightly slurred.

"You already have," she teased. But she wasn't as
calm as she appeared. Her nails dug into the mattress.
"Or have you forgotten?"

As if he could *ever* forget. "This time, I want to tap
straight from the source. Let me."

Her eyelids lowered to half mast, too heavy to hold
up. "Drink from me, then."

He slowly threaded his fingers around her ankles to
tug her toward him. She was his to devour. Their gazes
held as he placed her feet on his shoulders, leaving her
completely open to him.

He leaned in, anticipation burning him alive. Waiting…waiting until…she gasped his name, a benedic-
tion, and writhed her hips. Then he did it. Stroked his
tongue over the heart of her pleasure. She cried out, her
passion too great for her small body to contain. *I did
this, caused this.*

Pride coursed through him, even as the sweet, sweet
taste of her threatened to unman him. She was like
candy, a nectar he would crave all the days of his life.
An aphrodisiac. A torch to his discipline.

Destruction demanded more, and Baden was all too
happy to obey. He dove in for another taste but ended
up staying for the entire meal. He licked, sucked and
nibbled, and even thrust his tongue deep inside her,
mimicking sex. She writhed her hips faster, harder,

grinding against his face, chasing his mouth whenever he lifted his head.

"Baden… I want… I need…"

"I know." Yesterday and today she'd reduced him to a quivering mass of sensation. A live wire in need of contact. An outlet for the desire burning him from the inside out. It was only fair he should now return the favor.

As he sucked on her sweet little bundle of nerves, her thighs pressed against his temples. Goose bumps broke out over her luscious skin, and he knew she was close to climaxing. He eased the pressure and began to lap at her, easing her back from the ledge.

Not going to let her fall. Not yet, not yet.

"*Kretén*," she snarled, beating the mattress. Candlelight set her features aglow.

"Curse me all you like, *krásavica*. It won't do you any good. But don't worry. I'll let you have an orgasm… eventually."

She shivered. She cursed him again. "Such a cruel man. I may have to punish you."

"No, darling. You may have to beg me." He wanted her badly, wanted her more than he'd wanted anything or anyone, ever. And he wanted *everything* from her—including her total surrender. He stood and stroked his shaft from base to tip, knowing she liked when he did it. Her eyes gave her away. "You want this? Then ask me nicely."

The soft warmth of her chuckle proved as potent as a caress. "If you aren't careful," she said, pinching her nipples and arching her hips, "I'll make you watch me take my own pleasure—then I'll make you watch me leave you hard and aching."

He laughed, low and husky, surprised to find humor

in an act that had only driven him mad since his return to life. "Walking away will never be an option for you, *krásavica*. Let me show you why." He slid a finger deep inside her, for the first time feeling her inner walls clench around him without any kind of barrier. The heat…the wet…the softness…better than he'd imagined. "You need me inside you."

"And you need to *be* inside me."

More than anything. He fed her a second finger, thrilled as she stretched to accommodate him.

Moaning, she arched to follow his in-and-out glide. Though every cell in his body screamed with urgency, he set an easy pace.

"You were made for this," he praised. *Made for me.*

His sense of possession amplified—*mine, mine, all mine. Will never share.*

Will never let go.

He would keep her, now and forever, he decided. She would be more than a war prize. She would be *the* prize. Having endured a life of war and loss, a death that had brought him centuries of helplessness and captivity, a resurrection that had done the same, he deserved to have a woman—*this* woman—in his bed every night and in his arms every morning.

She was worth *any* hardship.

"Need more of you inside me," she gasped. "All of you. Please. I'm asking…begging so nicely."

She's killing me…but what a magnificent way to go. He worked in another finger, this time preparing her for his width.

"Wait." Gasping, she tried to shy away from his invasion. "Wait. Baden! Hold still for a second. That's not exactly pleasant."

He did as requested, but it cost him threads of his sanity.

Give me everything! Destruction demanded. *Now. Now! Won't hurt her. If we scare her, we'll never have this again.*

A crackling pause. *Ease her,* Destruction commanded next.

She breathed in and out, her walls remaining locked tight around his fingers, refusing to give. He bent and once again flicked his tongue against her tiny bundle of nerves. Another gasp left her, this one more about pleasure than pain.

"Better?"

"Yes, yes, so much better," she purred.

He sucked, hard.

"Yes! I'm close...so close..."

He sucked *harder*, bringing her to a swift and brutal climax. One he didn't allow her to enjoy for long. As she screamed, he withdrew his fingers—the scream became a whimper.

"Baden," she panted, so wonderfully wet she would soak him. "Please."

"You miss me already?" He craved the words almost as much as he craved her little body.

"Yes! I'm empty without you."

"Then you'll have me." His nerve endings were on fire for her. "All of me."

She pointed a trembling finger to the nightstand. "Condom. I was on the pill...not anymore...condom," she repeated when he remained unmoving.

He wasn't sure he could give her children, and the thought suddenly...angered him.

One day, she would want children. A family.

Aleksander could provide both.

Baden's anger prepared to detonate.

"Warrior." Katarina lifted her hips, a silent plea for his fiercest possession. "What are you waiting for? Get the condom and fill me."

Not asking now, but demanding. He liked this better.

He yanked open the only drawer in the nightstand, the contents spilling out. *Contain your strength.* Never had the outcome of a bedding been so important. Bending down, he swiped up a foil packet, ripped it open with his teeth and sheathed his entire length with latex, Katarina watching his every move with abject hunger. *That's my girl.*

He leaned over her and positioned himself for entry. He didn't thrust home, not yet, but flattened his palms at her temples. Their gazes held for several agonizing heartbeats.

"There's no going back after this," he told her. It was a warning. One she had best heed.

Take! Destruction demanded. *No going back, anyway.*

Again, they were in agreement.

"Good." She licked her lips, a sexy little kitty he couldn't resist. "I don't want to go back."

He wasn't sure she'd understood his meaning, and as sweat trickled along his back and chest he wasn't sure he had the control to explain it to her. No, he knew he didn't have the control.

He managed to grit, "You are mine, Rina."

"And you are mine," she whispered.

He could wait no longer. He surged inside her with a single, forceful stroke.

Crying out, she arched up to meet his thrust, sending

him even deeper. Her inner walls clutched him tighter than any fist, slicker than any mouth, and for a moment, incomparable bliss fogged his mind. Pleasure was pain and pain was pleasure, the two so intertwined he wasn't sure where one began and the other ended, only knew he loved every second.

"Pleasant?" he asked.

"Yes! Move in me," she pleaded. Her nails sliced at his back. She bit into his shoulder. "Move *fast*."

Her passion stripped him of any lingering desire to proceed slowly, to savor every second; he pulled back only to surge forward. Again she met his thrust with an arch. Her legs, which were still wrapped around him, squeezed his waist. She surrounded him, possessed him. Savaged him.

"Can't hold back much longer," he told her, hands already combing into her hair to fist the strands and hold her steady for his position. "If I hurt you…scream."

"*Drahý*, I'm going to scream no matter what you do. Give me everything you've got."

He. Was. An. Animal.

Katarina reveled in his every punishing thrust. The headboard bang, bang, banged into the wall, and pictures crashed to the floor. Springs squeaked in the mattress, the struts of the bed scraping against the wood floor.

With every in-and-out glide of his shaft, her nipples scraped against his chest; the friction threw kindling on the fire already spreading through her veins. He awoke sensations in her that she'd never dreamed possible, her nerve endings sizzling, her cells buzzing.

She'd never been so wet, never ached so thoroughly.

He was so big he stretched her and so strong he was probably bruising her, but she loved every second.

He'd once told her women wanted only two things from men: money and power. With him, she wanted affection and sex. Lots and lots of sex. But really, sex and power were synonymous right now, the maddened frenzy of his every stroke flooding her with a feminine prowess she'd never before known.

Weak? Not even close.

"Missing your sweet nipples," he said, his voice nothing but gravel. He paused long enough to bend his head and give each beaded tip a hard suck.

"Baden!" The pleasure! Mind-blowing!

He hooked his elbow under one of her knees and as he surged back up, his shaft slamming deep, he lifted her leg, opening her wider, allowing him to go even deeper. She cried out—then she screamed, an orgasm slamming through her with the force of a battering ram, shattering any fortifications she might have built against his allure.

The clenching of her inner walls soon drove him to the brink. He groaned and quickened his pace, moving faster and faster, harder and harder, prolonging her climax or sending her straight into a second, she wasn't sure which.

So good, so good, so freaking good. Every cell in her body exploded as if it was having an orgasm of its own. She was swept up, consumed, destroyed and remade.

With an animalistic roar, he surged into her a final time, releasing her leg to grip her hips and hold her steady as he jetted into the condom. He sank his teeth into the cord that connected her neck to her shoulder, something he clearly liked to do, pinning her more thoroughly, marking her, too, and she erupted all over again, clinging to him.

Finally, she sagged into the mattress and he collapsed atop her. They were both sweaty, both panting, and though she enjoyed his weight, he rolled over so that he wouldn't crush her.

She curled into his side because, without his body restraining hers, without his length deep inside her, she no longer felt complete—she needed some kind of connection with him...the first man she'd been with since Peter.

Reminders of her darling's death always saddened her. Today the sadness left her far too vulnerable.

Please, please don't let Baden's finish be as deplorable as last time.

When her heartbeat evened out, and he was still beside her, she decided to test the waters. "How do you feel?"

"You can't guess?" There was a teasing note to his tone, and she relaxed.

"Are you in pain?" She traced her finger along the edge of his butterfly tattoo. "Does this hurt you?"

"Ask me again when I awake from my pleasure coma."

She snickered, propping up on her elbow to meet his gaze. Hesitant, she drew her fingertip to his nipple, circling. He didn't flinch, and he didn't grimace, and satisfaction flowed over her like liquid sunshine.

When she lifted her hand, he grabbed her wrist to force her palm back to his chest.

From demanding she never touch him to insisting she never let him go. Oh, how their circumstances had changed!

"Next time," he said, "I'm going to kiss you while I take you."

She smiled at him. "So certain there will be a next time, eh?"

"With this face?" He patted his cheeks. "Yes."

She giggled as he removed the condom, tied it off and tossed it in the trash can. "You are marginally handsome… I suppose." *Always end on a positive note.* "But you are very, very good with your hands. And your mouth."

He stretched out at her side, as if the need to connect haunted him just as fiercely. "You forgot to mention my cock."

She leaned over and ran his earlobe through her teeth. "I didn't forget. I was saving the best for last."

"Were you now?"

"Mmm." She stood to shaky legs and held out her hand. "You've proven your skills in the bedroom. Now it's time to prove your skills in the kitchen. I'm hungry." They needed to be able to keep this good vibe in different situations.

"Nothing is ever free." He took her hand but not to let her pull him to his feet; he yanked her back on the bed—or rather, on top of him. "I'll make you a sandwich…for a price."

Baden puttered around the kitchen with a smile on his face. A smile! His head was clearer than ever, the beast calm, the tension drained from his body and a beautiful woman was asleep in his bed. This was the life he'd always dreamed for himself. The life he'd never thought he'd have.

"You look happy."

Fox. His smile faded. He hated that she'd approached without his senses being alerted—*won't happen again.*

Remembering his promise to Katarina, he nodded at her in greeting.

"The human is good for you," she said.

"Yes." He finished prepping the egg-and-cheese sandwich and returned the leftover ingredients to the refrigerator. "Tell me. Who do you distrust most this day?"

A pause. Then, "The human."

He stiffened. "Why?"

"She makes you happy...but for how long? She's a liability. And what if she's captured and tortured by your enemies? She'll flip faster than you can say *This is shit.* What if she's a spy? I've worked with Hunters, so I know the type. Goodie-goodie, but only on the outside. And what if a faction of Hunters has survived, operating in the shadows? She could be Bait, meant to lure you to your second death."

Was this how he'd sounded, all those centuries ago?

He knew what would come next: an attack against the one she distrusted.

She should fear *Baden.* If she harmed Katarina, he would harm her in turn. A thousand times over.

"Sit at the table," he commanded. "Now."

She forgot her torrent of suspicion long enough to grumble, "Wow. Are you always this affable?"

"Yes. Do you want my help or not?"

She sat with a huff.

He cracked the egg into a pan, saying, "When the demon hits you with thoughts of someone's possible betrayal, write down every good thing you remember about the person. Nice things they've said to you. Kind deeds they've done. The way they smile. Then read the list over and over until the demon shuts his foul, lying mouth." For years, those lists had been the only thing capable of stopping an attack against his best friends.

She regarded him warily. "If making lists is the golden ticket to peace, why did you allow yourself to be killed?"

She knew the truth? Katarina would not have told her.

Sensing the direction of his thoughts, Fox added, "Distrust shared the memory with me."

Of course. The bastard. "I abandoned my lists. Listening to the demon was just...easier. I'd been fighting for so long, I'd grown weary of it all." He'd allowed his light—his hope, the heart of him, the protective side so much a part of his nature—to be snuffed out.

A light Katarina had relit.

Will protect her at any cost.

Perhaps he should rename the beast Construction, he thought with an inner laugh. His other half no longer tore down but now built up.

Only with my human.

My *human.* Baden put the finishing touches on the sandwich.

Galen sailed into the kitchen. The blond paused when he spotted them and arched a brow. "Am I interrupting a gabfest, girls?"

"Yes," Fox said at the same time Baden said, "No." The eggs done, he dumped them atop the toasted bread. "I'm done."

"That's his impolite way of saying he can't be away from his precious another second," Galen remarked. "Oh! Breakfast sandwich!"

"Touch it and lose a hand." The ends of his fingers burned, the claws threatening to emerge—oops, they *had* emerged. They clanked against the porcelain.

Galen rolled his eyes. "BTW. Could you and the little missus keep it down the next time you go at it like rabbits? Some of us, and I'm not mentioning any names—" he hiked his thumb in Fox's direction "—need our beauty *Z*s."

"Some of us, and I'm not mentioning any names—" Baden pointed directly at Galen "—need a dagger through the heart."

"Haven't you heard? I don't currently have a heart." A tinge of bitterness seeped from his tone. "Word on the street is I've never had one."

"Here's an idea. Don't tattle on your friends after helping them plan a B&E, ensuring they get caught. Don't send human assassins after them when they curse you for your betrayal, and don't complain when one of them gets a little some-some while you have to rely on old faithful." He motioned to Galen's right hand.

The warrior surprised him, laughing rather than attacking. "Are you fifteen? A little *some-some*. Really? That's what we're calling it now?"

He shrugged. He'd heard his friends call the act many ridiculous things.

"Also," Galen added. "You need to work on forgiveness. Words hurt."

"So do daggers." To end the conversation, he flashed to the bedroom and placed the sandwich on the nightstand.

Katarina still slept. He was loath to disturb her, and yet need for her consumed him. He knew the bliss of her touch and now suspected there would never be a moment when he wouldn't crave it.

He decided to distract himself by granting her a boon she hadn't asked for…at the same time proving just how much she did, in fact, need him.

He made an adjustment in his mind. Because, according to Hades, he could always flash home. A loophole in the king's plan to keep him contained. For the next few minutes, he considered Aleksander's country estate his home. He flashed and stalked through the halls. Each of the male's closest advisors and guards had a room, and he flashed in and out so swiftly, he went unnoticed. It was only a matter of time before he found Katarina's brother, lying on a floor, a tourniquet tied to his arm, a needle sticking out of his vein.

The male was passed out, vomit pooling under his head. If he hadn't been turned on his side, he would have suffocated to death already.

Kill. A command born of anger rather than a possible risk to their survival.

No. Despite everything the male had done to Katarina, she would mourn him. Or rather, mourn the boy he'd once been.

Baden grabbed him by the hair and flashed to the cell where he'd kept Aleksander. Where Aleksander's severed hand still remained, he realized, allowing him to continuously flash without having to adjust his thought process. He then flashed in food, bottles of water and a bucket. Enough supplies to last a week.

He texted Torin to find out if anything else would be needed and ended up raiding a pharmacy to gather meds that would help with detoxing.

The male would get clean, whether he wanted to do so or not.

We'll be rewarded? Destruction asked.

Yes, and Baden knew just what he wanted…

21

"I handle my problems the old-fashioned way.
Gasoline and a match."

—Kane, former keeper of Disaster

Cameo's mind buzzed with depressing statistics as
she watched the clock. There were nearly two hundred
million orphans in the world, and nearly fifteen percent of them would commit suicide before turning eighteen. Over twenty thousand children died every year
due to poverty.

Naturally, every minute—every second—was agony.

But finally, blessedly, the last of her friends retired
to his bedroom. The coast was clear, her friends now
busy having sex.

Proof: soft laughter and breathy moans drifted from
cracks in the walls.

Let the marathon begin, she thought with no small
amount of envy. After the attack at the fortress, everyone was relieved to be alive and now that they were
healed, they were celebrating privately.

There were, of course, two stains on their happiness.
William's abduction of Gilly and Baden's most recent

move. Everyone worried he would be killed again. But Galen—the piece of shit—had been texting updates about the male, and so far all was well. There'd been no real problems, the human girl, Katarina, keeping Baden centered.

The way Lazarus once kept me centered?

Cameo had to know. Desperation clawed at her. Hope taunted her. She had the chance to taste happiness again—she *had* to taste happiness again.

And now, she had a plan.

According to what she'd been told, she'd met Lazarus when she was sucked into another realm. So, it stood to reason she could meet him again if she allowed herself to be sucked *back* into the other realm.

For such a journey, she needed three artifacts and a painting. The Cloak of Invisibility, the Paring Rod and the Cage of Compulsion. The painting had been done by Danika, the All-seeing Eye, who was able to see into heaven and hell. The pretty blonde gave life to the things she saw, those images acting as a guide through the realms. Without the right painting, Cameo could end up *farther* away from Lazarus.

The good news? When Keeley had flashed the women and children to the safe house, she'd flashed the artifacts and paintings, too.

The bad news? The artifacts and paintings were locked up, and Cameo hadn't been given a key.

Her friends knew her and had guessed her plan before she'd even conceived it. *I'm going back to him... going back to Lazarus.*

Her heart fluttered wildly, and a thousand butterflies danced in her stomach.

I know Lazarus, Strider had told her. *He might have*

scarified his life for mine, but his reasons were not altruistic. He's dangerous, the son of a creature known as the father of all monsters.

Did Lazarus's reasons for saving Strider really matter? He'd saved her friend. How bad could he truly be?

And really, Lazarus's sacrifice got him trapped in another realm and made him a spirit being. A spirit being she *must* have touched. How else would he have made her happy?

I want to touch him again. I want him *to touch* me.

Pleasure…oh, how she craved it.

I don't think you're hearing us, Kaia had piped up. *Lazarus is the consort of a Harpy. A Harpy who will come for him—and you!—if she discovers his spirit is out there and you're trying to get your groove on with it.*

One, from the info Cameo had managed to glean, Lazarus had never considered the Harpy his mate. And two, if there was even the slightest chance she could change the course of her life for the better, she had to go for it. Which meant she had to do a little breaking and entering tonight. Once she had the artifacts in her possession, she had to say goodbye to her friends.

This time, when she entered the realm, she might not be coming back.

Gillian knew she'd reached the end of the line. The last stop on the road of her life. The place where she would take her eternal dirt nap.

Stick a fork in me, I'm done.

She couldn't sleep, didn't even have the strength to toss and turn, and her body hurt as if countless needles had been plunged into every organ. Her hands and feet were ice-cold, making it impossible for the rest of her to get warm. Every time she managed to take a breath, she heard a strange wheeze.

Puck had told her she'd have a few weeks to live, but she hadn't even made it a full week.

Not ready. Have never really lived.

Tears burned her eyes. She'd spent the bulk of her childhood afraid of her stepdad and stepbrothers. She'd spent the past three years afraid of immortal warriors who'd never harmed her, who'd only ever protected her. She'd spent the past three years afraid of everything and everyone. Foolish! That fear had robbed her of so much, and she had no one but herself to blame. She'd chosen to hide in her room rather than go out with friends from school and create happy memories.

William was beside himself with worry and grief. This morning he'd paced beside her bed. He'd yelled at several doctors, and she was pretty sure he even killed a couple of them—or all of them. Cleaning crews had come in and out, ordered not to look at or talk to her, but her mind had remained in such a haze it had all seemed like a bad dream.

He'd even yelled at his father again.

Transform her! Now!

I can't.

You can.

All right, I can but I won't. It will kill her, son.

She's dying anyway.

This is true, but I won't be the instrument of her demise. You would never forgive me.

If she dies, I'll tear this world apart.

Bond with her, then.

I...can't. You know this.

Wrong. You won't, as you shouldn't. But this doesn't

have to be the end for her. You can capture her spirit when it leaves her body. I'll gift her with a pair of serpentine wreaths and—

No! I won't allow you to enslave or corrupt her.

I vow I will never call on her services, Hades had said, sounding offended.

You wouldn't be able to help yourself. The war with Lucifer heats daily. New players are taking sides. Pawns are being destroyed. The coming months in your court will be bad, and they'll be bloody. There will be major losses for both armies, and I won't allow her to witness such horrors.

When Hades reminded William that he was a prime target of assassins, that several attempts had already been made on his life while he'd scoured the world for doctors—and one of those attempts had nearly proved successful because he'd been distracted—Gillian had begun to cry in earnest. Her death would only distract him further.

"I'll find a way to save you," William said now, drawing her back into the present. How frantic he sounded. How agonized. "You just have to give me a little more time, poppet. Hold on for me. All right?"

Despite her attempt to comfort him, he was going to blame himself for her death, wasn't he?

Well, then. The first item on her bucket list suddenly crystallized. *Save William from himself.*

She had to survive this. No if, ands or buts.

So far, her best chance was marriage to Puck. William would never offer. He'd made that very clear. Maybe he'd rethink things now that the end was inevitable, but Puck had told her there was a chance she'd make her husband mortal. She couldn't risk weakening

William in such a way. Especially while his enemies circled like sharks that had scented blood.

Puck, however, was willing to take the risk. At least, he'd been ready…however long ago. Was he still?

If so, she would do it. She would marry him, she decided. She would live, even if she made him mortal.

The sex thing…if he insisted, she could maybe probably hopefully endure it. But maybe he wouldn't insist. He was the keeper of Indifference, would easily turn to someone else, someone other than his wife—despite his vows to the contrary.

William, on the other hand, would want sex. He would need it; he was a highly sexual creature with the drive of ten alpha males. But he also had a streak of honor he could hide from others but not from Gillian. He wouldn't turn to someone else after he'd pledged his life to hers, unless she granted him permission to cheat…

And she would. Wholeheartedly.

And she wouldn't even cry when he did it. Really.

But…a good husband would never stray, even with permission. Correct? Gillian's biological father—a saint!—never had, while her stepdad never stopped. He was one of the worst human beings ever to walk the earth.

Deep down, Gillian suspected she would grow to hate William if—when—he strayed. Which was ridiculous, considering her stance on the matter! But in the end, they would both be miserable.

So. Yes. Her husband had to be Puck. All she had to do was find him. Or rather, draw him here, because there was no way she could leave this bed.

She whimpered. How was she supposed to draw him here? She couldn't even lift her head…couldn't think… think…couldn't…

Her mind drifted in and out of a thick black cob-
web. The times she was aware, the wheezing in her
lungs grew worse.

Suddenly her body was lifted from the bed, the most
delicious heat surrounding her. Strong arms were now
banded around her, and a heart beat against her ear.
Confusion settled in. Was William taking her outside?
Going to let her die by the water?

"Gillian!" he roared, and he sounded far away.

Not in his arms, after all, she realized, the familiar
scent of peat smoke and lavender finally hitting her
awareness.

Sweet relief overtook her confusion. Puck had come
for her.

"Sorry, lass, but I've decided not to let you die. The
last time I left you, I felt something. I think it was regret, and I wish to experience it again."

His greatest aspiration was to feel *regret*? His life
was as sad as her own.

"Will…marry," she told him. She tried to track their
location, but everything was a blur. He must be doing
his too-fast-to-track thing. "What…need…do?"

"Just repeat after me." He turned a corner, her head
spinning. "I give you my heart, soul and body." He
waited until she'd echoed him, even though it took her
a while; she had to push out the words between panting breaths. "I tie my life to yours, and when you die,
I die with you."

The tone of his voice had deepened, as if the words
he'd just spoken carried more significance than any he'd
previously uttered.

The seriousness of what she was doing registered.
There would be no going back. Once they were bonded,

he would be her husband. They would be a unit. A family. And even if she *wasn't* having sex with him, he would have to come first. Puck before William.

The burn returned to her eyes. Was she really going to do this?

Her hands and feet grew colder by the second, but her muscles didn't have enough juice to shiver. She was so close to the end. Too close! So, yes, she was really going to do this.

Again, she echoed his statement.

He proceeded. "This I say, this I do."

"This I say, this I do."

When he said no more, she realized they were done. She expected something wondrous to happen. A tidal wave of strength. Warmth. Something! She got zilch, zero, nada.

"It didn't work," she managed to whisper.

"Don't worry, lass." Puck finally stopped running. He set her down on something soft then straightened, severing contact. The only bit of heat she'd had vanished. "We aren't done yet."

He pressed something even warmer against her lips. Something wet. A copper tang coated her tongue, and she gagged. Blood?

"Swallow," he commanded.

She shook her head in negation, the trickle sliding down her cheek rather than her throat.

"You will." He held her nose and jaw with one hand, preventing further movement, and held his wrist over her open mouth with the other, forcing her to obey.

Well. There was no way she was going to complete the ceremony now. He was too high-handed. Too uncaring about her plight.

But the blood slid into her stomach at last, and another black shroud covered her mind. This time, the gossamer fabric didn't send her into a state of unawareness. Puck lifted her arm, cut her wrist—the sharp sting made her cringe—then licked away the well of blood.

"Blood of my blood, breath of my breath," he said. "Until the end of time. Repeat the words."

"No."

"Then you die, and William and I will war for nothing."

Argh! She couldn't allow William to get sucked into another war. She repeated the words and finally, amazingly, the "thing" happened, and then some. Lance after lance of strength sped through her. The warmth inside her sparked hotter and hotter, and soon she felt as if she'd swallowed the sun.

A pang of sadness—she'd never experienced anything so magnificent, but she wasn't experiencing it with William.

The black faded from her mind completely and suddenly she could see. Sunlight! An open, airy bedroom. The decadent scent of lavender coated the air, stronger than ever before. She lay on a large bed, wisps of white fabric billowing from four posts.

I'm alive! Laughing giddily, she jolted upright. Puck perched beside her, watching her with a blank expression, and in a rush of sudden gratitude, she threw her arms around his neck to hug him. He'd saved her, despite the risk to himself—oh, no! The risk! Would William punish him?

No, no. Of course not. Puck had saved her, and that's what William—her friend—had wanted.

And since this was basically a marriage of convenience, she and Puck could even move into the fortress.

Or she could return without her husband in tow. Nothing had to change!

She tried to pull away, but his arms wrapped around her and held on tight. *Too sexual!* her mind screamed. Too much, too fast. She wrenched backward, cutting off all contact as her heart hammered a staccato rhythm. He frowned at her.

"I'm sorry," she muttered.

He said nothing, continued peering at her as sunlight washed over him. Maybe it was the bond but…he was somehow even more beautiful to her than before. The color of his skin seemed deeper, richer, and the silken strands of his hair gleamed. Even the razors braided throughout were lovely, the silver metal mesmerizing to her. She could make out every individual lash framing his gorgeous eyes. The sharpness of his nose gave his face an arresting strength only magnified by the hard slash of his lips.

He reached out and after a moment's hesitation, brushed a lock of her hair behind her ear. His fingers left a trail of fire in their wake, and she found herself leaning into his touch.

"You are exquisite," he said.

A blush burned her cheeks. "Thank you. And you—"

"Are not." His tone was a little harsher now. "I know."

"No. Don't put words—"

"Gillian!" William's roar echoed off the walls. He burst through the door a split second later, shards of wood raining in every direction. He had a dagger in each hand and the promise of death in his neon red eyes.

His dark hair billowed around his face, lifted by a wind she couldn't feel, and for a moment, she would have sworn lightning coursed under the surface of his skin. But the most shocking part of his transformation? The shadows stretching over his shoulders. William had wings!

He focused on Puck. "You're going to die—but not until you've begged for mercy for centuries to come. She's mine, and I protect what's mine."

Her mind snagged on one word. *Die.* "No," she said with a shake of her head.

"Actually, she's mine." Puck stood slowly, completely unafraid, and Gillian's mouth dried. "I would never harm my girl."

The lightning returned to William's skin. He stepped forward, lifting a dagger, ready to throw it.

Stretching out her arms to ward him off, Gillian leaped to her feet, making sure to shield Puck. "William. You can't hurt him."

His smile held different shades of evil. "Oh, poppet. I assure you I can."

"You don't understand. He saved me. He's…he's my husband." The word tasted foreign on her tongue. "Hurting him hurts me. I think. Right?"

Puck nodded at her.

A mix of shock and fury played over William's beloved features. "The bond," he said, tone now hollow. "You agreed to it."

Tears filled her eyes as she nodded. Things *were* going to change. "I didn't want to die, and you said you wouldn't bond with me. I heard you." But now that her head was clear, her body free of pain, she wasn't sure she'd made the right decision.

She might have ruined *everything*.

William might never forgive her for this. And Puck…

he might want to kill Torin, her friend. In her pain, she had forgotten his vengeance against the warrior.

"You have no idea what you've done," he told her quietly. "He's using you for something."

"I know." They were using each other.

"You know? Do you know you belong to him, and that the ties can never be broken?"

Yes, and it suddenly flayed her. "I'm sorry," she whispered.

Puck placed a possessive hand on her shoulder, and it felt...right. But it also felt wrong. She did her best to hide her dueling feelings from the two men.

William pressed one of the daggers flat against his heart and took a step backward, as if pushed. For the first time in their association, all pretense and civility were stripped from him. She saw desire, such intense desire, and wanted to sob and hug him and run from him and sob some more.

"I can lock him up," he told her, "keep him safe and keep him away from you."

A protest bubbled up; she bit her tongue, only a whimper escaping.

"Go ahead. Try." Puck's grip tightened on her.

I'm in a tug-of-war with two apex predators, and I'm no good for either of them.

And...and...why did William even want her? She was damaged goods. Messed up. Broken. Puck, on the other hand, she understood. She—her situation—elicited his emotions, however weak they were. However temporary.

How disappointed would he be if she failed to help him feel something new?

"Gillian. Do you want me to lock him up?" The words lashed from William.

The tears returned. She couldn't repay Puck's kindness with cruelty. "No. I'm sorry," she repeated.

In a snap, his expression blanked, and it broke her heart. He said nothing more, simply turned and strode out of the room.

What have I done?

With a sob, she fell back on the mattress. Puck sat beside her and ran his fingers through her hair.

"Do you love him?" he asked when finally she quieted.

Why lie? "Yes." Her tear ducts swelled and dried. "He's my best friend."

"I will be your best friend now."

As her husband—*still weird*—continued to run his fingers through her hair, she relaxed, a sense of calm enveloping her. No, not calm but…indifference? Just then, she didn't care about anything, and it was nice. The bond at work?

"Am I immortal?" she asked. "Or did I make you human?"

"I told you. I'm the dominant."

So. She was immortal. Now, she would live an eternity knowing she'd hurt William in the worst possible way. That she'd traded one hell for another.

"We will cement our bond now," he said, standing to remove his shirt.

She gave a violent shake of her head. "No. No sex. Ever. I give you permission to be with others. As many others as you want, but never me."

His frown returned. "We are husband and wife."

"I know, but I told you I never experienced desire and I meant it."

He thought for a moment, nodded. "Very well. It shall be as you wish." He turned on his heel and left through the same door William had taken, and the tear ducts she'd thought wrung dry welled with a new flood of moisture.

22

"Game of Thrones? No. Game of loans. I'm going
to loan my foot to your ass."

—Taliyah, the Cold Hearted

Katarina rested her head against Baden's shoulder and
petted her fingers along the ropes of strength in his
chest, her mind replaying the past few hours. First, he'd
read a text from Torin and cursed.

William is on a rampage. Gilly is better—but oops,
she's married to a dude named Pukinn/Puck/Dead Man
Walking. Oh, & she's maybe probably immortal so Willy's rage is gonna last FOREVER.

Baden told Katarina the bond had made the formerly
human girl immortal, the same way Ashlyn's bond to
Maddox had made her immortal, entwining their fu-
tures. Then he'd made sweet, sweet love to Katarina.
Afterward, he'd held her close and they'd whispered
silly secrets in the dark.

She'd told him how, when she was five years old,
her father convinced her she could magically change

stoplights. If she blew the lights a kiss, he'd said, red would turn to green. To this day, she blew kisses to the lights whenever she drove.

Baden told her how, centuries ago, he had allowed Paris to break his arm with a sledgehammer, because Paris had sworn up and down women loved nothing more than kissing an injury and making it better. Only, a kiss hadn't made it better. So he'd broken *both* of Paris's arms.

"You didn't kill him?" she'd asked. "Baden, I'm so proud of you!"

"The fact that I restrained myself is what earned my nickname. The Gentleman of Mount Olympus."

She'd laughed, and he'd tickled her. She'd begged him to stop, even as she'd hoped he would continue. He'd missed out on so much throughout the course of his life. Childish games, innocent fun…connection.

They'd made love again, and he'd fallen asleep with a smile—and the whisper of a single word on his lips. Marriage.

Was he considering making her immortal through the marriage bond? Was she?

No, no. Of course not. They were only temporary. That hadn't changed…had it?

She studied him now. Without the cares of the world and the demands of the beast pulling him in different directions, his features were almost boyish. And *she* had helped get him to that point.

"You stopped," he said, his voice deeper than usual, raspier, too. He turned his head to meet her gaze, and she gasped. His pupils consumed his irises, hiding the copper she found so beautiful. Flickers of red danced in the black. Blood stars. "Start again."

"Stopped what?" she asked, confused.

He clasped onto her wrist with a too-tight grip, as if he didn't know his own strength, and moved her hand up and down his chest. "Do this." He released her. "Do not stop again."

Baden wasn't usually so harsh with her and understanding suddenly dawned. Those eyes... She was talking directly to the beast, wasn't she? This wasn't the first time it had happened, either.

Tread carefully. The beast needed far more taming than Baden. He was wild, unpredictable. "You like being stroked?"

Short and sweet. Always end on a positive note.

"No."

She almost laughed. Almost. His expression held no hint of playfulness. "Why do you command me to continue, then?"

"I like being stroked *by you.* You are weak. No threat."

Argh! Not another naysayer. What would it take to prove to these people—and creatures—she possessed strength, just a different kind of strength than they possessed? "What else do you like?"

"Blood. Death. Vengeance. Never betray me, woman."

"As if I would dare," she said drily.

He glared at her. "You mock me?"

"I tease you. There's a difference. One is cruel, one is sweet. Sweet makes me happy."

Slowly the tension drained from him. "I think I like when you're happy."

"I'm glad. I like when you are happy, too."

"Only because you are frightened of me." He said the words as if they were an undisputed fact. "You are wise, at least. Sometimes."

"I'm not frightened of you," she replied, tracing her finger around one of his nipples, then the other. "Why should I be? We're friends."

His brow furrowed with confusion. "I have no friends. Friends are a hindrance."

"Friends are a blessing. They guard your back and—"

"I trust no one at my back." He barked the words, his anger pricked.

Still, she continued as if he hadn't spoken. No risk, no reward. "They stroke you when you need to be stroked."

Now he pursed his lips, unable to issue a rebuke without encouraging her to stop.

"They make you smile when you're sad," she added. "They fill you with joy when sorrow tries to overtake you. They shine light in your darkness."

"I can see in the dark," he grumbled.

The anger had left him, at least, the danger passed. She breathed a sigh of relief.

"Your brother hasn't guarded your back, and he hasn't been a blessing to you. He hurt you."

"Yes. There's no denying that. But I never said he was my friend."

A moment passed in silence as he pondered her statement. Then he said, "He won't hurt you again. He's now locked away, unable to buy drugs or even contact another human."

Destruction might as well have placed paddles over her heart. "He is?"

"We made sure of it. For you."

For me. "Thank you." Oh, she knew Dominik had to want to stay clean for this to succeed when he was freed, but this…this was a gift. "All right, big guy. We're going to do a trust exercise." Her gift to Baden *and* Destruction.

His frown returned in a hurry. "I trust—"

"No one. I know. But we're still going to do the exercise."

"Woman, you cannot force me—"

She placed her finger over his mouth, silencing him. His eyes widened, as if he couldn't believe her daring. "Your commentary isn't appreciated. Be quiet."

He nipped at her fingertip. "You are brave. And foolish."

Not so brave—and foolish—as determined to win this creature over. "Roll over."

"No." His teeth flashed in a scowl. "If you attempt to harm me, I will have to kill you."

Not a threat, but a promise. LGB? Pretty high. "Roll over," she repeated anyway, giving him a little push. "I'm going to stroke your back."

His muscles hardened into rocks. "You're stronger than before." He latched onto her wrist to bring her hand to his nose. As he sniffed, rage turned his pupils to smoke, dark tendrils wafting over his irises. "You carry the faint scent of hellhounds, and yet the race has been extinct for centuries. How is this possible?"

Hellhounds? Her? Impossible. Unless…

An idea took root, and she struggled to catch her breath. "I know so little about your immortal world, but I love dogs. Tell me about these hellhounds."

His distaste for the subject was keen. "Some secured the underworld while others hunted and captured spirits who managed to escape. They communicated telepathically—what one knew, they all knew—and they could flash between realms."

Her idea grew branches, horror sprouting at the ends like ripening fruit. "Were the people they bit... infected?" Her mouth dried. "Like, say, a werewolf."

"In a way. But there were very few bite-survivors. Once a hellhound tasted someone's blood, the need to feed on that specific person eclipsed everything else."

What a relief! Her dogs couldn't be hellhounds. If they'd actually bitten her, they would have devoured her. "How do you know this?"

"The male who imprisoned me controlled a pack. They...played with my limbs."

Her stomach roiled. She *ached* for the boy he'd been. "I'm so sorry." The words weren't good enough. *No* words were good enough.

His grip tightened enough to make her cry out in pain.

He gentled his hold, saying, "As children, immortals cannot regenerate. But I'm more than immortal. And I never forget a wrong done to me. If hellhounds managed to survive, they must be eradicated."

Despite her lingering horror about his past, protective instincts flared. To destroy an entire race for the crimes of a few? No!

—*You need help?*—

No, no. She projected her thoughts and prayed the animals heard. They were enclosed in the bathroom, but they were totally able to claw their way free. *I'm fine. Stay where you are.*

If she was wrong, if the race had changed, had learned to control the bloodlust and the pups were indeed hellhounds…if Destruction turned his wrath on them…

There would be hell to pay.

"Baden never mentioned a hellhound scent," she said.

"His senses aren't as highly developed."

Keeping her expression neutral proved to be a challenge, but she did it. "Well. As you said, hellhounds are extinct. Centuries have passed. Your nose could be playing tricks on you. Or maybe hellhounds once lived here. The place is old. Now. Stop stalling and—roll—over."

He obeyed at last, and she knew it wasn't because he'd suddenly decided to trust her. He probably intended to test her. A test she would pass with an A++, gold star, or whatever grading system he used.

She trailed her fingertips down the ridges of his spine, over the knots between his shoulders and down, down to the tight globes of his ass, continuing until he melted into the mattress. Soon, he began to purr.

"You're so hard and soft at the same time," she said.

"You like this." A demand, not a question.

"I do." She increased the pressure of her touch, massaging his muscles. His purrs soon became…snores? He'd fallen asleep? Really? A smile tugged at the corners of her lips. Clearly, this beauty had just bagged and tagged *two* beasts.

As morning sunlight poured into the bedroom, Baden tugged on a pair of battle fatigues. He was a bit unbalanced. Destruction was calm, almost content— would he next break out in song like a Disney princess?

I'm happy.

I know. And it's weirding me out.

Baden anchored weapons to his arms, his waist and

ankles, his focus remaining on Katarina as she ate the "thanks for your help" breakfast Fox had delivered. Pancakes and eggs. There were dark smudges on her forearms. Definitely not dirt. Probably bruises. Anger… He'd handled her roughly. Next time he would have to be more careful.

Her features were soft, luminous, her skin still flushed from this morning's debauchery.

The phone in his pocket vibrated, and he checked the screen. A text from Torin.

William wants revenge against the satyr & our help to get it

William would have to call in his favor if he desired Baden's help. Two birds, one stone. "Where are the dogs?" he asked Katarina.

Her head canted to the side, as if she were listening for the pitter-patter of their feet. "In the backyard playing. Why?"

He frowned at her. "You can hear them from here?" The windows were closed, the yard on the other side of the palace.

Though color stained her cheeks, she shrugged off the oddity as unimportant. "I'm a momma bear, and they're my cubs." She smiled at him, the sweetness not quite reaching her eyes. "You and Destruction better not hurt them."

Why would she say such a thing? "I would never. Why would you think otherwise?"

She licked her lips, clearly nervous. "Destruction mentioned his hatred for hellhounds, and I hope the hatred doesn't extend to all canines."

"The beast speaks to you?" Anger bloomed. "Without me?"

"Sometimes," she said with a shrug.

Baden hated the thought of the beast interacting with her without his aid. "He hates hellhounds for a good reason. His mother sold him to the Master of Dark Pleasures. The former king of the underworld kept young... sex slaves." Last night, the horrific memories had invaded his dreams. "Destruction ran and hellhounds gave chase...dragged him back to hell."

The color drained from Katarina's cheeks. "I *despise* the horrors he suffered. I do. But not all packs are—were—ambassadors of evil, I'm sure."

Katarina, forever the dog lover. "Our pups will never suffer at his hand."

Her eyes flared with hope. "You vow it?"

Her lack of trust cut at him, but he looked past it. From the beginning, he'd told this woman to fear him. He'd earned this. "I do."

"Thank you." Changing gears, she looked him over and whistled. "Sexy man. Are you headed out on another mission?"

"I am."

"Well. If you refrain from killing today, I'll do *very* naughty things to you...with my mouth."

Both he and Destruction roared with a desire so hot the flames might never be extinguished. "I want that. And I *will* have that. Today. I go to see Aleksander."

Her eyes widened. "You're going to let him live?"

"I am. But he must sever his tie with you. Afterward, I'll lock him away. He'll never be freed, will die in his cell."

Katarina set her plate on the nightstand and blew

him a kiss. "You, Baden, are a wonderful man. Oh! In all the excitement, I forgot to tell you Alek's mother is the one who gave him the coin."

His mother? Who was his mother, and how had *she* gotten it?

Destruction supplied the answer, pushing a memory through a dark miasma of rage, blood and death.

A harem took shape in Baden's mind. In his early days as king, Hades had kept a harem filled with beautiful women, immortals and humans alike. Anyone who'd caught his fancy.

I take what I want. No one stops me.

A blonde woman…one of his favorites, for a while, at least…was an angel who'd fallen for him, literally as well as figuratively, abandoning her home in the sky to live with him. Her wings had been removed by her sister, leaving thick, jagged scars on her back. He'd liked scars, and she'd liked the homage he paid them.

But she hadn't been content inside the harem, had been insulted every time she'd had to share him with others, and she'd eventually lashed out, killing his other women in cold blood. He'd come close to killing her in turn, but in a rare moment of mercy, he'd exiled her to the earth instead.

Soon after, he'd learned the coin he'd kept under heavy guard had gone missing. He'd known instantly who'd taken it. Her only means of vengeance.

He'd gone after her. No one he'd marked could hide from him. Ever.

That day, she'd laughed at him.

You want the coin? Too bad. You'll never find it. Especially if you kill me. The moment I die, it will be delivered to Lucifer.

He'd left her, then, sending one of his spies to remain near her at all times. Over the years, she'd married a human male and bore him a son—Aleksander—and by all accounts, the son who loved her had been the one who'd savagely torn out her insides. But, being only half immortal rather than fully, Aleksander would never have had the strength to overpower her. Which meant she'd allowed him to kill her.

Later that same day, Aleksander had cornered Hades's spy and told him to deliver a message: *I have the coin. I have no plans to use it—presently. But I, like my mother, have taken measures to ensure it's delivered to Lucifer upon my death.*

You should have told me sooner, Baden snapped at Destruction.

Sharing secrets is as new to me as it is to you.

In the present, Katarina climbed to her knees and wound her arms around his neck. "Where did you go, *drahý*?"

He loved when she called him darling. Even Destruction approved. The nickname told nothing of their strength but everything about the softening of their woman.

"I was right. Aleksander isn't human," he said. "His mother was a fallen angel."

"How do you know this?"

"Everything is here, thanks to Hades." He tapped his temple. "Sometimes I must dig. Sometimes the beast willingly offers."

She pressed her perfect breasts against his chest, and he lamented the shirt that prevented the skin-to-skin contact he now craved more than breath. "Again I wonder how I missed my husband's—"

He nipped at her lips. "That word is forbidden to you."

She smiled slowly at him. "Because you're jealous?"

More than he'd ever dreamed possible.

"Well, you basically have a husband, too," she pointed out. "You're bound to Hades."

Baden shuddered, and she laughed.

So beautiful...so bright. "Katarina," he said and cupped the back of her neck. His chest constricted. "Tell me you need me."

Her good humor faded, and she licked her lips. "No way. I won't lie."

"Tell me," he insisted.

"Never! I've trained dogs that would make you piss your pants in fear. I became their leader, the one *they* relied on for protection. I've spearheaded a business, taking it from a moderate success to an international phenomenon. And just so you know, showing mercy requires more strength than doling out vengeance. One fights an urge, the other indulges it."

He called himself a thousand kinds of fool for placing her in a defensive position. He eased off—for now—but he needed her admission like he needed the bands: both were crucial to his survival.

"Pandora has Aleksander. I'll resist the urge to hurt her. I'll even be gentle with her. Will that make you happy?"

"Yes." Katarina softened as she toyed with the ends of his hair. "But be careful out there. She's one wily bitch."

"You're beginning to sound as if you like me."

She pursed her beautiful lips before saying, "I... might."

A very Katarina answer. Stubborn while remaining mysterious.

"I'll return to you. Nothing in this world or any other can stop me." He placed a hard, swift kiss on her lips, then another, and her tongue came out to play with his. If he didn't flash now, he wouldn't flash at all, his shaft already throbbing for her.

He gave her a final kiss before leaving—that he could be parted from her was a miracle—and appeared in...what looked to be a horror movie.

Screams echoed from walls splattered with blood. Black goo flowed in rivers across a concrete floor, with organs floating along the surface. The scent of sulfur and brimstone saturated the air, stinging his nostrils. His lungs seized in an effort to expel the tainted particles.

Demons were here.

These particular minions had long, hairy limbs—some had claws, some had multiple horns—their different parts piled throughout the room. Pandora must have been fighting for hours.

There was a human arm amid the debris, a chain still shackled around the biceps.

Either Aleksander was free or Aleksander was dead.

Baden palmed his semiautomatics, the ones with axes protruding from the handles, and rushed down a winding hallway, following the sound of the screams. The lightbulbs had been busted from every source, the surrounding darkness thick, and yet he had no problem cataloging every detail as Destruction focused with laserlike intensity.

Lucifer tries again, the beast snarled. *And he will fail again.*

A toddler-size creature with eight legs dropped from the ceiling. It had been waiting for prey. Its mouth stretched wide, creating a cavernous hole big enough to fit a watermelon—or Baden's head. Its teeth were small but sharp and buzzed like a motorized saw.

Two quick shots, one to its eye and one to its mouth. Bits of enamel flew through the air like shrapnel. As Baden raced past it, he slashed through its head with the axes, ending its fight.

Inside the bedroom, four furry creatures dragged a bloody Pandora to the far wall, the tips of their legs as sharp as daggers. Daggers they shoved into her shoulders, torso and legs. Even under her serpentine wreaths, preventing the metal from touching her skin.

She was pinned in place. Warrior that she was, she continued to struggle using the only weapon she had left—her teeth. She bit at her captors, ripping off an ear then the tip of a chin. The taste of blood frenzied her. She fought for more.

Rage flared. Baden wasn't fond of Pandora, but no one else would ever be allowed to harm her.

Red eyes lit on him. Smaller creatures clawed free from the fur of the larger ones, cackling with glee. Considered him an easy target, did they?

They would learn.

As Baden strode deeper into the room, he crossed his arms at the elbows and slowly pulled them apart. His fingers remained on the triggers until his body formed a T, ensuring a steady stream of bullets sprayed. The creatures merely absorbed the hits and launched at him.

He twirled the guns so that he gripped the barrels. *Slash, slash, slash.* The axes removed multiple legs and even more daggered tips.

A sharp pain between his shoulders, followed quickly by another.

He ducked, twirling the guns once again and firing off another round. The creatures flew backward, screeching.

Destruction fought to take over, claws springing from the ends of Baden's fingers. The marks in his arms began to burn, as if doused with acid. Shadows began to rise.

All threats will die!

"Behind you!" Pandora shouted.

He spun—and took a dagger across the cheek. A hard push came next, flinging him across the room. He slammed into a wall. More disoriented than he should be. Dizzy. A ringing in his ears.

His surroundings blurred. He caught the scent of vanilla. Home?

No, he hadn't flashed unintentionally. He remained in the room with Pandora, had scented Katarina on his skin.

Poisoned claws, Destruction told him. *I'll burn it out.*

A moment later, he felt as if he'd swallowed a branding iron. As he lumbered to his feet, strength restored, another dagger was shoved under both of his bands. The marks cooled, the shadows thinned. The dizziness returned. Suddenly eight distinct voices rushed his mind with desires so sick and twisted he wasn't sure he would ever be able to cleanse their taint.

That kind of evil…it wasn't a gift, even if it saved him for a short time. Even if it seemed to protect him. The Sent Ones had spoken true. Evil infected. Evil ruined. Destruction had been able to contain it, but as this proved, even Destruction had his limits.

The beast had gone quiet.

The bands needed contact with his skin to work? Before Katarina, Baden would have wondered why. After last night, he knew the power of a simple touch. Knew the strength of the bond it created. The absolute sense of connection.

He slashed through the offending legs and yanked the daggers out from under the bands—Destruction roared, the other voices diminishing—but another creature lashed out at him…and another…and another. They came from every direction. Anytime he felled one, two more took its place, the goal always to shove more daggers under the bands.

When Destruction went quiet, the other voices once again filled his head with those disgusting desires. He fought so fervently, foam actually dripped from the corners of his mouth. But all the while, he continued hacking at the legs that bound him.

Finally! Free! He rolled toward Pandora.

If one warrior could put down ten of these creatures, two warriors could put down a hundred.

Despite her obvious pain, she struggled against her captors. Black blood leaked from her eyes, nose and ears, as if the thoughts inside her head were too much to bear.

"Behind you," she repeated, her voice weaker now.

He went low and twisted, firing the guns.

Click, click, click.

Out of bullets. Fine. He hacked at the creatures closest to him until they were nothing but bits and pieces and dove, using those pieces as a wall to block any oncoming stragglers. Midair, he ejected the empty cartridges and slammed the handles into new ones. When he landed, he popped to his feet and shot the creatures around Pandora.

They fell away from her as their legs detached from their bodies, but their daggers remained under her bands. She fought to remove them, but all too soon her knees gave out, and she collapsed.

Even writhing on the floor, she worked at the daggers, finally removing the last. She cried out with relief, the shadows springing from her arms.

With a hiss, they leaped at the creatures—now backing up. But not fully retreating. More amassed in the room, covering the ceiling, the walls, the floor, creating a sea of evil.

A war cry sounded amid the crowd. Creatures and shadows leaped into action and collided.

Baden yanked the remaining daggers out from under his own bands. When the last one slid free, his shadows joined the fray, Destruction now huffing and puffing.

His gaze met Pandora's as he extended a hand in her direction. She hesitated only a second before accepting.

He hefted her to her feet, asking, "Aleksander?"

"Taken."

He tried to flash to him, but failed. Too weak? He gathered his strength and tried again...failed again. Perhaps Aleksander had been killed?

A man could hope. "The coin?"

"No," she said, as though pulling the word through a lethal obstacle course. "I was unsuccessful."

A scream pierced the air. A limb plopped to the floor and black goo sprayed. The shadows were ravenous; he could feel the sharp pangs of their starvation as they feasted on the demons like the savages they were. Their teeth ghosted inside the creatures to rip at their spirits. Because that's what the shadows were. Spirit. Like to like. But what happened to the spirit must manifest in the body, the two connected; the creatures began to lose hunks of bone, muscle and skin.

They were being devoured from the inside out.

Sitting back and watching wasn't in Baden's nature. He was cut up and seeping his own black-as-night substance—were there specks of red mixed in?—but he dove into the heart of the battle, slashing, slashing, slashing. Pandora took a position at his six, stopping any ambush from behind.

We are...working together?

When the last creature was slain, the shadows returned to him and Pandora, sinking back into their proper places.

She hunched over. Panting, she said, "I could have... won without you."

"Yes. I'm sure. You could have won a second death."

She pursed her lips. "We need to retrieve the human."

"We?"

"A mistake," she rushed out. "I meant me. I'll retrieve Alek on my own."

"You won't. You had your night," he said. "Now he's mine."

"Bastard! You had more than a night and got less out of him. I think..." She gasped, closed her eyes to hide the disgust suddenly growing there. "I think we need to work together."

He didn't trust her. Even without Distrust coloring his thoughts, he would never trust her. Not fully. But...she was right. "Now isn't the time to go after him. There's no telling what kind of combat situation we'd face."

"So? He's weakened."

"*We're* weakened. Most likely the ones who took him are not." The truth was the truth, no matter how much he hated it. "I'm not giving him another opportunity to walk away. Or even to crawl. Next time, he loses." Everything.

She thought for a moment, reluctantly nodded. "We could use the wife to draw him—"

"No!" A roar. A threat, if she was smart enough to hear it. "You won't turn your sights to her or our dogs. And you won't use that title in reference to her, either."

"Title? You mean *wife*?"

She's mine! "Swear it or our truce is null and void."

She arched a dark brow. "We have a truce?"

"You're still alive, aren't you?"

She snorted. "Fine. Whatever. I swear it." She straightened, scrubbing a shaky hand down her face. "I never thought you'd commit to anyone, much less a human."

He could say the same. Humans were feeble, easily killed. And now, with as many enemies as Baden had racked up, he might as well paint a target on Katarina's back. If he wed her—bonded his life to hers as Puck had bonded his life to Gilly—she could become immortal, but would she also become a slave to Hades?

He couldn't risk it. There had to be another way.

One task at a time. First up: healing so that he was strong enough to protect her. "Have you learned to use a cell phone?"

"Am I a better warrior than you?" she replied drily.

"I'll take that as a no."

"It's a yes!"

He rattled off his number and stood to unsteady legs. "If Lucifer sends another ambush, let me know."

"Planning to save the day?" she sneered.

"You mean again? Yes."

She spun, kicking him in the stomach, but there was no actual anger to the strike and he simply lost his breath for a moment. "Bastard."

"Bitch."

"Pussy."

"Failure."

They peered at each other in silence, and he would have sworn the corners of her lips twitched, as if she was fighting a grin. "I'll text if I'm attacked," she said. "Or when I'm fully healed, whichever comes first."

"Until next time…" he said, and flashed away without problem.

23

"I mixed a vial of poison, called it Kindness…
and killed people with Kindness."

—Josephina, Queen of the Fae

Katarina praised Biscuit and Gravy liberally. They excelled at every game she initiated. Flirt pole. Fetch and catch. Hide-and-seek. Tug-of-war. But…did they excel *too* much?

Are they hellhounds or aren't they?

At every turn, the two maintained a high level of excitement and determination to win. They remained focused and never entered any of the emotional danger zones: anger, nervousness or fear.

Galen and Fox avoided her bedroom and the backyard, which was a good thing—for them. The more time that passed without Baden, the more Katarina's stomach churned. The more her stomach churned, the snappier she became. The snappier she became, the more aggrieved the dogs became.

She wanted her man home safe. She even wanted the beast home safe. The beast—who was a manifestation of Hades's tortured childhood. She'd never thought she would sympathize with the dark king who pulled Baden's strings. Or that she would fall prey to the old *he's just misunderstood, I should run* to *him not* from *him...should give him a hug.*

I want to hug him!

But. Despite her sympathy, she would never allow him to harm her pups.

"Are you hellhounds?" she finally asked as she stored the tug-of-war sleeve in a box at the foot of the bed. "You can tell me the truth."

—*Play! Play!*—

"Did you bite me? And if so, why didn't you feed on me?" Because they loved her? Love could overcome a multitude of compulsions. "Am I going to morph into one of your kind?"

—*Toy!*—

Biscuit scratched at the box. When that failed, he nosed the lid.

"Sit," she commanded, and both pups sat after only a slight hesitation.

Either they were too innocent to understand what she'd asked, or they didn't want to admit the truth.

"Where are your parents? Were they...killed? Are you on your own?"

Both ducked their heads, radiating sadness.

"You're not alone," she told them. "You've got me. And I'll love you even if you infected me, all right?"

Baden appeared in a flash of light, startling her. She pressed her lips together in a guilty line. The dogs didn't act surprised, at least, as if they'd sensed him; they simply watched him. But the real wonder? They remained in place, waiting for her command to rise. Such fast learners!

As she took in Baden's poor condition, a cry of dismay left her. He looked as if he'd been pitted against other junkyard dogs. His face, neck and arms were cut and bruised and caked with something thick and black that reeked of sulfur. His clothes were torn, and his limbs trembling.

She rushed to his side and wrapped an arm around his waist, offering support and comfort. "What happened?" She led him to the bed, determination giving her enough strength to hold him up when his knees buckled—the same strength Destruction had considered killing her for having.

She eased Baden onto the mattress and sat beside him, unwilling to stray from his side.

"Ambush," he said with a grimace.

"And Alek?"

"Captured by Lucifer's minions. I don't know whether he's dead or alive."

"What does Lucifer want with him?"

"The coin, I'm sure."

"But why? He already has a kingdom in the underworld."

"What's better than one kingdom? Two." Baden scrubbed a hand down his face. "He must be stopped, whatever the cost."

No. Not "whatever the cost." Baden's soul was more important than victory.

—*You need help?*—

"Yes," she replied without thought. "Go get Galen. Do you remember him? The blond man with miniwings." A simple wash wasn't going to help Baden. Not this time. She'd tended wounds of her own and wounds on her animals, but had no experience tending to an immortal. "Please."

The dogs bounded off, and she knew they'd understood her.

"They can follow such a specific order?" Baden asked with a frown.

"Yeah, I'm that good." *And, uh, they might be hellhounds, with powers beyond my understanding.*

He frowned, staring at the door. Trying to unravel the puzzle? "Call them back," he finally said. "I don't want Galen—"

"Let me stop you right there. I don't actually care what you want. Your well-being is more important than your reason for avoiding the man." Whatever that reason happened to be. "He can help you. I can't."

"He's an asshole," Baden muttered.

"You should adore him. *You* are an asshole."

As he glared at her, his pupils expanded, black with pinpricks of red. Destruction was making his presence known, and she couldn't have been happier, her relief palpable. If he had the strength to argue with her, to properly display his emotions, he had the strength to recover from his wounds.

And he had to recover.

To lighten the mood, she reached out to caress his cheek, just under the worst of the gashes. "Poor Baduction. You hurt your moneymaker."

His glare softened at the edges. "Are you saying you like the look of me?"

She chuckled as if he'd just told a joke. "I'm saying I have an *Outlander* fantasy you have yet to fulfill."

The glare returned full force, and he actually snarled

at her. "I learned the reference. I will only ever pretend to be me, and you'll thank me for it."

Yes. She probably would. "I don't think you have to pretend to be you, *pekný.*"

"You know what I meant," he grumbled.

So adorable. She liked this man. *Liked* liked. A lot. He was stubborn and grumpy and he had those murderous tendencies thanks to Destruction, but he could make her laugh when no one else was able.

Wow. He makes me laugh? Way to reach for the stars.

Well...he could turn her on with a single look. He challenged her and delighted her. And maybe she had a wild side she'd never before acknowledged or maybe she was just getting used to his world, because she liked that he would go to any means necessary to protect what he loved.

He doesn't love me.

But... I might be falling for him.

Tristo hrmenych! That wasn't a good thing. He would never age, but she would—yes? Despite the possible hellhound thing. Also, all the women his friends had picked were hardcore warriors, no matter how delicate they appeared. Katarina had sensed Ashlyn would morph into a snarling ogre if ever her children were threatened.

Baduction still considered Katarina weak.

I'm someone, damn it. I'm plucky!

"Are you hurt?" Baden asked, drawing her from her musings.

"No." She hooked a lock of hair behind his ear, connecting with him through touch. "Why?"

"You grimaced."

Galen saved her from having to think up a reply by

stumbling into the room. Biscuit shoved his muzzle into one leg and Gravy shoved his muzzle into the other to nudge Galen closer. Both canines stopped and panted, tongues hanging out of their mouths, only when Galen stood within reach of Katarina.

"Such good babies," she praised.

Scowling, Galen said, "If your dogs ever come after me again, I'll—"

Katarina leaped to her feet, the dogs jumping in front of her. His jaw dropped as she growled at him. Literally growled. Her gums burned. So did the ends of her fingers and even the ends of her toes, but she ignored the painful sensations, keeping her gaze locked on Galen.

"You don't want to finish that sentence," she told him.

The pups echoed her sentiment with a snarl. A sound unlike any they'd released before, deep and hungry, absolutely menacing, as if the warrior had just been placed on the dinner menu. An all-you-can-eat buffet.

"I don't think they like you," Baden remarked, his tone easy, almost amused.

The color drained from Galen's face as he held up his hands, palms out, and took a step back. "They are…"

"Going to tear off your face if you insult them? Yes. Or were you going to say they are angels? Because they are. Now zip your foolish mouth and help Baden." She motioned to the patient with a regal wave of her arm. "And you," she said, smiling at the dogs. "Guard my *pekný*."

The dogs jumped on the bed, taking up posts beside Baden. And okay, all right, not even she was this good, this fast. They were hellhounds, weren't they?

Hellhounds must be eradicated.

Over her dead body!

"All right. On that note…" Galen tentatively approached the bed and raked his gaze over Baden. "Here's my official diagnosis. With a little rest and a shower, he'll be fine. Just offer to screw his brains out as soon as he's on his feet. You'll have a healthy, happy boy by the end of the day." Galen winked at her before marching out of the room.

The words were both liberating and worrisome at once. She'd learned a few things about the warrior. As the keeper of False Hope, he enjoyed—and perhaps needed—to build people up only to tear them down. Even himself!

This could be a trick of the demon.

Well, she would make sure Baden did rest and recover. She gathered all the supplies she thought she might need: a bowl of hot water—which was always used in books and movies—rags, antibiotic ointment and bandages. Baden remained quiet, even pensive as she removed his shirt and got to work.

Finally he said, "I want to keep you. I *will* keep you."

Her heart kicked into a hard rhythm against her ribs. "Until the novelty wears off or until I'm old and gray?"

Angry, brooding eyes met hers, sending a shiver dancing through her. "I don't like the thought of you aging."

Well, that made two of them. This virile man didn't need a granny in a diaper clinging to his arm like a crutch. Not for a girlfriend. "No silver fox fantasies?" Half tease, half hope. Half plea for help.

And yes, she knew her math was off. Such an impossible topic called for skewed numbers.

"If I had sex with eighty-year-old Katarina, I would break her hip."

The deadpanned response broke through her growing upset, and she burst out laughing. "Most men would claim age doesn't matter."

He reached up and caressed her cheek. A touch he would not have initiated weeks before. A touch she thrilled to receive. "I'm not most men. I know how quickly the human body withers, have seen it happen too many times. And as I've mentioned, staying with me places you in danger. If someone were to hurt you... to injure you beyond repair..."

She struggled to maintain her composure amidst such a sensitive topic. "How about I stay with you until I get my first gray hair?" A little time together was better than no time at all.

"No." He shook his head with a determination that promised a battle if she dared disagree. "We'll find a way to make you immortal."

Tell him about the dogs.

No! She couldn't. Not outright. He wasn't just Baden, he was Destruction, too. She had to proceed with caution.

She petted his chest the way she knew he—they— liked. "Let's back away from the immortal thing for a bit. I'd rather talk about hellhounds and the people who survived their bite."

Baden gazed at her as if he'd give her anything she asked—and how heady was *that*? "I know of only two such cases. Zeus ordered his army to capture the males who'd been bitten, and we did. But they were stronger than before, with claws arcing from their fingers and toes. They were also crazy, constantly pulling at their hair and hitting their temples. On the way to Mount Olympus, a pack of hellhounds ambushed us. Many men died, including the bitten males. They were the main targets, the first killed."

"But why? The bloodlust alone?"

"I think the hellhounds wanted no outside tie. So many had tried to control them. Some, like Hades's tormentor, had even succeeded...for a time."

Now she withered. Was she soon to go crazed? Crave living beings for her meals? Would the pups begin to eye her as a meal-on-heels?

"Were the *hounds* immortal?" she asked.

"No. They had the life span of a human. To my knowledge, a hundred and twenty years is the longest one ever lived."

"What happened to them?"

"Hades took control of two underworld realms. His mother's and his tormentor's. He led his armies into battle against all the packs, eradicating the entire race."

A spark of anger burned her chest—some of those hounds had been innocent, surely. A spark she ignored. For now.

Where had Biscuit and Gravy come from? Were there more?

"About the immortal thing. I don't know if I want to live forever." Their relationship was so new. What if things ended in a month...a year...five years? She'd be stuck—alone—in a world she wasn't sure she liked. "And I'm not worried about the danger that comes with you."

"Because I am—"

"Because there will always be danger in the world. Making decisions based on fear only leads to regrets."

"You need me," he snapped. "With me at your side, you won't have to be afraid."

Oops. She'd poked the bear. Well, why not keep poking?

She stood, gathered cleaning supplies, stripped him of his soiled clothing and thoroughly washed him. "You *want* me to need you. There's a difference. I don't need you, and I'll never need you. Dependency isn't my thing. But I do desire you as fervently as you desire me."

He didn't erupt again, as part of her expected. He softened, saying, "For the first time in forever, I have hope for the future. At least, I think I have hope. It's been so long since I felt the emotion, I can't be sure." He rubbed his chest. "Whatever it is, you are at the center."

How sad was that? And how freaking sweet? She pointed to the wall, saying, "Biscuit, Gravy. To your own beds now, my loves."

They hopped off the mattress without pause and trotted to the pillows she'd stacked against the wall. After praising them for their obedience, she shimmied under the covers and stretched out beside Baden, careful of his injuries.

"We're talking about staying together, *being* together, but we've only ever been on one date. Which isn't fair— to me! I deserve to be wooed."

He draped his arm over her middle, pulling her closer. "I've never wooed a woman."

"Has a woman ever wooed *you*?"

"Many have tried."

"Okay. I'll bite." Perhaps literally, if she wasn't careful. "How did they try to woo you?"

"By sneaking into my home and waiting for me... naked in my bed."

Ha! "Please, *pekný*. I'm not that easy. Be naked in my living room, working a vacuum, and then we'll talk."

His raspy chuckle fanned warm, minty breath over her temples.

Screw being gentle because of his injuries. He was tough, and such toughness should come with a perk.

She traced her tongue around his nipple. "I'm in your bed... Perhaps I should get naked *now*."

His eyes flared with want. "You *should*," he said. The phone vibrated in his pocket, against her belly, but he paid it no heed. "Right now."

"First..." She took possession of the cell and checked the screen. Well, well. "Torin says William is demanding every demon-possessed warrior strike at Puck, without actually hurting Puck." A pause. "Who's Puck?" Would she ever learn all the players in this game?

"Puck married William's...potential soul mate? He's a satyr. Half goat," he added when she stared in confusion.

Goat? Seriously? "Could be worse for the girl, I suppose." But not by much, and suddenly Katarina was very glad her man simply shared his body with another presence.

"Gilly isn't the problem with this situation. William's focus is divided, making him an easy target. Lucifer will see this as the perfect opportunity to strike."

"William seems like the kind of guy who can handle himself, *whatever* the obstacles."

"If he's hurt... Hades loves his son. He will—" Baden frowned, suddenly pensive. Then he shook his head, as if dislodging the thought that had given him pause. "William's own sons will be distracted, too, putting many of my allies in jeopardy at once."

"William, who looks about thirty years old, has kids old enough to fight in a war?"

The smile he directed at her held a touch of indulgence. "They're old enough to destroy the world. They are the horsemen of the apocalypse."

Mind scramble! "Forget about naked vacuuming. If you want to woo me, write a book detailing who our enemies are, who our allies are, every immortal race, their strengths and weaknesses."

He nodded. "This I will do. For your protection."

"Because I need you, blah, blah, blah."

He ignored her, adding, "I'm afraid I can't forget about naked vacuuming. Anything that brings you pleasure, I will do."

A waterfall of warmth…so sweet… She leaned into him—only to halt when his phone buzzed a second time. A warrior was always on call. Sighing, she checked the screen. "Torin the cock blocker says you haven't checked in today, and he's seconds away from sending in the cavalry."

"I've been busy." Baden's hot gaze stroked her with delicious intent. "I'd like to be even busier."

Her nipples tightened, and her stomach clenched. "I'd like that, too, but not until we've sent him proof-of-life photos. I won't risk pop-in visitors while I'm rocking your world." She stood and snapped a few thousand pictures of him. "Make nice with the camera…good, good…now make hate with the camera. Yes! Just like that. Now make babies with the camera…"

He regarded her with a mix of amusement and exasperation.

She selected her favorite photo—one of him making hate with the camera—and texted it to Torin with a message: Baden is ATD (at the doctor's) and if he's feeling better later he might throw a BYOT party (bring your own teeth) TTYL (talk to you louder)

Send.

"What did you tell him?" Baden demanded.

"The truth."

The phone rang a second later, and Torin's picture popped up on the screen. Gorgeous white-haired immortal! Baden reached for the phone, but she backed away from the bed and answered for him, saying, "This better be important. You're interrupting my good time at Baden's expense."

Torin's chuckle crackled over the line. "You might be worse than my Keeley."

The Red Queen. Katarina missed the silly woman. "How is she?"

"All healed up. I'm calling to tell Baden we're going to help William. We owe him."

She repeated the words to Baden while twirling a lock of hair around her finger. "I don't understand how you can war with the goat-man…thing without actually hurting him."

"Easy," Torin said. "We go through his closest friends and family."

What! "That's horrible. They're innocent and—"

Baden snatched the phone away from her. "You have too much to do already, Tor. The box, the Morning Star. Lucifer."

Katarina reclaimed the phone and placed it on Speaker.

"No matter what Keeley tries," Torin said, "she can't

find the box or the Star. And now she can't even *look* for them."

"Why?" Baden demanded.

"The artifacts are missing. Three of them, at least. Danika is still with Reyes, but the painting of the office is missing, too."

Artifacts? What artifacts? Painting of what office?

The box, she could guess. Pandora's box. Why did the men want it back? Hadn't it caused enough trouble?

"Who would—" Baden began, but Torin cut him off.

"Cameo. Our girl kidnapped them. I'd say she planned to ransom them back to us just to mess with me, but the agonized look in her eyes the last time we chatted tells me otherwise."

The announcement enraged Baden. He punched the wall, cracking the stone and probably his knuckles. "Is no one going after her?"

"Are you kidding? She's a big girl. She texted to say this is something she has to do."

"The fool woman is going to get herself killed."

"You know better than anyone. We can't help those who won't help themselves."

Baden scrubbed his free hand through his hair, the strands proving stubborn and remaining in adorable spikes. "I'm sorry. I never meant to hurt you." He ended the call.

Katarina petted his arm, offering comfort, but he shrugged her off. The rejection stung, even though she knew its source. Self-recrimination.

Always end on a positive note.

Hands on her hips, she said, "You heard Galen's earlier orders. You need a shower…and I need to tease you sexually until you beg for mercy you'll never receive."

Baden frowned at her. "He never told you to make me beg."

"Well, good news, big boy." She winked at him. "I'm going to make you do it, anyway."

24

"I am the one who put *laughter* in *manslaughter*."

—Fox, keeper of Distrust

Sex in the shower, sex on the floor, and all I want...is more, more, more.

Katarina snickered as she snuggled deeper into Baden's side. She couldn't get enough of the man, and he obviously felt the same about her. He couldn't go a few minutes without touching her, and she loved it. Just like she loved—

Whoa. Slow down.

"I'm never letting you go, Katarina."

His startling confession left her shivering with delight. "Maybe I'll consider thinking about the possibility of maybe becoming immortal."

Once upon a time...

A new story. A new chance for happily ever after. But—*argh!*—she still couldn't get past the fact that this particular story would last for-freaking-ever. More time, more room for error.

"That isn't good enough. You *will* become immortal. One way or another."

An-n-nd goodbye happy mood.

"Ask nicely," she said, her nerves razed.

"Not this time. I'd rather deal with your anger than your death."

"I'm a grown-ass woman, Baden, and you don't get to make my decisions for me. My opinions matter. My *wants* matter. Whether you agree with me or not."

He wasn't deterred. "One day, you'll thank me for my insistence."

"I won't." *I won't reinforce his domineering tendencies.* "Now back off before you push me too far."

"I won't back off. I can't. This is too important. You're too young and too human to understand the—"

An animalistic growl sprang from deep inside her—a sound she'd never before made—and he went quiet. Not because of her, she realized, but because of the pups, who'd risen from their mound of pillows, the hair on their backs standing up.

Fury, a mirror to her own, pulsed off them.

The dogs dove for the bed—for Baden. Their teeth were bared, as if they planned to rip out his throat.

"No," she rushed out, and they twisted midair, soaring past Baden as he threw his body over hers.

"No?" He anchored his weight on his palms to loom above her, his beautiful features dark with anger and determination. "Do you hope to protect me? Or them?"

"Both. Though I can't fathom why I'd save you right now."

"Because I'm willing to do anything to see to your safety. Even go against your wishes. You might not like it, but some part of you must appreciate it."

Was *that* what she'd reinforced?

As the pups prowled around the bed, waiting for

her signal this time, Katarina forced herself to calm through every means possible. Deep breathing, counting to ten, imagining herself in a happy place—a field of wildflowers where her former pups could play with her new pups.

"How did we go from making love and cuddling to *this*?"

"Very easily. Making love, cuddling...you showed me the desires of a heart I'd thought long dead. And one day you might decide to take that away from me? One day someone might kill you or old age might get the better of you? No."

The romance of his words was ruined by the harshness of his tone. "Might? One day? Oh, no, *kretén*. I'm taking the desires of your heart away from you *today*. You're so hardheaded, my warning wasn't able to get through. Action is needed." He would learn a lesson, and she would calm down. "We're going to spend some time apart."

She stood and nuzzled the dogs to assure them all was well before dressing in a T-shirt and jeans. "When you deny my right to choose, you don't deserve me." She strode to the closet, grabbed an empty duffel and began to fill it with her clothing. "So I'm leaving. Going somewhere far, far away from you."

"No." He spat the denial as if it were poison. "You're staying here."

"Another command." She tsk-tsked. "You can't stop me without harming me. Because I *will* fight you."

He jumped up, copper eyes hot on her, and ripped the bag from her grip. A bag he tossed across the room. He backed her into the wall, a mix of carnality and acrimony as he flattened his palms beside her temples, caging her in.

She wasn't afraid…but might have been a little turned on. *Stay strong!* The long-term outcome was more important than the short-term pleasure.

To her surprise, the dogs remained quiet. Sensed no threat this time?

"Stay." Taking a page from her training manual, he began to pet her. "We're so good together."

He stroked her hair…down her arm…up her stomach and between her breasts… Only when she had gone taut with anticipation, the very air she breathed burning her with awareness only this man could elicit, did he circle her beaded nipple.

"If we're parted, I won't be able to touch you like this, and I desperately want to touch you. Stay," he repeated. "Please."

His resolve was a tantalizing throb against her skin. The problem? He'd couched the words as a request this time, and yet they were still a demand.

"Your *plea* is too little too late, warrior."

The gentleness evaporated from his expression. "You're a human. You don't know what's good for you."

"So you keep telling me." She pushed him away. "Well, I know beyond a doubt *you* aren't good for me. Now move!"

He moved, but only of his own volition, the bastard.

"What do you want from me?" he snapped.

"From you? Nothing." Head high, she bent to pick up the bag. She stuffed her belongings inside. "I want a man who sees me as his equal."

"That," he said, his voice now devoid of emotion, "is something I'll never do. I can't. Not when I could break you."

Just. Like. That. Hope that their relationship could

survive this withered. Disappointment and sorrow welled up and bubbled over. *Won't beg him to reconsider.*

She wasn't leaving to teach him a lesson and calm herself down, she decided. She was leaving, period. Their story was over. The end. She'd thought she could prove her worth. He'd just admitted he would never see it.

"We're done," she told him, and she meant it.

"We aren't done." He reached for her but let his arms drop before contact was made. "We will never be done."

Stay. Strong! The very strength he thought she didn't have. "When you start to miss me, and you will, don't come looking for me. This—" she waved a hand to indicate her body "—is now off-limits to you."

"No. No! I won't let you—"

"Katarina is still talking." She stomped her foot. "I'm done trying to train you. You failed my class. F plus plus."

His nostrils flared as he bared his teeth. "You were *training* me? Like one of your dogs?"

"Of course." She fluffed her hair. "You're a beast, are you not? Beautiful but deadly."

"I am. And now you'll see my worst." With a roar, his eyes glinting with red, he toppled the dresser. The drawers split down the middle, the contents spilling out. At the bed, he yanked the iron headboard until a bar came loose. A bar he hurled into the wall.

What had brought on this fit? Certainly not her admission to training him. It had made him angry, but not enraged.

The fact that she'd called him a beast?

Ignoring him as if she hadn't a care, she finished packing in silence, picking her garments off the floor.

Once upon a time...

Today, a new story began. One of her own making. She would use this heartbreak as an opportunity to patch herself up into a new and better person.

When she had everything she needed, she called, "Galen!"

Baden stopped his tantrum and glared at her. "He won't *dare* take you from me."

"He will. And you're going to give him the order or I swear to you now, I won't just fight you, I'll run every time your back is turned. I'll provoke this beastly side of you at every opportunity, and—"

"Enough." He was panting, his hands fisted. "You want to go? Very well. We'll let you go."

We, he'd said.

Relief battled with sorrow. *Don't want to lose another loved one.* But she didn't love him. She couldn't. "When my brother is well, you'll have Galen bring him to me, wherever I am."

Silence stretched between them. He nodded stiffly.

Galen soared into the room without knocking, irritation painting his features. "You rang, doodlepop?" He saw the naked Baden and covered his eyes. "Seriously, dude? Come on! If I'd wanted to be part of a sausage fest, I'd have visited my butcher."

The dogs moved to her side and licked at her hands. Chin trembling, she slung the bag over her shoulder and hooked leashes to the collars. "I'm ready to go."

"Uh, ready to go where?" Galen asked, confused.

Baden turned away, the muscles in his back knotted. "Take her somewhere else." He paused and gritted, "Somewhere safe."

"Somewhere of my choosing," she corrected. "And you won't tell Baden where I am. You won't *ever* tell him, even upon threat of death." There would be no sequel. She would make sure of it.

A sob brewed in the back of her throat.

Tears? For *him*? No!

Galen blinked, as if certain he'd misheard. "Are mommy and daddy getting a divorce?"

"Yes, and mommy has full custody of the fur children." She pasted a bright smile on her face, ignoring the thick veil of tension in the air. "Now let's go before I divorce your ass, too."

Baden battled an unholy rage. Katarina was gone. But even if she'd stayed, he would have lost her. She, like so many others, thought him beautiful on the outside but ugly on the inside. Despite her boast to the contrary!

His one bright light in a world of darkness now flamed out of reach.

He drove a fist into the wall again and again, creating new holes, tearing skin and cracking his knuckles.

Destruction prowled through his mind. *I want my woman back. Get her back!*

I will.

He must.

A hand came to rest on his bare shoulder. No pain. He whipped around, expecting to see Katarina. She'd realized her mistake! He came face-to-face with Fox instead.

"What?" he snarled, hating his desensitized skin.

Her gaze swept over his nakedness. "How about you get dressed? You're hot and all, but I prefer my men with a little less obsession for another woman."

He wasn't bashful or shy by any means, but he didn't like another woman's eyes on Katarina's property. He strode to the closet and tugged on a pair of pants. He would give Katarina time to calm. Then he would mount a charge to win her back.

Perhaps he shouldn't have ordered her to do his bidding, but damn it, remaining human wasn't an option for her. But he definitely should have waited to force the issue until he had a way to change her.

"What?" he repeated with just as much heat.

"I heard yelling, and thought I could help you out. I didn't realize offering aid would be such a terrible crime. My mistake."

"I don't need your help. Also, what happens in my life isn't your business." Cultivating a friendship with the keeper of Distrust? Not ever going to happen. He may have given her advice, but that had been at Katarina's request. Now he just wanted to kill someone.

"I'm not your enemy, Baden."

"You're right. You're worse. You're a reminder of a past I cannot change."

"Yes, and you should be grateful! You're stronger now. You're wiser. And I'm a fucking mess."

"Through fault all your own. You welcomed the demon. You wanted it."

"I wanted power. You have no idea what life was like for me, an immortal born without—" She sucked in a breath, quieted. What had she stopped herself from revealing?

She was an immortal of indeterminate origin. She'd never shifted into an animal form that he'd seen. Her voice wasn't a weapon, like a siren, and she didn't have wings like a Harpy, Sent One or angel. She had no fangs to mark her as vampire, or whatever Pandora had become, and no aura of power, like a witch.

"I wanted power," she repeated.

"You acquired an illusion of power. And a new weakness."

"I know that. *Now*."

True power was friendship—strength in numbers. True power was love—a willingness to sacrifice for others.

Love often ran red.

True power was hope for a better tomorrow—which he no longer had. True power didn't have to spring from violence, he realized. It could be as gentle as a woman's touch.

Perhaps he *was* wiser now. And yet, he'd still allowed his determination to possess Katarina to drive her away. To keep her safe, yes, but also to care for her on his own terms.

He yanked a shirt from a hanger and pulled the material over his head. "You need to go."

"Look. Whether you want my aid or not, you're going to get it. I know something about Hades's sons." She rubbed the back of her neck, shifted from one booted foot to the other. "William and Lucifer used to wear the bands, too."

How could she know that? And William would never keep such a secret—

No, not true. William was a selfish prick, easily amused by the ignorance of others. Even his friends.

William had even warned Baden away from Fox. Because she knew his secret.

"You should have told me sooner," he said.

"I didn't want you asking questions about my past."

"Oh, I won't. I'll be too busy killing the man I

thought was my friend." Baden grabbed two daggers and made an adjustment in his mind.

Home—wherever William is. He ended up in a spacious bedroom. The walls were covered in claw marks, the furniture busted into jagged pieces, shards of glass littering the floor.

Maddox, Paris and Sabin were doing their best to pin William as he raged, while Strider and Lucien guarded the door to prevent an escape. Did they not remember the male could flash? Or could William not flash while his emotions were in such turmoil?

He fought with a skill beyond lethal, his every movement precise and methodical despite his volatility.

By some miracle, Maddox was able to latch onto one arm while Strider was able to latch onto the other, allowing Paris to come in from behind to perform a headlock. They wouldn't be able to restrain the male for long. Already William was close to gaining his freedom.

Baden closed the distance in a hurry and slammed one of his daggers deep into William's heart. Finally, the male stilled, glaring at Baden as literal flames flickered in his eyes.

"Mistake, Red. Big mistake."

Baden slammed the other dagger into William's gut.

William laughed with manic glee while the others gaped in astonishment. "I've been meaning to come to you. To collect the favor you owe me."

Baden sensed the opposite was true. "You want your favor? Tell me to release you, and I will."

Eyes of crystalline blue darkened until jet black. Black that spread to his cheekbones, reminding Baden of one of the kings he'd seen in Hades's chamber.

I'm staring into the abyss.

"No," William said. "I think I'd rather wait."

"Very well." Baden twisted the daggers deeper. "Then let's discuss the reason for my visit. Were you or were you not once bound by Hades's bands?"

In a shocking move, William surged forward, pushing both daggers deeper. One more step, and Baden's hands would come out the other side.

"Does this feel like a sharing moment to you?" the warrior demanded, deceptively calm, even as bolts of lightning flashed underneath his skin.

"Answer me, anyway," Baden said.

"Or what? You'll stick me with a third dagger?"

Bastard. Was there nothing he feared? "You think you're the only one with problems?" A question the male had once asked him.

"I'm the only one with a problem I care about."

"Tell me what I want to know or—"

"Or what?" The words were whispered, more lethal than the blades. "Tell me. I'm figuratively dying of curiosity."

This was Hades's son. Threats wouldn't work, as proven. Appeals to a softer side wouldn't work, either. He had no softer side. Or rather he'd had a softer side, but she'd been taken away from him.

Baden yanked out the daggers, one at a time, removing bits of heart and liver, too. Oops. "Do you know if Gilly and Puck registered? Want to make sure I buy the right toaster."

William narrowed his eyes, and it was clear he struggled to retain his composure. "Yes, Red. I wore the bands, just like you. They made me Hades's son, and if you live long enough, they'll do the same to you—brother."

25

"Go ahead and eat your weight in ice cream. You'll just give him more of you to love."

—Haidee, former keeper of Hate

Galen, the *chruno*, refused to take Katarina and the dogs to Bratislava, where she could find a new place to live and start over. Instead, he took her little ragtag group straight to Keeley and Kaia. According to Galen, Keeley had horrifying powers her enemies feared so greatly, they wouldn't even speak her name except in hushed whispers, and Kaia could chew through an entire army without breaking a sweat. Details Baden had left out during intros.

This was another perfect example of why Katarina needed a book of who was who to whom in the worlds.

Not that Baden would provide such a tome now.

The backs of her eyes began to…no, surely not… but she couldn't deny—or fight—the burn for long. Trembling, she patted her cheeks. They were still dry. Good, that was good. She would *not* cry for him. Her parents and Peter deserved her tears. Her precious dogs deserved her tears. Baden did not.

Suck it up. Move on.

"Here. She's your problem now, ladies. Protect her if you want. Or not. My part is done." Galen vanished without another word.

Keeley stared at her, confused. "Who are you?"

Was that a joke? "You know me. We hung out just last week."

Keeley shook her head. "No way. I'd remember. Wait." She rubbed her temples. "The deets are coming back to me. You're Baden's girl… Katrina. He absconded with you after the attack on our home."

A pang in her heart, the burn returning to her eyes. "I *was* Baden's girl." She pointed to a cozy spot in the corner, and the dogs trotted over to lie down. "We decided to part ways because he's an asshole. And my name is Katarina."

"Katrina is better," Kaia said with a nod. "Fewer syllables."

Katarina gave her a false smile. "I'll call you KiKi, then. It's prettier."

Got to make the best of a bad situation.

She took in her surroundings. The decor could have been plucked from the set of a porno. Dark, intimate and suggestive, with mirrors on the ceiling and walls. "What is this place?"

"A nightclub for immortals," Keeley said. "Known as Downfall."

Appropriate. According to the hours of operation displayed on the wall, the bar wasn't set to open for hours. Well. No wonder it was currently devoid of other patrons.

"Why are you here after hours?" she asked.

"Long story short, I was testing the club's security,

seeing if it was possible to break and enter. Hint: it is."
Kaia moved behind the bar and mixed a concoction she
named the Shame Spiral. "Slight hiccup. I didn't actually tell the owners I would be doing them such a massive favor. Here. Drink."

"I'll be honest with you," Katarina said. "This might
as well be cardboardeaux. I can't tell the difference between a well-mixed drink and a piss-poor one."

"Then you're probably the only person in the world
who will appreciate the enormity of my talent."

Well, then. "Bottoms up." She downed her glass
in a single gulp and coughed as her throat and stomach burned. The room spun for a moment. "I think we
should rename the drink Bad Decisions."

Kaia fist-pumped the air. "Change approved! Now
drink another." She slid a second glass in Katarina's direction. "It'll help get your mind off things."

"If I'm arrested for stealing liquor…" The first drink
she could justify. *Just had my heart crushed.* This second one? Not so much.

"Dude. The worst Thane will do is stake us to his
front lawn. He's one of the three owners, and staking
is a specialty of his." Kaia flicked her mass of red hair
over her shoulder. "But he'd have to catch us first, and
that ain't happening."

Keeley nodded with enthusiasm. "My girl speaks
true. I can flash, and she can fly like the wind. Besides,
you'll lag behind, and he'll turn his efforts to you. We'll
be forgotten."

So comforting. "Your immortality isn't fair." And
she wasn't jealous. Really. That ship had sailed.

The pink-haired vixen tapped her chin with blunt-tipped nails painted ivy-green. "There's got to be a way we can even the playing field and make you immortal."

"Baden said the same thing."

"He's right. I mean, Hades has the ability, and I'm stronger and better than him. I'm almost certain I did something to Gilly…"

Wait. "The girl who got sick and had to marry a goat-man to survive?"

Kaia ran her finger across her neck in a *dude, shut your piehole* motion. "We aren't supposed to talk about that, Keys."

"Someone got sick? Why am I always the last to know?" Keeley downed her newest drink then motioned to Katarina to do the same.

She obeyed, the heat was more delectable than painful this time, causing fireworks to explode and spew flames in her head. "I don't want to have to marry a monster." Or a beast.

Longing leveled her. *Going to wipe Baden from my memory. Never going to think about him again. Or crave him. Or dream of him. Or fantasize about him.* Nope. Never. He'd pulled the he-man card, and she'd had to exit the game.

"Oh! I remember now." Keeley pouted, saying, "How was I supposed to know helping Gilly become immortal would maybe possibly harm her?"

Kaia threw her arms into the air. "Uh, maybe because you told me, *Kaia, this might harm Gilly* right before you secretly slipped the elixir in her drink." Speaking of drinks, she poured another round. "You considered the risk worth the reward. Aka William's eternal happiness versus his eternal hatred."

Keeley shrugged. "Win some, lose some."

Katarina stared at her new drink in horror. "Did you elixir me?"

"No! Or probably not. I'm pretty certain I've learned my lesson." Keeley reached over the bar and grabbed a black bottle labeled Ambrosia. She popped the cork with her teeth and spit the thing across the room. "Only time will tell."

Kaia wagged a finger in Katarina's face. "What is confessed at Downfall stays at Downfall. Snitches get stitches."

"Understood. Trust me." Otherwise, William was likely to murder both women for their deeds. "In case I haven't made myself clear, I've decided I don't want to be immortal. No matter how many perks come with the transformation."

Keeley drained half the bottle then wiped her mouth with the back of her hand. "Baden messed up that badly, huh?"

"He ordered me to do his bidding, no matter how I felt about the matter."

"Well. I say take the high road," Kaia said with a nod. "That way, you won't clog up the low road. I prefer a free path."

Katarina drained her glass. If she was elixired, she was elixired. She'd deal. Besides, continuing to drink was an excellent idea. The best! Her brain was now a strobe light!

Keeley bumped her shoulder, nearly pushing her to the floor. "All our names start with a K. Coincidence? Or are we part of a secret club and just didn't know it?"

"Secret club." Kaia clapped. "The girls most likely to steal candy from a baby."

"No way." Keeley thought for a moment. "The girls

most likely to cause an accident due to their stunning good looks."

The debate continued.

Kaia: "Girls most likely to become president of the PTA. People That Amaze."

Keeley: "Girls most likely to attend an Immortals After Dark convention. Dibs on Lothaire!"

Kaia: "Girls most likely to skinny-dip in public."

Keeley: "Girls most likely to make a coffee run after killing an enemy."

The two girls wrestled quite brutally over who was right and who was wrong, drawing blood, before Keeley decided Katarina would look so "amazeballs" with a "ward." Something to temporarily prevent pregnancy. "Someday you'll thank me for this. Trust me."

"Can Baden even—never mind." She wasn't with Baden anymore. He wasn't her boyfriend, and she wasn't his girlfriend. They would never have sex again. One day, she'd have a new man in her life. A new story. "Give me the ward."

For the other man, she thought, defiant.

Keeley pulled the necessary equipment out of a giant purse—or suitcase. "I never leave home without the proper tools."

The ward, as it turned out, was nothing more than a tattoo on the back of Katarina's neck; the swirling black symbol would be hidden under her hair whenever she left the wavy mass down. She wasn't sure how it would prevent pregnancy—or if it wouldn't prevent pregnancy—but what else was new? At least the pain of the etching helped distract her from her troubles.

"Whenever you're ready to pop a few buns out of your oven," Keeley said, "we'll fill in the ward. Oh! I can give you a protection ward. And a locator ward, and oh! Oh!" She jumped up and down. "I know. A ward to prevent anyone from using their powers against you."

"Nah." She didn't want another ward until she'd learned more about them. "I'm good."

"I hope you don't mind," Kaia piped up, "but I invited my older sis Taliyah to join us. I think I hear her in the courtyard. She should pass through the door any—"

The front door swung open and a tall, slender blonde strode into the club, two huge men flanking her sides. Both males had large white wings with striations of gold, the most beautiful things she'd ever seen. *Must touch!*

The dogs had other ideas. Awake and alert, they raced over to take a post in front of her.

"Boo hiss," Kaia called. "You told me you'd be alone."

Taliyah hiked her thumbs at the guys. "These jerk-offs were on the way to bust up the festivities. I had a choice. Kill them or invite them to tag along." Her pale blue gaze landed on Katarina. "Excellent. The woman I've been hunting. I owe Baden a little payback, and you're going to help me."

"Hey." Kaia stomped her foot. "You can't murder my new friend."

"Don't be ridiculous. I *soooo* can. But where's the fun in that? She's a puny human."

The dogs snarled.

Katarina snarled, rage bubbling up from a cauldron of hurt. That—was—it! She wasn't puny, weak or feeble, and she was sick and tired of being labeled as such.

Taliyah stopped. Kaia and Keeley regarded her warily.

"I. Am. Not. Puny!" She threw the words as if they were daggers, her gums and the tips of her fingers and toes burning. She looked and discovered her nails had lengthened, thickened and sharpened. They were claws. Claws! With a flick of her tongue, she learned her teeth had undergone the same metamorphosis. She had fangs.

Shock was a cool cascade inside her, but it wasn't enough to calm her.

"Someone get Baden," Kaia said. "Pronto."

"No!" Katarina snarled. "The first person to leave is the first person to die." Issuing threats now? What the hell was happening to her? Was she finally morphing into a hellhound?

Keeley's eyes went wide. "Uh, I'd go out on a limb and say our Katarina isn't exactly human. The hellhounds did something to her. But how? Hellhounds are extinct. Hades killed them."

Hades. Everything always came down to Hades. "You knew the pups were hellhounds?" she demanded.

"Keys, you're not really helping," Kaia said.

"Oh! I remember! I knew they were hellhounds from moment one," Keeley replied with a shrug. "I wasn't with Hades when he first began his war with the packs, but I was with him before it ended. I hid as many as I could find. Pets are adorable. And I knew Hades would one day thank me."

Katarina growled. Baden thought *she* would thank *him* for his domineering attitude. He was wrong!

In a blink, both Harpy sisters were hanging from the ceiling in the far corner of the room. The winged "jerk-offs" pulled swords of fire out of the air.

"We're best friends, remember, Katarina?" Kaia called. "You love me."

"Katrina," Keeley corrected. "I remember how much she hates being called by the wrong name. And maybe I should flash in Baden, despite her protests?" She chugged from the bottle of ambrosia, as if she hadn't a care. "Wait. If she were to kill him, Torin would be upset. All right, that's a no-go."

Katarina pointed a claw at her. "Do *not* go against my wishes."

"We have to do something," one of the winged men said. "Without hurting her. Hellhounds weren't always evil. Once, they retrieved and saved souls from the underworld."

The two looked to be in their midthirties. One was white and scarred from head to toe, his only spot of color his crimson eyes. The other was bronzed with rainbow eyes. Both were as beautiful as their wings in an eerie nonhuman way.

"What to do, what to do." Keeley brightened. "I know! I gave her a ward to prevent pregnancy…and a ward that's essentially an off switch. Because I'm awesome, and I always think ahead. Three cheers for me!"

What! "You tricked me." And she would pay.

"Well," Taliyah snapped. "Flip the switch!"

Katarina swiped out her arm, intending to claw through the pink-haired beauty's throat.

Keeley smiled at her. "Sleep," she said, and a second before contact, it was lights out for Katarina and both of the dogs.

Music filled the nightclub as a live band played on stage. Crowds of people—scratch that, crowds of immortals—packed every inch of the place. Katarina sat at a corner table, pre-hungover but post-buzz. The dogs lounged at her feet, licking her ankles every few minutes to let her know they were on guard.

She'd awoken from her impromptu snooze about an hour ago and found herself and the dogs in an unfamiliar but lavish office, sprawled across a plush leather couch. She'd remembered what had transpired in the bar and had gone in search of Keeley, grateful for the preemptive measures the girl had taken, a lot miffed, but desperate to apologize. For one brief moment, she'd wanted to kill the girl. Kill her. As in, end her for all eternity.

If she'd done so, Katarina never would have forgiven herself.

Was that the same kind of struggle Baden endured on a daily…hourly…basis?

She'd discovered she was still inside Downfall and though Keeley had taken off, Kaia, her sister Taliyah and Bjorn and Xerxes—Sent Ones, the winged warriors were called, a species *in charge* of angels—had still been present, preparing for the club to open.

"Don't worry about the Red Queen," Bjorn had said. "She's already forgotten you."

"Sit, relax," Xerxes had said, escorting her to the table she now occupied. "Enjoy the show."

"Aren't you worried she and her canine entourage will eat your guests?" Kaia had asked. "I mean, they're hellhounds! Do you know how many of my clan died because of those things?"

Was Katarina to be hated, even ostracized? "I can go."

Taliyah had patted her on the shoulder. "Don't be dumb. I'm thinking about becoming gay for you. You're worth knowing now. And as long as we keep your se-cret, no one will come after you and your dogs."

Now Katarina watched the happenings inside the club with wide eyes. These people—immortals—par-tied like rock stars high on a cocktail of crank, adren-aline and top-of-the-line steroids. They danced with abandon, hands wandering, bodies gyrating. Some of the creatures had wings, but every set was different and specific to each immortal. Some wings were feathered while some were made of membrane and bone. And the colors! Everything from snow-white to jet-black. Rain-bows everywhere probably wept with envy.

Some of the immortals had horns. And not just on their heads. Some had snakes rather than hair. *Living* snakes. An instinct she hadn't possessed before the pups changed her told her not to look those snakes in the eye. Some of the immortals had fur rather than skin. It was as if every fairy tale she'd ever read was represented here. Mythical creatures she would have sworn were the product of an overactive imagination—or nightmares, yeah, mostly nightmares—walked by her.

The most startling thing? She now belonged among them. She might not fully shift into a hellhound, and she might still be susceptible to age and death, but she was too dangerous to be around humans, her temper a little too hot to handle. If ever she lost control and used her razor-sharp teeth and claws…

She *was* strong enough for Baden, physically and every other way. Not that he would ever know it. The bastard! But…

The truth was, she already missed him, and *tristo hrmenych*, she still ached for him. Was *he* thinking of *her*? Regretting his commands?

The burn returned to the backs of her eyes, though once again, no tears formed. Deep breath in…out.

She studied her new world more intently, grateful for the distraction. Whatever the origins of the immortals, none of the beings were afraid to throw down. In fact, three fights had already broken out. The worst one had begun when someone shouted "son of a troll whore." The biggest guy Katarina had ever seen had broken things up with only a look.

Baden could take him, she thought with a stab of pride.

Ugh. *Have to stop thinking about him.*

A vampire approached her table and licked his lips. His fangs were bright white—had he used strips?

"Hallo, pretty. Fancy a rub and tug?"

Her defenses kicked into high gear. "Not interested."

Bjorn and Xerxes swooped out of nowhere and "escorted" the vampire away. Such sweethearts, she thought, smiling when they returned to her side.

Bjorn tugged on a lock of her hair. "You are a new participant in the war, and you're on our side. We will allow nothing to happen to you while you're here."

"But I'm not a participant in anything. I'm just—"

"Say cheese." Taliyah snapped a few dozen pictures of their group on her cell phone. She winked at Katarina, saying, "Thanks. I think that'll do the trick." Then, as quickly as she'd appeared, she was gone.

Xerxes sighed. "The girl hopes to cause trouble."

"Don't they all," Bjorn remarked.

On the dance floor, Katarina caught a glimpse of— Baden?

Her first thought: *He's come to apologize!*

Heart drumming erratically, she jumped to her feet.

"Excuse me, gentlemen. Stay," she told the dogs, not wanting them to become lost in the crowd or to be overlooked and stampeded. She stalked across the room, pushing her way through the crowd…but Baden wasn't where she'd seen him.

Frowning, trying not to wilt with disappointment, she spun, searching for him. There! In the back, by a closed door. She raced forward—but Baden wasn't at the door, either. Inside the room? She tested the knob. No lock. Tentative, she entered…an office. Different than the one she'd woken in.

"Hello?"

No response.

There was a desk, two plush chairs and a wall of monitors showing different areas of the club. As she stepped deeper inside, a gust of wind slammed the door shut, and she gasped.

A tall, leanly muscled man with dark hair—no, light hair…no, dark…no, red…no, light again—stepped into view. He wore an expensive suit tailored to his body, and to be honest, he was probably the most beautiful male she'd ever seen. He exuded sex and sophistication and yet, something about him made her shudder with distaste.

"Greetings, Katarina." His voice was as seductive as the rest of him and drew another shudder from her. "So nice to meet you in person at last."

"Who are you?" The way he'd just changed his hair… realization struck. He'd pretended to be Baden, hadn't he? He'd led her back here on purpose. But to what aim?

"I'm the man who wants to help you."

"Why would you want to help me?"

"Perhaps I misspoke. We can help each other." He

eased into the chair behind the desk and kicked up his legs, revealing Italian loafers. "You might know me as Lucifer."

Hades's enemy. *Baden's* enemy. Basically: the devil she'd heard about in church.

"Please, have a seat." He waved a graceful hand. "I'm here to bargain with you, not hurt you."

Any bargain this male offered would profit him alone, no matter how amazing it seemed to her.

Deception was his specialty.

"No way, no how." She shook her head in negation. "I'm not interested in anything you have to offer."

He smirked at her, as if he knew a secret she did not. "The stories about me are exaggerated, I assure you."

Would say anything…

"You have no interest in saving your man from death?" he asked.

In lieu of an answer, she grabbed the door handle and twisted. Of course, *now* it was locked.

"Maybe this will change your mind." He waved his hand a second time, and between one second and another, a dead body appeared on the desktop.

She gasped, horrified. This was a fresh kill, blood still wet and dripping.

Lucifer held up his pinky, a long nail growing from the tip. Gaze on her, he dug the sharpened end into the dead man's eye socket. As her stomach roiled, he popped the eyeball into his mouth and chewed.

She barely stopped herself from gagging, knowing instinctively he would enjoy such a reaction.

He smiled. "The gooey center is always my favorite. Would you like a taste?"

She ignored the offer, saying, "If only you could see the world through your victim's point of view."

"Oh, I can. I do. And I savor every second."

He's worse than I expected.

"I'll *never* bargain with you." How did one fight a liar? With truth. Time to hit him where it hurt. "Why would I? You're weak." She, better than anyone, knew just how sharply that particular taunt could land. "You failed to defeat the king of angels and got yourself thrown out of the heavens. You can't even defeat Hades, or you'd have done so already."

Smoke wafted from his nostrils as he jackknifed to his feet. "You would do well to fear me, little girl."

"Fear is your way in. The door you sneak through. I choose to remain at peace."

He stepped around the desk, his body nothing but a husk for murderous rage. "I want to help your man. He and his friends fight their darkness when they should embrace it. Only then will they know true freedom and strength."

True strength. The way to Baden's heart.

The burn returned to her gums and fingertips, reminding her she wasn't helpless. She was armed. "What do you know of freedom? You, who are bound to your pride, want only to enslave others."

Biscuit, Gravy. Come!

"I *will* bring Baden to heel. I owe him," he said. "Perhaps I'll start by giving you to my army, allowing them to sate their baser needs with you. The warrior will be distraught, I'm sure, and—"

The dogs burst through the door, wood shards raining in every direction. They stopped to flank her sides, strange buzzing sounds accompanying their growls. She looked down, praying the pups were okay.

Flabbergasted, she reeled back. Their teeth…their teeth *moved*. They had two rows up top and two rows on bottom, and both rows spun round and round like the blades on a chain saw.

Lucifer looked at the pups, then at Katarina. His eyes narrowed with calculation. "I collect information, and I've heard things. If you want Baden to bend to your will, I can arrange it. I can also make you immortal."

The bend to her will thing? Not just no, but never. What a hypocrite she would be, superseding his right to choose. But the immortality thing… *Was only fooling myself when I said no, letting fear lead me.*

Fear this male must have sensed.

Because, if she'd agreed to try, but Baden couldn't find a way, she would have to live with disappointment and he would have to live with failure.

"What do you say, Miss Joelle?" A slow smile bloomed. "Shall we bargain?"

26

"There is no theory of evolution. Only a list of creatures I've allowed to live."

—Xerxes, Sent One

Can't purge this rage.

Destruction's roar was an endless scrape against Baden's mind. The beast craved blood, pain and death as never before—or barring that, he craved satisfaction with Katarina. He needed one or the other, and nothing else would do.

"I'll ask again." Baden lifted Galen off his feet, pinning him to the wall. "Where is she?"

Galen's mouth opened and closed, but he could only gasp for breath.

"Where. Is. Katarina?" William had flashed away seconds after referring to Baden as his brother, without telling him anything more about the wreaths. Soon after that, Taliyah had arrived at the safe house with pictures of Katarina. She'd smirked as he'd viewed the images of his woman smiling at Bjorn and Xerxes, as if the two were her favorite heroes.

When she left me, she looked at me as if I was a monster.

Taliyah had said, "Don't bother going to the club. She'll be gone before you arrive. I'll make sure of it."

He *had* tried to flash to the club, thinking of the place as his home—*will murder the Sent Ones for touching what's mine!*—but it had been futile. Now he wondered if Hades had somehow fixed the loophole.

Next, he'd tried flashing to Aleksander, but it had proved futile, too. He'd tried flashing to Dominik with the same abysmal result.

Had he somehow lost the ability to flash entirely?

"We need her," he shouted. "She's our calm." Their sanity.

"We? Our?" Galen finally managed to push out. "You want me to betray your girl?" He wedged his feet between their bodies and kicked. "We both know you'd kill me for that."

Baden stumbled backward, losing his grip. "You don't care about her, and you don't care about me. Stop pretending."

"You're right. I've never cared about anyone but myself." Galen straightened his collar and brushed an invisible piece of lint from his shoulder. "Do you want to know where I was the day of the assassin's attack?"

"Not anymore. Tell me where Taliyah has taken Katarina!" *Before I snap.*

The warrior pretended not to hear him, saying, "I was in town talking to a therapist about the best way to help Legion."

"I don't need to know—"

"Yes, you do need to know. You don't want to change your opinion of me. You don't want to believe I'm trying to be the right man for her—the right friend for you. To you all. I would have brought you here, would have helped you, without any incentive, but you offered the one thing I couldn't refuse. Now I'm going to help you whether you want me to or not."

"The only way to help me is to tell me where Katarina has been taken."

Galen's smile was cold. "That, I can't do. Not because I don't want to. Taliyah isn't sending me updates."

He scrubbed a hand over his face. This was his fault, not Galen's. Katarina had wanted to be an equal with her man, as any sane person would, while he'd expected her to cave to his desires. As if her desires were somehow less important than his.

It hadn't taken long to see his own stupidity. She was his most precious treasure. Why would he treat her— any part of her—with anything other than reverence?

"Go away," he muttered. "I hate you, but I don't want to hurt you."

"You don't hate me. You're just a fan in denial."

A flash of light erupted behind Galen, who turned swiftly, withdrawing a dagger from the sheath at his waist. Baden was at his side a split second later, his own trusty daggers in hand. But it was Keeley who appeared, not an enemy. She wore a matching bra-and-panty set and had rollers in her hair. Had she forgotten her clothing? This wouldn't be the first time.

"Hey, guys." She smiled and waved as if they'd bumped into each other at the supermarket. "Wait. I forgot you two even existed, so how did I—"

"Because of me," Galen interrupted. "I've made sure to send you daily reminders. So. Why are you here? Alone?"

"Oh! Right. Taliyah left her with the Sent Ones, thought it'd be funny to send Baden on a wild-goose chase while Katarina was where he assumed she wasn't, but the warriors called me back because of an emergency. I mentioned the emergency, right?" Keeley flashed to his broken nightstand and with a wave of her hand, fixed it. "I'm afraid I'm the bearer of bad news, fellas. Something marginally horrible has happened, but we'll overcome it together. Because we're family and that's what families do. Or so I've been told by Torin."

Destruction clawed at Baden's skull.

"If the Sent Ones harmed a single hair on Katarina's head…" They would be dead by sunrise.

"There's a vein throbbing in your forehead," Keeley remarked. "Are you having a stroke? Or did I not mention the situation is only *marginally* horrible?"

"Keeley." Galen's mouth curled at the corners. "Concentrate."

"Right. The emergency. Lucifer offered to make Katarina immortal in exchange for her soul and—"

"What!" Baden roared. Such a bargain would come at too high a cost, no matter how much he wanted her to live forever. She would most likely become Lucifer's slave, the way Baden was Hades's slave. The vile deeds such an evil male would order her to do…

"Will no one allow me to finish?" Strands of her hair lifted with a breeze he couldn't feel.

"Please," Galen said, ever the gentleman. "Continue."

"*And* the smart girl refused. I'm so proud of her!"

Only then was Baden able to breathe properly. "Tell me the horrible part."

"Well. Lucifer has put a price on her head. She's being hunted."

Was she in danger even now? "Why are we still talking? Take me to her."

"Wow. No wonder she left you. You think you're king of everyone's castle." Keeley's grin put Galen's to shame, far colder than ice. "Good luck with that." A second later, both Keeley and Galen vanished—and Katarina appeared.

Relief bathed him, a shower that washed away his anger. Even Destruction calmed. She had no cuts, no bruises, and was still in possession of each of her limbs.

Her anger clearly remained, however. Her gaze met his and slitted. "You!"

"Me." He took a step toward her, but she swiped a dagger from the nightstand to ward him off. He dropped his own weapons, the ensuing thud echoing through the bedroom. "Where are our dogs?"

"*My* dogs are with Kaia."

"They are mine, just as you are mine. Though I'm not commanding it be so. I'm simply hoping."

"Oh, no! You aren't—"

"I'm sorry. So very sorry. I missed you with every fiber of my being, Katarina. Your opinions matter. I will defend them with my life."

She raised her chin and waved the dagger. "Interrupt me again, and see what happens. I *dare* you."

A bolt of lust slammed into him, completely surpassing his previous anger. Her unwillingness to back down…her show of strength in the face of a dangerous situation…*my beautiful female.*

"I can take care of myself," she said. "Today, I've proven it."

He forced himself to admit the truth. "You don't need me." She could survive the world without him. She could *thrive* in the world without him. "But you still want me, and *I'll* prove *that.*" He cupped his growing length and stepped toward her. "If you'll let me. Please, let me."

"No." The tremor in her voice betrayed her. "No!"

He took another step toward her. "I'm begging, Rina." He offered the words with ragged desperation. "Cut me if you must. Hurt me. But make love to me, too. I'm nothing without you."

Her eyes sparkled. "How long will this sweet man remain with me?"

"Forever."

"Because you still expect eternity, despite what I've said?" She hissed at him, again waving the dagger. "*Kretén!* You're right. I do still want you. You made my body hunger for you."

Her admission made him hard—as—stone, his erection swelling over the waist of his pants, a bead of moisture rolling from the tip.

She added, "But you also made my mind despise you."

He could work with that. "I'll do anything you demand. And, if you let me, I'll make your body come and your mind forgive me. I just need a chance."

She tossed the dagger to the floor. "Yes to the former, never to the latter. What I want from you? For you to remember making me come doesn't mean anything or change anything. This is hate sex, nothing more. One last time. A final goodbye. Closure."

Even as she spoke, he ripped off his shirt, tore the zipper of his pants and kicked the material from his legs. "Not goodbye," he said. "You make your choice, and I make mine. I'll follow you to the ends of the earth."

"Oh, this is *definitely* goodbye." Her motions jerky, she stripped, as well. "All stalkers will be shot on sight."

Part of him missed the innocent human who'd vomited at the sight of blood, who'd beseeched him not to commit acts of violence. But he reveled in her bravery.

"You aren't the only one whose body hungers, Rina." His aches worsened as he drank her in. The rosy flush that darkened her skin. The plump breasts with the dusky tips. The flat plane of her stomach, the sensual dip of her navel. The heart-shaped flare of her hips, and the tiny patch of dark curls. Those long, endless legs.

No woman was more perfect.

"If you're done with the inspection," she said primly.

"For now." He stalked forward, slow and purposeful. Determined. He was starved for her, wouldn't spook her.

She backed up, doing her best to maintain a bit of distance. Not because she was scared of him, he saw no fear in her eyes, but calculation. The woman enjoyed taunting him. She planned to make him work for her.

He would love every second.

Anticipation drove him; he slanted to the right, sending her toward the full-length mirror in the corner. As soon as her back met the cool glass, she gasped, delighting him. He pounced, taking her by the shoulders and spinning her to face her reflection. *Their* reflection.

Destruction was already under her thrall.

With her back pressed against the heat of Baden's chest, he positioned her the way he wanted her: her hands gripping the edge of the mirror, her legs braced apart. What a sight they were. A contrast of colors. His hair a deep red, hers a glossed onyx. His skin bronzed, hers burnished brown, poreless, flawless...made for his tongue, his hands. Every part of him. He belonged to her.

They were a contrast of textures. Where he was rough, she was smooth. Where he bulged with muscle, she teemed with softness.

He breathed her in as he cupped her breasts and brushed his thumbs over her rigid nipples. "I missed these."

"No talking." The breathless rasp of her voice fogged the mirror. "Only doing."

"I can multitask." He drew her earlobe through his teeth. "And Rina? You may be able to survive the world without me, but I can't survive the world without you. *We* can't. You keep us calm. You are our home." And maybe that was why he hadn't been able to flash. *Home is where the heart is.* He could no longer make any adjustments in his mind about what was and wasn't his home. It was her, plain and simple. Always and forever.

She sucked in a breath, her eyes wide. "That's…you just admitted to having a weakness."

"I just spoke true."

Slowly, she softened against him. She even rested her head on his shoulder, giving him better access to her elegant neck. He took full advantage, kissing and licking the succulent column with abandon, savoring her taste.

"You are the sweetest candy." After giving her nipples a loving pinch, he traced his fingers down…down her stomach, stopping to dabble at her navel. All the while he ground his erection between the globes of her ass. "Last time, I took you without kissing you and vowed never to make such a mistake again. Please… I want your mouth."

She shook her head. "No kissing. This is hate sex, remember?"

Harsh words, but her breathlessness buoyed him.

"Hate kiss me, then." He would take her however he could get her. "Your taste is sure to be my ruin."

Tremors rocked her against him. "There's no such thing as a hate kiss."

"Prove it." And while she did, he would make her come so hard she screamed the house down.

She began to pant. A sheen of sweat glistened on her skin. She tilted her head up...and he waited, unable to breathe...desperate...

"I'll kiss you, but only because you need to accept the truth. Give me your mouth."

He smashed his mouth into hers before she could change her mind. His tongue moved on hers, and she moaned, meeting the ferocity of his feasting with a ferocity all her own. They ate at each other.

"C-convinced?" she asked.

"Not even close. Keep trying."

She snagged his lips for another brutal kiss. His hand trailed down...down...and he speared his finger deep inside her. She was hot—searing—and she was wet—soaking.

"I think your body *loves* me," he rasped.

Love. The word echoed in his mind, and longing unlike any he'd ever known welled inside him. He craved her love?

She ground into his finger. "More."

"Your demand, my pleasure." He pierced her with a second digit, and she cried out. He watched her reflection, fascinated by her reactions to him. Her features were soft with wanting, her hips arching to follow the thrust of his hand. Had any woman ever been so uninhibited? Satisfied because he was the man with her, and not someone else?

She reached around him, grabbing his ass and holding on tight, her nails cutting into his flesh. *She can't get enough of me. She's mine for the taking.* His control—already on edge—frayed. Madness ruled him.

He dove in for another kiss, pressing the heel of a palm against the source of her desire while cupping and kneading her breast with the other. More cries escaped her, and as one minute bled into another, the sounds came faster and faster.

She wiggled against him. "Baden. Please."

Rapture flowed through his veins. Sweat slicked over him, over her, creating an easy glide. She released his ass to lift her arms and tangle her fingers in his hair.

Yes, yes. Her breaths turned shallow as she tugged the strands, angling his head the way *she* wanted it, silently demanding he possess her mouth harder, faster, deeper.

"Going to give you everything, Rina." The need for release plagued him. *Been too long without her.* A day—an hour, a single minute—was too long. He slid his fingers out of her.

In protest, she bit his bottom lip with enough force to sting. Naughty girl. He flipped her hair out of the way, placed the hand wet with her essence on her nape and applied pressure, forcing her to lean forward until her cheek met the glass.

"Want you bare," he said. She'd taught him to crave skin-to-skin contact.

"Yes. Please. No worries…the ward…can't get pregnant…please."

Ward? Keeley must have tattooed her with a symbol used by the Curators, the Red Queen's people. A powerful race somehow able to both strengthen and weaken themselves with their mystical wards. Symbols from a time before the creation of humans.

As he dove down to lick the essence he'd left on Katarina's skin, he positioned himself for entry—then drove all the way in.

Her climax was instant and all-consuming, her inner walls squeezing his length, milking it. He fought his own release, not ready for this to end, barely able to breathe, wanting—needing—more of her. But the more he pounded into her, the more fighting his climax ceased to be an option; in fact, it became nothing but an afterthought. Her climax still raged, still squeezed at him, his name a continuous purr on her lips, and a thick fog fell over his mind.

Mine. She's mine. Will keep. Will have, again and again.

Yes, yes. So good. Nothing better. Will mark. Brand. Possess.

Control...lost.

He gripped her hips to hold her steady and thrust deep inside her one last time. He felt every wave of sublime pleasure as it left him, his body shuddering with the force.

Only when he was emptied out did her own orgasm end.

Her legs trembled, and he knew it was only a matter of seconds before she collapsed. He pulled out and scooped her up in his arms.

Panting, she rested her head on his shoulder. "See? Didn't change anything."

Only fooling yourself, krásavica.

"Sleep if you wish." He laid her across the bed then gathered the proper supplies to clean their bodies. As soon as he finished, he tucked her under the covers. "I'll protect you from anyone foolish enough to try and claim Lucifer's bounty."

"Don't need—"

"I know. You're strong." He smoothed a hand over her brow. "And Rina?"

"Yes?"

"Kaia texted me about the change in you. The fangs and the claws." He wished he'd seen the transformation. How beautiful she must have been. "The pups are hellhounds."

She stiffened, saying, "That was supposed to be a secret."

"Considering the questions you once asked me, I'm assuming they bit you at some point."

Defensive, she said, "They didn't do it to hurt me."

"I know." He knew Hades had been bitten by hellhounds, and now wondered if Pandora bore that part of him, thanks to the bands. The way Baden bore the Berserker. "If they'd wanted to hurt you, you would have been hurt. Badly. They must have done it to bond with you."

"Like the goat-man bonded with Gilly?"

"In essence. I want you to know, whatever changes the bond causes, my opinion of you won't be altered. I like you."

Destruction liked her, too, *despite* the hellhound thing. He'd been without her, and never wished to experience such a horror again.

"No," she said, sounding bitter, "you like me now that I'm stronger."

"You've always been strong." He stroked his finger along her jaw. "I pretended not to see it so that I'd have an excuse to protect you. But even the strongest of warriors need a watchman. Let me have the honor of being yours. I know I would love for you to be mine."

Heavy-lidded eyes stared up at him, more green than gray at the moment. Her lips were red and swollen from his abundance of kisses, her cheeks pink from his stubble. "Maybe…maybe what just happened between us changed a *few* things," she admitted, "but I'm still furious with you."

He blew her a kiss. "Don't worry. That makes two of us."

27

"The best defense is killing the other team's offense."

—Bjorn, Sent One

Baden did his best to barricade the desert palace from
every immortal race—those who would attack from the
sky, those who would attack from the ground and those
who would attack from the *under*ground. He built traps
along the perimeter and stocked the arsenal with weapons Hades had given him. Weapons he'd never before
seen and wasn't yet sure how to use.

When you had a price on your head, every weapon
was welcome.

After he'd told his friends about the bounty Lucifer
had placed on Katarina, they'd decided to help William
later and Baden now. They were here, in the Realm of
the Forgotten, placing traps beyond the house.

So far, no one had found a way into the realm without a key or an invitation from Galen. An invitation he
hadn't extended to Pandora.

Yesterday, Baden met her in a neutral location: the
rubble in Budapest. He'd flashed, the ability working
again. He'd simply thought of Pandora's bands, how

they were part of Hades and now, part of Baden. She'd done the same.

Another loophole? Maybe.

Like him, she'd healed from her injuries and had suffered no other demon ambushes. They'd discussed their current predicament. How neither had a desire to kill Hades. Or each other.

I don't know how this happened, she'd said with more than a little disgust, *but... I don't hate you.*

Prepare to gag, he'd replied. *Because I'm beginning to think of you as...a sister.*

She *had* gagged. *I know—brother. Will these feelings change when the bands are removed? Or is Hades's essence too firmly entrenched in us?*

She hadn't known about the hellhounds or the Berserker, and Baden had explained before answering her question. *Probably too firmly entrenched.* How else would they survive the removal of the bands?

And Hades would want them to survive. They were part of his family now.

We must defeat Lucifer, Baden had said. Lucifer had come after Baden's woman—*our woman, do not forget again*—and the bastard would pay for it.

Mess with Katarina, suffer the consequences. Let the world know.

When Pandora had mentioned the bounty on Katarina's head—*why does Lucifer want her dead?*—Baden had almost killed her. The woman he'd just admitted was the closest thing he had to a sister. If she made a play for the human... But Pandora had merely laughed at him. Laughed. Because the situation put him at a serious disadvantage.

She'd said, *We're currently tied. As distracted as you*

are, I'm sure I'll pull ahead any day. For that alone, I wish your human well. I like you, Baden, but I still plan to trounce you. Because, if we're wrong and Hades doesn't feel affection for us, one of us will die. Again. I'm determined to live.

As am I. He wanted a life with Katarina. Who would still age, despite her connection to the hellhounds. But that was a worry—a trial—for another day.

Last night, after another assassin job for Hades, Baden had asked the male to make Katarina immortal. The response?

Not going to happen, Red. Not now, not ever. If I turn your woman after refusing to turn William's, my son would help Lucifer simply to spite me.

Am I not also your son? he'd almost asked. Almost. But he'd held his tongue. Like Pandora had said, if they were wrong and Hades felt no affection for them...

"What are you doing up there, Baden?" Katarina called.

"My duty. My honor." He was high in a tree, anchoring cameras to different limbs so that he would have a view of the desert from every angle.

Katarina and the pups entered the backyard. The trio of glaring suns stroked her lovingly. And why not? She wore a white bikini that displayed her delectable curves to perfection; she was a temptation like no other.

Destruction licked hungry lips. *Must have her again. Must wait until she comes to us.*

Something they'd learned: Katarina's willingness was the key to their pleasure.

As Baden worked, his gaze returned to her again and again, his every muscle knotting, his shaft throbbing behind his zipper.

Sunglasses hid her eyes, but he thought she might be watching him, too. She stretched out on the grass, rubbed her knees together and shifted restlessly. Her nipples were beaded and clearly defined as she poured a cup of water down her chest in an effort to cool off.

"I want you, Rina."

She winced, all *how embarrassing for you.* "That's obvious, *drahý.*"

"And still you're going to deny me?"

"I mentioned my anger with you, yes?"

"No, you didn't." Vengeful women were a nuisance. And sexy. Mostly sexy. "You mentioned fury. You must be cooling off."

She sputtered for a moment, before settling on, "Don't you prefer me hot?"

Must have her soon.

Each day, Katarina and the pups had done their own thing. She'd taught them to play fetch and other games, had worked on their manners and obedience, and had even ensured they practiced biting and tugging on a padded sleeve. Her love for the animals was obvious. She constantly smiled at them, petted them and welcomed their sloppy kisses. Baden, she'd ignored.

He missed her smiles. He yearned for her pets.

"Where are Tweedledee and Tweedledum?" she asked.

Galen and Fox. They'd helped him set many of the traps and had only flipped him off a dozen times a day when he'd double-checked their work. "They're hanging cameras in front of the house."

Laboring with Galen had reminded him of the days they'd spent in Olympus, when they'd guarded Zeus.

They'd fought together, bled together, partied and laughed together.

Still can't afford to trust him.

Baden climbed higher in the tree to place the final camera—and movement just over the wall stopped him. He palmed his cell phone rather than a gun. Many of the traps he'd set were controlled remotely and with the press of a few buttons, he could blow sections of the realm to hell and back.

His finger paused over the keyboard, and he watched, ready, but the scenery remained the same.

He finished his work and dropped, landing with considerable force but absorbing impact without missing a beat. "Let's go inside and—" His bands heated, emitting a soft red glow.

A summons.

As Destruction snarled with irritation, Baden said, "I'd like you to go inside. Katarina? At least until I return—"

The backyard vanished and as usual, Hades's throne room came into view.

"Enough," Baden barked. "If you wish to see me, call. Text. Now send me back."

"When have protests ever helped you?" The king was shirtless, blood and other things streaked over his chest. Bits of tissue hung from dark strands of his hair. He wore black leather pants that had been ripped at the knees, and he had on one boot, the other missing.

Calm, steady. "I'd like to go back. Please." Begging hadn't worked with Katarina, but then, she was far more stubborn than the king of darkness.

Hades stood a few feet away, giving Baden an up close and personal view of the tattoos covering his body.

Like the ones on the Iron Fist, they *moved*, slithering like snakes. "Worried about your female, eh?"

Something about his tone… Had he learned the truth about the pups?

Will kill him if we must, Destruction said. Oh, how allegiances had changed.

"Well, you can stop worrying," the king added. "I've sent a message to those who think to hurt one of mine in order to collect Lucifer's bounty. To harm the girl is to die by my hand. Or my mouth. I'll make the decision on a case by case basis."

Hades knew. Maybe not everything, considering he was protecting Katarina rather than attempting to slay her, but he knew something. "*My* hand. *My* mouth. She's mine." Even Destruction bristled at the male's claim.

"Semantics. You are mine, and what's yours is mine."

Be at ease. The more time Katarina spent in the Realm of the Forgotten, the more likely this world—this king included—was to forget her. "I'm not here to discuss her, I'm sure."

"True. I have your next task." Hades reached into his pocket and withdrew the necklace Baden had stolen from Poseidon's concubine. "Give this to the water king. If—and only if—he agrees to support me during the war. If not, you have my permission to cut him into little pieces. But you'll need this." He tossed a weapon; Baden caught the hilt. "Deliver the pieces to every other immortal king in existence."

You've got to be kidding me. He studied the new weapon. A mini-scythe, with a curved golden blade.

"The weapon needs only a taste of your target's blood," Hades said. "After that, it can hack at the target all on its own. You have only to release it."

444 The Darkest Torment

Nice. "Poseidon *won't* agree. I stole the necklace. He'll only want to fight me."

"That sounds like a you problem," Hades said. Like father, like son. He clapped his hands. "Pippin."

The robed man materialized with his stone tablet and placed a pebble in Hades's hand. Once Baden inhaled the ash, he gained the ability to flash directly to Poseidon. He also gained the ability to survive in the water-world, just in case Poseidon happened to travel there.

"Before you go, we have one more piece of business." Hades drummed his fingers together, a true evil overlord. "The coin."

Baden stiffened. His greatest failure. "I will—"

"Aleksander has agreed to give the coin to Lucifer."

Aleksander still lived, then. Was still bound to Katarina. Destruction bucked like a bull before the blare of a horn. "I'll stop him before he can keep his word."

"Lucifer has blocked your ability to flash to the male. And he's already kept his end of the bargain, granting Aleksander an immortal army."

"Armies can be destroyed."

"Yes, and so can you."

The male *worried* for him. It was suddenly as clear as newly cleaned glass, and he wondered how he'd ever questioned Hades's affection.

No more waiting, he decided. The time had come to present his questions. "I know the bands make me your son. What do you plan for me—for Pandora— after the war?"

Hades peered at him for a long while, silent, as if debating the wisdom of his next words. Eventually he called, "Leave us."

Pippin, the guards and every creeping thing Baden

hadn't noticed before—snakes, spiders and snake-spider hybrids—rushed from the room as if their feet were on fire.

"I'll give you the answer you seek." Hades side-eyed him. "But I desire a boon in return."

Something he couldn't command Baden to do? That should prove interesting. "You have my full attention."

"You know you are...bonded to me." The admission came grudgingly. "And I know your woman trains hell-hounds." Those words—they came smugly.

Both Baden and Destruction brimmed with anger—*will protect, no matter the cost.* "You will not harm her or the pups."

The king smiled at him. "I don't want to harm them, Baden. I want to use them."

"I won't involve them in the war."

"They're *already* involved."

"No!" An explosion from Baden, accompanied by a snarl from Destruction. "Never."

"I can command you to bring her here." Hades worried his jaw with two fingers. "If she denies me, I can threaten to kill you. She'll change her mind fairly quickly, I'm guessing."

As Baden seethed with the urge to lash out, every muscle in his body locked up, preventing movement.

The king sighed. "But such threats usually only work for a short while. She'll look for ways to escape me. No. I desire her loyalty."

"Loyalty cannot be forced. Not even with the wreaths."

Hades flicked his tongue over an incisor, an action Baden caught *himself* doing. "One conversation with the girl. That's what I desire."

If he resisted Hades in this, *would* the male force the issue? "You may speak with her as long as I'm present, but you must vow not to harm her or the pups in any way—or to allow anyone else to harm them—no matter her answer to you."

A stiff nod, as if Hades had expected no less but still resented the restrictions. "So be it. Now. Your answers." He strode to his throne and sat. Every inch the royal, he said, "You aren't my son...yet. But you could be. The potential is there. Everything hinges on you. The bands start outside your flesh but burn their way inside as your will supersedes mine. Once they're fully entrenched, I'll have no anchor for my power and lose my tether of control."

No anchor, but because of Destruction, Baden and Hades would be forever bonded—Destruction would forever be a part of him. "Branded, I'll remain tangible to those with bodies?"

"You will."

Baden reeled, and reeled hard. Both he and Pandora could supersede Hades's will, becoming his children before the game ended. Hades would lose his control over them while they retained the benefits of the bands.

That. That was what Baden wanted. His life once again his own—with the exception of the beast. But he'd already learned to deal with the creature, thanks to Katarina; they weren't two anymore, but one.

Hades waved him away. "I suggest you complete today's task and prepare your woman for our meeting."

Almost giddy, Baden anchored the necklace in place and hid the mini-scythe beneath his shirt.

"Oh, before you go," Hades said. "Your methods

have been a bit…rough in the past. You're dealing with a royal this time. Try to be diplomatic."

"As you wish. Daddy."

Baden flashed. He ended up in a bedroom, the walls painted black. There were two windows, and both peered into the bottom of an ocean. The water was clear and smooth, coral glistening and fish swimming. Above, the domed ceiling also revealed an open view of the ocean—and the mers raptly watching whatever was taking place on the bed. A four-poster with wisps of black cloth shielding every side.

The race had always been big on public displays. Sex, punishments, disagreements, nothing was taboo.

When the mermaids and mermen spotted Baden, they beat at the glass in an attempt to gain Poseidon's attention. Judging from the increased moans and groans that drifted through the air, the sea king assumed his audience liked his moves and grooves.

Baden debated leaving and returning a little later— bad form, interrupting a man before climax—but why risk flashing into an ambush after the people warned their king of his unwanted visitor?

Destruction still seethed from the encounter with Hades. *Concentrate! Finish this and return to Rina. Protect what's ours.*

Yes. Striding forward, Baden tightened his grip on the scythe. He stealthily parted a section of the cloth and took in the scene. A naked woman was tied to the posts, spread completely, her body forming an X. Her eyes were covered with a mask and a ball gag was stuffed in her mouth. Not the forest nymph.

Poseidon knelt behind her, pounding inside her with wild abandon. Was this a punishment or a pleasure?

Either way, this was probably going to send Poseidon straight to Lucifer's side.

No. The mer king will die first.

Cold-blooded murder wasn't always the answer. But sometimes, in his world, it was.

Baden threw the scythe—and the king swung around and threw a dagger. The scythe nicked Poseidon's biceps, and the dagger embedded in Baden's shoulder.

He removed the weapon, dropped it to the floor, and like a boomerang, the scythe returned to him. He gripped the hilt and grinned as vibrations radiated up his arm. The weapon hungered for more; he could *feel* it.

The water king paled when the weapon's identity clicked. "You are Hades's enforcer."

"I am." Was that *pride* in his tone?

"The position won't save you. Leave now or suffer."

"I'm not the one who will suffer." He waved the gold blade.

The lover struggled against her bonds, uncertain what was happening around her, and Poseidon slapped her on the side of her buttocks, his gaze remaining on Baden.

"I'm here to return the necklace," Baden said. "A gift from Hades. In exchange, you'll agree to back him in the war against Lucifer."

"I'm…interested. We have much to discuss." Poseidon pulled from the girl, swung his legs over the side of the bed and stood, reaching for a robe.

"Slow and steady. My grip is loosening."

"I'm sure," was the wry response.

Behind him, banging sounded at the door. The guards had been alerted and would bust in at any moment. Obviously the king of the sea had no desire to chat, only to stall. Baden doubted a mention of Pandora would do the trick.

Take care of him, before we rage.

He almost—almost—conceded control to the beast. His methods were madness, but they were quick and the results undeniable. He released the scythe, instead, and the blade flew at Poseidon with a speed for the record books. Slices appeared on his face, chest, and thigh, beads of crimson welling.

Tried to be diplomatic. Failed.

Baden opened his hand and the weapon returned. "You'll vow to back Hades in the war or I let the blade devour you. The choice is yours. Either way, you have five seconds to agree. One."

Bang, bang, bang.

Poseidon lifted his bloody chin. "I won't be forced."

"Two. Three."

"Lucifer has offered me your head on a silver platter if I aid him."

So. The bastard was playing every angle.

The door at last burst open and armed men—on legs—rushed inside the room. No one took a shot at Baden. Yet. They surrounded him, awaiting the command from their king.

"Four." Baden popped the bones in his neck, preparing for battle. And he wasn't the only one. The tips of his fingers burned, and the marks on his arms writhed, the shadows rising.

Poseidon noticed and scowled. "Tell Hades I would be *honored* to aid him."

28

"All of my friends are bitches. Including the men!"

—Gillian Bradshaw

—*Momma! Daddy!*—

The words bounced through Katarina's mind, courtesy of the pups. She was still in the backyard, though she'd been in the process of heeding Baden's request and herding her group inside. The excited cry had stopped her.

"Where?" she asked, spinning.

—*Beyond the wall!*—

Seriously? She scaled the tree to get a peek at—oh, wow! An entire pack of hellhounds glared at her. And she knew they were hellhounds. They were massive, as big as horses, and all different colors. Some were solid while others were speckled. All had fangs—lots and lots of fangs. Their tails were long, coiled like whips and resting on their backs, ready to strike.

Maybe—hopefully—they were impressed with Katarina's courage. After all, she didn't soil her pants or faint. Yet.

All the hounds were clearly older than Biscuit and Gravy—who should probably be named Blood and Shed.

Trembling, she climbed down. The pups leaped at her feet. If the pair wanted to return to their pack, she would understand. And cry. Mostly cry. There was another burn at the backs of her eyes as she crouched down, and this time…yes. Moisture actually trickled down her cheeks.

She'd built a family here. Even as mad as she'd been at Baden, *they'd* built a family here. And now her family was going to be ripped apart. Again!

"So." She petted the tops of their heads. "That's your momma and daddy out there, huh?"

—*Momma! Daddy!*—

"They are good to you? Don't hurt you?"

—*Love!*—

"How were you separated from them?"

—*Sensed the bad man. Wandered off, even after Momma said to stay.*—

They'd sensed Hades in Baden, she realized. And the pack would never forgive Hades for his crimes— understandable—which meant they would never accept Baden—a travesty—which meant they would never accept her. A gut-punch!

"Why didn't you tell me before? I could have helped you find your parents."

—*Didn't want to leave you.* Never *want to leave you.*—

"Sometimes what we want isn't what we need." Her tears flowed more freely as she wrapped her arms around the dogs. A hug goodbye.

Some of their excitement drained.

—*Not goodbye! You come! You come!*—

"No, babies," she said gently. "I can't go with you. I have to stay here." Had to fix things with Baden, once and for all. He and the beast needed her, and she kinda sorta…loved them. Loved them more and more every day. Every hour. Every minute. They were the center of her story. The only path to her happily-ever-after.

I have to give my guys another chance, don't I?

"I have to stay here," she repeated, and this time she meant it with every fiber of her being. "Baden is my man, and he needs me."

The pups shook their heads no, adamant.

—*You come! You come!*— Frantic now.

The tears *raced* down her cheeks.

Be strong. The words she'd had to tell herself every time one of her dogs had gone to live with a new family. "Your momma and daddy miss you very much. You're going to be happy with them."

—*You come! You come!*—

A sob burst from her, and she buried her face in their soft, sweet-smelling fur. She cried for what she would lose today, and for what she'd already lost. Her parents and Peter, and the boy her brother had once been. She cried as she realized it was okay for her to live. To feel the emotions her loved ones couldn't.

She hiccupped when she calmed and told the pups, "I miss my mom and dad *so much*, and if I could bring them back, I would. You've been given a second chance with yours, a brand-new story. I won't stand in your way."

As she wiped away *their* tears, she almost broke down again.

"Well, well. If it isn't my little wife and her new pets." The hated voice drove her to her feet. Her gaze landed on Aleksander. He stood a few yards away, black-clad guards lined up behind him, blocking the door to the house.

Stay calm! A command for herself, and for the pups. Baden had taken precautions, had placed cameras throughout the realm. Surely Galen and Fox had—or would—spot the intrusion and sweep in to even the odds.

Biscuit and Gravy growled, and an answering growl rose from her. Maybe Katarina had disapproved of Baden's methods for disposing of his enemies, but there were two things she'd always admired about him: he stood up for himself, and he never backed down.

I'm done cowering because of Alek and his threats. The only power he has over me is what I allow.

I am strong, and now I'll prove it.

"How did you find me?" she demanded. "How did you get here?"

"Finding you wasn't easy. I knew I had a wife, but couldn't recall her name. Until Lucifer helped remind me."

Bastard!

Alek stepped toward her, only to stop when the pups issued another warning.

Each of the guards—*can't be human, too big, too menacing*—raised a big, angry-looking gun and aimed at the animals.

She placed Biscuit behind one of her legs and Gravy behind the other. *Stay.* "Don't hurt them," she shouted at Alek. "They've done nothing wrong."

He grinned coldly at her. "But you have, haven't you, *princezná*?" He didn't wait for her reply, but added, "Because of your failure to pick the lock or find the key needed to free me, I had to promise the coin to Lucifer. In exchange, he'll give me an army and a kingdom under his. I won't be a king, merely a prince. Today is just a taste of my reign."

Or he'd been tricked. "If Lucifer truly has such amazing power, why aren't you a prince right this very second?"

A flicker of red in the depths of his eyes. "I have yet to reveal the coin's location. I insisted on a visit with you before I fully align with him."

No, there was more to it than that. Lucifer hadn't liked Katarina's refusal to bargain, and he wouldn't want to risk her alliance with Hades. But given Baden's bands, there was no way around that. Except through her death.

Why not send Alek to see to the deed, since he'd controlled her in the past, without giving the human/ immortal hybrid what he wanted?

Is today the end for me? Even with her newfound strength, she couldn't take on all these men. Not on her own.

Well. If she went down, she would take Alek with her.

—*Bad people. Bad people* die.—

The pups spoke into her mind, and the desire to fight bombarded her. Her gums and fingers began to burn.

Alek frowned, as if he sensed something about her had changed but he couldn't quite pinpoint what it was. "You," Alek told her while taking another step in her direction, "will be my concubine, not my wife. I know you gave yourself to the redhead—"

"You told me to!" she couldn't help but remind him.

His hands curled, reminding her of hammerheads.

Was he imagining hitting her? "Therefore, you're no longer worthy of bearing my name. I hereby disavow my claim to you." He stretched out his arm and waved his fingers at her. "Now come."

If she refused, would he murder the dogs?

Can't let his actions affect mine. Won't back down. Not again.

She had enough regrets in her past. No reason to add more.

"I'm not going with you, *blázon*." Crazy man. She threw the words at him like daggers. "Not now, not ever. You disgusted me before the wedding, and you've disgusted me every day since. You're a worm, destined to be food for others."

His nostrils flared as he took another step forward. The pups pawed the ground—and they weren't the only ones. Her foot slid over the grass of its own accord.

Growls sprang from every direction.

Gasping, she spun. Hounds were now perched all along the wall. They'd climbed? Jumped? The hairs on their backs were raised, creating lethal-looking spikes. The tiny hairs on the back of her neck were raised, as well. Their tails were uncoiled and sticking straight up, braided ropes hanging from the ends.

Fear radiated from the guards, their hands trembling.

"Hold," Alek snapped.

In a situation like this, fear had the potential to take over, causing the guards to strike before orders were given.

"Don't you dare shoot the animals," she said with a tone sharp enough to draw blood.

Alek glared at her. "Or?"

—Attack?—

"Or I'll tell them to rip you apart piece by piece."
Mmm. Piece by piece. The perfect buffet. She licked
her lips at the thought, only to blanch. Eating an opponent would never be an option.

Pale as a ghost, Alek shouted, "Shoot them. Shoot
all of them. No survivors."

Oh, hell no!

"Attack!" she shouted, launching forward. Halfway,
her fangs and claws sprouted fully. She wanted Alek's
throat in her mouth, and she wouldn't stop until she
had it.

Oh, goodie. Eating an opponent *was* an option.

The first gunshot boomed, many others following.
Too many to count. But she wasn't hit—no, she moved
too swiftly, able to watch the bullets fly and easily
dodge. The same must have been true for the hounds,
who swarmed the yard, beating her to the men.

Blood. So much blood. A sea of it. A never-ending
ocean.

Screams echoed in Katarina's ears, despite the quiet
that had descended over the yard. The bloodlust had left
her only a few moments ago. Now she stood in place,
her feet like boulders, her legs quaking. Carnage surrounded her.

Here, there, everywhere were severed limbs, heads
and organs. The horde of hounds still gorged, chomp-
ing on the different body parts.

How many men had *she* bitten?

Alek lay before her. He was still alive, but that would
change at any moment. Or maybe not—he'd regrown the
hand Baden had removed. He wasn't human, and had

never been. When she'd bitten him—again and again—she'd sampled the power in his veins. Dark power.

He reached for her, his hand juddering. "Help." He was missing a leg and his torso was split open, what was left of his intestines spilled out beside him.

"The coin." How she spoke past the lump in her throat, she didn't know. "Where is it?"

"Help," he repeated. "Please."

"Tell me what I want to know, and I'll help you." Just not the way he probably hoped.

A tear trickled down his cheek. "My mother was… fallen angel. My father…human… I was going to die one day…she forced me to kill her…to take the coin and…hide it inside my…body."

His body. The coin was still in there, perhaps even acting as life support. Which meant, if she removed it, he would lose his life, his only bargaining chip and his new kingdom all at once.

"Help." He choked on a gurgle of blood. "P-promised."

"You're right. I did." Steeling herself for what needed to be done—*no other way*—she dug inside his chest cavity, searching for the coin. "Don't worry. Your pain will end."

He fought her with what little strength he had left. Too little too late.

In a chamber of his heart, she encountered something hard, cold and round. She had to tug to remove it, breaking a few of his ribs, but his protests ceased, and his head lolled to the side.

He was dead. Once and for all. She felt no relief.

She stared down at her bloody palm, at the quarter-size piece of gold Alek had killed and died to possess. How could something so small and pretty cause so much trouble?

She couldn't allow anyone else to find it or use it and perhaps aid Lucifer. Or Hades. Not even Baden. He'd grown to like Hades, and even she had to admit he was the lesser of two evils. The beast was trainable; Lucifer, who wanted Baden to embrace darkness, was not.

The problem was, Hades had once eradicated hellhounds. He couldn't be allowed to take another shot at them.

Maybe...maybe she could use the coin to protect the dogs? But what if he punished Baden for her daring?

Then again, if she used the coin to save Baden, severing his tie to the king, Hades could punish the hounds.

If she wished for immortality, she might be strong enough to protect both Baden and the hounds. She might not.

Every option presented a major risk. She needed time to think, to consider all the pros and cons.

A paw scratched at her thigh. One of the dogs sat in front of her, his dark eyes intelligent, stormy—and locked on her. He had long, thick scars on his muzzle. One of his ears was missing. His speckled fur was matted with blood and fleas.

—*I am Roar.*—

"I'm Katarina," she replied softly.

—*The pups are mine. I am father. Werga is mother. We...thank you.*—

The appreciation was unexpected and unnecessary. "They are wonderful—" If she said "dogs" would he take offense? "Pups." As he'd called them. "I loved every minute I spent with them."

—*Agree they are wonderful, but they have done*

the unthinkable. Drank your blood and shared theirs with you.—

They had…yes, they sure had. She remembered tasting pennies when she'd awoken from their bite. But… what would that mean for them? Would they be punished? "The fault is mine. Any repercussions are mine to endure."

—They knew our rules. You did not. No links. Kill what you taste. No survivors. No witnesses. Ever.— His mouth pulled back in a scowl, revealing his fangs. They were a lot bigger than hers. *—The three of you are linked and will remain so…until death.—*

"My death, I'm guessing." Her dry tone clearly surprised him, but she'd had one too many death threats lately. This was just more of the same.

—No, girl. You misunderstand. Your death would bring theirs.—

What!

"Katarina!" Baden's voice sawed through the tension.

She spun as new growls rang out, her heart seeming to soar and drop at the same time as she stuffed the coin in her pocket. "Don't hurt him," she shouted. "Please. He means you no harm."

—He is yours?—

"He is."

—He smells of another pack. A pack we thought long dead.—

Biscuit and Gravy had mentioned the fact that Baden smelled like Hades. And if Hades smelled like another pack… Was *Hades* connected to hellhounds?

Maybe. But if the male were, in fact, bonded to them,

he would have died when they'd died. Yes? Unless…
had he found a way to sever the bond?

To her shock, the dogs remained in place, simply
watching Baden as he stalked across the sea of carnage to reach her.

His hair stuck out in spikes. His skin was bleached
of color, but his eyes were brighter than ever, a frothing mix of fury and concern.

"Are you all right? You're bleeding. Why are you
bleeding? And you're fucking *crying*?" He wiped his
thumbs over her cheeks, collecting her tears. "What
have they done to you?" He whipped his attention to
Roar. "I'll kill you in ways you've never imagined."

The promise earned him another chorus of growls.

Katarina gripped his forearms and forced his attention to return to her. "I'm fine." For now. "The blood
I'm wearing belongs to others. Alek is dead." She motioned to what remained of her tormentor's body. "See
for yourself."

Baden glanced down at the motionless husk, silent
for a moment. He withdrew a dagger, crouched down
and sliced through Alek's neck, until the head detached.
"Now the bastard can't regenerate." He straightened.
"But why the tears?"

"My family," she told him, then turned to Roar.
"Spare my man. He had no part in my dealings with
the pups."

"*I* will do the sparing. But only if I'm assured the
hounds will *never* attack you." Baden stepped in front
of her, her sword and her shield, but she was far past
the need. She moved to his side, where she belonged.

—*The pups can no longer exist without you*— Roar
scowled at her. —*Which means you're stuck with the*

rest of us. We'll stay with you, and we'll guard you.
Your man is safe from us.—

She gasped as the implications of his words dawned.
The hounds were coming out of hiding, and there would
be no keeping Hades in the dark.

She would have to do something. With or without
the coin.

"What's wrong?" Baden hadn't heard Roar's speech,
and must have assumed the worst, considering her reaction. "Tell me before I lose control."

"The hounds...they're going to...they're mine, all of
them. My family. Now and always." But they were Hades's enemy, and Baden was Hades's man; that wasn't
going to change anytime soon. If ever.

There had to be a way to coexist. There just had to
be.

A flood of possessiveness...ferocity...filled her, her
inner hellhound making itself known.

I will protect what's mine—till my dying breath.

29

"I apologize for offending you. Be assured, it won't happen again. Oh, and by the way. You're a pussy."

–Neeka, the Unwanted

A sharp rap at the door. Cameo stalked across the hotel room to welcome the delivery boy inside. The two-story suite was the best of the best, complete with luxuries that would make anyone joyous. Anyone but her. She saw only a means to an end. A way to get to Lazarus.

I'm coming for you...

There were two benefits a hotel such as this one provided for its wealthier guests. One, she could get anything she wanted or needed simply by picking up the phone, and two, privacy was a given. Even the maids couldn't enter without her express permission.

She scanned the immediate area as she turned the knob—all weapons were hidden.

She waved the male inside. He wheeled the tray into the small kitchen and she began to hope the encounter would end without any exchange of words.

She should have known better. Good things rarely happened to her.

"Are you having a nice day, ma'am?"

Ma'am. That's *what I've become?*

She could have nodded. She could have ignored him or pretended to be deaf. Three things she'd done in the past. Not exactly feeing charitable, she said, "Yes."

That was it. One word. Tears began to pour from his eyes as if he'd sprung a leak.

Humans! Breakable little flowers, all of them. Besides the deaf human she'd once loved—the human who'd betrayed her to Hunters, nearly ending her life— the only beings who'd been able to spend any length of time with her were the demon-possessed immortals she lived with. But even with them, she had to limit what she said.

So many words were trapped inside her!

One day, those words would reach the tipping point and spew out—and the world would probably end as misery spread, suicides and homicides abounding.

The man wiped his eyes with a look of surprise. "I'm sorry. I have no idea what's come over me."

If ever he learned the truth, he would either die of a heart attack, or he'd crap his pants.

No time to bury the body, no desire to launder his clothing.

She escorted him to the door without saying a word. As he raced down the hall, embarrassed by his tears, she sealed herself inside the suite, only then relaxing enough to smell the creamy pasta and steamed vegetables. As a possible last meal it would be...adequate. But then, no food had ever tasted like anything more than powder to her. Except for chocolate, of course. That, she enjoyed, but she limited her intake because she needed *something* to look forward to and the more she indulged, the easier it would be for Misery to ruin it.

Except…this time, even the thought of chocolate caused warmth to spill through her. She tingled, she ached…with the ghost of a memory? Had Lazarus drizzled chocolate sauce over her entire body and licked her clean?

A girl could dream.

Excitement for the future filled her—and agonized Misery. The demon, in turn, did what he always did when she experienced anything other than sadness, reminding her of the biggest obstacle in her way.

No one could stand her for long. Why would Lazarus be any different?

Because he's mine?

Her friends had overcome centuries of evil when they'd met their women. Without the box, without her freedom, going to Lazarus was the best—the only—way to succeed and find what the others had: someone to love.

Maybe. Was he even mate material?

Not knowing agonized her.

And, having no idea what she would face during her quest to find him, she had to keep her strength up; she ate every crumb, even as the food settled like lead balls in her stomach. When she finished, she entered the bedroom where she'd stored the three artifacts and Danika's painting.

She took a minute to send a group text to her friends,

telling them where she'd ended up. They needed to know where to find the artifacts when she was gone.

Don't try to stop me. I have to do this. I'll return if I can, but if I can't, know that I'm doing my best to live the life I've always wanted.

The guys would give her an hour, maybe two, before they burst into the room. They worried for her safety far too much to wait much longer. They always had, even in the heavens.

Within seconds, everyone had texted her back with either curses or entreaties to be careful. Torin, the best friend she'd ever had, texted step-by-step instructions about what she'd done last time. He also cautioned her.

The artifacts stopped working for Keys. They might not work for you. If they do… I wish you the best, Cam, I really do. But please remain on guard. There are whispers that Lazarus lives by stealing the lives of others. If he takes yours, nothing will save him from us. Nothing.

Whispers weren't always true. For another moment of happiness? Worth the risk.

Even if she would only forget again.

Torin added: I love you, Cam. Come back to us. And maybe bring Viola with you. Or not. Yeah, probably not.

Viola. The keeper of Narcissism. She'd been a prisoner of Tartarus when the extra demons in the box had been handed out. She was annoying, irritating and, through no fault of her own, completely self-absorbed. She had also been trapped in the Rod, found and saved.

Recently she'd entered the Rod again—on purpose. No one knew why. Once again, she needed saving.

Cameo replied: I love you, too. I'll find her. And if all goes according to plan, I WILL return...with a smile. AND Viola. Prepare yourself.

She knew him, knew he would laugh when he read it.

Another text came in, this one from Baden: I watched him. Lazarus is more a monster than I've ever been. This will not end well for you, Cameo. He will destroy you.

Maybe. Maybe not. Either way, not going to him would be worse. She would always wonder what she could have had.

Thanks for the vote of confidence, she replied. And now, she was done communicating.

Time for action.

She tossed the phone on the desk. Trembling now, she climbed into the Cage of Compulsion. The Cloak of Invisibility, Paring Rod and painting were already inside, waiting for her. With Torin's instructions rolling through her mind, she placed the Cloak over her head and peered at the painting. The canvas depicted an office like any other. Except for the box—Pandora's box, made from the bones of the goddess of Oppression, able to enslave *anything*—resting on a bookshelf.

Cameo reached for the Rod, the final step, hoping, dreading. The moment she made contact, her entire world went black.

My honeymoon. Yay for me.

Gillian wrapped her arms around her middle as she huddled before a crackling fire. Heat radiated from the flames, but it did her no good. The realm's frigid temperature had formed a wall behind her, turning her backside into an icicle.

As soon as William had left, Puck had taken her hand and led her out of the sand castle at a pace that had allowed her to finally see her surroundings—pretty, mystical and fantastical—and through a "portal" to this other realm. Ice hell. He'd done it despite her wish to return to her friends!

He didn't want to live with William, which she now understood. But he didn't need to live with *her*, either. Not that he'd listened. Not that he ever listened.

Even though she'd asked him to stay with her, he'd taken off an eternity ago to procure lunch, which had already come and gone.

Now the dinner hour was upon her and there was still no sign of him. Darkness reigned. Silence, too. The only noise was the crackle of the logs as they burned… and her thunderous heartbeat. At this point, she kind of hoped Puck didn't return. Not until morning, at least.

This was their first night as man and wife. Would he change his mind and make a pass at her? Demand sex with her?

No, surely not. He knew her stance on the matter. Had said he respected her wishes.

Then again, he was a guy and guys tended to get stupid when they got hard.

Just…grin and bear it. She'd done it before. She could do it again.

Big hands roving over her small body…

She gagged.

I'm immortal now. I have to live with those memories forever.

I'm an idiot!

I've never even been on a date and now I'm married? Stupid *idiot!* She should have died while she'd had the chance.

A strange sound registered—the clomp of hooves? She stiffened. Next the scent of peat smoke and lavender drifted to her.

Puck had returned, after all.

He stepped into the firelight, his features as indifferent as always. And yet, he made her pulse quicken. There was something about him…

Their new connection, probably. And his inhuman beauty.

He looked as if he was wearing eyeliner. His lashes were long and black and curled at the ends, giving him soulful eyes despite his lack of expression. What would he look like if ever he cared about something? Anything? About…her?

"Lunch and dinner." He dropped two dead rabbits in front of her. "Clean and cook them while I bathe."

Excuse me? He'd been gone for hours, and that was all he had to say to her? "I'm not cleaning them." Or eating them.

He frowned at her. "You aren't hungry?"

"I'm starved, but—"

He cut her off, saying, "Then clean, cook and eat them. Problem solved."

Was this how things were going to be between them? He gave orders and expected absolute compliance? "No," she said with a shake of her head. "I don't want to touch a dead animal. I don't want to *eat* an animal. I'm a vegetarian."

He shrugged, completely apathetic. "You'll do what I command. Nothing else is acceptable." He walked away then, disappearing in the shadows.

Grimacing, she toed the animal carcasses out of her way, her stomach weeping even as her anger spiked. She was Puck's greatest investment! He'd married her for a reason and that reason hadn't changed. He needed her. So, he could freaking take care of her.

Should probably try to take care of...myself?

Definitely. And she would. Of course she would. Later. After he'd fed her a proper meal.

Oh, wow. She sounded every one of her eighteen years. How embarrassing—for her!

But she had passed hungry and now hangry, so what the hell.

She jumped to her feet and stalked after him, knowing he'd gone into the very cave he'd forbidden her from entering during his absence because "you never know what's nesting inside."

Drip, drip. The warm, damp air was fragrant with— she sniffed. Orchid oil? A dreamy scent she followed until she reached a bubbling hot spring. A whimper of longing escaped her. She could have stayed in here the entire time rather than freezing out there. Obviously, nothing was nesting.

Puck stood in the middle of the water that reached his waist, his back to her, his long hair plastered to his skin; through the strands she could see a crimson butterfly tattooed from the base of his neck to the curve of his ass. The gossamer wings looked as if they would actually lift and flutter.

And...she frowned. In many—*many*—places, Puck's

flesh was raised. With scars? A lump grew in her throat. Poor baby. What had happened to him? For scars to have formed on an immortal, the injuries had to have occurred during his childhood, before his body had developed the ability to regenerate, or had to have been so horrific, so fierce, even his ability to regenerate couldn't heal him fully.

Poor baby? Who am I?

Stay strong. She stomped her foot, saying, "You are my…my husband. You will feed me. It's your duty."

Ugh. That *was staying strong? Acting like a child?*

Slowly he turned to face her. Droplets of water trickled down his cheeks, falling onto the wide bulk of his shoulders. "I may not care about much of anything, lass, but I live by certain rules. I have to." Just then, he was an Egyptian prince with an Irish accent, and he was more confident, more commanding, than she'd ever been in her entire life. "My rules are the only reason I've survived my affliction—the only reason the people around me have survived."

She licked her lips, his gaze following the motion of her tongue.

"The one you need to memorize?" he continued— did he sound a smidge less confident? "You will work or you will starve."

A standard she would normally support. "I told you. I'm a vegetarian. I don't mind working for my food, as long as it's food I can eat."

"You *can* eat what I provided, you simply prefer not to. What you don't yet understand is this. You don't have to like the tasks I give you, lass, but you must do them."

"I would rather starve to death."

He shook his head. "That will never be an option for you."

"But—"

"You'll do as you're told, or you'll suffer."

William would never threaten her this way. He wouldn't force the issue, ever. He would provide for her—fruits, nuts, even twigs if that was all he could find—no questions asked. She'd gone from the ultimate pampered life—and a man who valued her—to this, a laborious life with a man who couldn't care less about her.

Biggest. Mistake. Ever.

"You would hurt me?" she asked through chattering teeth.

His answer was a succinct, "Yes."

She backed away from the hot spring. "I'll hate you."

"And as you've probably figured out, I won't be bothered by it."

Fear gave way to anger and incredulity, and she balled her fists. He couldn't…he wouldn't…

Actually, he could and he would. "I want to go home."

"*I'm* your home."

"I want to go to my old home."

"No. You'll go to mine."

And find herself surrounded by others of his kind? "We don't have to live together."

"We do."

Argh! He never backed down. About anything!

Clearly, she'd handled the situation the wrong way. Besides, this was a poor start to their marriage. She remembered her mom and biological dad. They'd loved each other. They'd complemented each other and sweetly touched each other. They'd worked together and the rare times they'd fought, they'd compromised.

"Fine. I'll gather twigs and search for berries and—"

"Twigs are for fire and there are no berries in this realm."

Her brow furrowed. "What did the rabbits eat, then?"

"They aren't rabbits, lass."

Won't ask. Probably best not to know. *Find a new way to reach him.* "Your situation has changed. Shouldn't you change your rules, too?"

Puck thought for a moment. He waved his fingers at her and though she had no desire to close the distance, she did just that. He patted the stone ledge, and she sat, her legs crossed. With slow, careful movements, he removed her boots and socks. She flinched at first contact and couldn't bring herself to relax, not until he dipped her bare feet into the hot, bubbling water.

Her eyes closed as the suds caressed her skin and massaged sore, tired muscles. She couldn't *not* enjoy it.

"Why do you not eat meat?" he asked. "Meat makes you strong."

Why not tell him the truth? "When I was younger, my stepbrothers would whisper to me at the dinner table. If we had hamburgers, they would ask how long I thought the cow had screamed before it died? If we had chicken, they would ask if I imagined its chicks crying for their momma?" She shuddered.

He stroked his chin. "You are far more damaged than I realized."

Most people probably would have taken offense, but she knew what she was and knew he spoke true. She *was* damaged. "I know," she said and sighed. "Maybe we could…bargain? If you'll find me something to eat—besides animals!—I'll do my best to make you feel an emotion."

Compromise, the only way to build a bridge between them.

He pursed his lips. "You'll do your best anyway."

She flicked water at him. "Is that something you can force me to do?"

"No." The word lashed like a whip.

Well, well. Look at me. Already making him angry. "Then this deal is the only way to guarantee my cooperation. And then, after I make you feel, you'll take me home—to the home of my choosing." She remembered what William had once said about him and his desire for vengeance. "And you won't hurt Torin. Ever."

Motion clipped, he spread her legs and moved between them. Again, she tensed. The position was suggestive. Too suggestive. *Far* too suggestive. She placed her hands on his chest to push him away, but he merely flattened his own atop hers and held firm.

"How will you make me feel emotion?" he asked.

Can't think like this. "I—I'll tell you jokes and sad stories."

He gave a single shake of his head. "Others have tried the same and failed."

"Had those others ever made you feel anything previously?"

"No." A grudging admission.

"Then I already have an advantage."

His gaze dropped to her legs. "What if I want to feel something other than happy or sad?"

Her mouth dried in an instant. "I don't... I can't..."

"How else will you do it?" he asked. To distract her? *Really, really can't think right now.* "You'll just have to wait and see." *As will I.*

"If you fail, will you try what I suggest?"

Those suggestions would be sexual, wouldn't they? The look in his eye...

Just have to make sure I don't fail. "Yes," she croaked. "I will."

"Very well." He nodded, releasing her and moving to the other side of the spring. "I won't force you to eat meat. And you...when we reach my homeland, you will make me feel something...one way or another."

30

"If you hope to defeat me, you're going to need a bigger pair of balls. Would you like to borrow a pair from my case?"

—Thane, Sent One

In his bedroom, Baden stripped himself, then stripped Katarina. He tossed their soiled garments into the unlit hearth, planning to burn them later and scatter the ashes.

"Wait!" She rushed to the clothes and dug through the pile. A moment of insanity? Understandable, considering everything that had transpired today.

She stood, radiating relief, and strode to the bed, where she straightened the pillows.

"The bed is fine as is." He picked her up and carried her into the bathroom…placed her in the shower stall. Hot water sprayed and steam thickened the air. He climbed in behind her to wash the blood from her, still rocked to the core that she'd cried today.

Rocked to the core, and torn to shreds. The beast prowled through his mind, on edge and inconsolable.

They could have lost her. The way Baden's friends had once lost him.

And really, Baden could have lost Galen and Fox, too. Hellhounds had had the pair pinned in the kitchen, ready to attack. As exasperating as both warriors were, he'd realized he liked having them in his life.

Thankfully, upon seeing Katarina, the hounds had backed down and joined their pack in the yard, where they had remained.

"Everything's going to be all right." He cupped her cheeks, wet skin against wet skin. "The dogs are your personal army now. You'll never be in harm's way again."

"I'm not afraid," she muttered.

"Tell me what's wrong, then, and I'll fix it." He would fix it and every other problem for the rest of her life. She was his. His to pleasure and to pamper. His to protect, right alongside the dogs. *Will always protect.*

Never letting her go.

She gazed up at him through water-beaded lashes. "I don't want to talk right now. I want to enjoy you, to make a memory that will last forever."

If she wanted a memory, he would give her a memory.

He sat on the bench, pulling her onto his lap. She straddled his thighs, the showerhead at her back. Without preamble, he thrust a finger deep inside her.

She was ready for him. But then, desire remained on constant simmer between them.

"I need inside you."

"Yes."

He gripped her by the waist, lifted her, and impaled her with a single thrust. No foreplay. Just raw passion.

Crying out, she arched her hips, moving sensuously on him. He grit his teeth and forced her to wait, motionless. Sweat rolled from him, the strength he displayed superhuman. The lack of friction was agonizing, but it was an agony he willingly endured.

"Well," she said and nipped his bottom lip. "That is certainly interesting."

"You have no idea. And I'm only getting started."

"Mmm. I hope so." Her eyelids lowered to half mast. She placed kisses along the line of his jaw. "I've never wanted you more."

She wanted him, not because he was a weapon to be used, but because he was a man. Her man. He had worth, not because of what he could do for her, but because of who he was to her. A truth as powerful as it was humbling.

"You'll get your climax." *Eventually.*

He angled his arm, two of his fingers finding her bundle of nerves. He stroked and stoked her desires. She moaned. She groaned. She breathed his name and writhed her hips in an attempt to follow his movements. When that failed, she grinded on his shaft—or tried to. He continued to hold her immobile.

"Baden!" She beat at his shoulders. "You're determined to kill me, yes?"

"I *am* an assassin, desire my weapon."

"Move!"

Her inner walls clenched his length tighter and tighter, growing hotter and hotter, wetter and wetter. Destruction wanted to give in. *Baden* wanted to give in. But the outcome was far too important.

Eternity versus momentary. Eternity won.

"I'll move," he vowed. "After we talk."

She unleashed a string of Slovak profanity.

Destruction laughed, delighting in her temper. The beast knew, like Baden, she would never betray them.

"Bodaj ta porantalo." I wish you got a stroke. *"Z chujem się na głowy pozamieniałeś."* You swapped heads with your own dick. *"Idź pan w chuj."* Go to the dick.

"That's twice you've mentioned my dick," he told her. "Are you, perchance, trying to tell me you wish to give me my reward at long last? To take me down your throat?"

"Čo ti jebe?" Are you insane? "You tease me now?"

"I'm not teasing, but I *am* determined. You're going to tell me what's wrong with you. And I'm not demanding, mind you. I'm simply giving you a reason to *want* to tell me."

"Such a dirty trick." She attempted to maneuver to her knees. When it proved unsuccessful, she leaned into the waterfall. He merely followed her, fitting his mouth around a succulent nipple and suckling, tasting her sweetness.

The curses stopped—until *he* stopped.

"Chod materi do pice." Fuck off.

"I will fuck *you*…just as soon as you give me what I want. Like for like. Nothing is free in this world."

She melted against him and combed her fingers through his soaking hair. "You are a diabolical fiend… but…but…oh! Please."

Please…yes… He suckled her nipple while once again rubbing his fingers between her legs…but when she gasped, close to falling over the edge, he forced himself to stop.

Eternity wins.

Destruction banged at his skull—*more!*—as Katarina banged her little fists into his shoulders a second time.

"Your decision, Rina," he prompted. His mind was so fogged with arousal, his every nerve ending shouting; he wasn't sure where he found the strength to remain immobile. "Talk or stay just…like…this."

More beating before she finally gave up, wrapping her arms around him and resting her head against the hollow of his neck.

Panting for breath, she told him, "I have the coin."

He stiffened. Well, he stiffened worse. "When did you find it?"

"Today. Alek hid it inside his black heart."

The one place Baden hadn't thought to look.

"My options are limited. Use it to free you from Hades's rule. Save the hounds from his ire. Or become immortal and be with you. I can have one, but not all."

"There is no decision, *krásavica*. While I wear the bands, I won't bond with you. I won't allow you to fall under Hades's command. So you must use the coin to become immortal, and together we will save the hounds." He would have her always and forever.

Creases formed in her brow. "What happens when the bands are removed?"

"Not removed, but absorbed. I'll become Hades's son. A supernatural adoption. He won't hurt what's mine."

She looked hopeful, but shook her head. "I can't trust—"

"Trust *me*." Finally Baden moved, sliding in and out of her once…twice…before stopping again. She clung to him. "Promise me."

Her claws scratched his back, every mark stinging.

"I'll do what I think is best." That said, she bit his ear and then, oh, *then*, she turned the tables on him, whispering all the things he made her feel, telling him how deeply she ached for him, how only he could satisfy her.

How had he ever thought this woman unsuitable for him? How had he ever thought her weak?

Of the two of them, she was stronger. By far. She had tamed the beast. She had walked away from a bargain with Lucifer. She had won the allegiance of a hellhound pack. There was nothing she couldn't do.

And there was one thing *Baden* couldn't do: stay still. Not any longer.

"Rina." He flashed her to their bed, because there, with her, was home. He pinned her underneath him, his shaft still buried hilt-deep. "Will you wrap your legs around me?"

The moment she complied, he gripped the headboard and pulled out, farther and farther, until he almost slid free—then he slammed back in. He repeated the action again and again…moving in and out of her. *My woman. Mine to pleasure.*

Every thrust of his hips was a promise. Every gasp of his name was a new tie between them. A new bond: a man and his woman…a man and his greatest treasure.

Over the years, Baden had experienced the worst life—and death—had to offer. She had made everything better. She had made every trial, every battle, worth fighting.

Control slipping, he pinned her hands over her head. Their fingers wove together. He slowed…slowed his thrusts…until every inward glide lasted an endless eternity, her hips lifting as high as she could get them to greet him. Sweat slicked their bodies and her nipples teased his chest, the friction delicious, like running matches over a hard surface. Flames sparked.

He held her gaze, letting the tenderness only she elicited shine bright and true, without hindrance. "There will always be something, some reason we shouldn't be together, but there will never be a good time to live without you. I will cherish you, Rina. I will never hurt you, not again. And I will show you the world—my world. Our world."

Tears welled in her eyes, wrecking him. He settled on his haunches and pulled out of her.

Moaning, she reached for him. "Empty, come back."

He fell to his back and lifted her above him. When she straddled him, he leaned against the headboard and clasped his length. "Taste me. Taste your honeyed sweetness on me. See how good we are together."

She eyed his shaft as if he'd just presented a starving woman with a banquet. "You are naughty, but lucky, lucky you, I am, too. I'm thrilled to give you your reward."

Slowly she lowered her head. With her gaze locked on his, she sucked his shaft into her mouth and moved her tongue under the crown. The light scrape of her teeth had him hissing in agony…and rapture.

"Hurt you?" she asked.

"Only hurts when you stop."

"Like for like," she said and chuckled softly when he cursed. With another suck, she took him into her mouth and slid down, down until she had him at the back of her throat.

He cupped her nape, his fingers tangling in her hair. "Been so long since I've had this," he managed to croak. "But never this good."

A happy purr vibrated along his length. His sac drew up tight.

"Harder, Rina. Faster. *Please.*"

She obeyed, her hand coming into play, squeezing his base as her mouth slid up and down, again and again, leaving wet and heat and aches behind.

"Sucking me so good," he praised. The beast purred in the back of his mind.

Her free hand sank under him, her nails digging into his ass. *Going to come...*

No. Not without her.

Baden pinched her chin and lifted her head. She was panting, her lips swollen, red and damp.

"Want more," she said, wrenching free of his hold with every intention of fitting her mouth over his cock once again.

My woman. My prize. Craves my taste. Was there anything hotter?

"I'll give you more." He sat up, gripping her hips and turning her around. As he leaned against the pillows, he took her with him, dragging her hips higher and higher up his chest, leaving a path of liquid fire in her wake.

When her sweet, honeyed core was positioned directly over his face, he rasped, "We do this together."

Understanding, she braced her hands outside his thighs and sucked his shaft back into her greedy mouth. At the same time, he pierced her opening with his tongue. Her teeth clenched on his shaft, pleasure racing through him.

Urgency filled him, and passion drove him. He licked at her, sucked on her. The sweetest candy, the finest wine.

"Baden." Tremors in her voice. "I'm close."

"Hold on, Rina. I'm not done with you." *Will never be done.*

She set upon his length in a maddened frenzy, every motion hard and dirty. He wanted to last, wanted this—her—forever, but in seconds, she pushed him over the edge of satisfaction. As he jetted into her mouth, roaring his satisfaction, he pierced her core with two fingers and pressed his tongue against her swollen little core. When he sucked, hard, her scream of pleasure filled the room. They shattered and shuddered together.

When he was tapped out, she licked him lazily, as if she couldn't get enough. He picked her up and fit her against his side. His heart had yet to slow. *Content in every way.* He doubted he would ever recover from this.

A soft snore rose from Destruction, drawing a laugh from Baden.

"Ashlyn told me how she and Maddox got together," Katarina said, tracing her fingertip over his chest. "I know how *all* your friends got together with their women, actually."

Baden gently smoothed a lock of hair behind her ear. "What are you trying to tell me?"

"Well, at the center of every story, there's one thing in common. They sacrificed something for each other."

He'd had the same thought once. Love sacrificed.

Katarina peered up at him. "Baden... I want you to know... I love you. I really do."

He went still, the ability to breathe abandoning him. He'd once thought he and Katarina had no real foundation. Which, he realized now, was absurd. She was his foundation. His *only* foundation. *"Krásavica—"*

But she wasn't done. "I'm not sure how it happened

or even when. All I know is that it should have been impossible. My captor became my life raft."

"I lo—"

"No. Don't say anything. Let me get this out."

He frowned but nodded. He loved her, too. Loved her with all his heart—the very heart she'd revived from the dead. He should have realized sooner. His possessiveness. His desire to be with her. His connection to her.

She was his light. His only hope. The way out of the darkness.

"You are strong, intelligent and honorable," she said. "And I've come to accept you will always solve problems with your fists and sometimes daggers. You have to. You're at war. But there are some things you can't—"

"Katarina," he said, stopping her. He cupped her cheeks, caressing her silken skin with his thumbs. "You are—"

"Bored with this conversation? Yes." Hades's voice brutally murdered the tender moment. "Also, I thought a literal tit for tat was only fair. Now we're even."

Destruction came awake with a jolt and a desire to slaughter.

Baden scrambled from the bed, throwing a sheet over Katarina, who shoved her hands under the pillow she'd straightened earlier.

He glared at the king. "You made a mistake, coming here like this."

"What are you going to do? Spank me? I'd probably like it. What you won't do? Renege on our bargain. I'm ready for my conversation with the girl."

A loud *bang* erupted at the door, as if it had just been hit by a Mack truck. *Bang, bang.* The wood cracked and split, and two large hellhounds prowled inside the room, their gazes locked on Hades, who stared at them with shock.

"It's true, then," he said, slack-jawed. "My hounds are—"

A menacing rumble rose from the pair, all *not yours, never yours.*

Hades narrowed his focus to Katarina.

Wrapped in the bedsheet, she stood, a vision of strength and courage, unwilling to back down in the face of danger. "They are *mine.*"

Hades turned his glare to Baden. "You have five minutes to dress and bring the girl to my throne room. You won't like what happens if you're late."

31

"Baduction might be a brute, but he's my brute."

—Katarina Joelle, newly minted member of the
hellhounds

Katarina's stomach filled with acid as she dressed in a clean T-shirt and pants, the coin clutched tightly in her fist. When the beautiful dark-haired man—Hades—had first appeared, she'd feared he'd come for it, meaning to snatch it before she could use it.

But he hadn't. Now she had to deal with him. She had to use the coin, which meant she had to decide what mattered most. Since Baden no longer despised his bands, she could use it to become immortal, as he wanted, so they could share a future, or she could use it to save the dogs once and for all.

Baden dressed in his customary black shirt and camo pants before strapping weapons all over his body. He took hold of her wrist, staring at the hand clasping the coin—debating what to do?—before framing her cheeks with his big hands.

"I want you immortal." His tone was firm, unbending. That he hadn't simply tried to take the coin...well, it proved just how much he trusted and admired her.

"I know," she said softly.

But he wasn't done. "I love you, and I must have you in my life. Without you, I have nothing. Without you, I *am* nothing."

I am his strength, she realized, her eyes growing wide.

"And I don't want to put any pressure on you, but without you I will destroy the world and everyone in it."

She choked on the combination of a laugh and a sob.

Once upon a time...

He is my new story.

Love changed everything, didn't it?

She gave him a gentle kiss, a silent moment of communion. "I love you. Love being with you. But I also love the hounds."

As she lifted her head, Roar nudged her leg.

—*You go to Hades,* we *go to Hades*—

"No." She shook her head. "I don't like the thought of you in danger."

"Imagine how I feel about the possibility of *you* in danger," Baden began.

Roar prodded him out of the way, letting the warrior know he wasn't part of the conversation. —*Hades knows we follow you. He will want you in his employ and will stop at nothing to get you. Do not agree. Our ancestors* bled *to free themselves from his rule. We will not make light of their sacrifice and submit to him.*—

"Was he cruel to them before he killed them? Your ancestors, I mean." How much pain and misery had he dished?

—He blamed the entire race for the centuries he spent imprisoned.—

So, yes. Yes, he'd been cruel. Probably more so than she could even imagine.

"The man Hades is today isn't the man he was in the past," Baden said. He couldn't hear the hound, but he could guess what had been said based on her response. "There's good in him. I've sensed it, even seen it."

And had come to love it, she thought. Had come to love the man himself.

—Your mate is blinded by his bands.—

Or the hounds were blinded by their hate.

—We will go with you. Get used to the idea.—

"All right. But I'll have to hold on to you when Baden flashes me."

Roar gave her a *just try it* look and shook his head, dead fleas falling from his fur. First order of business when she returned: giving the entire pack a bath.

Wonder how they'll react to that.

—I know you've only just met me, girl, but surely even you can sense my power. We will never *need the warrior's help.—*

Great. She'd offended him.

"We must go." Baden tugged her to his side. "Whatever happens, remember that I love you, that you are my top priority, and I will allow no one—*no one*—to hurt you or the hounds."

"I love you, too." She rested her head on his shoulder, trusting him, and by the time she'd wrapped her arm around his waist, he'd already flashed them to Hades.

A new room took shape—a throne room. The sight of it shocked her and, before she'd met Baden, might have made her vomit. Blood splattered the walls. Screams sounded in the distance. A pile of dead bodies rested in the corner. The pungent scent of what could only be brimstone stung her nostrils. And the throne itself—compiled of human bones—was a monstrosity. Now she merely thought: *Hades should fire his decorator.*

The male sat on that throne with a bored expression, as if he hadn't ordered their attendance. An old man wearing a robe stood at his right, and four warriors were lined up at his left. Those warriors were a lot like Baden: scary-ass sexy.

Every man on the royal dais stared at her, taking her measure.

She released Baden to give them all a double-birded salute.

They were *amused.*

Roar and Werga appeared in front of her, and the group stopped laughing.

Hades canted his head at the hounds. "Told you."

The other males stared with awe—and maybe horror.

"Onward and upward." Hades spread his arms in welcome. "You are Katarina Joelle and—"

"She is mine," Baden announced. "My woman."

"I am Hades," the man continued as if he hadn't been interrupted. "I'm sure you've heard of me. I'm the king of the underworld."

"You mean the king of *this* realm," one of the men piped up.

Hades pursed his lips. "Yes. The men at my left are kings within their own domains."

Five royals in total, here to witness the coming events. Wonderful. "Well, who among you is the strongest?" she asked. "He's the one I'd like to speak with."

This time Hades was *not* amused. "You're a clever

girl, aren't you? Sow dissent and watch us fight for the title of strongest, allowing you to walk away unscathed. One day, we shall fight for the title, but today is not that day." He stood, his big body encased in an Italian suit. "We're still waiting for—"

A flash of light had her turning—and facing Pandora. The woman wore a scarlet gown, the silk clinging to her curves like a second skin. Her black-as-night hair hung pin-straight around her face, hitting just above her shoulders.

"Excellent." Hades nodded with satisfaction. "Everyone is here."

Katarina noticed one of the kings peered at the warrior woman with white-hot desire.

How interesting.

She met Pandora's glare. The woman who'd attacked her without provocation, who'd fought with Baden and betrayed him, as well as befriended him, and kept him sane during the worst years of his life—and death. They nodded at each other with grudging respect.

"First order of business," Hades said. "The game. My players are tied. Whatever am I to do?"

"Kill them both," the tallest of the kings called.

"Give them to me," another said, his gaze still on Pandora.

Steps slow and measured, Hades glided from the dais. *Have you realized the enormity of the gift I gave you?*

His voice…he'd spoken straight into her head, just like the hounds. And judging by the confusion on Baden and Pandora's faces, he'd spoken into their heads, as well.

Not just a piece of me, but a different version of

me. Baden, the berserker. Pandora, the hellhound. He smiled a predator's smile at the warrior woman. *Don't think I haven't noticed your meal choices lately. But. While I will allow you both to live, you'll have to fight for the privilege. Here and now. Show me who's strongest, bravest. Him—or her—I will reward.*

He held out his hands to Katarina. "While Baden and Pandora beat each other into blood and pulp, you and I will chat, get to know each other better."

"No." Baden moved in front of her. "I told you. She's mine. You won't speak to her without me by her side."

Hades waved his hand and Baden dropped to his knees, where he remained. "You'll fight Pandora, as commanded."

He bared his teeth as tension pulled his skin taut. Was he battling the compulsion to obey? Was Pandora? She bore the same pained look.

Katarina's heart shuddered in her chest. She'd thought she'd had options. She didn't. Not really. She could only trust Baden would keep his word to protect the hounds.

"I have a better idea," she announced. "You will release Baden and Pandora from your control. *Without* hurting or killing them."

Hades laughed. So did the men on the dais. Men who were killers. They had to be. They had dead eyes. Eyes that proclaimed: *I take what I want, when I want, damn the consequences.*

"Katarina," Baden grated. "Don't…"

"I'll grant your request," Hades said to her, ignoring Baden. "*If* you agree to live here with me—with your hellhounds."

A line of hair stood up along the spine of both Roar and Werga.

"No," she said. "You'll agree to my terms because of this." Smug, she tossed the coin at him.

He caught it without glancing away from her—and he smiled. "You found it."

She gave a single nod. "I did."

"Well, I hate to be the bearer of bad news—oh, who am I kidding? I love it. Someone misinformed you, darling. Probably because I misinformed everyone who's ever asked about the coin. It doesn't buy you whatever you want. Not even a single wish."

No. He was lying. He had to be lying, trying to trick her. To force her to back down.

Baden grabbed her hand, pulling her down beside him, hugging her and whispering, "The hounds will take you somewhere—anywhere—else. I'll fight Pandora, and I'll find you."

"No. I'm not leaving you, and I'm not letting you hurt your...whatever Pandora is to you. But I also can't enslave the dogs. I just can't. They would rather die."

"Katarina," he said, his tone grave. "I'll win. I'll claim my reward. The safety of the hounds."

Yes, but at what cost to his soul?

Sharp fingers tangled in her hair, yanking her to her feet. She cried out. Baden and the beast snarled in unison. The dogs growled.

She growled and twisted to bite Hades's hand. Infecting him the way she'd been infected? Or did the link require conscious thought?

The king released her, stepping away from her.

She jumped to her feet, demanding, "What *does* the coin buy me?"

He rubbed the wound she'd caused. "A chance to fight and kill me and *take* my crown."

Her stomach dropped. Fight Hades? How could she ever hope to beat him?

"Don't you dare," Baden shouted at the male. "You touch her, and I'll kill you."

"If only you could back up your threat with action," Hades told him.

Roar and Werga moved to Katarina's side, brushing her calves to claim her attention. She looked down and met Roar's troubled gaze.

He rubbed his face against her biceps, his teeth scraping, cutting her skin, and a wave of dizziness hit her.

—We are now linked for the rest of our lives.— Anger roughened his tone. She'd gotten them into this mess, and they couldn't kill her to get out of it.

Werga nuzzled her other arm before biting into her muscle. More dizziness…but it was accompanied by strength. Power. Animalistic, wild and savage. A burn at the ends of her fingers, worse than ever before. Little claws grew at the ends, and she couldn't stop them. Inside her mouth, her teeth sharpened, cutting her gums.

"What's happening?" Hades demanded.

"Did they just…link with her?" one of the warriors on the dais asked. "Willingly?"

—Hades tried to force a link before he slaughtered our ancestors. He soon learned it cannot be forced.—

She heard Roar's voice so clearly now, as if he'd actually spoken the words, no filter between them.

"They did," Hades said, emotionless. "Well, Miss Joelle. I accept the coin *and* your challenge. Weapons are lady's choice. If your hounds enter the fray, my allies will behead Baden without hesitation. I adore the male, but I've learned to prioritize."

He was going to fight her?

Likelihood of Getting Bitten: 100%. Yes, she was scrappy and had fought kids in school, but she'd never been in an all-out brawl. How was she supposed to defeat a monster? "I don't want to fight you."

"Too bad. The challenge was made as soon as you presented me with the coin. You can stand there if you'd like. I'm happy to do all the work."

Okay. There was no way out of this. She had to defeat him, despite the odds, and that was that. The pups—as well as Roar and Werga—now counted on her.

"No," Baden shouted, struggling with all his might to stand. "Fight me instead. I'll be her proxy."

"Denied." Hades removed his shirt, revealing row after row of muscles, his strength deadly, his tattoos strange. "You'll stay right where you are, warrior."

More and more hellhounds jumped past an invisible curtain and landed inside the room. They raced around her, each scraping her with sharp teeth before darting away from her.

No longer was dizziness a problem. She was too strong for it. So strong she wasn't sure how her body contained it, wasn't sure how she hadn't morphed into the Hulk.

"I'm waiting," Hades snapped.

Jealous of her connection to the hounds? "I choose hand-to-hand combat," she said. With the claws, she wasn't sure she could actually grip a weapon.

"No. No!" Still Baden struggled, straining so forcefully a vein burst in his forehead. "Don't do this. Please."

She tuned him out. She had to. Beating Hades would save her pups and Baden and Pandora. Two goals, one trial. No prob.

She was so juiced on power the battle began to sound like the best—idea—ever. When she stepped forward, Baden's struggles increased so forcefully, she could hear his bones popping out of place.

Not tuned out, after all.

—*Focus! Let our instincts guide you. You'll never survive otherwise.*—

Wonderful. She met Hades in the middle of the room. "I'm ready."

"Whenever you decide you've had enough," he said with a smile, "all you have to do is pledge your life to my service and the pain will end. Until then…" He struck.

Words Keeley had once spoken to Baden filled his head: *If you have two wreaths and one immortal, how many problems will he face? Gold. Obviously. Because the heart bleeds secrets and doggies have claws.*

The problem—one gold coin, trapped in a bleeding heart.

Then Pandora's situation took center stage. In essence, she was a hellhound. Like Katarina. If Pandora was linked to a hound, hurting her could hurt Katarina. Maybe. Probably. He wasn't sure how it worked, only knew he didn't want to risk harming his woman. Ever.

Then… Hades punched Katarina.

His woman recoiled from the impact. Baden roared loud enough to puncture a lung.

Free myself, flash her to safety, kill Hades.

As he fought the king's compulsion, he popped both shoulders out of joint and fractured several ribs.

A frenzied Destruction *helped* him.

Hades drew back his fist, intending to launch a second strike.

"No!" Baden shouted.

Too late. Hades struck Katarina in the face. Beautiful, delicate Katarina flew across the room. When she landed, she rolled with her momentum, shockingly graceful, and came up on all fours, like an animal.

As blood dripped down her cheek, another roar ruptured Baden's lungs. He knew Hades wasn't fully engaged; he wasn't surrounded by shadows. But it wouldn't take much to kill a human. Even one bolstered by hellhounds.

Have to stop this.

He unsheathed a dagger and stabbed into his shoulder, reworking his plan.

Remove my arms, remove the bands. Tackle Hades with what's left of my body.

Hades operated in the human and spirit realm. Baden, even as a spirit—which he would be without the bands—would be tangible to him.

Shadows sprang from the marks on his other arm, eating at the dagger, protecting themselves. Without his body, they would have no host.

"More?" Hades asked Katarina.

Without a word, she launched forward and slammed into him. No, not just slammed. Ripped. She bit into his neck and tore out his trachea. As he fell, she spat the bloody cartilage and tissue on the floor.

Baden stilled. Destruction gaped.

Sweet Katarina could…win?

Hades's body had repaired itself by the time he landed. He grabbed Katarina by the ankles and tripped her. The moment *she* landed, he was at her side, grabbing her by the hair and tossing her across the room. She crashed into the wall, cracking stone. Dust thickened the air. Miraculously, she didn't pause to catch her breath; she simply dove at Hades, snarling as she bit him.

That's our woman!

"Take out his eyes *then* his throat!" Baden shouted, his voice layered, the beast just as determined to save her.

She managed to claw out one of Hades's eyes before he was able to bat her away. She only came back for more. He batted her away again and again, but she always came back. He couldn't get rid of her. She came in high, clawing and biting his face and neck, and she came in low, clawing and biting his ankles and calves in a nearly successful attempt to hobble him. Her ferocity staggered Baden.

"Pledge your life to me," Hades demanded, "before I decide to end you for good."

"No!" Baden shouted. "Don't do it." The hellhounds would hate her, and she would never forgive herself.

Snarling, she jumped on Hades and tore off his ear—with her teeth.

Shadows began to rise from the male, and Baden knew they would destroy her. Not even the hounds could defeat them.

No. No, no, no. Can't let her die. Can't. "Don't let the shadows near you, Rina."

Baden put every bit of his remaining strength in breaking free. He would rather die than lose his Katarina. He would rather suffer eternally. Would rather cease to exist.

Love for her consumed him, his desire to help her completely superseding the bond he shared with Hades. The bands on his arms began to heat…and heat…burning his skin…singeing and blistering. Sinking inside him. *Branding* him.

The pain! His flesh cooking! Smoke wafted from him, but finally, blessedly, the bands disappeared, leaving only the tattoos behind, and he began to cool.

Suddenly Hades threw back his head and roared to the rafters, as if he'd just had an organ removed. Or had a new one sewn inside him.

Katarina used his distraction to her advantage, tearing out his throat yet again. Hades fell, the shadows disappearing, and Baden threw himself between the two combatants.

His glamour girl tried to shove him out of the way, still snapping and snarling at Hades, who leaped to his feet, his throat already on the mend.

Baden's first thought: *I'm still tangible*.

His second: *Finish this*.

"You might be able to kill me," Katarina spat at Hades, still trying to get through Baden, "but I'm going to take you with me."

The two were cut and bleeding, clothes tattered and stained. Both were panting.

"No more," Baden said, cupping the back of Katarina's neck and drawing her into his side. As Destruction mewled, glad to have her near, he petted her hair and whispered words of praise in her ear.

Gradually she relaxed against him.

The dogs lined up at his sides, glaring at Hades, perhaps even preventing him from making another move against her.

"Do you trust me?" Baden asked Katarina.

Her gaze, now filled with a wealth of vulnerabilities, met his. "You know I do."

Someone had to win the war with Lucifer, and he would rather it be Hades. "If Hades agrees to our terms, will you allow him to live?" He wanted to kill the man—and still might—but better to err on the side of caution today. They could always kill him later.

She drew in a breath, slowly released it. She nodded.

Baden kissed her on the forehead before facing the king. "I'm no longer yours to command, but I'll continue to be your ally in the war against Lucifer. In return, you won't harm Katarina or the hounds. You won't pressure them to aid your cause. If they forgive you for what transpired this day—and in the past—they forgive you. If not, it's your loss. The choice belongs to them. You won't get me any other way."

Hades looked Baden over with...pride?

If he liked that, wait until he heard the rest. "You fought my woman, and I *will* punish you." It would be bloody, and it would be violent. Hades had *much* to answer for. But it would happen after the war, when a worse enemy had been dealt with. "No bond matters more than the one I share with Katarina."

"Yo, Baden," Pandora called. "I want in on this."

He couldn't help with her bands. She had to find the strength to overcome them on her own. But he could give her *something*. "Pandora will be given a kingdom of her own to rule." It was what she'd wanted, what she'd hoped for.

Hades shocked him to the depths of his soul by nodding. "All shall be as you've asked. Your strength has proven your worth…my son."

What happened next happened quickly. Katarina could taste the tang of copper in her mouth, could hazily recall what she'd done and how she'd viciously attacked and bitten Hades, so she was a little unprepared for the smile he leveled on her.

"You've earned your immortality, girl. More than that, you have the strength to endure it. Pippin." He clapped his hands.

The old man in the robe removed several stones from his tablet and handed them to Hades. She thought… she thought she saw a gorgeous young man under the wrinkles. Perhaps she'd had a screw knocked loose in the fight.

Each stone burst into flames, the ashes floating, floating toward Katarina, and then they were there, in her face, and all she could do was breathe them in.

A wave of dizziness hit her, stronger than all the others combined. It nearly swept her off her feet, but Baden tightened his hold, preventing her from falling. She moaned, and the hounds moaned with her, each of them toppling over as if drunk. Were they becoming immortal, too, through the link?

And was she immortal *right now*? Had the inhalation of ashes truly changed the makeup of her DNA?

"William will hate me for this," Hades said. "But you, Katarina Joelle, are worth the trouble. And yes. This means I'll allow you to keep Baden. You're welcome."

"You don't control me, *kretén*, and you never will. But I appreciate the vote of confidence." For once!

"She is Katarina Lord now," Baden proclaimed. "I claim her as my wife."

Maybe that would have been enough to make her immortal, the way Ashlyn's bond to Maddox had made her immortal, but probably not. Maddox hadn't been a spirit bound to wreaths.

And neither was Baden. Not now.

He peered deep into her eyes. "If you'll have me."

Her love for him was a wild thing, and yet as pure as newly fallen snow. Denying him would have been tantamount to denying her body food. "I will."

He blessed her with a radiant smile, one so bright it made her eyes water.

Would the waterworks *ever* stop?

Hades cleared his throat. "You, Katarina Lord, will help heal the breach I created with the hounds all those centuries ago."

—*Never.*—

Roar ran his paws across the floor.

"The things you did to them—" she began.

"Are hardly worth mentioning." Hades waved a hand through the air. "I merely put all of their ancestors down—or thought I did—after they killed my— well. It doesn't matter now. The past is the past. We march on toward the future."

A growl rose from her. So dismissive. *I will*—

Baden stepped in front of her, meeting the gaze of his…father. Drawing attention away from her. "I want the seed of Corruption removed."

Hades protested, but Baden shook his head, adamant.

"Very well." Hades gripped his arms, and the shadows slithered from Baden's arms to coil on Hades's wrists.

"Thank you." Baden faced Katarina. "Let's go check on your brother, *krásavica*."

She sighed. She knew what he was doing, and she was going to let him do it. There would be no more fighting. At least, not today. "Yes. Let's."

"Afterward, we'll go home."

"To the Realm of the Forgotten?" Where the slaughter of Alek and his army had taken place. Where... someone else lived. What was his—her?—name?

"No. To my—our—friends. I want to share our happiness with them. You are happy, yes?"

She wound her arms around him. "More than I ever thought possible, *pekný*." He was the start of her story, and he would be the end of it. *A happy tale.*

Once upon a time...and forever after.

Epilogue

Baden reclined next to the fireplace, a glass of whiskey in hand, watching as his beautiful Katarina taught Maddox's children how to properly play with hellhounds. The entire group had moved into a new fortress—one located in Budapest, like the other, but higher in the mountains, hidden by a wealth of trees.

Torin had paid the former owners a fortune to leave in a hurry.

The Lords were already making memories here.

Just last night, Katarina had given the entire hellhound pack a bath. The animals had protested, loudly, but she'd told them they weren't allowed inside the new home until they were clean and flea-free. She'd stood in the backyard with a water hose and one by one the hounds had allowed her to do her thing.

A funnier sight Baden had never beheld. Hounds feared the worlds over for their strength, prowess and desire to eat their enemies—as well as their friends— had trembled while a slip of a female lathered them with shampoo.

His life was more than he'd ever dreamed possible, even though not everything had worked out the way he would have liked. The war in the underworld still raged, and it was only heating. No one had heard from Cameo. William hadn't returned to the fortress, but word on the street was he had followed Puck to his homeland.

Katarina's brother had lived through the worst of his withdrawals and had started down the road to recovery. He'd apologized for all the horrible things he'd done to her and her dogs, and Baden knew she'd begun to have hope for him and for their relationship, but as soon as he was released from the dungeon, he'd snuck out to buy heroin. Katarina had asked one of the hounds to follow and guard him, but in her heart, she'd let him go.

After she'd overcome her own wreaths, Pandora had opted to stay in the underworld with Hades to build her kingdom there. Baden wondered if she'd stayed because of affection for her new father...or an attraction to one of the other kings. She had secrets and she wasn't sharing them with him...her brother.

Would he ever grow used to the term?

Maddox plopped into the chair next to his. "Well, my friend. I can tell you've learned your lesson. No matter how dark and painful the present, the future can be brighter. You just have to hold on."

"This isn't a Hallmark moment." Baden flipped him off, earning a laugh. "No matter how calm the present, the future can be stormy."

His friend sobered, nodded. "Hades and Lucifer are still lining up their players."

"It's only a matter of time before they finish and true combat starts."

Maddox reached out, patted his hand. "Our side will win. Then we'll help you punish Hades for his battle with Katarina."

Baden's chest constricted. "You're a better friend than I deserve."

"I learned from the best," Maddox said, and for a moment, Baden was transported back to their days in the heavens. When a Titan army ambushed the royal soldiers tasked with guarding Zeus.

Maddox had been hit right away, a myriad of spears and arrows cutting through his chest and exiting out his back. More spears and arrows fell, ready to take out the rest of them. Baden could have run for cover, but he'd run to Maddox instead, carrying him to safety.

"We have the artifacts back in our possession," Maddox said. "We'll keep searching for Cameo, Viola, the box and the Morning Star."

Only then could his friends be freed from their demons. The ultimate goal.

Galen stalked into the room, gaze secured on Baden. "Think you can renege on our deal, prick?" His wings were larger than before, arching over his shoulders, snow-white down covering every inch. "I want my date."

"You promised to date him?" Maddox punched Baden in the arm. "Good luck with that. Katarina will protest."

"Katarina will demand they kiss in front of her—with tongue," the girl in question called.

Baden pushed to his feet. He wasn't surprised Galen had shown up. He was only surprised Galen hadn't shown up with Fox at his side. The girl hadn't stopped texting Baden questions about Distrust.

How do I know what's instinct and what's demonic paranoia?

Are you plotting against me? Be truthful.

Does the demon make me look fat in these jeans?

This morning, after a little prompting from Katarina—*you needed help with Destruction, would have probably perished without me, and now she needs help with Distrust. Do your part*—he'd finally given in and agreed to be Fox's mentor.

"Take a walk with me," he said to Galen.

As they strode out of the living room, Baden looked back at Katarina and blew her a kiss.

"Stop disgusting me." Galen yanked him out the door. "And start talking."

Cool air brushed his bandless arms. "Aeron refuses to tell me Legion's current location."

"So?"

"So," Baden added. "My wife happens to lead the hellhounds."

"I know, I know. She's wonderful, and you're the luckiest immortal in the history of the universe. What does that have to do with my plight?"

"Those hounds tracked Legion."

Stopping abruptly, Galen gripped him by the shoulders and shook him. "Tell me."

"First, I need your vow. You cannot hurt her—"

"Don't insult me again. I would *never* hurt her. She is to me what Katarina is to you."

In this, Baden believed him. The man was utterly besotted.

Baden rattled off the address. Galen jumped into the air a second later—and never landed. His wings took him into the clouds.

Biscuit and Gravy came barreling around a corner, running straight for Baden. They plowed into him, and if he'd been a weaker man, he would have fallen. A laughing Katarina raced after them.

"They didn't want to leave you unprotected," she said as he caught her in his arms.

"They like me now?"

"Not even a little. But they love me."

"As do I." As the pups chased their tails and sprinted circles around him, Destruction rubbed against his skull, desperate to get his hands on her. "As does the beast."

She traced her fingertips over his temples. "Does he need me?"

"We both do." Baden bent and pushed his shoulder into Katarina's middle, hoisting her up on his shoulder. "And we're going to have you. Perhaps make you scream."

She laughed all the way to their bedroom, earning winks and good-natured jabs from his friends, but by the time he threw her atop the mattress, she was panting.

"I usually keep my training sessions short and sweet," she said, "but with my sweet Baduction... I think I'll devote several hours."

"Oh, no, *krásavica*. You're going to devote eternity. Nothing else is acceptable."

* * * * *

Lords of the Underworld

INSIDER'S GUIDE

Dear Reader,

I hope you're ready for a peek behind the Lords of the Underworld curtain. When Katarina asked Baden for a Who's Who to Whom in the Underworld, well, the big, bad warrior demanded I take care of the task. That's right. Me. As if I exist simply to do his bidding. I don't. Really! When I threatened to leave him—to pull a "Katarina"—he laughed. And then he took off his shirt. I said, "When would you like the guide completed?" His response of "Yesterday" notwithstanding, I became a woman on a mission, determined to bring him—and you—the latest dish on the dark, sensual immortal warriors and their collection of "mine." Not to mention their numerous enemies and the ever-heating war.

Warning! Warning! If you hate alpha sexiness, stop reading. Things are about to get HOT in here.

Love,
Gena Showalter

Who's Dating Whom?

*Maddox was the first to fall, giving his heart to Ashlyn.
The beauty's sacrifice broke his curse and expertly
defeated the villain.*

*With only one dance, Lucien was snared by the wild
Anya, and "you belong to me" became their favorite
mantra.*

*Reyes turned his sights to the protection of Danika,
and it wasn't long before the two were practicing his
dark erotica.*

*Sabin rescued Gwen and obsession quickly grew,
and now there's nothing the two will not do.*

*Naughty Aeron taught the innocent Olivia how to sin,
and in the process learned how empty his life had
once been.*

*Gideon and Scarlet shared a faux secret past,
and soon realized their love was unsurpassed.*

Amun gave Haidee the worst of his hate,
but she soon won him over...after all, she is his mate.

Strider tried to ignore Kaia and the burn of lust in
his blood, but love for the redhead rushed through
him like a flash flood.

Paris wanted Sienna but tried to resist...
resistance that melted the first time they kissed.

Kane was supposed to wed Josephina's greatest foe,
but Josephina won him at the very first hello.

When Torin and Keeley met, they nearly came to blows.
But it wasn't long before they were tearing off each
other's clothes.

Baden could not protect himself from Katarina's
sweet heart, and now he's vowed they'll never be
apart.

What's next for the Lords, we can't really say.
But with Cameo, William and Galen on the block,
prepare for a little cray-cray.

The Darkest Day

Before sitting down to write The Darkest Torment, *I drafted a scene to 1) get me back into the
Lords of the Underworld universe, 2) let myself
(and readers) know what's been going on since
the release of Torin's book,* The Darkest Touch,
*and 3) watch the sexy Maddox throw a punch or
twelve. What? I did it for him. He needed to let
off a little steam. Anyway. "The Darkest Day" is
that scene. I hope you enjoy!*

—*Mere days after Baden's return*—

Maddox hammered his fists into the punching bag
so fast and with so much force the chain ripped from
the ceiling and the leather tore, sand spilling out as the
bag flew across the gym. *An-n-nd there goes another
one.* With a curse, he tore off what remained of the tape
covering his knuckles. He needed to find a new way to
let off steam. Today all he'd done was sweat. Droplets
ran down his chest as he turned to his friend Strider,
who sprinted on the treadmill.

"Hit on me."

Frowning, Strider jerked the earbuds from his ears. "Excuse me? You want me to *hit* on you?"

"Yes, please. And make it hurt."

"You mean hurt so good. Fine, but what happens in the gym stays in the gym." With the press of a button, Strider stopped the treadmill and lowered the incline. "Is your dad a baker? Because you've got some nice buns."

Maddox took a moment to process the words he'd just heard. *Mis*heard? He arched a brow at him. "Are you kidding me?"

"Wait. I can do better." Strider cleared his throat. "Are you a magician? Because whenever I look at you, the rest of the world disappears."

"Wow. You aren't kidding, but you *are* a moron. You know that, right? I wanted—want—you to use me as a punching bag. Hit me with your fists, not your supposed man prowess."

"No way I'm punching you." Strider grabbed a towel from the rack on the wall and wiped the back of his neck. "Ashlyn will punish me by replacing the oh-so-delicious Oreo filling with toothpaste. Again."

"Well, I'll replace your teeth with my fist if you don't."

"You'd do that either way."

He wasn't wrong.

"Besides," Strider added. "Your wife is scarier than you."

Again, he wasn't wrong. Ashlyn looked like an angel, but when it came to the protection of her loved ones, she had the temper of an entire demon horde.

"I need a good fight." The urge to hurt and be hurt had overwhelmed Maddox more and more lately, and he feared what he would do if ever he snapped. Anyone weaker than himself—meaning *everyone*—would be in danger.

He carried the demon of Violence inside his body, and the fiend was hungrier than ever. Starved. Even buzzing with gleeful anticipation, as if it sensed something Maddox did not—impending danger.

As the keeper of Defeat, Strider would ensure Maddox—and therefore Violence—experienced a total knockout. Because, if Strider lost, *he* would experience a total knockout. The worst of the worst for a guy like him. When he was unconscious, anyone could kick his ass, making his suffering a thousand times worse.

I suck. Maddox shouldn't have asked him to help.

With a roar of frustration, Maddox strode to the defunct punching bag and kicked it…into Strider's chest, knocking the guy to his ass. *Oops.* "My bad."

"Well, that's something to cross off my bucket list," Strider said drily. "Magic sandbag ride."

"Sorry." Maddox hopped from one foot to the other, more amped by the second.

Sabin, the keeper of Doubt, and Reyes, the keeper of Pain, stalked into the gym, stopping abruptly when they spotted Maddox practically foaming at the mouth and Strider, who'd pushed free of the bag and now stood in a growing pile of sand.

Both Sabin and Reyes grinned with relish.

"Came to work out, but my spidey senses tell me something better is afoot." Sabin rubbed his hands together. "Does someone need an old-fashioned beating?"

"Yes. Let's start with you." The guy was within reach. Maddox swung his arm with considerable force. *Crack!* His fist slammed into Sabin's jaw, sending his

The Darkest Day

friend staggering to the side. At the moment of impact, Maddox's thin thread of control snapped. He—utterly—unleashed.

He punched and kicked, and Sabin and Reyes punched and kicked in turn. He never ducked, but accepted every blow as his due. When furniture got in his way, he destroyed it.

You can't win. Stop. Stop now.

Sabin's demon whispered doubts through his mind. Maddox laughed and delivered a punch so powerful he broke Sabin's neck.

Oops again.

This wasn't the first time they'd fought to such an extreme, and it wouldn't be the last. However, Sabin was usually the one who broke *Maddox's* neck in order to end a rampage. Today, with darkness driving him, Maddox wasn't sure he *could* be stopped.

Besides, the guy would heal…in a few days.

Reyes delivered a hard jab to Maddox's throat. A dirty move. Also welcome. As Maddox gasped for breath, Strider jumped on his back and jackhammered a fist into his temple. As Maddox stumbled from the impact, Reyes sealed the deal by knocking his feet out from under him. By the time he hit the ground, two others had joined the fray. William the Ever Randy, and Cameo, the keeper of Misery.

Well, well. A boot party.

As different members of the group took turns kicking him, the demon hummed with happiness. This. This was what it had craved.

Cameo pressed a booted foot into his throat. "Had enough?"

"Not yet." The words were slurred, his lips and tongue wonderfully swollen.

"Let me help with that." William straddled his waist and grinned down at him. "You want action, shithead? I'll give you action. Too bad you're not going to like it." He punched, his fist somehow pushing past skin, muscle and bone and reaching Maddox's spirit—reaching the demon.

Maybe Maddox *could* be stopped. Shrieks of pain sounded in his head just before darkness swallowed him whole...

What seemed a mere second or two later, voices woke him. Water sloshed around in his ears, so he couldn't make out the actual words. He blinked open his eyes, shook his head—good, movement. As he rolled his shoulders and bent his legs to check that he still had use of them, the water—nope, blood, he realized—drained out of his ears.

"...is going on with everyone?" demanded Paris, the keeper of Promiscuity. "We finally got Cameo and Baden home, and as of yesterday morning, Cameo has no memory of her time away from the fortress and Baden, the Gentleman of Olympus, has morphed into a cold-as-ice bastard. He's plowing through women as if there's a going-out-of-business sale and, dude, his temper grows worse by the day. He even puts Maddox to shame."

Something rained over Maddox and, judging by the smell, he guessed it was popcorn.

He sat up, shaking off a round of dizziness. To his delight, Violence remained quiet.

He looked around the gym. Every piece of equipment had been shattered, and there was a fresh crop of holes in every wall. He noticed most of his friends had congregated in the room. The wives and children were missing, though. Lucien, keeper of Death, had probably flashed them away from the fortress the moment the fight had broken out before returning alone to wait for everything to calm.

Even Galen was here. Once the hated enemy, now the tolerated enemy, he stood off to the side, watching the others interact with something akin to envy in his eyes.

Maddox ignored him. It was either that or kill him. *Might have forgiven his crimes but haven't forgotten the results.* He focused on Cameo. "You lost your memory?" It wouldn't be the first time. In fact, it happened whenever she experienced a moment of happiness.

She grabbed a handful of popcorn from the bowl on Torin's lap and said, "Yep."

One word, and still he cringed, all the world's sorrows seeping from her voice. Whatever had overcome the demon's sadness, even for a moment, well, it must have been a miracle.

Maddox stood up and stepped over the still unconscious Sabin to grab a handful of popcorn for himself.

Torin moved the bowl out of reach. "Dude! I'm done sharing with you guys. You're ungrateful assholes. Which is my least favorite kind of asshole! Get your own buttery goodness."

"Fine. I will." Maddox stepped on the guy's nuts, using them as a ladder as he reached for all that "buttery goodness." Rather than taking a scoop of kernels, he took the entire bowl. "Got my own."

Torin punched him in the thigh with a gloved fist. "Jackass." As the keeper of Disease, he could start a worldwide plague just by touching another living being skin-to-skin. Thankfully, they'd discovered a cure a few weeks ago, which had given all of them a new sense of freedom.

Maddox jumped back when Cameo reached for a second scoop, barking, "Mine!"

She smiled without humor. "Want me to make you sob so hard you lose your appetite?"

As he shuddered, he threw a handful at her. "Here. Eat and *stop talking*."

Baden strode into the room, every step measured and intent. He was one of the tallest and most stacked with muscle among them, with dark red hair and a face Cameo liked to call "Jamie Fraser beautiful." He used to host the demon of Distrust and, despite that, he used to be nice. As Paris had said, the Gentleman of Olympus was now a bastard.

Baden was rarely without a scowl that promised pain and bloodshed.

Miserable SOB. He was giving Cameo a run for her money. Several thousand years ago, he'd been beheaded, and his spirit sent to a prison realm. The bands circling his arms somehow made him tangible to the living.

His head tilted to the side. "I finally come back from the dead and you guys turn my home into a shithole?"

Nearly everyone else in the room deadpanned, "You're welcome."

Bastard or not, he was still a brother by circumstance, and they'd treat him as such.

"Typical." Baden tripped over a blow-up doll, cursed and lifted the plastic beauty for all to see. "Did Paris order a stripper?"

"Lola!" Paris leaped toward the doll to draw her in

for an exaggerated hug. "Where you been, girl? Why you been ducking my calls?"

Aeron, the former keeper of Wrath, grabbed the doll and tossed her across the room like a beach ball. "Probably because your wife would stab your precious Lola with a butcher knife. Meanwhile, my wife would patch her up and I'd be stuck with another stray."

That, right there, was the difference between marrying the current keeper of Wrath—Paris's wife—and an actual angel—Aeron's wife.

As everyone laughed, Maddox met Baden's dark gaze. The guy motioned to the hallway with a slight tilt of his chin. Understanding, Maddox finished off the popcorn and tossed the empty bowl at Gideon, keeper of Lies.

"Make more," Maddox commanded.

"Yeah." Lucien kicked Gideon out of his chair.

"Don't worry." The blue-haired punk flipped them both off simultaneously. "I won't spit in the kernels."

Gideon couldn't speak a word of truth without suffering agonizing pain, so Maddox heard the unspoken truth. There would be a special topping on the new kernels—exactly what he'd hoped to hear. Or not hear. Whatever!

"Fine," he said, being sure to grumble. "I'll make more." He strode toward the door, bumping shoulders with Baden along the way. His friend stiffened, even hissed upon contact, and Maddox frowned. "Why don't you pretend to be useful and help me?"

"Wow. It takes two guys to work a microwave?" Cameo asked.

Moans and whimpers rang out. The girl could tell

the funniest joke in the world, but everyone around her would only want to stab their ears with a pencil.

Baden followed Maddox into the hall, maintaining distance between them to prevent any more contact.

As soon as the others were out of hearing range, Maddox said, "What's wrong?"

"An easier question to answer is what *isn't* wrong."

Been there. "Why don't you start with the reason you cringe every time someone touches you."

Baden ran his hands over the serpentine wreaths now circling his biceps. They were a gift from Hades, the king of the underworld. "I spent multiple millennia without having contact with another person. Yes, Pandora was with me in the other realm, and, yes, we constantly fought, but we rarely touched. Now my skin feels as if my every nerve ending is exposed."

Okay. That made sense. "But you've slept your way through a baker's dozen and—"

"Only one part of my anatomy has to touch a woman," Baden interjected, "and with a condom, we aren't exactly skin-to-skin. Besides, the pleasure is worth the agony."

Maddox considered the things he would do to get inside Ashlyn. Actually, what *wouldn't* he do? With her, any amount of pleasure would be worth any amount of agony.

"What about your new temper?" he asked.

Baden hung his head. "I'm not demon-possessed anymore, but I feel an evil presence inside me."

"Because of the wreaths?"

"That, or something was done to me during my stint inside Lucifer's prison. Like Cameo, my memory is fading."

Lucifer was the worst of the worst, evil in its purest form, and certainly capable of doing something horrible to Baden. "Take off the wreaths. Return to the spirit world. We can find another way to get you back." Even as he spoke the words, denial screamed through his head. *Just got my friend back. Can't lose him.*

"I can't. I've tried."

Relief poured through him, as did fear. Baden wanted to leave them? "Is the evil constant or can you pinpoint triggers?"

"There are definitely triggers, and they start and end with my temper, which is getting worse by the day. That's the main reason I wanted to talk with you. How do you control yours?"

Maddox laughed without humor. "I don't. Not anymore." And now that he thought about it, whatever Baden was dealing with might be the root cause of his own problem. Evil fed off evil, after all. The more it consumed, the more it wanted.

That impending sense of doom…

If evil overtook Baden… Yeah, they'd *all* be in danger. In more ways than one.

The guy would have to be locked away. For his own good, yeah, but also for the rest of the world. And if that didn't work, he'd have to be killed. Again. Neither idea appealed to Maddox.

Baden's thoughts must have taken a similar journey. "I don't know what I've brought into your house. Maybe I should leave the fortress. I could be putting you guys—your families—at risk."

"Not my house, our house. You're staying." The words blasted from Maddox with the force of a cannonball. "We finally got you back. We can't lose you again. Whatever's going on with you, we'll figure it out. Together. We'll *fight* it together."

Silence.

He sighed. "In the meantime, have you tried deep breathing?"

"No. Because I'm a moron," Baden snapped. He paused to punch the wall, dust pluming the air as cracks formed in the stone. "Sorry. I'm sorry."

Please. This little man fit was nothing. "Don't worry about it."

They descended the stairs and veered right, soon entering the kitchen.

"There is one thing that has always helped me, no matter how far gone I am," Maddox said.

Baden stepped in front of him, consuming his personal space. Desperation radiated from him as he said, "Tell me."

"I think of Ashlyn, Urban and Ever." His wife and his twin babies, the top three reasons he breathed.

Disappointed, Baden turned to brace against the marble countertop. "You love them. You know they're fragile, that you could hurt them, but you don't want to hurt them so you do whatever it takes to protect them. I can't do the same because I love no one."

"You love me." Maddox bumped his shoulder—screw lack of contact—before heading into the closest pantry to grab a package of popcorn. "You love my family. And don't try to deny it. I've seen you with the twins."

Maddox's heart had nearly burst out of his chest as the big, bad warrior had sat down to play beauty shop with Ever, allowing her to braid his hair, lacquer his face with makeup and paint his toenails princess pink.

Afterward, he'd played chess with Urban. Game after game, teaching the boy strategy—the only thing Urban loved as much as his girls, as he called them. His mama and his sister.

"Why don't you start looking for companionship rather than sex, so you *can* fall in love with a female?" Maddox asked. "Let the girls put your profile up on E-ternity or something."

"The dating site for immortals?" Baden shuddered. "No."

"But—"

"You want revenge against me, don't you? That's what this dating-site nonsense is about. I let myself be killed all those centuries ago, and now you want me to suffer your wrath."

Maddox hadn't known Baden had let himself be killed all those centuries ago, but he'd suspected. They all had. Having that suspicion confirmed was worse than taking a blade to the heart. He should know!

He took his own advice and did a little deep breathing before he placed the popcorn bag in the microwave and said, "Why did you do it?"

The ensuing pause was so heavy they both struggled with their next breaths.

Baden bowed his head. His voice soft, he said, "That's not important. Not anymore."

"It is to me."

"Drop it, Maddox. Please. Our reunion is strained enough. We don't need the past rising up to make things worse."

He didn't point out the obvious. If the past wasn't dealt with, it would rise up regardless. Instead, he gave a clipped nod. "Whatever you need."

"Thanks."

Beep. He grabbed the steaming bag from the microwave, burned his fingers and cursed as the bag slipped from his grip and hit the floor. "Two-second rule," he said, and picked it up by pinching the corner between his fingers.

After pouring the kernels into a bowl, he met Baden's gaze. "If left unchecked, evil grows. You know that as well as I do. At this rate, things are only going to get worse for you. Be prepared."

Baden offered a clipped nod of his own, and for the first time, Maddox realized there was something missing from his friend. A gleam of hope in his eyes.

The coming months were going to be tough for *all* of them.

Better enjoy the calm while it lasts. Maddox patted the warrior on the shoulder. "Come on. Let's go back to the gym and have ourselves a real party. You've missed out on a lot of shit since your death, and I'm making it my personal mission to ensure you do everything."

"Yeah?"

"Yeah. Starting with beer pong."

Before they'd taken a step, the sounds of stampeding buffalo echoed from the stairs. A few seconds later, the entire group entered the kitchen, bringing the party to them.

"Did I hear someone say beer pong?" Paris asked. "Let's make things interesting. Strip pong!"

A chorus of "no" rang out.

Baden even slugged Paris in the arm. "Keep your clothes on. Seeing your ass is on my Oh, No list, not my To Do list."

"Oh, look at that." Paris shook his head, his expression all about pity. "The big man thinks he's funny."

Reyes gave Paris's arm a second punch and said, "He is. He's also right. Your ass? No!"

Paris wasn't deterred. "Not seeing it pains you, don't even try to deny it, and pain is your jam. That's the only reason you can live without getting a peek at my goods and services."

Maddox watched as the guys set up shop on the counter and smiled, a sense of contentment finally settling over him...for now.

The Authors Want To Know

I started writing with a goal to publish over fifteen years ago. In that time, I've had the pleasure of meeting— and falling in love with—a myriad of authors. These women have become my best friends, my confidants, my cheerleaders and sounding boards, my most admired, not to mention my source for the most incredible books! Gimme! I asked each author what she'd most like to know about the Lords of the Underworld. Here's what the awesome women had to say:

Nalini Singh: What do you love most about writing a long-running series with recurring characters?

GS: Every time I sit down to tackle a new Lords of the Underworld book, I feel as if I'm transported straight into a holiday. Family comes together, inside jokes abound, and fights break out. In my case: *The last cookie is mine!* In the Lords' case: *I get to kill him!* I'm once again surrounded by boundless affection and unbreakable loyalty. And let's face it. I enjoy torturing these immortal warriors. Without heat and pressure there would be no diamonds. Also, I like pairing the men with women they never dreamed they could love. I like figuring out what the warriors hate most—and then making it happen to them. But most of all, I like the end result of their tests and trials: they are worthy of the love they've been given.

PC Cast: Gena, my love kitten, you write awesomely hot sex scenes. How do you keep them spicy and unique book after book?

GS: Before I can tackle the question, I just have to get this out of the way: *purrrrrrr*. Okay, now I'm ready, LOL. I remove myself from the love scenes completely, letting the characters drive every motion and word. From the first moment of eye contact—that first spark of awareness—to the final, well, explosion, they are in charge. And really, every character has a different past, different likes and dislikes, different hopes and dreams, different experiences. Those differences keep everything fresh. (Fresh. Ha! See what I did there?)

Karen Marie Moning: Is there a supernatural or mythological race you've always dreamed of introducing to the world, either as a love interest or a kick-ass secondary character?

GS: Yes, oh yes! I wanted to introduce the Harbingers to the Lords of the Underworld universe and in *The Darkest Torment* I finally had the chance. Well, to at least mention the Harbingers. In the next Lords of the Underworld book, the war between Hades and Lucifer will hit a new level of dangerous, and I'll be able to delve more deeply into the Harbinger mythology.

I'm bubbling over with excitement. Get ready for my freakiest, deadliest race yet!

JR Ward: Gena, I need to know—which Lord would you play Never Have I Ever with? And which one would you NOT do it with? Wait. That sounds dirty. Also what's your never ever??? Okay, okay, I'll stop!

GS: Ha! I think I would hate playing Never Have I Ever with… Strider. Actually, *hate* is too strong a word. Dislike, maybe? The dude is keeper of Defeat and he can't lose a single challenge without suffering agonizing pain. I imagine he'd bust a freaking nut in his effort to outdo me, and I'd laugh and then he'd curse at me and then I'd throw something at him. And my never ever…this is probably horrible to admit but when it comes to these warriors I don't think I have a never ever, LOL. Gimme some sugar!

Jeaniene Frost: If you could go back, would you change anything in the series?

GS: Every time I've sat down to write a new Lords of the Underworld book, I've wanted to go back and change something *so badly*. Now, without a manuscript in front of me and certain rules influencing the direction I can go, I would limit my changes to a handful of character arcs. I would rewrite Sienna's journey. I would pair Paris with Viola, even though a lot of readers would revolt. I would do Gideon speak differently. But most of all, I would plot out the entire series before ever writing book one—*The Darkest Night*—so that I would have a clear path to follow.

Kathryn Smith/Kady Cross: Knowing how much you love your fur kids, and animals in general, which Lord would you trust to babysit your pets?

GS: Oh, man! Trust one of those naughty men with my babies? I never say never…until today. Never! Okay, okay. They aren't that bad. When they love a woman, they are willing to die to protect her and everything she holds dear. So I'd go with Baden. Now that he's hooked up with Katarina, the alpha of the hellhounds, all canines are precious to him. He'd take excellent care of my pack…and I'd enjoy watching him on my nanny cam.

Kresley Cole: My dearest, glorious Gena, moon of my life, my sun and stars, which Lord would you like to be stuck with on a deserted tropical island? (Keep in mind that I would be paddling madly to reach said island to join you two.)

GS: Because I love and adore you—my darling love bunny—I'd be willing to share my bounty with you! We'd need to pick the Lord most likely to 1) hunt and prepare our every meal 2) give us daily massages 3) build the best shelter for us 4) never attempt to escape our clutches, and 5) not get jealous when I choose to spoon you instead of him. With all of that in mind, I think I'd go with… Lucien! He can see into the spirit realm as well as the natural realm, so he can better stop any threat to our paradise. He can flash in the best food, and he's very good with his hands… (P.S. bring a laptop because I will insist you write stories for me!)

Jill Monroe: I know so many of your characters are based on me, but are there others based on real people?

GS: My inspired-by-JM characters are my favorites! As for the other characters…well, none are based solely on one person, but I do take bits and pieces/personality traits from the people I love. I mean, I just happen to have the most amazing cast of family and friends in the history of the universe, so why not share the gold? In fact, my youngest sister once called to tell me she'd read my book and discovered a line she'd once said to our mother.

Roxanne St. Claire: Describe the Lords of the Underworld series in three compound words. Must use hyphens!!

GS: Racking my brain… Okay, I've got it! I'd go with: Mouth-watering, ride-or-die and redemption-not-optional.
   I asked my editor (the wonderful Allison Carroll) the same question and here's what she had to say:
   Un-put-downable, magically-delicious and epically-alpha.

Kristen Painter: Which Lord is most likely to become a crazy cat guy?

GS: I have to go with… Paris! He's such a lady magnet. Females the world over—whether human or otherwise—flock to him. They just can't help themselves. But now I'm kicking myself for not writing cats into the storyline! I can see them all over the fortress, bugging the warriors while they train. Okay, don't be surprised if this happens in future stories!

Deidre Knight: Which Lord would you like to take on vacation—and where?

GS: I'd have to go with… Strider! Even though he'd be the last person I picked for playing games, the keeper of Defeat would ensure I had the best time ever. (Because I'd challenge him, of course.) And I think I'd want to go to a cabin in the mountains, surrounded by snow. Cuddles by the fire…seclusion… Oh, oh! Maybe I'd tour Scotland and Ireland instead. I've always wanted to visit, and Strider would look oh, so delicious in a kilt.

Amy Lukavics: Which Lord surprised you the most?

GS: I'd have to say… Torin! Because he hosts the demon of Disease, he's spent his life locked inside the fortress, interacting with people through a computer screen. He feared kicking off another plague. The moment he was forced out of his comfort zone, however, a ferocious, battle-loving bad-ass overtook him—the warrior he'd locked up on the inside as surely as he'd locked himself in the fortress. I was as shocked as I was delighted.

Lily Everett: Katarina is such a dynamic heroine and she's absolutely perfect for Baden! In particular, her background as a dog trainer and her relationship with the hellhounds is genius. How did you pick such an inspiring profession for Baden's heroine?

GS: When I sat down to write *The Darkest Torment*, I knew I wanted to create a beauty and the beast storyline. But in order for Katarina Joelle to survive this particular beast—an immortal who could snap her neck like a twig with a single twist of his wrist—she had to have an edge. Plus, I loooooved the idea of a woman training a fearsome Lord of the Underworld like a dog. I chuckled like a schoolgirl from start to finish.

Kelli Ireland: Every fan has a favorite Lord (or, ahem, four). Then there's William the Ever Randy. Can you tell us something about William that the Lords—and we—don't know yet? Maybe something William really doesn't want anyone to know.

GS: Oh, Willy. My sweet Willy. I knew his threads in *The Darkest Torment* would anger some of my readers. I also knew the threads would utterly enrage William. But what happened, well, it had to happen. William is so freaking stubborn. He needed a kick in the pants (and now he needs someone to kiss his wounds and make him better, LOL). As for a secret…

We learned how William became Hades's son. But what about his biological parents? What about other blood relations? They're out there…and they are looking for him…

Beth Kendrick: What's your favorite Lords of the Underworld quote?

GS: There have been lines that made me laugh out loud, lines that made me gasp. Lines that made me shiver.

But one of the ones that stands out the most actually comes from this book.

William: You can't fight the darkness.
Baden: I am the darkness.

To me, it shows the terrible state Baden is in, his lack of hope. Little does he know, light is on the way!

Recruit or Kill?

*FROM THE PRIVATE FILES OF HADES,
ONE OF THE NINE KINGS OF THE UNDERWORLD*

Ruling an army isn't a job for the weak. Ruling a legion of armies is a job only for the strongest of the strong. I am that male. The general. The puppeteer. The ultimate gamer. The head coach. The master of all I survey.

Call me whatever you wish. I'm all that, and more.

But if you aren't for me, you are against me. If you are against me, you are as good as dead. Either way—if you're alive or dead—I'll get my hands on you.

If you're good enough to make my team, congrats. You win an award: you get to keep your head. If you prove unworthy, well, you'll get benched and benched players get cut. Literally.

Now it's time to decide which of the Lords of the Underworld qualify…

—Hades, the king other kings fear

Maddox

Demon: Violence
Height: 6'4"
Hair: Black
Eyes: Violet when (almost) happy, red when angry
Tramp stamp: Scarlet butterfly on his upper left shoulder, wrapping around to his back
Other distinguishing marks: The demon's skeletal face is visible through Maddox's skin when the two are angered. (Side note: Emotions are for pussies.)
Preferred weapon: Fists
(Note to self: Ask him if he enjoys a good fisting. Try to keep a straight face.)
Demon naughtiness: Stabbed Pandora to death, which led to the disappearance of the box. In modern society the offspring of Violence is responsible for street-gang warfare, rape, murder and terrorism.
My thoughts: Rape will never be tolerated within my ranks. The demon must be eliminated—through violence? Hmm. A paradox. A new puzzle to solve.
Warrior's background: When he killed Pandora, he was cursed to die every night only to be resurrected the next day, knowing he had to die again. The curse was broken through "love."

What is love?

He still erupts into fits of violence. He's volatile and

highly dangerous. I'm beginning to like him. He enjoys classical music and carving.

An-n-nd there goes the like.

Achilles' heel: Technology. Emotional attachment to human female Ashlyn Darrow, former para-audiologist for the World Institute of Parapsychology. Also his twin children, Urban and Ever.

(Note: Kids are dirty little creatures. Avoid!)

Placement: Second string

Lucien

Demon: Death
Height: 6'6"
Hair: Black, shoulder-length
Eyes: Mismatched—one brown (normal eye) and one blue (allows him to see into the spiritual world…my world)
Tramp stamp: Black butterfly on his upper left shoulder and front of chest
Other distinguishing marks: One side of his face is covered in scars. He emits a strong odor of roses—a drugged scent that calms a soul just before he escorts it to the afterlife.
Preferred weapon: Knives with poisoned tips
Demon naughtiness: Death ushers souls into hell like a boss.
Side note: Rumors suggest there are humans who don't consider Death a demon. They call his actions a "natural progression of life." Ridiculous! Humans weren't created to die but to live forever. I like that they're so blinded from the truth, however. Perhaps I should send demons out to ensure these rumors grow. The more a human thinks death is natural, the less that human will fight when I choose to add his—or her—soul to my army.
Warrior's background: Calm and stoic, the former Captain of the Immortal Guard (Zeus's army). He's the

one who disfigured his face. He did it centuries ago in a fit of rage, indicating an unstable temperament and a harmful nature. His spirit can slip in and out of his body with ease. He can flash. He has been called The Dark One, Malach ha-Maet, Yama, Azreal, Shadow Walker, Mirya, and King of the Dead. He's the one who opened Pandora's box after it was stolen.

Achilles' heel: Three of note. The first, when his soul leaves his body, his flesh is vulnerable. The second, his attachment to Anya, minor Greek goddess of Anarchy. He has abilities he hasn't even tapped into yet, probably because he has no idea he has them. Once I teach him…

Placement: First string

Reyes

Demon: Pain
Height: 6'5"
Hair: Dark brown
Eyes: Brown
Tramp stamp: A ruby, onyx, and sapphire butterfly on his chest and neck
Other distinguishing marks: Deeply tanned skin; frequently sports scabs caused by self-mutilation
Preferred weapon: Daggers, sword, guns
Demon naughtiness: Physical pain and suffering throughout the ages. Acts of random cruelty.
Notable background: He goes to amazingly excruciating lengths to cause himself pain, i.e. jumping off rooftops and cutting his flesh.
Achilles' heel: Once again, an attachment to a female. Danika Ford, the All-seeing Eye. He throws up when flashed. He needs some kind of physical pain at least once an hour.
Placement: First string

Paris

Demon: Promiscuity
Height: 6'8"
Hair: Varying shades of brown and black
Eyes: Blue
Tramp stamp: Butterfly on his lower back
Other distinguishing marks: Pale skin. He's widely regarded as the most physically "appealing" of all the Lords. I call foul. None of the warriors can compare to me.
Preferred weapon: Sword. (The one in his pants? Snicker.)
Demon naughtiness: Out-of-wedlock pregnancy, sexually transmitted diseases and infidelity. He can use his voice to project images into a human mind. He can emit the scent of chocolate and champagne to attract a lover.
Notable background: Without frequent physical release, he's weakened. He passes out when flashed.
Note to self: Might be fun to experiment. If I hack off his arms and lock him inside a room, will his balls literally turn blue? Will his cock spontaneously explode?
Achilles' heel: Sienna Blackstone, the new keeper of Wrath
Placement: Second string...unless I need an assassin to infiltrate a woman's bedroom.

Aeron

Demon: Formerly Wrath
Height: 6'6"
Hair: Military-cropped, brown
Eyes: Violet
Tramp stamp: Butterfly in the middle of his back, and the name Olivia tattooed over his heart, plus countless others—all hold special meaning to him
Other distinguishing marks: Hugely muscled. He used to have a pair of black gossamer wings that could be hidden behind slits in his back when not in use. He has two eyebrow rings.
Preferred weapon: He doesn't discriminate but embraces any weapon at his disposal. My kind of guy.
Demon naughtiness: n/a
Note to self: Could be fun to secretly give him another demon, placing him under my reign. Food for thought.
Notable background: He was beheaded and given a new body by the Sent Ones. His wife, Olivia, is a fallen Sent One. His ties are to Team Good.
Achilles' heel: His wife and a former demon minion Legion
Placement: A possible cut

Torin

Demon: Disease
Height: 6'5"
Hair: Silver-white, shoulder-length (brows are black)
Eyes: Green
Tramp stamp: Onyx butterfly framed in crimson, located on his stomach. At certain angles, the entire tattoo appears black.
Other distinguishing marks: He wears long black gloves like a Victorian maiden. He's ugly as hell and witless. Carries the All-key inside him, which means he can't be confined in any way—I'm sure there's a reason that trait sucks ass and I'll think of it soon.
Preferred weapon: Does it matter? He can't fight worth a damn.
Demon naughtiness: Disease is responsible for a myriad of plagues that resulted in thousands of casualties. He is also at the root of cancer and all additional pestilence, most recently the dreaded Ebola pandemic.
Notable background: The warrior used to think he couldn't touch another living being skin-to-skin without infecting him/her/it with disease, not knowing he simply had to share his blood or semen to create an immunity. Idiot! Also, he's engaged to my former fiancée.
Achilles' heel: His woman, who used to be my woman. Long live the Red Queen!

Placement: I have no room for him on my team. ~~I'll kill him at my earliest convenience. I'll get the Red Queen's permission to kill him at my earliest convenience.~~ I'll pretend he doesn't exist.

Sabin

Demon: Doubt
Height: 6'7"
Hair: Brown
Eyes: Gold-brown
Tramp stamp: Violet butterfly on right rib cage and waist
Other distinguishing marks: Rough-hewn face. Wears a necklace given to him by Baden, former keeper of Distrust.
Preferred weapon: He used to rely on knives, guns, throwing stars et al, but now prefers to unleash his Harpy bride. He finds her methods of killing amusing. I must concur.
Demon naughtiness: Whispers insecurities into the ears of anyone within reach and causes crippling—at times life-threatening—self-doubt. Responsible for multiple suicides.
Notable background: His demon tortured me when I was a child, something he must answer for. He can project his voice into the minds of others (human and immortal).
Achilles' heel: His single-minded devotion to Gwendolyn the Timid, his Harpy wife. Can't see great distances. Left knee was injured centuries ago and didn't heal correctly.
Placement: ~~Rip out his demon, kill it with my bare hands~~. Demon can be used to my advantage. First string. Lucifer's biggest weakness is his pride. If I can prick it…

Gideon

Demon: Lies
Height: 6'3"
Hair: Dyed metallic blue
Eyes: Blue, kohl-rimmed
Tramp stamp: Butterfly on his right thigh, a pair of red lips on his neck, and a pair of eyes above his heart. On his waist, the words "To part is to die" are tattooed above a bouquet of red flowers.
Other distinguishing marks: Multiple piercings and general Goth appearance.
Preferred weapon: All of them. He has no specific preference, using whatever is nearby.
Demon naughtiness: Lies has infiltrated politics worldwide, resulting in false promises from world leaders and the disintegration of modern society. The demon has even convinced most of the human race "white lies" are harmless. He is insidious. Devious.
Notable background: Warrior is unable to tell the truth without experiencing terrible pain. He's had his feet and hands removed at different points in his life, actions I've experienced as well. Like mine, his appendages grew back.
Achilles' heel: Am I a broken record? His woman. Scarlet, the keeper of Nightmares. Also, he vomits when he's flashed and he's afraid of spiders.
Placement: Despite his insidious deviousness, can I trust him? Requires further thought.

Cameo

Demon: Misery
Height: 5'7"
Hair: Long, black
Eyes: Silver
Tramp stamp: Glittery butterfly on her lower back, with wings that spread around to both hips
Other distinguishing marks: Her voice drips with the sorrows of the world. There is an oval-shaped mole on her right hip.
Preferred weapon: Semiautomatic, long-range rifles
Demon naughtiness: Misery is responsible for depression and anxiety. The fact that both are reported at higher rates today than ever before suggests the demon's reach is increasing.
Notable background: She's caused profound emotional anguish in everyone around her. She loved a human, but lost him to Hunters. She dated both Kane and Torin. When at her worst, she'll quote depressing statistics.
Achilles' heel: Her inability to remember the things that make her happy.
Placement: My bedroom?

Amun

Demon: Secrets
Height: 6'6"
Hair: Brown
Eyes: Brown
Tramp stamp: Butterfly on his right calf
Other distinguishing marks: The darkness of his skin and eyes. He is leanly muscled and rarely speaks. Photos of him are always distorted. His image can't even be drawn.
Preferred weapon: Things of an exotic nature.
Demon naughtiness: Fosters a lack of communication in everything from marriages to national security. With him, true peace can never be achieved.
Notable background: The warrior is unable to speak without the secrets of the world pouring from his mouth. The listener hears the voice of the person whose secret is being revealed. He is now mated to Haidee, one of the former keepers of Hate, now one of the keepers of Love. Two Horsemen of the Apocalypse (my adorable grandchildren!) owe him a year of servitude.
Achilles' heel: Revealing his own secrets—and mine.
Objectives: Avoid or cut from the team

Strider

Demon: Defeat
Height: 6'5"
Hair: Blond
Eyes: Blue
Tramp stamp: Sapphire butterfly on his left hip
Other distinguishing marks: His overall asshole-ness.
Preferred weapon: He embraces all weaponry.
Demon naughtiness: Defeat is determined to win no matter the cost. He has brought about the downfall of athletes worldwide, encouraging illegal tactics—like steroids—in order to obtain a win.
Notable background: He can't lose a battle or even an argument without succumbing to intense physical agony and prolonged sleep. Loves cinnamon.
Achilles' heel: His woman, and his inability to lose gracefully.
Placement: First string, on a trial basis. If he challenges me, he'll have to be cut. Literally. Lads need to be taught proper lessons so they grow into better men.

Kane

Demon: Formerly Disaster
Height: 6'4"
Hair: Mixture of brown, black and gold
Eyes: Hazel
Tramp stamp: Black butterfly on his right hip
Preferred weapon: Rifles and other long-range weaponry
Demon naughtiness: n/a
Notable background: He's married to the queen of the Fae. Possible new army to utilize?
Achilles' heel: His woman, of course.
Placement: Will depend on treaty talks with the Fae.

Galen

Demons: Jealousy and False Hope
Height: 6'5"
Hair: Blond curls
Eyes: Sky blue
Tramp stamp: A butterfly on both of his pecs
Other distinguishing marks: Some claim he looks like a warrior angel. White wings are in the process of regeneration.
Preferred weapon: Sword of red fire
Demon naughtiness: Known for ruining relationships, inciting silly shows of pride, and placing people on the wrong road, headed in the wrong direction
Notable background: He was the last Lord created. He's the one who suggested the Lords steal the box before he turned on them and told Zeus. Once aligned with Rhea, queen of the Greeks. Once coleader of the Hunters, humans who sought to kill the Lords of the Underworld. The father of Gwen, Sabin's wife.
Achilles' heel: His obsession with Legion, former demon girl turned human girl
Placement: Requires further study

Baden

Demon: Formerly Distrust
Height: 6'8"
Hair: Red, with a slight curl. The strands used to catch fire when he became angered. (Note to self: help him regain the ability, shouldn't be difficult but like a muscle memory…he'll need it.)
Eyes: Copper
Tramp stamp: Butterfly on his chest
Other distinguishing marks: One of the most beautiful males on the planet
Preferred weapon: Everything. A male after my own heart.
Demon naughtiness: n/a
Notable background: He was the first Lord of the Underworld to be created. He is now the son of the greatest king in existence, and he wisely married Katarina, the Alpha of the Hellhounds.
Achilles' heel: His woman. Because of Katarina's abilities, Baden's connection to her is a strength.
Placement: At my side, as my son

Pandora

Demon: n/a
Height: 6'
Hair: Black, straight
Eyes: Gold
Tramp stamp: Butterflies tattooed along her forearm, a kill list
Other distinguishing marks: She now has the strength and agility of a hellhound
Preferred weapon: Chain saw, claws and teeth
Demon naughtiness: n/a
Notable background: Was the strongest female warrior in Mount Olympus, charged with guarding *dimOuniak*. Killed by Maddox, who stabbed her six times upon the possession of Violence.
Achilles' heel: Her anger and her curiosity. I must teach her to temper both before she gets herself killed.
Placement: By my side, as my daughter

OTHER DEMON-POSSESSED WARRIORS OF NOTE
(non-mates)

VIOLA: Keeper of Narcissism and the minor goddess of the Afterlife. Long silver-blond hair with cinnamon-colored eyes. Can appear in a puff of white smoke. 5'3". Pierced navel. Smells of roses like Lucien, only sweeter. When the demon overtakes her, she grows two horns, red scales, fangs, claws; her eyes turn red and she smells of sulfur. Her butterfly tattoo is pink. The front is along her chest, stomach and legs while the back stretches across her shoulders, thighs and calves. She has a pet Tasmanian devil/vampire named Princess Fluffikans. Before her possession, she fed on souls.

PUKINN: Keeper of Indifference. Looks to have an Egyptian heritage. Dark eyes with long, straight black hair. Horns. Hands that are permanently clawed. Furred legs. Part satyr. Irish accent. Now bonded to Gillian Bradshaw.
    To kill for stealing from William or not to kill?

CAMERON: Keeper of Obsession. Bronze hair and skin, with lavender eyes rimmed in silver. He still mourns the death of a woman—I need more details about this. He chronicles each of his imprisonments with tattoos, and he collects stories from other people and tells them as his own.

WINTER: Keeper of Selfishness. Bronze skin and hair, with lavender eyes rimmed in silver. Sister to Cameron.

She has long legs and a curvy body. She also has fangs. Does she like to bite? (Note to self: find out!)

MATES TO THE LORDS OF THE UNDERWORLD

JOSEPHINA "TINK" AISLING: Queen of Seduire. Half Fae, half human. Black hair. Blue eyes. Bronze skin. Pointy ears. Scar on cheek and chest. Smells of rosemary and spearmint. Daughter of Tiberius and Glorika. Half sister of Synda. Formerly a blood slave. Has the ability to temporarily steal others' abilities with her hands, and to project into others' thoughts. Now has the powers of a Phoenix. Married to Kane; pregnant.

HAIDEE ALEXANDER: Former Hunter used as Bait to kill Baden. Stabbed by Strider when she helped kill Baden. Petite. Shoulder-length blond hair with pink streaks. Gray eyes. Silver stud in brow. Sleeve of tattoos on one arm—the tattoos are faces, numbers, addresses, names ("Micah," "Viola," "Skye") and phrases ("Darkness always loses to light," "You have loved and been loved.") On her back is a tattoo scorecard that says "Lords: IIII, Haidee: I". She grows ice-cold and can exhale mist. Hates snakes. Throws up after flashing. The demon of Hate killed her mother, father and little sister. Was once the keeper of a small piece of Hate, but now holds a piece of Love. Mated to Amun.

ANYA: Minor goddess of Anarchy. Tall. Long white hair. Blue eyes. Pixie face. Daughter of Dysnomia and Tartarus. Has a weakness for lollipops. Helped break Maddox's curse. Strongest source of power is chaos. Immortals are immune to her commands. Stealing soothes her. She gave up the All-key to help her beloved Lucien.

SCARLET: Keeper of Nightmares. Shoulder-length black hair, black eyes and red lips. 5'9". Multiple tattoos. "To Part is to Die" above a bouquet of red flowers, and a jewel-tone butterfly on her upper thighs. She is the daughter of Rhea and a Myrmidon warrior and married to Gideon. Born and raised inside Tartarus. Disappears into shadows. Weakened during daylight hours. Smells like night flowers. Her demon is mated to Lies. She is pregnant with a game changer (not that she knows it).

SIENNA BLACKSTONE: Keeper of Wrath. Queen of the Greek gods. Wavy brown hair, hazel eyes and overly full lips. Lots of freckles her husband, Paris, is particularly obsessed with licking. Black wings rise above her shoulders and end in sharp tips perfect for slicing an enemy to ribbons. A black butterfly tattoo surrounds the base of the wings. Her blood is liquid ambrosia.

ASHLYN DARROW: From North Carolina. Light brown hair, honey-colored skin and eyes. 5'5". Only twenty-four years old when she met Maddox. Wherever she stands, she hears every conversation that has ever taken place there. Worked as a para-audiologist for the World Institute of Parapsychology since the age of five. After breaking Maddox's curse, her life span bonded to his. She is the mother to twins Ever and Urban.

DANIKA FORD: All-seeing Eye. A blonde with green eyes and freckles. An artist. Once the Hunters recruited her as Bait, hoping she would kill the Lords, but she mated to Reyes instead. She is a portal into both heaven and hell, and one of the four keys needed to find Pandora's box.

KEELEYCAEL: A Curator. The Red Queen. Known as Keeley to her friends. Her appearance changes with the seasons. Winter: blue hair, skin and eyes. Autumn: red hair with brown streaks, amber-gold eyes, peaches-and-cream skin. Summer: blond hair, blue eyes, tanned skin. Spring: white skin, light pink hair with green chunks framing her face, and blue eyes. Once engaged to Hades. Now married to Torin.

OLIVIA: Once a Sent One. A joy-bringer for her charges—now a joy-bringer for her husband, Aeron. Has long wavy brown hair and sky-blue eyes. Pale skin. Her wings were cut from her back. She was given a new pair, but they only pop from the slits in her back with strong emotion.

GWENDOLYN SKYHAWK: Harpy known as Gwendolyn the Timid. Long red hair with blond streaks. Eyebrows are dark auburn. Eyes are amber with sparkling gray striations. Button nose. Petite. Twenty-seven years old. Raspy voice. Raised in Alaska. Was imprisoned by Hunters for a year. Mated to Sabin. Youngest sister of Bianka, Taliyah and Kaia. Daughter of Tabitha and Galen.

KAIA SKYHAWK: Harpy. Bright red hair. Golden eyes mixed with gray. Twin of Bianka. Sister of Taliyah and Gwen. Daughter of Tabitha and a Phoenix. Works as a mercenary. Formerly known as Kaia the Disappointment, now known as Kaia the Wing-Shredder. Married to Strider. When she goes Harpy, she has an azure glow and her eyes turn red and black. She controls fire.

KATARINA JOELLE: Once a human, but now the immortal Alpha of Hellhounds. Her father was black, her mother white; both are deceased. She has dark hair and gray-green eyes. She's tall and slender with delicate features. Known as "Rina" to her mate, Baden.

Top Ten Hellhound Rules for Humans

1. Do not, under any circumstances, refer to a Hellhound as a "dog." "Warrior" is always appropriate. So is "Master."

2. What you eat, your Hellhound eats. When you eat, your Hellhound eats. When you don't eat, your Hellhound eats.

3. Every time you issue a command, you get bit. It's a rule. Deal with it.

4. If a Hellhound wakes you in the middle of the night simply to lick your face, say thank you. You're still alive.

5. Where you sleep, a Hellhound sleeps. The floor is NEVER acceptable.

6. If a Hellhound barks or growls to get your attention, say thank you. You still have your limbs.

7. Strike the words "sit," "stay" and "good boy" from your vocabulary. Forever.

8. If a Hellhound tells you to "sit," "stay" or calls you a "good boy" say thank you. Your face hasn't been used as a chew toy. Yet.

9. What belongs to you belongs to your Hellhound. What belongs to your Hellhound belongs to your Hellhound.

10. The term "bath time" will now be referred to as "the day you die badly."

The Who's Who to Whom

Aeron—Lord of the Underworld; former keeper of Wrath; husband to Olivia

All-key—a spiritual relic capable of opening any lock

All-seeing Eye—Godly artifact with the power to see into heaven and Hell

Amun—Lord of the Underworld; keeper of Secrets; husband to Haidee

Anya—(minor) goddess of Anarchy, engaged to Lucien

Ashlyn Darrow—human female with supernatural ability; wife to Maddox; mother of Urban and Ever

Axel—Sent One with a secret

Baden—Lord of the Underworld; former keeper of Distrust; companion to Destruction (newly resurrected); husband to Katarina

Bait—human females, Hunters' accomplices

Bianka Skyhawk—Harpy, sister of Gwen, Taliyah and Kaia; wife to Lysander

Bjorn—Sent One

Black—one of the four horsemen of the apocalypse; child of William

Cage of Compulsion—Godly artifact with the power to enslave anyone trapped inside

Cameo—Lord of the Underworld; keeper of Misery

Cameron—keeper of Obsession

Cloak of Invisibility—Godly artifact with the power to shield its wearer from prying eyes

Cronus—former king of the Titans; former keeper of Greed; husband to Rhea

Danika Ford—human female; wife to Reyes; known as the All-seeing Eye

dimOuniak—Pandora's box

Downfall—nightclub for immortals owned by Thane, Bjorn and Xerxes

Elin—Phoenix/human hybrid; mate to Thane

Ever—daughter to Maddox and Ashlyn, sister to Urban

Fae—race of immortals descended from Titans

Flashing—transporting oneself with just a thought

Fox—immortal of unknown origin; associate of Galen's; keeper of Distrust

Galen—Lord of the Underworld; keeper of Jealousy and False Hope

Geryon—once the guardian of the gate to Hell; deceased yet in spirit form; companion to goddess of Oppression

Gideon—Lord of the Underworld; keeper of Lies

Gillian Bradshaw—human female recently made immortal; bonded to Pukinn

Greeks—former rulers of Olympus

Green—one of the four horsemen of the apocalypse; child of William

Gwendolyn Skyhawk—Harpy; wife of Sabin; daughter of Galen

Hades—one of the nine kings of the underworld

Haidee Alexander—former Hunter; keeper of Love; mated to Amun

Hera—Queen of the Greeks; wife to Zeus

Hunters—mortal enemies of the Lords of the Underworld; disbanded

Josephina "Tink" Aisling—Queen of the Fae; wife to Kane

Juliette Eagleshield—Harpy; self-appointed consort of Lazarus

Kadence—the goddess of Oppression; deceased yet in spirit form; companion to Geryon

Kaia Skyhawk—part Harpy, part Phoenix; sister of Gwen, Taliyah and Bianka; consort of Strider

Kane—Lord of the Underworld; keeper of Disaster; husband to Josephina

Keeleycael—a Curator; the Red Queen; engaged to Torin

Lazarus—an immortal warrior; only son of Typhon and an unnamed gorgon

Legion—demon minion in a human body; adopted daughter of Aeron and Olivia; aka Honey

Lords of the Underworld—exiled immortal warriors now hosting the demons once locked inside Pandora's box

Lucien—coleader of the Lords of the Underworld; keeper of Death; engaged to Anya

Lucifer—one of the nine kings of the underworld; son to Hades; brother to William

Lysander—elite warrior angel and consort of Bianka Skyhawk

Maddox—Lord of the Underworld; keeper of Violence; father to Urban and Ever; husband to Ashlyn

Melody—siren; blind; works for Hades

Morning Star—created by the Most High. With it nothing is impossible. Hidden in *dimOuniak*.

Neeka Eagleshield—part Harpy, part Phoenix, known as The Unwanted

Never-ending—a portal to hell. 1 regular day is 1000 years in the Never-ending.

Olivia—fallen warrior angel; mated to Aeron

Pandora—immortal warrior, once guardian of *dimOuniak* (newly resurrected)

Pandora's Box—aka *dimOuniak*; made of the bones from the goddess of Oppression; once housed demon high lords; now missing

Paring Rod—Godly artifact with ability to rend soul from body

Paris—Lord of the Underworld; keeper of Promiscuity; husband to Sienna

Phoenix—fire-thriving immortals descended from Greeks

Pukinn—satyr, keeper of Indifference; alias: Irish; bonded to Gillian

Red—one of the four horsemen of the apocalypse; child of William

Reyes—Lord of the Underworld; keeper of Pain; husband to Danika

Rhea—former Queen of the Titans, former keeper of Strife; wife to Cronus

Sabin—coleader of the Lords of the Underworld; keeper of Doubt; consort of Gwen

Scarlet—keeper of Nightmares; wife of Gideon

Sent Ones—winged warriors; demon assassins

Sienna Blackstone—former Hunter, current keeper of Wrath, current ruler of Olympus; beloved of Paris

Strider—Lord of the Underworld; keeper of Defeat

Taliyah Skyhawk—Harpy, sister of Gwen, Bianka and Kaia

Tartarus—Greek god of Confinement, also the immortal prison on Mount Olympus

Titans—rulers of Titania; children of fallen angels and humans

Thane—Sent One; mate to Elin

Torin—Lord of the Underworld; keeper of Disease; husband to Keeleycael

Urban—son of Maddox and Ashlyn; brother of Ever

Viola—Titan; (minor) goddess of the Afterlife; keeper of Narcissism

White—one of the four horsemen of the apocalypse; child of William; deceased

William the Ever Randy—immortal warrior of questionable origins; aka The Panty Melter and William of the Dark

Winter—keeper of Selfishness

Xerxes—Sent One

Zeus—King of the Greeks; husband to Hera

REQUEST YOUR FREE BOOKS!

2 FREE NOVELS
FROM THE SUSPENSE COLLECTION,
PLUS 2 FREE GIFTS!

YES! Please send me 2 FREE novels from the Suspense Collection and my 2 FREE gifts (gifts are worth about $10). After receiving them, if I don't wish to receive any more books, I can return the shipping statement marked "cancel." If I don't cancel, I will receive 4 brand-new novels every month and be billed just $6.49 per book in the U.S. or $6.99 per book in Canada. That's a savings of at least 18% off the cover price. It's quite a bargain! Shipping and handling is just 50¢ per book in the U.S. and 75¢ per book in Canada.* I understand that accepting the 2 free books and gifts places me under no obligation to buy anything. I can always return a shipment and cancel at any time. Even if I never buy another book, the two free books and gifts are mine to keep forever.

191/391 MDN GH4Z

Name   (PLEASE PRINT)

Address   Apt. #

City   State/Prov.   Zip/Postal Code

Signature (if under 18, a parent or guardian must sign)

Mail to the **Reader Service:**
IN U.S.A.: P.O. Box 1867, Buffalo, NY 14240-1867
IN CANADA: P.O. Box 609, Fort Erie, Ontario L2A 5X3

Want to try 2 free books from another line?
Call 1-800-873-8635 or visit www.ReaderService.com.

* Terms and prices subject to change without notice. Prices do not include applicable taxes. Sales tax applicable in NY. Canadian residents will be charged applicable taxes. Offer not valid in Quebec. This offer is limited to one order per household. Not valid for current subscribers to the Suspense Collection or the Romance/Suspense Collection. All orders subject to credit approval. Credit or debit balances in a customer's account(s) may be offset by any other outstanding balance owed by or to the customer. Please allow 4 to 6 weeks for delivery. Offer available while quantities last.

Your Privacy—The Reader Service is committed to protecting your privacy. Our Privacy Policy is available online at www.ReaderService.com or upon request from the Reader Service.

We make a portion of our mailing list available to reputable third parties that offer products we believe may interest you. If you prefer that we not exchange your name with third parties, or if you wish to clarify or modify your communication preferences, please visit us at www.ReaderService.com/consumerschoice or write to us at Reader Service Preference Service, P.O. Box 9062, Buffalo, NY 14240-9062. Include your complete name and address.